"Plenty of action and intriguing characters keep this fun. In the increasingly crowded field of kick-ass supernatural heroines, Mercy stands out as one of the best." —*Locus*

"Briggs's world, in which witches, vampires, werewolves, and shapeshifters live beside ordinary people, is plausibly constructed, the characters are excellent, and the plot keeps the pages flapping." —*Booklist*

"Briggs has created a believable alternative world populated with strong, dynamite characters, deadly adversaries, and cunningly laid plots that leave the reader looking for more." —*Monsters and Critics*

PRAISE FOR
MOON CALLED

"An excellent read with plenty of twists and turns. [Briggs's] strong and complex characters kept me entertained from its deceptively innocent beginning to its can't-put-it-down end. Thoroughly satisfying, it left me wanting more." —Kim Harrison, *New York Times* bestselling author

"Patricia Briggs always enchants her readers. With *Moon Called*, she weaves her magic on every page to take us into a new and dazzling world of werewolves, shapeshifters, witches, and vampires. Expect to be spellbound." —Lynn Viehl, *New York Times* bestselling author

"A suspenseful read that will have you on the edge of your seat as you burn through the pages. Ms. Briggs weaves paranormal and mystery together so deftly you can't put the book down. The cast of characters is wonderfully entertaining, and Mercy's emotional struggles will pull on your heartstrings. For lovers of the paranormal, this is a must-read." —*Romance Junkies*

"A strong story with multidimensional characters . . . Mercy is, at heart, someone we can relate to." —*SFRevu*

P9-DNE-410

Titles by Patricia Briggs

The Mercy Thompson Novels
MOON CALLED
BLOOD BOUND
IRON KISSED
BONE CROSSED
SILVER BORNE

The Alpha and Omega Novels
ON THE PROWL
(with Eileen Wilks, Karen Chance, and Sunny)
CRY WOLF
HUNTING GROUND

MASQUES
WOLFSBANE
STEAL THE DRAGON
WHEN DEMONS WALK

THE HOB'S BARGAIN

DRAGON BONES
DRAGON BLOOD

RAVEN'S SHADOW
RAVEN'S STRIKE

continued . . .

"Mercy is not just another cookie-cutter tough-chick urban fantasy heroine; she's got a lot of style and substance and an intriguing backstory. Series fans will appreciate the resolution of some ongoing plotlines, and the romantic tension is strong."
—*Library Journal*

"[Mercy is] one of the best of the kick-ass heroine crop." —*Locus*

"An excellent book with all of the elements I really like in a story: action, romance, emotional growth of the characters, and a deeper knowledge of the world in the series." —*Vampire Genre*

PRAISE FOR

IRON KISSED

"The third book in an increasingly excellent series, *Iron Kissed* has all the elements I've come to expect in a Patricia Briggs novel: sharp, perceptive characterization, nonstop action, and a levelheaded attention to detail and location. I love these books."
—Charlaine Harris, #1 *New York Times* bestselling author

"Briggs's third novel featuring Thompson is another top-notch paranormal mystery; her well-balanced contemporary world, where humans live uneasily among werewolves and fae, is still a believably lived-in world; the ever-present threat of government legislation against nonhumans (though familiar to *X-Men* fans) adds weight to her paranormal elements, and thoughtfully researched mythology adds rich detail. Thompson is a sharp, strong heroine, and her lycanthropic love triangle is honest and steamy. Briggs never shies from difficult material, and she moves effortlessly from werewolf pack psychology to human legal proceedings, making this a tense, nimble, crowd-pleasing page-turner."
—*Publishers Weekly*

PRAISE FOR

BLOOD BOUND

"Once again, Briggs has written a full-bore action adventure with heart . . . Be prepared to read [it] in one sitting, because once you get going, there is no good place to stop until tomorrow."
—*SFRevu*

SILVER BORNE

PATRICIA BRIGGS

ACE BOOKS, NEW YORK

THE BERKLEY PUBLISHING GROUP
Published by the Penguin Group
Penguin Group (USA) Inc.
375 Hudson Street, New York, New York 10014, USA
Penguin Group (Canada), 90 Eglinton Avenue East, Suite 700, Toronto, Ontario M4P 2Y3, Canada
(a division of Pearson Penguin Canada Inc.)
Penguin Books Ltd., 80 Strand, London WC2R 0RL, England
Penguin Group Ireland, 25 St. Stephen's Green, Dublin 2, Ireland (a division of Penguin Books Ltd.)
Penguin Group (Australia), 250 Camberwell Road, Camberwell, Victoria 3124, Australia
(a division of Pearson Australia Group Pty. Ltd.)
Penguin Books India Pvt. Ltd., 11 Community Centre, Panchsheel Park, New Delhi—110 017, India
Penguin Group (NZ), 67 Apollo Drive, Rosedale, North Shore 0632, New Zealand
(a division of Pearson New Zealand Ltd.)
Penguin Books (South Africa) (Pty.) Ltd., 24 Sturdee Avenue, Rosebank, Johannesburg 2196,
South Africa

Penguin Books Ltd., Registered Offices: 80 Strand, London WC2R 0RL, England

This is a work of fiction. Names, characters, places, and incidents either are the product of the author's
imagination or are used fictitiously, and any resemblance to actual persons, living or dead, business
establishments, events, or locales is entirely coincidental. The publisher does not have any control
over and does not assume any responsibility for author or third-party websites or their content.

SILVER BORNE

An Ace Book / published by arrangement with Hurog, Inc.

PRINTING HISTORY
Ace hardcover edition / April 2010
Ace mass-market edition / February 2011

Copyright © 2010 by Hurog, Inc.
Map illustration by Michael Enzweiler.
Cover art by Daniel Dos Santos.
Cover design by Judith Lagerman.

ISBN: 978-0-441-01996-0

ACE
Ace Books are published by The Berkley Publishing Group,
a division of Penguin Group (USA) Inc.,
375 Hudson Street, New York, New York 10014.
ACE and the "A" design are trademarks of Penguin Group (USA) Inc.

PRINTED IN THE UNITED STATES OF AMERICA

10 9 8 7 6 5 4 3 2 1

*To Long-Suffering Editors who never lose their cool,
Husbands who feed horses, Children who drive
themselves and fix their own meals, to Vets who take
panicked phone calls at all hours, and to all of you
who give of your time, talents, and energy to
help others and to be there when you are needed.
My thanks.*

ACKNOWLEDGMENTS

There are many people who helped with this book. Thank you to Michael and Susann Boch, my friends in Germany who fix my German and provided Zee with his magic. Thank you to the two women who work at KGH and helped me find a safe space for Samuel. My apologies for losing the scrap of paper I wrote your names down on. If you catch me again, I will include your names in the next book. Thank you to Sylvia Cornish and the ladies of the book club who answered my questions about warrants. My thanks also go to Sgt. Kim Lattin of the Kennewick Police Department, who answered a number of urgent questions for me. To my awesome husband, who choreographed many of the fight scenes (in this and other books). To Tom Lentz, who has a Kel-Tec and with Kaye and Kyle Roberson gave me excellent gun advice. As always, a very grateful author acknowledges the editing talents of the people who read, critiqued, commented, and argued along the way: Mike Briggs, Collin Briggs, Michael Enzweiler, Debbie Lentz, Ann Peters, Kaye and Kyle Roberson, Sara and Bob Schwager, and Anne Sowards.

As always, any and all errors in this book are the responsibility of the author.

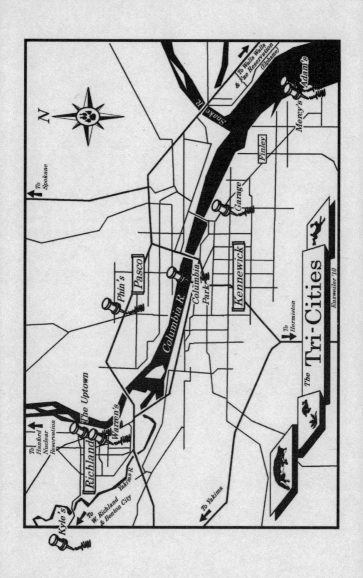

1

~~~

THE STARTER COMPLAINED AS IT TURNED OVER the old Buick's heavy engine. I felt a lot of sympathy for it since fighting outside my weight class was something I was intimately familiar with. I'm a coyote shapeshifter playing in a world of werewolves and vampires—outmatched is an understatement.

"One more time," I told Gabriel, my seventeen-year-old office manager, who was sitting in the driver's seat of his mother's Buick. I sniffed and dried my nose on the shoulder of my work overalls. Runny noses are part and parcel of working in the winter.

I love being a mechanic, runny nose, greasy hands, and all.

It's a life full of frustration and barked knuckles, followed by brief moments of triumph that make all the rest worthwhile. I find it a refuge from the chaos my life has been lately: no one is likely to die if I can't fix his car.

Not even if it is his mother's car. It had been a short day

at school, and Gabriel had used his free time to try to fix his mother's car. He'd taken it from running badly to not at all, then had a friend tow it to the shop to see if I could fix it.

The Buick made a few more unhealthy noises. I stepped back from the open engine compartment. Fuel, fire, and air make the engine run—providing that the engine in question isn't toast.

"It's not catching, Mercy," said Gabriel, as if I hadn't noticed.

He gripped the steering wheel with elegant but work-roughened hands. There was a smear of grease on his cheek-bone, and one eye was red because he hadn't put on safety glasses when he'd crawled under the car. He'd been rewarded with a big chunk of crud—rusty metal and grease—in his eye.

Even though my big heaters were keeping the edge off the cold, we both wore jackets. There is no way to keep a shop truly warm when you are running garage doors up and down all day.

"Mercy, my *mamá* has to be at work in an hour."

"The good news is that I don't think it's anything you did." I stepped away from the engine compartment and met his frantic eyes. "The bad news is that it's not going to be running in an hour. Jury's out on whether it will be back on the road at all."

He slid out of the car and leaned under the hood to stare at the Little Engine That Couldn't as if he might find some wire I hadn't noticed that would miraculously make it run. I left him to his brooding and went through the hall to my office.

Behind the counter was a grubby, used-to-be-white board with hooks where I put the keys of cars I was working on—and a half dozen mystery keys that predated my tenure. I pulled a set of keys attached to a rainbow peace-sign keychain, then trotted back to the garage. Gabriel was back to sitting behind the wheel of his mother's Buick and looking sick. I handed him the keys through the open window.

"Take the Bug," I told him. "Tell your mom that the turn signals don't blink, so she'll have to use hand signals. And tell her not to pull back on the steering wheel too hard or it will come off."

His face got stubborn.

"Look," I said before he could refuse, "it's not going to cost me anything. It won't hold all the kids"—not that the Buick did; there were a lot of kids—"and it doesn't have much of a heater. But it runs, and I'm not using it. We'll work on the Buick after hours until it's done, and you can owe me that many hours."

I was pretty sure the engine had gone to the great junkyard in the sky—and I knew that Sylvia, Gabriel's mother, couldn't afford to buy a new engine, any more than she could buy a newer car. So I'd call upon Zee, my old mentor, to work his magic on it. Literal magic—there was not much figurative about Zee. He was a fae, a gremlin whose natural element was metal.

"The Bug's your project car, Mercy." Gabriel's protest was weak.

My last project car, a Karmann Ghia, had sold. My take of the profits, shared with a terrific bodyman and an upholsterer, had purchased a '71 Beetle and a '65 VW Bus with a little left over. The Bus was beautiful and didn't run; the Bug had the opposite problem.

"I'll work on the Bus first. Take the keys."

The expression on his face was older than it should have been. "Only if you'll let the girls come over and clean on Saturdays until we get the Bug back to you."

I'm not dumb. His little sisters knew how to work—I was getting the better of the bargain.

"Deal," I said before he could take it back. I shoved the keys into his hand. "Go take the car to Sylvia before she's late."

"I'll come back afterward."

"It's late. I'm going home. Just come at the usual time tomorrow."

Tomorrow was Saturday. Officially, I was closed on the weekends, but recent excursions to fight vampires had cut into my bottom line. So I'd been staying open later and working on the weekend to make a little extra money.

There is no cash in battling evil: just the opposite in my experience. Hopefully, I was done with vampires—the last incident had nearly gotten me killed, and my luck was due to run out; a woman whose best talent was changing into a coyote had no business in the big leagues.

I sent Gabriel on his way and started the process of closing up. Garage doors down, heat turned to sixty, lights off. Till drawer in the safe, my purse out. Just as I reached for the final light switch, my cell phone rang.

"Mercy?" It was Zee's son, Tad, who was going to an Ivy League college back East on a full scholarship. The fae were considered a minority, so his official status as half-fae and his grades had gotten him in—hard work was keeping him there.

"Hey, Tad. What's up?"

"I got an odd message on my cell phone last night. Did Phin give you something?"

"Phin?"

"Phineas Brewster, the guy I sent you to when the police had Dad up on murder charges and you needed some information about the fae to find out who really killed that man."

It took me a second. "The bookstore guy? He loaned me a book." I'd been meaning to return it for a while. Just . . . how often do you get a chance to read a book about the mysterious fae, written by the fae? It was handwritten and tough to decipher, slow going—and Phin hadn't seemed anxious to get it back when he'd loaned it to me. "Tell him I'm sorry, and I'll return it to him tonight. I have a date later on, but I can get it to him before that."

There was a little pause. "Actually, he was a little unclear as to whether he wanted it back or not. He just said, 'Tell Mercy to take care of that thing I gave her.' Now I can't get through to him; his phone is shut off. That's why I called you instead." He made a frustrated noise. "Thing is, Mercy, he never turns that damn phone off. He likes to make sure his grandmother can get in touch with him."

Grandmother? Maybe Phin was younger than I'd thought.

"You are worried," I said.

He made a self-deprecating noise. "I know, I know. I'm paranoid."

"No trouble," I said. "I ought to get it back to him anyway. Unless he keeps long hours, he won't be at the store by the time I can get there. Do you have a home address for him?"

He did. I wrote it down and let him go with reassurances. As I locked the door and set the security alarm, I glanced up at the hidden camera. Adam would probably not be watching—unless someone triggered an alarm, mostly the cameras ran all by themselves and simply sent pictures to be recorded. Still . . . as I started for my car, I kissed my hand and blew it to the tiny lens that watched my every move, then mouthed, "See you tonight."

My lover was worried about how well a coyote could play with the wolves, too. Being an Alpha werewolf made him a little overbearing about his concern—and being the CEO of a security contracting firm for various government agencies gave him access to lots of tools to indulge his protective instincts. I'd been mad about the cameras when he'd first had them installed, but I found them reassuring now. A coyote adapts; that's how she survives.

PHINEAS BREWSTER LIVED ON THE THIRD FLOOR of one of the new condo complexes in West Pasco. It didn't seem like the sort of place where a collector of old books would live—but maybe he got his fill of dust, mold, and mildew at work and didn't need it in his home.

I was halfway between my car and the building when I realized that I hadn't brought the book when I got out of the car. I hesitated but decided to leave it where it was, wrapped in a towel on the backseat of the Rabbit. The towel was to protect the book—in case I hadn't gotten all the grease off my hands—but it worked okay to disguise it from would-be thieves, which seemed unlikely here anyway.

I climbed up two sets of stairs and knocked on the door marked 3B. After a count of ten, I rang the doorbell. Nothing. I rang the doorbell one more time, and the door at 3A opened up.

"He's not there," said a gruff voice.

I turned to see a skinny old man, neatly dressed in old boots, new jeans, a button-down Western shirt, and a bolo tie. All he was missing was a cowboy hat. Something—I think it was the boots—smelled faintly of horse. And fae.

"He isn't?"

Officially, all the fae are out to the public and have been for a long time. But the truth is that the Gray Lords, who rule the fae, have been very selective about which of them the public gets to know about and which ones might upset the public—or are more useful posing as human. There are, for instance, a few senators who are fae in hiding. There is nothing in the Constitution that makes it illegal for a fae to be a senator, and the Gray Lords want to keep it that way.

This fae was working pretty hard at passing for human; he wouldn't appreciate me pointing out that he wasn't. So I kept my discovery to myself.

There was a twinkle in the faded eyes as he shook his head. "Nope, he hasn't been home all day."

"Do you know where he is?"

"Phin?" The old man laughed, displaying teeth so even and white they looked false. Maybe they were. "Well, now. He spends most of his time at his store. Nights, too, sometimes."

"Was he here last night?" I asked.

He looked at me and grinned. "Nope. Not him. Maybe he bought up some estate's library and is staying at the store while he catalogs it. He does that sometimes." Phin's neighbor glanced up at the sky, judging the time. "He won't answer the door after hours. Closes himself in the basement and can't hear anyone. Best wait and go check at the shop in the morning."

I looked at my watch. I needed to get home and get ready for my date with Adam.

"If you have something for him," the old man said, his eyes clear as the sky, "you can leave it with me."

Fae don't lie. I used to think it was *can't* lie, but the book I'd borrowed made it pretty clear that there were other factors involved. Phin's neighbor hadn't said he was working at the store. He said maybe. He didn't say he didn't know where Phin was either. My instincts were chiming pretty hard, and I had to work to appear casual.

"I'm here to check up on him," I told him, which was the truth. "His phone is off, and I was worried about him." And then I took a chance. "He hasn't mentioned any of his neighbors—are you new?"

He said, "Moved in not long ago," then changed the subject. "Maybe he left the charger at home. Did you try the store phone?"

"I only have one number for him," I told him. "I think that was his cell."

"If you leave your name, I'll tell him you stopped in."

I let my friendly smile widen. "No worries. I'll run him down myself. Good to know he has neighbors who are watching over him." I didn't thank him—thanking a fae implies that you feel indebted, and being indebted to a fae is a very bad thing. I just gave him a cheerful wave from the bottom of the stairs.

He didn't try to stop me, but he watched me all the way out to my car. I drove out of sight before pulling over and calling Tad.

"Hello," his voice said. "This is my answering machine. Maybe I'm studying; maybe I'm out having a good time. Leave your name and number, and maybe I'll call you back."

"Hey," I told Tad's answering machine. "This is Mercy. Phin wasn't home." I hesitated. Safely back in my car, I thought that I might have overreacted about his neighbor. The better I know the fae, the scarier they seem. But it was probable that he was harmless. Or that he was indeed really scary—but it had nothing to do with Phin.

So I said, "Met Phin's neighbor—who is fae. He suggested calling the store. Do you have the store's number? Have you tried calling him there? I'll keep looking for him."

I hung up and put the Rabbit in gear with every intention of going home. But somehow I ended up on the interstate headed for Richland instead of Finley.

Phin's mysterious call to Tad and the suspicion I felt toward Phin's neighbor made me nervous. It was a short trip to Phin's bookstore, I told myself. It wouldn't hurt to just stop by. Tad was stuck on the other side of the country, and he was worried.

The Uptown is a strip mall, Richland's oldest shopping center. Unlike its newer, upscale counterparts, the Uptown looks as though someone took a couple dozen stores of various styles and sizes, stuck them all together, and surrounded them with a parking lot.

It houses the sorts of businesses that wouldn't thrive in the bigger mall in Kennewick: nonchain restaurants, several antiques (junk) stores, a couple of resale clothing boutiques, a music store, a doughnut shop, a bar or two, and several shops best described as eclectic.

Phin's bookstore was near the south end of the mall, its large picture windows tinted dark to protect the books from sun damage. Gilt lettering on the biggest window labeled it: BREWSTER'S LIBRARY, USED AND COLLECTIBLE BOOKS.

There were no lights behind the shades in the windows, and the door was locked. I put my ear against the glass and listened.

In my human shape, I still have great hearing, not quite

as sharp as the coyote's, but good enough to tell that there was no one moving around in the store. I knocked, but there was no response.

On the window to the right of the door was a sign with the hours the shop was open: ten to six Tuesday through Saturday. Sunday and Monday hours by appointment. The number listed was the one I already had. Six had come and gone.

I knocked on the door one last time, then glanced at my watch again. If I skirted the speed limit, I'd have ten minutes before the wolf was at my door.

MY ROOMMATE'S CAR WAS IN THE DRIVEWAY, looking right at home next to the '78 single-wide trailer where I lived. Very expensive cars, like true works of art, shape the environment to suit themselves. Just by virtue of being there, his car made my home upper-class—no matter what the house itself looked like.

Samuel had the same gift of never being out of place, always fitting in, while at the same time he conveyed the sense that here was someone special, someone important. People liked him instinctively, and trusted him. It served him well as a doctor, but I was inclined to think it served him a little too well as a man. He was too used to getting his way. When charm didn't cut it, he used a tactical brain that would have done credit to Rommel.

Thus, his presence as my roommate.

It had taken me a while to figure out the real reason he'd moved in with me: Samuel needed a pack. Werewolves don't do well on their own, especially not old wolves, and Samuel was a very old wolf. Old and dominant. In any pack except his father's, he would be Alpha. His father was Bran, the Marrok, the most überwerewolf of them all.

Samuel was a doctor, and that was more than enough responsibility for him. He didn't want to be Alpha; he didn't want to stay in his father's pack.

He was lone wolfing it, living with me in the territory of the Columbia Basin Pack but not part of it. I wasn't a werewolf, but I wasn't a helpless human either. I'd been raised in his father's pack, and that was close to being family. So far he and Adam, the local pack's Alpha—and my lover—hadn't killed each other. I was moderately hopeful that would continue to be the case.

"Samuel?" I called as I rushed into the house. "Samuel?"

He didn't answer, but I could smell him. The distinctive odor of werewolf was too strong to be just a leftover trace. I jogged down the narrow hall to his room and knocked softly at the closed door.

It was unlike him not to acknowledge me when I got home.

I worried about Samuel enough to make myself paranoid. He wasn't quite right. Broken but functional, I thought, with an underlying depression that seemed to be getting neither better nor worse as the months passed. His father suspected something was wrong, and I was pretty sure the reason Samuel was living with me and not in his own house in Montana was because he didn't want his father to know for certain how badly broken Samuel really was.

Samuel opened his door, looking his usual self, tall and rangy: attractive, as most werewolves are, regardless of bone structure. Perfect health, permanent youth, and lots of muscle are a pretty surefire formula for good looks.

"You rang?" he said in an expressionless imitation of Lurch, dropping his voice further into the bass register than I'd ever heard him manage. We'd been watching a marathon of *The Addams Family* on TV last night. If he was being funny, he was all right. Even if he wasn't quite meeting my eyes, as if he might be worried about what I'd see.

A purring Medea was stretched across one shoulder. My little Manx cat gave me a pleased look out of half-slitted eyes as he stroked her. As his hand moved along her back, she dug in her hind claws and arched her tailless butt into the air.

"Ouch," he said, trying to pull her off, but she'd gotten her claws through his worn flannel shirt and was hooked onto him tighter than Velcro—and more painfully, too.

"Uhm," I told him, trying not to laugh. "Adam and I are going out tonight. You're on your own for dinner. I didn't make it to the grocery store, so the pickings are meager."

His back was to me as he leaned over his bed so if he managed to unstick the cat, she wouldn't fall all the way to the floor.

"Fine," he said. "Ouch, cat. Don't you know I could eat you in a single bite? You wouldn't even—*ouch*—even leave a tail sticking out."

I left him to it and hurried over to my own room. My cell rang before I made it to the doorway.

"Mercy, he's headed over, and I've got some news for you," said Adam's teenage daughter's voice in my ear.

"Hey, Jesse. Where are we going tonight?"

Thinking of him, I could feel his anticipation and the smooth leather of the steering wheel under his hands— because Adam wasn't just my lover; he was my mate.

In werewolf terms, that meant something slightly different for every mated pair. We were bound not just by love, but by magic. I've learned that some mated pairs can barely perceive the difference . . . and some virtually become the same person. Ugh. Thankfully, Adam and I fell somewhere in the middle. Mostly.

We'd overloaded the magic circuit between us when we'd first sealed our bond. Since then it had proved to be erratic and invasive, flickering in and out for a few hours, then gone again for days. Disconcerting. I expect I'd have gotten used to having the connection to Adam already if it were consistent, as Adam assured me it should have been. As it was, it tended to take me by surprise.

I felt the wheel vibrate under Adam's hand as he started the car, then he was gone, and I was standing in my grubbies talking to his daughter on the phone.

"Bowling," she said.

"Thanks, kid," I told her. "I'll bring back an ice-cream cone for you. Gotta shower."

"You owe me five bucks, though ice cream wouldn't hurt," she told me with a mercenary firmness I could respect. "You'd better shower fast."

Adam and I had a game, a just-for-fun thing. His wolf playing with me, I thought, because it had that feel: a simple game with no losers was wolf play, something they did with the ones they loved. It didn't happen often in the pack as a whole, but among smaller groups, yes.

My mate wouldn't tell me where he was taking us—leaving it for me to discover his plans by whatever means necessary. It was a sign of his respect that he expected me to be successful.

Tonight, I'd bribed his daughter to call me with whatever she knew, even if it was just what he was wearing when he walked out the door. Then I'd be appropriately dressed—though I'd act astonished that we matched so well when I hadn't a clue where he was taking me.

Play for flirting, but also play designed to distract both of us from the reason we were dating instead of living together as mates. His pack didn't like it that his mate was a coyote shifter. Even more than their natural brethren, wolves don't share territory well with other predators. But they'd had a long time to get used to it and were mostly resigned—until Adam brought me into the pack. It shouldn't have been possible. I've never heard of a non-werewolf mate becoming pack.

I set out clothes to wear and hopped into the shower. The showerhead was set low, so it wasn't hard to keep my braids out of the full force of the water as I scrubbed my hands with pumice soap and a nailbrush. I'd already cleaned up, but every little bit helped. A lot of the dirt was ingrained, and my hands would never look fashion-model tended.

When I emerged from the bathroom in a towel, I could

hear voices in the living room. Samuel and Adam were deliberately keeping it soft enough that I couldn't hear the words,
but it didn't sound like there was any tension. They liked each
other just fine, but Adam was Alpha and Samuel a lone wolf
who outpowered him. Sometimes they had trouble being in
the same room together, but evidently not tonight.

I started to reach for the jeans I'd laid out on my bed.
Bowling.

I hesitated. I just couldn't see it in my head. Not the bowling part—I was sure that Adam enjoyed bowling. Throwing a
weighty ball at a bunch of helpless pins and watching the resultant mayhem is just the kind of thing that werewolves love.

What I couldn't see was Adam telling Jesse he was taking me bowling. Not when he was trying to keep it from
me. The last time all she'd been able to do was tell me what
he was wearing when he left the house.

Maybe I was just being paranoid. I opened my closet
and looked at the meager pickings hanging there. I had
more dresses than I'd had a year ago. Three more.

Jesse would have noticed if he'd dressed up.

I glanced at the bed where my new jeans and a dark blue
T-shirt summoned me with their comfort. Bribes can go both
ways—and Jesse would find it amusing to play double agent.

So I pulled out a pale gray dress, classy enough that I
could wear it to all but the most formal of occasions and
not so dressy that it would look out of place at a restaurant
or theater. If we really went bowling, I could bowl in the
dress. I slipped into the dress and quickly unbraided my
hair and brushed it out.

"Mercy, aren't you ready yet?" asked Samuel, a touch
of amusement in his voice. "Didn't you say you had a hot
date?"

I opened the door and saw I hadn't gotten it quite right.
Adam was wearing a tux.

Adam is shorter than Samuel, with the build of a wres-
tler and the face of . . . I don't know. It is Adam's face,

and it is beautiful enough to distract people from the air of power that he conveys. His hair is dark, and he keeps it short. He told me once that it is so the military personnel that he has to deal with in the course of his security business feel comfortable with him. But these last few months, as I've gotten to know him better, I think it is because his face embarrasses him. The short hair removes any hint of vanity, and says, "Here I am. Let's get down to business."

I would love him if he had three eyes and two teeth, but sometimes his beauty just hits me. I blinked once, took a deep breath, and brushed off the need to proclaim him *mine* so I could pull my mind back to interactive mode.

"Ah," I said, snapping my fingers, "I knew I'd forgotten something." I ran back to my closet and snagged a sparkly silver wrap that dressed the gray up appropriately.

I came back out to see Samuel giving Adam a five-dollar bill.

"I told you she'd figure it out," Adam said smugly.

"Good," I told him. "You can pay Jesse with that. She told me we were going bowling. I need to find a better spy."

He grinned, and I had to work to keep my face annoyed. Oddly enough, given his face, it wasn't the beauty of Adam-with-a-smile that delighted me when he grinned—though he really was spectacular. It was the knowledge that I'd made him smile. Adam was not given to . . . playfulness, except with me.

"Hey, Mercy," Samuel said, as Adam opened the front door.

I turned to him, and he gave me a kiss on the forehead.

"You be happy." The odd phrase caught my attention, but there was nothing odd in the rest of what he said. "I've got the red-eye shift. Most likely I won't see you when you get back." He looked up at Adam, meeting his eyes in a male-to-male challenge that had Adam's eyes narrowing. "Take care of her." Then he pushed us out and closed the door before Adam could take offense at the order.

After a long moment, Adam laughed and shook his head.

"Don't worry," he said, knowing the other wolf would hear him through the door. "Mercy takes care of herself; I just get to clean up the mess afterward." If I hadn't been watching his face, I wouldn't have seen the twist on his lips as he spoke. As if he didn't like what he was saying very much.

I felt suddenly self-conscious. I like who I am—but there are plenty of men who wouldn't. I am a mechanic. Adam's first wife had been all soft curves, and I am mostly muscle. Not very feminine, my mother liked to complain. And then there were those idiosyncrasies that were the aftermath of rape.

Adam held out his hand to me, and I put mine in his. He had gotten very good at inviting my touch. At not touching me first.

I looked at our clasped hands as we went down the porch stairs. I'd thought that I was getting better, that the involuntary flinching, the fear, was leaving. It occurred to me that maybe he was just getting better at working around my fears.

"What's wrong?" he asked, as we stopped beside his truck.

It was so new there was still a sticker on the rear-seat window. He'd replaced his SUV after one of his wolves had dented the fender defending me—followed by a separate incident when an ice elf (honking huge fae) who was chasing me dropped the front half of a building on it.

"Mercy—" He frowned at me. "You don't owe me for the damned truck."

His hand was still holding mine, and I had a moment to realize that our fickle mate bond had given him an insight into what I was thinking, before a vision dropped me to my knees.

IT WAS DARK, AND ADAM WAS AT HIS COMPUTER in his home office. His eyes burned, his hands ached, and his back was stiff from so many hours of work.

The house was quiet. Too quiet. No wife to protect from the world. It had been a long time since he'd loved her—it is dangerous to love someone who doesn't love you in return. He'd been a soldier too long to put himself deliberately in danger without a good reason. She loved his status, his money, and his power. She'd have loved it better if it had belonged to someone who did as she told him.

He didn't love her, but he'd loved taking care of her. Loved buying her little presents, loved the idea of her.

Losing her had been bad; losing his daughter was much, much worse. Jesse trailed noise and cheer everywhere she went—and her absence was . . . difficult. His wolf was restless. A creature of the moment, his wolf. There was no way to comfort it with the knowledge that he'd have Jesse back for the summer. Not that he derived much comfort from that either. So he tried to lose himself in work.

Someone knocked on the back door.

He pushed back the chair and had to pause. The wolf was angry that someone had breached his sanctuary. Not even his pack had been brave enough these past few days to approach him in his home.

By the time he stalked into the kitchen, he had it mostly under control. He jerked open the back door and expected to see one of his wolves. But it was Mercy.

She didn't look cheerful—but then, she seldom did when she had to come over and talk to him. She was tough and independent and not at all happy to have him interfere in any way with that independence. It had been a long time since someone had bossed him around the way she did—and he liked it. More than a wolf who'd been Alpha for twenty years ought to like it.

She smelled of burnt car oil, jasmine from the shampoo she'd been using that month, and chocolate. Or maybe that last was the cookies on the plate she handed him.

"Here," she said stiffly. And he realized it was shyness

that pinched in the corner of her mouth. "Chocolate usually helps me regain my balance when life kicks me in the teeth."

She didn't wait for him to say anything, just turned around and walked back to her house.

He took the cookies back to the office with him. After a few minutes, he ate one. Chocolate, thick and dark, spread across his tongue, its bitterness alleviated by a sinful amount of brown sugar and vanilla. He'd forgotten to eat and hadn't realized it.

But it wasn't the chocolate or the food that made him feel better. It was Mercy's kindness to someone she viewed as her enemy. And right at that moment, he realized something. She would never love him for what he could do for her.

He ate another cookie before getting up to make himself dinner.

ADAM SHUT DOWN THE BOND BETWEEN US UNTIL it was nothing more than a gossamer thread.

"I'm sorry," he murmured against my ear. "So sorry. F—" He swallowed the obscenity before it left his lips. He pulled me closer, and I realized we were both sitting in the gravel driveway, huddled next to the truck. And the gravel was really cold on my bare skin.

"Are you all right?" he said.

"Do you know what you showed me?" I asked. My voice was hoarse.

"I thought it was a flashback," he answered. He'd seen me have them before.

"Not one of mine," I told him. "One of yours."

He stilled. "Was it bad?"

He'd been in Vietnam; he'd been a werewolf since before I was born—he'd probably seen a lot of bad stuff.

"It seemed like a private moment that I had no business seeing," I told him truthfully. "But it wasn't bad."

I'd seen him the moment that I'd become something more than an assignment from the Marrok.

I remembered feeling stupid standing on his back porch with a plate of cookies for a man whose life had just gone down in the flames of a nasty divorce. He hadn't said anything when he answered the door—so I'd assumed that he'd thought it stupid, too. I'd gone back home as fast as I could without running.

I had had no idea that it had helped. Nor that he saw me as tough and capable. Funny, I'd always thought I looked weak to the werewolves.

So what if I still flinched if he forgot and put a hand on my shoulder? Time would fix that. I was already a lot better: daily flashbacks to the rape were a thing of the past. We'd work through it. Adam was willing to make allowances for me.

And our bond did its rubber-band thing, which it did sometimes, and snapped back into place, giving him access to my thoughts as if my head were clear as glass.

"Whatever you need," he said, his body suddenly still as the evening air. "Whatever I can do."

I relaxed my shoulders, burying my nose against his collarbone, and after a second, the relaxation was genuine. "I love you," I told him. "And we need to talk about me paying you for that truck."

"I'm not—"

I cut off his words. I meant to put a finger against his lips or something tender like that. But I'd jerked my head up in reaction to his apology and slammed my forehead into his chin. Shutting him up much more effectively than I'd meant to as he bit his tongue.

He laughed as he bled down his shirt, and I babbled apologies. He let his head fall back against the truck door with a thump.

"Leave off, Mercy. It'll close up quick enough on its own."

I backed up until I was sitting beside him—half laughing

myself, because although it probably hurt quite a bit, he was right that his injury would heal in a few minutes. It was minor, and he was a werewolf.

"You'll quit trying to pay for the SUV," he told me.

"The SUV *was* my fault," I informed him.

"You didn't throw a wall on it," he said. "I might have let you pay for the dent—"

"*Don't* even try to lie to me," I huffed indignantly, and he laughed again.

"Fine. I wouldn't have. But it's a moot point anyway, because after the wall fell on it, fixing the dent was out of the question. And the ice elf's lack of control was completely the vampire's fault—"

I could have kept arguing with him—I usually like arguing with Adam. But there were things I liked better.

I leaned forward and kissed him.

He tasted of blood and Adam—and he didn't seem to have any trouble following the switch from mild bickering to passion. After a while—I don't know how long—Adam looked down at his bloodstained shirt and started laughing again. "I suppose we might as well go bowling after all," he said, pulling me to my feet.

2

WE STOPPED AT A STEAK HOUSE FOR DINNER first.

He'd left the bloodstained coat and formal shirt in the car and snagged a dark blue T-shirt from a bag of miscellaneous clothes in the backseat. He'd asked me if he looked odd wearing a T-shirt with tuxedo pants. He couldn't see the way the shirt clung to the muscles of his shoulders and back. I reassured him, truthfully—and with a straight face—that no one would care.

It was Friday night, and business was brisk. Happily, the service was fast.

After the waitress took our orders, Adam said, a little too casually, "So what did you see in your vision?"

"Nothing embarrassing," I told him. "Just one time when I brought cookies over to you."

His eyes brightened. "I see," he said, and his shoulders relaxed a bit, even if his cheeks reddened. "I was thinking about that."

"We okay?" I asked him. "I'm sorry I intruded."

He shook his head. "No apologies necessary. You're welcome to whatever you pick up."

"So," I said casually, "your first time was under the bleachers, huh?"

He jerked his head up.

"Gotcha. Warren told me."

He smiled. "Cold and wet and miserable."

The waitress plunked our food down in front of us and hurried on her way. Adam fed me bites of his rare filet mignon, and I fed him some of my salmon. Food was good, company better, and if I had been a cat, I'd have purred.

"You look happy." He took a sip of his coffee and stretched out a leg so his foot was against mine.

"You make me happy," I told him.

"You could be happy all the time," he said, eating the last bite of baked potato, "and move in with me."

To wake up next to him every morning . . . but . . . "Nope. I've caused you enough trouble," I told him. "The pack and I need to come to . . . détente before I'm moving in. Your home is the den, the heart of the pack. They need a place where they feel safe."

"They can adjust."

"They're adjusting as fast as they can," I told him. "First there was Warren—did you hear that after you let him in, several other packs have allowed gay wolves to join, too? And now there's me. A coyote in a werewolf pack—you have to admit that's quite a lot of change for one pack to take."

"Next thing you know," he said, "women will have the vote or a black man will become president." He looked serious, but there was humor in his voice.

"See?" I pointed my fork at him. "They're all stuck in the eighteen hundreds, and you're expecting them to change. Samuel likes to say that most werewolves have all the change they can deal with the first time they become wolf. Other kinds of change are tough to force on them."

"Peter and Warren are the only ones who've been around since the eighteen hundreds," Adam told me. "Most of them are younger than I am."

The waitress came and blinked a little as Adam ordered three desserts—werewolves take a lot of food to keep themselves fueled up. I shook my head when she looked my way.

When she left, I took up the conversation from where I'd left off. "It won't hurt us to wait a few months until things settle down."

If he hadn't basically agreed with me, I'd have been sleeping in his house already instead of making do with dates. He understood as well as I did that pulling me into his pack had caused a lot of resentment. Maybe if it had been a healthy, well-adjusted pack beforehand, things wouldn't have gotten so tense.

A few years ago, some of his pack had started harassing me—a coyote living next door. Werewolves, like their natural brethren, are territorial, and they don't share their hunting ground easily with other predators. So to put a stop to it, Adam declared me his mate. I hadn't known at the time why the harassment abruptly stopped—and Adam hadn't been in a hurry to tell me. But pack magic demanded that the declaration be answered, and Adam bore the cost when it wasn't. It left him weaker, crabbier, and less able to help his pack stay calm, cool, and collected. By bringing me in as a member of his pack at virtually the same time our mating bond connected, Adam hadn't given his people a chance to get their feet underneath them before throwing them back onto uncertain ground.

"One more month," he said finally. "And then they—and Samuel, too—will just have to get used to it." His eyes, the color of bitter dark chocolate, were serious as he leaned forward. "And you will marry me."

I smiled, showing my teeth. "Don't you mean, 'Will you marry me?' "

I meant it to be funny, but his eyes brightened until little gold flecks were swimming in the darkness. "You had your chance to run, coyote. It's too late now." He smiled. "Your mother is happy that she'll be able to use some of the stuff from your sister's wedding that wasn't."

Panic swelled my heart. "You didn't talk to her about this, did you?" I had visions of a church filled with people and white satin everywhere. And doves. My mother had had doves at her wedding. My sister had eloped to get away from her. My mother is a steamroller, and she doesn't listen very well . . . to anyone.

The wolf left his eyes, and he grinned. "You're okay with marrying a werewolf who has a teenage daughter and a pack that's falling apart—and your mother panics you?"

"You've met my mother," I said. "She ought to panic you, too."

He laughed.

"You just weren't around her long enough." It was only fair that I warn him.

————————

WE WERE LUCKY AND GOT OUR SCORING TABLE to ourselves, as the women who had the lane to our left were packing up when we got back from choosing our bowling balls from the available stack. Mine was bright green with gold swirls. Adam's was black.

"You have no imagination," I told him smugly. "It wouldn't hurt if you found a pink ball to bowl with."

"All the pink balls have kid-sized holes in them," he told me. "The black balls are the heaviest."

I opened my mouth, but he shut me up with a kiss. "Not here," he said. "Look next to us."

We were being observed by a boy of about five and a toddler in a frilly pink dress.

I raised my nose in the air. "As if I were going to joke about your ball. How juvenile."

He grinned at me. "I thought you'd feel that way."

I sat down and messed with player names on the interface on the scoring table until I was satisfied.

"Found On Road Dead," he said dryly, looking over my shoulder.

"I thought I'd use our cars as names. You drive a Ford now. F-O-R-D."

"Very Woo-hoo?"

"Not a lot of cool words start with a 'W,' " I admitted.

He leaned over my shoulder and changed it to "Vintage Wabbit," then into my ear, he said, "Very wicked. Mine."

"I can live with that." His warm breath on my ear felt very wicked, all right.

Until Adam, I'd always felt like his black bowling ball—boring but useful. I'm nothing special in the looks department, once you get past the slightly exotic coloring my Blackfoot father gave me. And Adam . . . Heads turn when Adam walks by. Even in the bowling alley, he was attracting attention.

"Go throw your boring black ball," I told him sternly. "Flirting with the scorekeeper won't help you because the computers keep score now."

"As if I needed help," he smirked, walking backward a few steps before he turned around to pay attention to the poor, helpless bowling pins.

He bowled with the deadly earnestness and decisive style with which he did everything else. Controlled power, that was Adam.

But I started noticing something other than admiration in the gazes of the people who were beginning to look at us. At Adam. He wasn't really a celebrity; he tried to stay out of the news. But Adam was one of the wolves who was out to the public—a sober, successful businessman whose security company protected American nuclear technology from foreign hands: a good guy who happened to be a werewolf. All fine and dandy when they read about it in the newspapers, I guess. But it was different to see a werewolf at their bowling alley.

They are afraid of him.

The thought was so strong it felt as if someone were whispering into my ear, bringing with it worry.

Look at them. I saw the men bristling over their women, the mothers hastily gathering their children to them. In a moment, there would be a mass exodus—and that was assuming that some of the young men I saw coming to their feet about four lanes down didn't do something stupid.

He hasn't noticed yet.

Adam gave me a sly, pleased grin at his strike as he walked back—a strike more remarkable because there were no shattered pins, no broken equipment. Too much power can be as great a disadvantage as not enough.

Look beside you.

I took up my green ball and glanced at the people next to us. Like Adam, they were too involved in their game to notice the growing murmuring. The young boy was crawling under the chairs, and his parents were bickering over something on the scoreboard. Their too-cute toddler— with her pink dress and little pink lions in the two-inch ponytails that stuck out from the back of her head—had climbed up on the bowling platform and was playing with the ball-return blowers designed to dry sweaty palms. She wiggled her little hands over the cool air and laughed.

Adam will feel bad when he notices that people are leaving because he's here.

Sweat gathered on my forehead, which was ridiculous because it was cool inside. I paused halfway to the throw line (or whatever it was called) and, imitating Adam, I brought the ball up and held it in the middle of my chest.

Perhaps there's a way to show everyone that he's not a monster, he's a hero.

I glanced over my shoulder and watched the toddler

bang on the air vent. Her brother had wandered back through the seating area and was playing with the balls on the racks. His mother had just noticed he'd gotten away from her and had gotten up to go get him.

I turned my attention back to the pins.

"Are you watching?" I asked Adam. The urge to do something for Adam was so strong it made my hands clench.

"My eyes are peeled," he said. "Are you going to do something amazing?"

I swung the ball awkwardly, as if I'd never bowled before, missed the release, and sent it zipping backward toward the little girl playing with the air.

As soon as it left my fingers, I couldn't believe what I'd done. Sweating, shaking, and horrified, I turned. But as quick as I was, I'd missed the action.

Adam had caught the ball a good two feet short of the toddler.

She looked up at Adam, whose noisy fall to the ground had disturbed her play. When she saw that there was a strange man so close, her eyes got big, and her bottom lip stuck out.

Adam is mostly uninterested in children (other than his own) until they are teenagers or older and, as he told me once, capable of interesting conversation.

"Hey," he said, looking very uncomfortable.

She considered him a moment. But she was female and Adam was . . . well, Adam. So she put her hands in front of her mouth and giggled.

It was adorable. Darling cute. He was a goner, and everyone who was watching could see it.

The miniature conqueror squealed as her father grabbed her up and her mother, little boy in tow behind her, babbled out thanks.

And you are the villain of the piece. Poor Mercy.

Of course I was the bad guy; I'd nearly smooshed a toddler. What had I been thinking? If she'd taken a step back, or if Adam hadn't been fast enough, she could have been killed.

She wasn't in any danger. You didn't throw it at her, just rolled it past her. It wouldn't have hit her. You saved him, and he didn't even notice.

He frowned at me after we moved over a lane (for the safety of everyone, though the anxious manager didn't actually come out and say that). We restarted the game, and he let me bowl first.

I carefully rolled the first ball down the gutter, where it wouldn't be likely to hit anyone. I don't know if I did it for my own sake or to reassure anyone watching me.

All you were trying to do was keep Adam happy. And this is the thanks you get.

Almost squishing babies wasn't exactly an act I expected thanks for. I rubbed my forehead as if it would help clear my thoughts.

It wouldn't have hit her. You made sure of it. Even if Adam had missed, it would have rolled harmlessly past.

Adam watched me thoughtfully, but he didn't say anything to me as I engineered my loss by a hundred bazillion points. I could hardly bowl well after my spectacular failure, or someone would figure out I'd done it on purpose.

I *had* done it on purpose, hadn't I?

I couldn't believe I'd done something like that. What was wrong with me? If Adam had looked more approachable, I might have talked to him about it.

He doesn't want to hear what you have to say. Best just keep quiet. He'd never understand anyway.

I didn't mind, didn't object anyhow, to the way Adam made sure to stand where he could field my ball if I lost control again. After all, his rescue of the baby looked better if he seemed to think I was an idiot, right?

Four turns in, Adam stepped in front of me, and said in a low voice that wouldn't carry beyond us, "You did it on purpose, didn't you? What in the *hell* were you thinking?"

And for some reason, even though I agreed with him, his question made me mad. Or maybe that was the voice in my head.

He should have understood sooner. He should understand his mate better than anyone. You shouldn't have to defend yourself to him. Best not to say anything at all.

I raised an eyebrow and stalked past him to pick up my ball. Hurt fed anger. I was so mad I forgot myself enough to get a strike. I made sure it was the last point I made in the game—and I didn't say a word to him.

Adam won with a score over two hundred. When he finished bowling the last frame, he took both our balls back to the rack while I changed my shoes.

The teenage boys (by then five lanes away) stopped him and had him sign an autograph for them. I took my shoes back to the desk and turned them in—and paid for the game, too.

"Is he really the Alpha?" asked the teenage girl behind the counter.

"Yep," I said through clenched lips.

"Wow."

"Yep."

I left the bowling alley and waited for him by the side of his shiny new truck, which was locked. The temperature had dropped by twenty degrees as soon as the sun went down, and it was cold enough to make me, in my heels and dress, uncomfortable. Or it would have been if my temper hadn't kept me nice and warm.

I stood by the passenger door, and he didn't see me at first. I saw him lift his head and sniff the air. I leaned my hip against the side of the truck, and the movement caught his attention. He kept his eyes on me as he walked from the building to the truck.

He'd thought you'd deliberately endanger a child to make him look good. He doesn't understand that you'd never do such a thing. She wouldn't have gotten hurt; the ball would have rolled past her harmlessly. He owes you an apology.

I didn't say anything to him. I could hardly tell him that the little voices made me do it, could I?

His eyes narrowed, but he kept his mouth shut, too. He popped the locks and let me get myself in the truck. I paid attention to the buckle, then settled back in the seat and closed my eyes. My hands clenched in my lap, then loosened as a familiar shape inserted itself and my hands closed on the old wood and silver of the fae-made walking stick.

I'd gotten so used to its showing up unexpectedly, I wasn't even surprised, though this was the first time I'd actually felt it appear where it hadn't been. I was more preoccupied with the disaster of our date.

With the walking stick in my hands, it felt as if my head cleared at last. Abruptly I wasn't angry anymore. I was just tired and I wanted to go home.

"Mercy."

Adam was angry enough for the both of us: I could hear the grinding of his teeth. He thought I would throw a bowling ball at a little girl.

I couldn't blame him for his anger. I moved the walking stick until the base was on the floor, then rubbed my thumb on the silver head. There was nothing I could say to defend myself—I didn't want to defend myself. I'd been recklessly stupid. What if Adam had been slower? I felt sick.

"I don't understand women," he bit out, starting the car up and gunning the gas a little harder than necessary.

I gripped the fairy stick with all my might and kept my eyes closed all the way home. My stomach hurt. He was right to be angry, right to be upset.

I had the desperate feeling something was wrong, wrong, wrong. I couldn't talk to him because I was afraid I'd make everything worse. I needed to understand why I'd done what I'd done before I could make him understand.

We pulled into my driveway in silence. Samuel's car

was gone, so he must have headed into work earlier than he meant to. I needed to talk to him because I had a very nasty suspicion about tonight. I couldn't talk to Adam—because it would sound like I was trying to find excuses for myself. I needed Samuel, and he wasn't here.

I released my seat belt and unlocked my door—Adam's arm shot in front of me and held the door closed.

"We need to talk," he said, and this time he didn't sound angry.

But he was too close. I couldn't breathe with him this close. And right then, when I could least afford it, I had another panic attack.

With a desperate sound I couldn't help, I jerked my feet to the seat and propelled myself up and over the front seat and into the back. The back door was locked, too, but even as I started to struggle with the latch, Adam popped the lock, and I was free.

I stumbled back away from the truck, shaking and sweating in the night air, the fae stick in one hand like a cudgel or a sword that could protect me from . . . being stupid. Stupid. Stupid. Damn Tim and all that he'd done for leaving me stupidly shaking while I stood perfectly safely in the middle of my own stupid driveway.

I wanted to be myself again instead of this stranger who was afraid of being touched—and who had little voices in her head that made her throw bowling balls at children.

"Mercy," Adam said. He'd gotten out of the truck and come around the back of it. His voice was gentle, and the sound of it . . . Abruptly I could feel his sorrow and bewilderment—something had happened, and he didn't know what it was. He just knew he'd screwed up somehow. He had no idea how it had gone so badly wrong.

I didn't want to know what he was feeling because it only made me stupider—and more vulnerable.

"I have to go in," I told the stick in my hand because I couldn't look up at Adam's face just then. If I'd looked at him, I think I would have run, and he'd have chased me. Some other day, that might have been fun. Tonight, it would be disastrous. So I moved slowly.

He didn't follow me as I walked to my door but said from where he stood, "I'll send someone over to stand guard."

Because I was the Alpha's mate. Because he worried about me. Because of Tim. Because of guilt.

"No," he said, taking a step closer to me, telling me the bond was stronger on his side at that moment. "Because I love you."

I shut the door gently between us and leaned my forehead against it.

My stomach hurt; my throat was tight. I wanted to scream or punch someone, but instead I clenched the walking stick until my fingers hurt and listened to Adam get in his truck and back out of my driveway.

I looked down at the walking stick. Once—maybe still— it made all the sheep its bearer owned have twins. But it had been fashioned a long time ago, and old magic sometimes grew and developed in strange ways. It had become more than just a walking stick with agricultural applications. Exactly what that meant, no one really knew—other than it followed me around.

Maybe it was a coincidence that the first time I'd felt like myself since walking into the bowling alley was when I'd grabbed it in Adam's truck. And maybe it wasn't.

I've had a lot of fights with Adam over the years. Probably inevitable given who we were—the literal as well as figurative Alpha male and . . . me, who was raised among lots of dominant-type males and had chosen not to let them control me (no matter how benign that control might have been). I'd never felt like this after a fight, though. Usually, I feel energized and cheerful, not sick and scared out of my skin.

Of course, usually the fight is my idea and not someone using the pack bonds to play with my head.

I could be wrong, I thought. Maybe it had been some new kind of nifty reaction to my run-in with the not-so-dearly-departed Tim—as if panic attacks and flashbacks weren't enough.

But, now that it was over, the voices tasted like the pack to me. I'd never heard of pack being able to influence someone through the bonds, but there was a lot I didn't understand about pack magic.

I needed to shed my skin, free myself for a little while of the pack and mate bonds that left too many people with access to my head. I could do that: maybe I couldn't get rid of everything, but I could shed my human skin and run alone, clear my head for just a little bit.

I needed to figure out for certain what had happened tonight. Distance didn't always provide me with solitude, but it usually worked to weaken the bonds between Adam and me—and also between the pack and me. I needed to leave before whoever he decided to send over to guard me arrived, because they certainly wouldn't let me run off on my own.

Without bothering to go to my bedroom, I stripped. Setting down the walking stick took more effort, which told me that I'd already convinced myself that it had served to block whoever had been influencing me.

I waited, ready to pick up the walking stick again, but there were no more voices in my head. Either they had lost interest because Adam was gone and they'd succeeded in their efforts. Or else distance was as much of a factor as I believed. Either way, I would leave the stick behind because a coyote carrying such a thing would draw too much attention.

So I slid into my coyote-self with a sigh of relief. I felt instantly safer, more centered, in my four-pawed form. Stupid, because I'd never noticed that changing shape interfered with either my mate bond or pack bond in the least. But I was willing to grab onto anything that made me feel better at this point.

I hopped through the dog door Samuel had installed in my back door and out into the night.

Outside smelled different, better, clearer to me. In my coyote skin, I took in more information than the human me. I could scent the marmot in her nearby den and the bats who nested in the rafters of my garage. The month was half-gone, and the moon was a wide slice that was orange—even to my coyote color-impaired eyes. The dust of the last of the harvest was in the air.

And a werewolf in lupine form was approaching.

It was Ben, I thought, which was good. Darryl would have sensed my coyote, but Ben had been raised in London and had lived there until a year and a half ago. He would be easier to fool.

I froze where I stood, resisting the temptation to drop flat or hide. Motion attracts attention, and my fur is colored to blend in with the desert.

Ben didn't even glance my way, and as soon as he rounded the corner—obviously heading toward my front porch—I took off through the sagebrush and dry grass, off into the desert night.

I was on my way to the river, to a rock beach where I could be alone, when a rabbit broke out of the brush in front of me. And it was only then I realized how hungry I was.

I'd eaten a lot at dinner—there was no reason for me to be hungry. Not just a little hungry. Starving. Something was wrong.

I set that thought aside as I gave chase. I missed that rabbit, but not the next, and I ate him down to the bones. It wasn't nearly enough. I hunted for another half hour before I found a quail.

I don't like to kill quail. The way the lone feather sticking up on top bobs in opposition to their heads when they walk makes me smile. And they are silly, without a sporting chance against a coyote, at least not against me. I suppose they can't be that vulnerable, because I'm not the only coyote around and there are a lot of quail. But I always feel guilty about hunting them.

As I finished my second kill, I planned what I'd do to the person who made me so hungry I had to eat quail.

A werewolf pack can feed off of any of its members, borrowing energy. I wasn't sure exactly how it worked, though I'd seen it often enough. It's part of what makes an Alpha wolf more than he was before he took on that mantle.

None of that had ever affected me before I'd become a member of Adam's pack, so I hadn't worried about it. No one had been able to get inside my head and make me think that throwing a bowling ball at a toddler was a good idea. Or make me take out my frustration on Adam.

Finished and full, I made it to my final destination without further incident.

I don't know if anyone owned this little bit of the river; the nearest fence was a hundred yards away, the nearest house a little farther than that. There were a few old beer cans scattered around, and if the weather had been a little bit warmer, I might have run into people.

I climbed on the big rock and tried to feel the pack or Adam. I was alone. Just me, the river, and, far up on the Horse Heaven Hills, the little lights from the windmill farms. I don't know if it was the distance or if there was something special about this little bit of ground, but I'd never been able to feel the touch of the mate or pack bond here.

Thank goodness.

Only when I was certain Adam couldn't hear me did I let myself dwell on how creepy it was to have someone else in my head, even Adam, whom I loved. Something I would never, if I could help it, allow Adam to know.

Oddly, because Adam had been a wolf for longer than I was alive, I accepted him as a werewolf more easily than he did himself. Knowing that I was freaked-out by the greatest gift any wolf could give another wouldn't surprise him (as it did me), but it would hurt him needlessly. I would adjust in time—I didn't have any choice if I wanted to keep him.

If I had to deal with only the mate bond between Adam and me, it would be easier. But he'd made me pack, too, and when the link worked as it was supposed to, I could feel all of them there, with me. And with that bond, apparently, they could suck energy from me and make me fight with their Alpha.

Alone in my head, it was easy to look back and see how it had happened—a nudge here, a push there. I would do a great deal to keep Adam from being hurt, but not endanger an innocent—and I have never in my life given anyone the silent treatment. Anyone who offends me deserves to hear exactly how they trespassed—or needs to be lulled into a false sense of security before the sneak attack when they aren't paying attention. But silence had been Adam's ex-wife's weapon of choice.

Whoever had worked on me was trying to drive us apart.

So who had it been? The whole pack? Part of the pack? Was it deliberate—or more that the whole pack hated me and was trying to force me away? Most important of all, to me anyway, was: how did I stop it from ever happening again?

There had to be a way—doubtless if a werewolf could influence a pack member as easily as they'd influenced me, Alphas would have much tighter control of their packs than they did. A pack would run more like a cult and less like a bunch of testosterone-laden wild beasts momentarily subdued by the threat of immediate death under their leader's fangs. That or they'd have killed each other off entirely.

I'd needed Samuel to be home so I could ask him about how things worked. Adam doubtless knew, but I wanted to go into this conversation knowing how to approach him.

If Adam thought one of his pack members was trying mind-influencing tricks on me . . . I wasn't certain what the rules were for something like that. That was one of the things I wanted to find out from Samuel. If someone was going to die, I wanted to make sure I approved, or at least knew about it before I pulled the trigger. If someone *was* going to die, I might just keep this to myself and create a suitable punishment of my own instead.

I'd have to wait until Samuel got back from work. Until then, maybe I'd just keep a good hold on the walking stick and hope for the best.

I stayed out on the little rocky beach watching the river in the moonlight as long as I dared. But if I didn't get back before Ben realized I was gone, he'd call out the troops. And I just wasn't in the mood for a pack of werewolves.

I stood up, stretched, and started the long run back home.

———

WHEN I ARRIVED AT MY BACK DOOR, BEN WAS pacing back and forth in front of it uneasily. When he saw me, he froze—he'd started realizing something was wrong, but until he saw me, he hadn't been sure I wasn't there. His upper lip curled, but he didn't quite manage a snarl, caught as he was between anger and worry, dominant-male protective instincts and the understanding that I was of higher rank.

Body language, when you know how to read it, can be more expressive than speech.

His frustration was his problem, so I ignored him and hopped through the dog door—much, much too small for a wolf—and went straight to my bedroom.

I changed out of my coyote form, grabbed underwear and a clean T-shirt, and headed for bed. It wasn't horribly late—our date had been very short, and my run hadn't taken much longer. Still, morning came soon, and I had a car to work on. *And* I had to be in top form to figure out just how to approach Samuel so he wouldn't tell Adam what I was asking.

Maybe I should just call his father instead. *Yes*, I decided. I'd call Bran.

——————

I WOKE UP WITH THE PHONE IN MY EAR—AND thought for a moment that I'd completed the task I'd decided upon before falling asleep, because the voice in my ear was speaking Welsh. That didn't make any sense at all. Bran wouldn't speak freaking Welsh to *me*, especially not on the phone, where foreign languages are even harder to understand.

Muzzily, I realized I could still almost remember hearing the phone ring. I must have grabbed it in the process of waking up—but that didn't explain the language.

I blinked at the clock—I'd been asleep less than two hours—and about that time I figured out whose voice was babbling to me.

"Samuel?" I asked. "Why are you speaking Welsh? I don't understand you unless you talk a lot slower. And use small words." It was kind of a joke. Welsh never seems to have small words.

"Mercy," he said heavily.

For some reason my heart started beating hard and heavy, as if I were about to get some very bad news. I sat up.

"Samuel?" I addressed the silence on the other end of the phone.

"Come get—"

He fumbled the words, as if his English were very bad, which it wasn't and never had been. Not as long as I'd known him—which was most of my thirty-odd years of life.

"I'll be right there," I said, jerking on my jeans with one hand. "Where?"

"In the X-ray storeroom." He barely stumbled over that phrase.

I knew where the storeroom was, on the far end of the

emergency room at Kennewick General, where he worked. "I'll come for you."

He hung up without saying anything more.

Something had gone very wrong. Whatever it was, it couldn't be catastrophic if he was going to meet me in the storeroom, away from everyone. If they knew he was a werewolf, there would be no need for storerooms.

Unlike Adam, Samuel was not out to the public. No one would let a werewolf practice medicine—which was probably smart, actually. The smells of blood and fear and death were too much for most of them. But Samuel had been a doctor for a very long time, and he was a good one.

Ben was sitting on my front porch as I ran out the door, and I tripped over him, rolling down the four steep, unyielding stairs to land on the ground in the gravel.

He'd known I was coming out; I hadn't tried to be quiet. He could have moved out of my way, but he hadn't. Maybe he'd even moved into my way on purpose. He didn't twitch as I looked up at him.

I recognized the look though I hadn't seen it from him before. I was a coyote mated to their Alpha, and they were darned sure I wasn't good enough.

"You heard about the fight tonight," I told him.

He laid his ears back and put his nose on his front paws.

"Then someone should have told you that they were using the pack bonds to mess with my head." I hadn't meant to say anything about it until I had a chance to talk to Samuel, but falling down the stairs had robbed me of self-control.

He stilled, and the look on his face was not disbelief, it was horror.

So it was possible. *Damn. Damn. Damn.* I'd hoped it wasn't, hoped I was being paranoid. I didn't need this.

Sometimes it felt like both the mate and the pack bonds were doing their best to steal my soul. The analogy might be figurative, but I found it nearly as frightening as the literal version would have been. Finding out that someone could use the whole mess to make me do things was just the flipping icing on the cake.

Fortunately, I had a task to take my mind off the mess I was in. I stood up and dusted myself off.

I had planned on waiting and talking to Adam directly, but there were some advantages to this scenario, too. It would be a good idea for Adam to know that some of the pack were . . . active about their dislike of me. And if Ben told him, he couldn't read my mind to figure out that I wasn't weirded out only by the mind control, but also by the whole bond thing, pack and mate.

I told Ben, "You tell Adam what I said."

He would. Ben could be creepy and horrible, but he was almost my friend—shared nightmares do that.

"Give him my apologies and tell him I'm going to lie low"—Adam would know that meant stay away from the pack—"until I get a handle on it. Right now, I'm going to get Samuel, so you're off duty."

3

~~~~

I DROVE MY TRUSTY RABBIT TO KGH AND PARKED in the emergency lot. It was still hours before dawn when I walked into the building.

The trick to going wherever you want unchallenged in a hospital is to walk briskly, nod to the people you know, and ignore the ones you don't. The nod reassures everyone that you are known, the brisk pace that you have a mission and don't want to talk. It helped that most of the people in triage knew me.

Through the double doors that led to the inner sanctum, I could hear a baby crying—a sad, tired, miserable sound. I wrinkled my nose at the pervading sour-sharp smell of hospital disinfectant, and winced at the increase in both decibels and scent as I marched through the doors.

A nurse scribbling on a clipboard glanced up at my entrance, and the official look on her face warmed into a relieved smile. I knew her face but not her name.

"Mercy," she said, having no trouble with mine. "So

Doc Cornick finally called you to take him home, did he? About time. I told him he should have gone home hours ago—but he's pretty stubborn, and a doctor outranks a nurse." She made it sound like she didn't think that should be the proper order of things.

I was afraid to speak because I might thrust a hole into whatever house of cards Samuel had constructed to explain why he had to go home early. Finally, I managed a neutral, "He's better at helping people than asking for help."

She grinned. "Isn't that just like a man? Probably hated to admit he trashed that car of his. I swear he loved it like it was a woman."

I think I just stared at her—her words made no sense to me.

Trashed his car? Did she mean he had a wreck? Samuel had a wreck? I couldn't picture it. Some werewolves had trouble driving because they could be a little distractible. But not Samuel.

I needed to get to Samuel before I said something stupid. "I better—"

"He's just lucky he didn't get hurt worse," she said, and turned her eyes back to whatever she was writing. Apparently she could carry on a conversation at the same time, because she continued. "Did he tell you how close he came? The policeman who brought him in said that he almost fell into the water—and that's the Vernita bridge, you know, the one on Twenty-four out in the Hanford Reach? He'd have died if he made it over—it's a long way down to the river."

What the heck had Samuel been doing all the way out at the bridge on the old highway north of Hanford? That was clear on the other side of the Tri-Cities and then some, and nowhere near any possible route between our house and the hospital. Maybe he'd been running out in the Reach, where people were scarce and ground squirrels plentiful. Just because he hadn't told me that he was going out hunting didn't mean he hadn't. I wasn't his keeper.

"He didn't say anything about danger to him," I told her truthfully and followed it with a small lie designed to lead her into telling me more details. "I thought it was just the car."

"That's Doc Cornick," she snorted. "He wouldn't let us do anything other than get the glass out of his skin—but just from the way he's moving, you can tell he did something to his ribs. And he's limping, too."

"Sounds like it was worse than he told me," I commented, feeling sick to my stomach.

"He went all the way through the windshield and was hanging on to the hood of the car. Jack—that's the policeman—Jack said he thought that Samuel was going to fall off the hood before he could get there. The wreck must have dazed Doc because he was crawling the wrong way—if Jack hadn't stopped him, he'd have gone over."

And then I understood exactly what had happened.

"Honey? Honey? Are you okay? Here, sit down."

She'd pulled out a chair when I wasn't watching and held it behind me. My ears were ringing, my head was down between my knees, and her hand was on my back.

And for a moment, I was fourteen again, hearing Bran tell me what I'd already known—Bryan, my foster father, was dead—his body had been found in the river. He'd killed himself after his mate, my foster mother, had died.

Werewolves are too tough to die easily, so there aren't many ways for a werewolf to commit suicide. Since the French Revolution pretty much unpopularized the guillotine in the eighteenth century, self-decapitation just isn't all that easy.

Silver bullets have some difficulties, too. Silver is harder than lead, and the bullets sometimes blow right through and leave the wolf sick, in pain, and alive. Silver shot works a little better, but unless rigged just right, it can take a long time to die. If some busybody comes along and picks all the shot out—well, there's all that pain for nothing.

The most popular choice is death by werewolf. But that wouldn't be an option for Samuel. Very few wolves would take up his challenge—and those that would . . . Let me just say I wouldn't want to see a fight between Samuel and Adam. Even odds aren't what suicidal people are looking for.

Drowning is the next most popular choice. Werewolves can't swim; their bodies are too dense—and even a werewolf needs to breathe.

I even knew why he'd chosen the location he had. The Columbia is the biggest river in the area, more than a mile wide and deep, but the three biggest bridges over it—the Blue Bridge, the suspension bridge, and the interstate bridge—all have two heavy-duty guardrails. There is also a fair bit of traffic on those, even in the middle of the night. Someone is sure to see you go over and attempt a rescue. It takes a few minutes to drown.

The bridge he'd chosen instead was not as heavily traveled and had been built before bridges were designed so that even morons would have a hard time driving off of them. The river is narrower at that point—which means deeper and faster—and the drop-off is . . . impressive.

I could see it, Samuel on the nose of the car and the police officer running up. It had been sheer dumb luck that the only other vehicle on the road was a police car. If it had been an ordinary bystander, he might have been too fearful for his own safety to attempt a rescue and would have let Samuel drown. But a policeman might just follow him in and try to rescue him. Might put his life at risk for Samuel.

No, Samuel wouldn't have fallen once the police officer found him.

No matter how much he wanted to.

My dizziness was fading.

"You be happy," he'd told me when I'd left on my ill-fated date. A wish for my life and not for the date.

The jerk. I felt the growl rise in my throat and had to work to swallow it.

"He's all right," the nurse assured me. I pulled my head out from between my knees and noticed on the way up that her name tag read JODY. "We got the glass out, and though he's moving stiffly, he hasn't broken anything major or he wouldn't have lasted this long. He should have gone home, but he didn't want to—and you know how he is. He never says no but sends you on your way without ever saying yes either."

I knew.

"I'm sorry," I told her, standing up slowly so as to give the appearance of steadiness. "It just caught me off guard. We've known each other a long time—and he didn't tell me it was anywhere near that bad."

"He probably didn't want to scare you."

"Yeah, he's considerate like that." *My aching butt he was considerate. I'd kill him myself—and then he wouldn't have to worry about suicide.*

"He said he was going to find a quiet place and rest for a minute," Nurse Jody said, looking around as if he ought to appear from thin air.

"He said I could find him in the X-ray storage room."

She laughed. "Well, I guess it is quiet in there. You know where it is?"

I smiled, which is tough when you're ready to skin someone. "Sure." Still smiling, I walked briskly past curtained-off rooms that smelled of blood and pain, nodding to a med tech who looked vaguely familiar. At least the baby's cries had muted to whimpers.

Samuel had tried to commit suicide.

I knocked on the storage-room door, then opened it. White cardboard file boxes were piled up on racks with a feeling of imposed order—as if somewhere there was someone who would know how to find things here.

Samuel sat on the floor, his back against a stack of boxes. He had a white lab coat on over a set of green scrubs. His arms rested across his knees, hands limp and hanging. His head was bowed, and he didn't look up when I came in. He waited until I shut the door behind me to speak, and he didn't look at me then either.

I thought it was because he was ashamed or because he knew I was angry.

"He tried to kill us," Samuel said, and my heart stopped, then began to pound painfully in my chest because I'd been wrong about the bowed head. Very wrong. The "he" he was talking about was Samuel—and that meant that "he" was no longer in charge. I was talking to Samuel's wolf.

I dropped to the ground like a stone and made damned sure my head was lower than the werewolf's. Samuel the man regularly overlooked breaches of etiquette that his wolf could not. If I made the wolf look up at me, he'd have to acknowledge my superiority or challenge me.

I change into a thirty-odd-pound predator built to kill chickens and rabbits. And poor, silly quail. Werewolves can take out Kodiak bears. A challenge for a werewolf I am not.

"Mercy," he whispered, and lifted his head.

The first thing I noticed was hundreds of small cuts all over his face, and I remembered Jody, the nurse, saying that they'd had to get the glass out of his skin. That the wounds weren't healed yet told me that there had been other, more severe damage his body had to address first. Nifty—just a little pain and suffering to sweeten his temper.

His eyes were an icy blue just this side of white, hot and wild.

As soon as I saw them, I looked at the floor and took a deep breath. "Sam," I whispered. "What can I do to help? Should I call Bran?"

"No!" The word left him in a roar that jerked him forward until he was crouched on both hands, one leg knee up, one leg still down on one knee.

That one knee on the ground meant that he wasn't, quite, ready to spring on me.

"Our father will kill us," Sam said, his voice slow and thick with Welsh intonation. "I . . . We don't want to make him do that." He took a deep breath. "And I don't want to die."

"Good. That's good," I croaked, suddenly understanding just exactly what his first words to me had meant. Samuel had wanted to die, and his wolf had stopped him. Which was good but left us with a nasty problem.

There is a very good reason that the Marrok kills any werewolves who allow the wolf to lead and the man to follow. Very good reasons—like preventing-mass-slaughter sorts of reasons.

But if Samuel's wolf didn't want them to die, I decided it was better he was in charge. For a while. Since he didn't seem to want to kill me yet. Samuel was old. I don't know exactly how old, but born sometime before the *Mayflower* at least. Maybe that would allow his wolf to control himself without Samuel's help. Maybe. "Okay, Sam. No calls to Bran."

I watched out of the corner of my eye as he tilted his head, surveying me. "I can pretend to be human until we get to your car. I thought that would be best, so I held this shape."

I swallowed. "What have you done with Samuel? Is he all right?"

Pale ice blue eyes examined me thoughtfully. "Samuel? I'm pretty certain he'd forgotten I could do this: it has been so long since we battled for control. He let me out to play when he chose, and I left it to him." He was quiet a moment or two, then he said, almost shyly. "You know when I'm here. You call me Sam."

He was right. I hadn't realized it until he said it.

"Sam," I asked again, trying not to sound demanding, "what have you done with Samuel?"

"He's here, but I cannot let him out. If I do, he'll never let me get the upper hand again—and then we will die."

"Cannot" sounded like "never." "Never" was bad. "Never" would get him killed as surely as suicide—and maybe . . . probably a lot of other people along the way.

"If not Bran, what about Charles's mate, Anna? She's Omega; shouldn't she be able to help?"

Omega wolves, as I understand them, are like Valium for werewolves. Samuel's sister-in-law, Anna, is the only one I've ever met—I'd never heard of them before that. I like her, but she doesn't seem to affect me the way she does the wolves. I don't want to curl up in a ball at her feet and let her rub my belly.

Samuel's wolf looked wistful . . . or maybe he was just hungry. "No. If *I* were the problem, if I were ravaging the countryside, she might help. But this is not impulse, not desperation. Samuel just feels that he no longer belongs, that he accomplishes nothing by his existence. Even the Omega cannot fix him."

"So what do you suggest?" I asked helplessly.

Anna, I thought, might be able to put Samuel back in the driver's seat, but, like the wolf, I was afraid that might not be a good thing.

He laughed, an unhappy laugh. "I do not know. But if you don't want to try to extract a wolf from the emergency room, it would be good to leave very soon."

Sam rocked forward to get up and stopped halfway with a grunt.

"You're hurt," I said as I scrambled up to give him a hand.

He hesitated but took it and used me to give him better leverage so he could get all the way to his feet. Showing me his weakness was a sign of trust. Under normal circumstances, that trust would mean I was safer with him.

"Stiff," Sam answered me. "Nothing that won't heal on its own now. I drew upon your strength to heal enough that no one would know how bad the injuries were."

"How did you do that?" I asked, suddenly remembering the fierce hunger that had resulted in a rabbit-and-quail dinner on top of the salmon I'd had with Adam. I'd thought it had been someone in Adam's pack—for the very good reason that borrowing strength was one of those things that came with a *pack* bond. "We aren't pack," I reminded him.

He looked directly at me again, then away. "Aren't we?"

"Unless you . . . Unless Samuel's been conducting blood ceremonies when I was asleep, we're not." I was starting to feel panicky. Claustrophobic. I already had Adam and his pack playing with my head; I didn't particularly want anyone else in there.

"Pack existed before ceremonies," Sam said, sounding amused. "Magic binds more obviously, more extensively, but not more deeply."

"Did *you* mess with my head on my date with Adam?" I couldn't keep the accusation out of my voice.

"No." He tilted his head, then snarled, "Someone hurt you?"

"No," I said. "It's nothing."

"Lies," he said.

"Right," I agreed. "But if it wasn't you who did it, the incident is something for Adam and me to handle."

He was still a moment. "For now," he said.

I held the door open for him, then walked beside him through the emergency room.

As we moved through the walkway and out the door, Sam kept his eyes on me, and his regard had a weight to it. I didn't protest. He did it so that no one would see the change in his iris color—but also because when a werewolf as dominant as Samuel meets someone's gaze with his wolf in the fore, even humans bow their knees. That would be pretty awkward and hard to explain. At this point, we were operating with the hope that it would matter to Samuel that he could come back and practice medicine here again.

I helped him into the backseat of the Rabbit—and noticed that the towel-wrapped book was still there. I wished that getting it back to its owner was the extent of my troubles. I grabbed it and put it in the far back, out of harm's reach. Hopping in the front, I drove out from under the parking-lot lights as soon as I could. It was still the wee small hours, but Samuel was a big man, and it would be hard to miss him stripping in the back of my little car.

It didn't take him long to dispose of the clothes and begin his change. I didn't look, but I could tell when he started because the noises turned from shredding fabric to pained whines. What the wolves go through when they change is one of the many reasons I am very grateful to be what I am instead of a werewolf. For me, the change from coyote to human or back is virtually instantaneous. The side effects are nothing more annoying than tingles. For a werewolf, change is painful and slow. From the grunts he was making, he hadn't yet fully finished his shift by the time I drove into my driveway.

Home wasn't the safest place to bring him. No werewolf who saw him would miss what had happened, and Adam's house—visited often by members of his pack—was just behind my back fence. But I couldn't think of anyplace better.

Eventually, we'd have to tell Bran—I knew it, and I suspected that Samuel . . . Sam knew it, too. But I'd give him what time I could—assuming he didn't go on a rampage and start eating people.

That meant keeping him out of sight of Adam and his pack. *My* pack. My mate and my pack.

It felt wrong to hide things from him. But I knew Adam, and one thing he was very good at was honor and duty. It was one of the reasons I'd grown to love him—he was a man who could make the hard choice. Duty and honor would force him to call Bran. Duty and honor would force Bran to execute Samuel. Samuel would be dead, and two good men would suffer as well.

Luckily for all of them, my sense of duty and honor was more flexible.

I got out of the car and turned in a slow circle. I caught Ben's scent, fading. Otherwise, we were alone with the more mundane creatures of the night: bats, mice, and mosquitoes. The light was on in Adam's bedroom, but it went dark as I was watching. Tomorrow, I'd need to come up with a better place for Sam.

Or a good reason to avoid the pack.

I opened the back door of the Rabbit, keeping it between Sam and me in case he came out of the change in a bad mood. The pain of the change does not make for a happy wolf—and Sam was already hurt when he started. But he seemed okay. When he hopped out, he waited politely for me to close up the car, then followed me to the door.

He slept on the foot of my bed. When I suggested he might be more comfortable in his room, he regarded me steadily with ice-colored eyes.

Where does a werewolf sleep? Anywhere he wants to.

I thought it would bother me, thought it would scare me. It ought to have bothered me. But somehow I couldn't work up the energy to be too worried about the big wolf curled up on my feet. It was Sam, after all.

MY DAY STARTED OUT EARLY DESPITE MY LATE night.

I woke up to the sound of Sam's stomach growling. Keeping him fed had attained a new priority level, so I bounced up and cooked him breakfast.

And then, because cooking is something I do when I'm upset or nervous—and because it sometimes helps me think, especially if the cooking involves sugar—I indulged myself with a spate of cookie baking. I made a double batch of peanut butter cookies, and while they were in the oven, I made chocolate chip, for good measure.

Sam sat under the table, where he was out of my way, and watched me. I fed him a couple of spoonfuls of dough even though he'd eaten several pounds of bacon and a dozen eggs. He *had* shared the eggs with my cat, Medea.

Maybe that was why he was still hungry. I fed him some of the baked cookies.

I was in the middle of putting cookies into baggies when Adam called.

"Mercy," he said. His voice was fuzzy with fatigue, his tone flat. "I saw the light was on. Ben told me what you said. I can help you with that."

Usually, I follow Adam's conversations just fine, but I'd had less than three hours of sleep. *And* I was preoccupied with Samuel, which he could not know anything about. I rubbed my nose. Ben. Oh. Adam was talking about how the pack had screwed up our date. Right.

I had to keep Adam away. Just until I figured out some brilliant plan to keep Samuel alive . . . And here before me was the perfect excuse.

"Thank you," I said. "But I think I need a break for a few days—no pack, no . . ." I let my voice drift off. I couldn't tell him I needed space from him when it wasn't true. Even over the phone he might pick up the lie. I wished he was here. He had a way of making things black-and-white. Of course, that meant that Samuel should be killed for the good of the wolves. Sometimes gray is the color I'm stuck with.

"You need some distance from the pack—and me," Adam said. "I can understand that." There was a small pause. "I won't leave you without protection."

I looked down. "Samuel's off for a couple of days." I needed to call before heading to work and get him time off, but that didn't change the fact that he wasn't going to be at work for the next couple of days. The wreck made a convenient excuse. "I'll keep him with me."

"All right." There was an awkward pause, and Adam said, "I'm sorry, Mercy. I should have noticed there was something wrong." He swallowed. "When my ex-wife decided I'd done something she didn't like, she'd give me the silent treatment. When you did it . . . it threw me."

"I think that was the point someone was aiming for," I said dryly, and he laughed.

"Yeah. I didn't stop and consider how unlikely a tactic that was from you," he agreed. "Sneak attacks, guerilla warfare, but not silence."

"Not your fault," I told him, before I bit my lip. If I didn't need to keep him away from Sam, I'd have said more. A lot more, but I needed time for Samuel to fix himself. "I didn't figure it out until we were almost home."

"If I'd realized something was up while it was still happening, I could have found out who it was," said Adam, a growl in his voice. He took a deep breath and let it out. When he spoke again, his voice was calmer. "Samuel will know how to stop them, too. While he's escorting you around, why don't you ask him to teach you how to protect yourself? Even when it's not deliberate—" He had to stop again. "The needs and desires of the pack can influence you quite a bit. It's not too hard to block if you know how. Samuel can show you."

I looked at the white wolf sprawled out on the kitchen floor with Medea cleaning his face. Sam looked back at me with pale eyes ringed in black.

"I'll ask him," I promised.

"See you," he said, but continued in a rush. "Is Tuesday too soon?"

It was Saturday. If Samuel wasn't better by Tuesday, I could cancel. "Tuesday would be really good."

He hung up, and I asked Sam, "Can you teach me how to keep the pack out of my head?"

He made a sad noise.

"Not without being able to talk," I agreed. "But I promised Adam I'd ask." So I had three days to fix Samuel. And I felt like a traitor for . . . I hadn't really *lied* to Adam, had I? Raised among werewolves, who are living lie detectors, I'd long ago learned to lie with the truth nearly as well as a fae.

Maybe I had time to make brownies, too.

My cell phone rang, and I almost just answered it, assuming it was Adam. Some instinct of self-preservation had me hesitate and glance at the number: Bran's.

"The Marrok is calling," I told Samuel. "Think he'll wait three days? Me either." But I could delay him a little by not answering the phone. "Let's go work on some cars."

SAM SAT IN THE PASSENGER SEAT AND GAVE ME a sour look. He'd been mad at me since I put his collar on—but the collar was camouflage. It made him look more like a dog. Something domesticated enough for a collar, not a wild animal. Fear brings violence out in the wolves, so the fewer people who are scared of them, the better.

"I'm not going to roll the window down," I told him. "This car doesn't have automatic windows. I'd have to pull over and go around and lower it manually. Besides, it's cold outside, and unlike you, I don't have a fur coat."

He lifted his lip in a mock snarl and put his nose down on the dashboard with a thump.

"You're smearing the windshield," I told him.

He looked at me and deliberately ran his nose across his side of the glass.

I rolled my eyes. "Oh, *that* was mature. The last time I saw someone do something that grown-up was when my little sister was twelve."

AT THE GARAGE, I PARKED NEXT TO ZEE'S TRUCK, and as soon as I got out of the car, I could hear the distinctive beat of salsa music. I have sensitive ears, so it was probably not loud enough to bother anyone in the little houses scattered among the warehouses and storage units that surrounded the garage. A little figure at the window waved at me.

I'd forgotten.

How could I have forgotten that Sylvia and her kids were going to be cleaning the office? Under normal circumstances, it wouldn't have been a problem—Samuel would never hurt a child, but we weren't dealing with Samuel anymore.

I realized that I'd gotten used to him, that I was still thinking of him as though he was only Samuel with a problem. I'd let myself forget how dangerous he was. Then again, he hadn't killed *me* yet.

Maybe if he stayed with me in the garage . . .

I couldn't risk it.

"Sam," I told the wolf, who'd followed me out of the car, "there are too many people here. Let's—"

I'm not sure what I was going to suggest, maybe a run out somewhere no one would see us. But it was too late.

"Mercy," said a high-pitched voice as the office door popped open with a roar of bongos and guitars, and Gabriel's littlest sister, Maia, bounced down the short run of steps and sprinted toward us. "Mercy, Mercy, guess what? Guess what? I am all grown-up. I am going to pretty school, and I—"

And that was when she caught a glimpse of Sam.

"Ooo," she said, still running.

Samuel is not bad-looking in his human form—but his wolf is pure white and fluffy. All he needed was a unicorn's horn to be the perfect pet for a little girl.

"Pretty school?" I asked, stepping forward and to the side, so I was between the werewolf and Maia. Maia stopped instead of bumping into me, but her eyes were on the wolf.

The next-oldest girl, Sissy, who was six, had emerged from the office a few seconds after her sister. "*Mamá* says you can't run out of the office, Maia. There might be cars who wouldn't see you. Hi, Mercy. She means preschool. I'm in first grade this year—and she is still just a baby. Is that a dog? When did you get a dog?"

"Pretty school," repeated Maia. "And I'm not a baby." She gave me a hug and launched herself at Sam.

I would have caught her if Sam hadn't bounded forward, too.

"Pony," she said, attacking him as if he weren't a scarily huge wolf. She grabbed a handful of fur and climbed on top of him. "Pony, pony."

I reached for her, but froze when Sam gave me a look.

"My pony," Maia said happily, oblivious to my terror. She thumped her heels into his ribs hard enough I could hear the noise. "Go, pony."

Maia's sister seemed to understand the danger as well as I did. *"Mamá,"* she shrieked. *"Mamá*, Maia's being stupid again."

Well, maybe not as well.

She frowned at her sister and—while I stood frozen, afraid that whatever action I took would be the one that sent Sam over the edge—told me, "We took her to the fair, and she saw the horses—now she climbs on every dog she sees. She almost got bitten by the last one."

Sam, for his part, grunted the fourth or fifth time Maia's heels hit his side, gave me another look—one that might have been exasperation—and started toward the office, for all the world as if he were a pony instead of a werewolf.

"Mercy?" Sissy said.

I suppose she'd expected me to say something—or at least move. Panic left me with cold fingers and a pounding heart—but as it faded, something else took its place.

I've seen any number of werewolves whose wolf had superseded the man. Usually, it happens in the middle of a fight—and the only thing to do is to lie low until the man takes back control. The other time it often occurs is with the newly Changed wolves. They are vicious, unpredictable, and dangerous even to the people they love. But Sam hadn't been vicious or even unpredictable—except in the best sense of the word—when Maia had hopped up to play Wild Horse Annie.

For the first time since I'd walked into that damned hospital storeroom last night, I felt real hope. If Sam the wolf could keep to civilized manners for a few days, maybe I would have a chance to persuade Bran to give us a little more time.

Sam had reached the office door and stood patiently waiting for me to let him in while Maia patted him on the top of his head and told him he was a good pony.

"Mercy? Are you okay?" Sissy looked in my car—I often brought cookies. I'd brought the ones I made this morning out of habit. I usually make a lot more cookies than any one person can eat, so when I have a baking fest, I bring the cookies for customers. She didn't say anything when she spotted the bags sitting on top of the book I still needed to deliver to Phin, but she got a big smile on her face.

"I'm fine, Sissy. Want a cookie?"

WHEN I OPENED THE OFFICE DOOR, WHICH WAS A fading orangish pink and needed to be repainted, the blaring music was overwhelmed by "Mercy" and "Look, dog!" And what seemed like a hundred small bodies piled on us.

Sissy put her small fists on her hips, and said in a picture-perfect imitation of her brother, "Barbarians." And then she took a bite of the cookie I'd given her.

"Cookie!" shrieked someone. "Sissy has a cookie!"

Silence fell, and they all looked at me like a lion might look at a gazelle in the savanna.

"You see what happens?" asked Gabriel's mother, not even glancing up from scrubbing the counter. Sylvia was about ten years older than I, and she wore those years well. She was a small woman, delicate and beautiful. They say Napoleon was small, too.

"You spoil them," she told me in a dismissive tone. "So it is your problem to deal with. You must pay the price."

I pulled the two bags of cookies from where I'd hidden them in my jacket. "Here," I gasped, holding them out over the horde's reaching hands toward their mother. "Take them quick before the monsters get them. Protect them with your life."

Sylvia took the bags and tried to hide her smile as I wrestled with little pink-clad bodies that squealed and squeaked. Okay, there weren't a hundred of them; Gabriel had five little sisters. But they made enough noise for ten times that many.

Tia, whose name was short for Martina, the oldest girl, frowned at us all. Sam, sitting beside her, had been abandoned for the possibility of a cookie. He seemed amused, more amused when he caught my wary glance.

"Hey, we're doing all the work," Rosalinda, the second-oldest said. "You *chicas* start scrubbing right this moment. You know you won't get cookies until *Mamá* says."

"Sissy got one," Maia said.

"And that is all anyone will get until it is clean," proclaimed Tia piously.

"You're no fun," Sofia, the middle girl, told her.

"No fun," agreed Maia with her bottom lip sticking out. But she couldn't have been too upset because she bounced away from me to crawl back onto Sam, her fingers clutching his collar. "My puppy needs a cookie."

Sylvia frowned at Sam, then at me. "You have a dog?"

"Not exactly," I told her. "I'm watching him for a friend." For Samuel.

The wolf looked at Sylvia and wagged his tail deliberately. He kept his mouth closed, which was smart of him. She wouldn't be happy if she got a good look at his teeth— which were bigger than any dog's I've ever seen.

"What breed is it? I've never seen such a monster."

Sam's ears flattened a bit.

But then Maia kissed him on the top of his head. "He's cute, *Mamá*. I bet I could ride him in the fair, and we would win a ribbon. We should get a dog. Or a pony. We could keep it in the parking lot."

"Uhm, maybe he's a Great Pyrenees mix?" I offered. "Something big."

"Abominable Snow Dog," suggested Tia dryly. She rubbed Sam briskly under one ear.

Sylvia sighed. "I suppose if he hasn't eaten them yet, he won't."

"I don't think so," I agreed cautiously. I looked at Sam, who seemed perfectly fine, more relaxed than I'd seen him since I walked into the storeroom at the hospital.

Sylvia sighed again, theatrically, her dramatically large eyes glittering with fun. "Too bad. It would be much less trouble if I had a few less children, don't you think?"

"Mamá!" came the indignant chorus.

"There aren't as many as there seem to be when they are running around shrieking," I told her.

"I've noticed. When they are asleep, they are a little bit cute. It's a good thing, or none of them would have survived this long."

I looked around. They'd already been working for a while. "You know, people are going to walk in—and turn around and walk back out because they won't recognize the place. Are Gabriel and Zee in the shop?"

"Sí, yes, they are. Thank you for the use of your car."

"No troubles," I told her. "I don't need it right now. And you can do me a favor and tell me about anything you notice is wrong with it."

"Besides the steering wheel popping off?"

I grimaced. "Yep."

"I will do so. Now you and that . . . elephant you brought . . . need to go into the shop so my little monsters can get back to work."

Obediently, I lifted Maia off the wolf. "Let's go to work," I told him.

Sam took two steps with me, then lay down in the center of the office with a grunt. He stretched out on his side and closed his eyes.

"Come on, S—" I bit my lip—what was the name Samuel kept on his collar? Right. "Come, Snowball."

He opened a single white eye and stared at me.

I swallowed. Arguing with dominant wolves could have unpleasant results.

"*I* will watch the puppy," declared Maia. "We can play cowgirls, and I will teach him to fetch. We shall have a tea party." She wrinkled her nose. "And then he won't get all dirty playing with the greasy cars. *He* doesn't like being dirty."

Sam closed his eye as she patted him on the nose.

He wasn't going to hurt her.

I took a deep breath. "I think he likes the music," I told Sylvia.

She huffed. "I think you want him out of your way."

"Maia wants to babysit," I said. "It'll keep her occupied."

Sylvia looked at Sam thoughtfully. She shook her head at me but didn't fuss when I left him lying there.

Zee had shut the door between the office and the shop— he's not fond of Latin music. So when I went in, I closed it behind me, too.

4

THE FIRST THING I HEARD WHEN I EMERGED FROM the bathroom with my working overalls on was Zee swearing in German. It was modern German because I could understand about one word in four. Modern German was a good sign.

The Buick was in the first bay. I couldn't see Zee, but from the direction of his voice, he was under the car. Gabriel was standing on the far side of the vehicle; he looked up when he heard me come in, and relief flashed across his face.

He knows Zee is . . . well, not harmless, but that Zee won't hurt him. But Gabriel is too polite—and as a result, he has to put up with a lot more of Grumpy Zee than I do.

"Hey, Zee," I said. "I take it that you can fix it, but it'll be miserable, and you'd rather haul it to the dump and start from scratch."

"Piece of junk," groused Zee. "What's not rusted to pieces is bent. If you took all the good parts and put them in a pile, you could carry them out in your pocket." There was a little pause. "Even if you only had a small pocket."

I patted the car. "Don't you listen to him," I whispered to it. "You'll be out of here and back on the road in no time."

Zee propelled himself all the way under the car so his head stuck out by my feet.

"Don't you promise something you can't deliver," he snarled.

I raised my eyebrows, and said in dulcet tones, "Are you telling me you can't fix it? I'm sorry. I distinctly remember you saying that there is nothing you can't fix. I must have been mistaken, and it was someone else wearing your mouth."

He gave a growl that would have done Sam credit and pushed himself back under again, muttering, *"Deine Mutter war ein Cola-Automat!"*

"Her mama might have been a pop machine," I said, responding to one of the remarks I understood even at full Zee-speed. "Your mama . . ." sounds the same in a number of languages. "But she was a beauty in her day." I grinned at Gabriel. "We women have to stick together."

"Why is it that all cars are women?" he asked.

"Because they're fussy and demanding," answered Zee.

"Because if they were men, they'd sit around and complain instead of getting the job done," I told him.

It was a relief to do something normal. In my garage, I was in control . . . Well, Zee was really in charge when he came in. Even though I'd bought the shop from him and now paid him to come in, we both knew who was the better mechanic—and he'd been my boss for a long time. Maybe, I thought, handing him sockets size ten and thirteen, that was the real relief. Here I had a job I knew how to do and someone I trusted giving me orders, and the result would be a victory for goodness and order. Fixing cars is orderly—unlike most of my life. Do the right thing, and it works. Do the wrong, and it doesn't.

"*Verdammte Karre,*" Zee growled. "*Gib mir mal—*"

The last word was garbled as something heavy went thump, thump, bang.

"Give you what?" I asked.

There was a long silence.

"Zee? Are you all right?"

The whole car rose about ten inches off the jacks, knocking them over on their sides, and shook like an epileptic. A wave of magic rose from the Buick, and I backed away, one hand locked in Gabriel's shirt so he came with me as the car returned all the way to the ground with a bang of tires on pavement and the squeak of protesting shocks.

"I feel better now," said Zee in a very nasty tone. "I would be even happier if I could hang the last mechanic who worked on it."

I knew that feeling—ah, the unparalleled frustration of mismatched bolts, miswired sending units, and cross-threaded parts left for me to discover: things that turned what should be a half-hour job into an all-day event.

Gabriel was pulling against my hold as if he wanted to get farther from the car. His eyes were wide, the whites showing all the way around his irises. I realized, belatedly, that it might be the first time he'd seen Zee really work.

"It's okay. He's through now, I think." I let go of Gabriel's shirt and patted his shoulder. "Zee, I think the last mechanic who worked on it was you. Remember? You replaced the wiring harness."

Zee rolled out headfirst again, and there was a black grease mark running from his forehead to his chin where something had rolled across his face. A spot of blood lingered on his forehead, and there was a lump on his chin. "You may shut up anytime you choose, *Kindlein,*" he advised me sharply. Then he frowned. "I smell cookies, and you look tired. What is wrong?"

"I made cookies," I told him. "I saved a bag in the car for you to take home. I brought more with me, but the horde is in possession."

"Good," he said. "Now, what is robbing you of sleep?"

He used to leave me alone. But ever since Tim . . . ever since I'd been hurt, he coddled me in his own way.

"Nothing you can help me with," I said.

"Money?"

"Nope."

He frowned, his white eyebrows lowering over his cool gray eyes.

"Vampires?" He snapped it out. Zee didn't like vampires, much.

"No, sir." I saluted his tone. "Nothing you can do anything about."

"Don't you sass me, girl." He glowered at me. "I—"

One of Gabriel's sisters screamed. I had a terrible vision of Sam chewing on one of the kids, and I was running.

I had my hand on the door and the door mostly open when Tia shouted, *"¡Mamá, Mamá, una pistola! Tiene una pistola."*

Inside the office there were kids all over: hanging from shelving, standing on the six-inch sill at the bottom of the big window, on the floor wrapped around Sam.

A man, a huge man with a nasty-looking automatic in a steady two-handed grip, stood in the doorway between the outside and the office, holding the door open with one black leather-booted foot. The rest of him was dressed in black, too, with some sort of bright yellow design on the left shoulder of his leather pseudomilitary jacket. The only outlier in his generally soldier-of-fortune appearance was the shoulder-length silver-threaded red hair that flowed from his head in a manner that would have done credit to a romance novel cover model.

Just behind him, I caught a glimpse of another man, dressed in a button-up shirt and slacks. But the second man's body language told me at a glance that it was only the first man, the man with the gun, who was a threat. The second man held something on his shoulder, but, beyond determining that it wasn't a weapon, I ignored it and him to focus on the dangerous one.

Sylvia held a broom in her hand, but she was frozen because the barrel of the gun was aimed right at the littlest Sandoval. Maia was locked onto Sam with both hands and screaming Spanish in a manner that might be overly dramatic if there hadn't been an automatic pointed at her.

I expect it was worry for her that kept the wolf motionless on the floor of the office, his eyes narrowed on the barrel of the gun as the skin over his muzzle moved in a soundless snarl.

If I'd had time to be scared, it would have been then, looking at Samuel. At Sam. Already I could see the tightening of the muscles in his hindquarters that preceded an attack. Gun or not, Maia or not, he wasn't waiting long.

All of this I saw the first instant I opened the door, and I was moving even as I took in the scene. I snatched Sylvia's broom, rounded the corner of the counter, and brought the broom handle down on the gunman's wrists. It hit with a crack, knocking the gun loose before he, or anyone else in the room, had a chance to react to my entrance.

Aside from turning into a coyote when I feel like it, my superpowers are limited to an inconsistent resistance to magic and a turn of speed that is a bit on the far side of humanly possible. From the time I heard the first scream, I used every ounce of speed I had.

I swung at the man a second time, this time aiming at his body as if the broom were a Louisville Slugger, saying urgently, "Stay *down*, Sam."

All that karate was good for something, I thought, as the man grabbed the handle and jerked back. I let it go. Off balance because he was braced for resistance, he took a step back, and I kicked him in the stomach, knocking him down the stair and onto the blacktop outside. Not incidentally, he took the guy who'd been behind him with him to the ground.

Now, if only the werewolf listens.

I snatched up the gun our intruder had dropped on the floor and stepped into the doorway, holding the door open as he had, with one foot. I pointed the gun at the stranger's face—and waited for the real terror to begin.

But there was no roar behind me, no further screams as Sam shook off the air of civilization that made people look at him and think "pet" rather than "monster."

I took a moment to breathe then, half-stunned by Sam's restraint. It took me a moment to figure out what to do with the best-case scenario I'd been unexpectedly gifted with.

I could hear noise behind me, but I ignored it. Zee was there; no enemy could come at me from that direction. The sobs and frightened voices softened and stopped. Sam wasn't growling. I wasn't sure if it was a good sign or not, but decided to think positively.

"Sylvia, call the police," I told her after a half second of consideration. We were in the right. And thanks to Adam, who littered my workplace with security cameras, we'd have proof. As an added bonus, there were no werewolf attacks to explain away. No reason for Sam to play any role in this at all. "Tell them what happened and ask them to hurry."

"Hey, lady, you don't want to do that," said the second man, breathlessly. He was beginning to struggle to get out from under the gunman—who was assessing me with cool eyes while his assistant kept talking. "You don't want the police involved. This will go better the quieter we can keep it."

If he hadn't sounded so patronizing, I don't think I would have pulled the trigger.

I shot to the side, far enough that there was no way it would hit either of them, near enough that the blacktop that was dislodged by the bullet hit them both.

"I'd stay still if I were you," I said, adrenaline making my voice shake. My hands, the important part, were steady.

"I am calling Tony," said Sylvia behind me in a low voice that the two men lying on their backs at the base of my steps wouldn't hear. "That way there will be no mistakes made." Her voice was calm and unhurried. All those years as a police dispatcher coming to her aid. Tony was my friend, Sylvia's friend—and we both trusted him.

With the intruders under control, I became aware that there were other people outside. Not customers these. They stood by a full-sized black van that managed to look wicked and elegant in a custom paint job.

There were three people—two (one man, one woman) dressed like the gunman, right down to the flowing locks, and a girl in a gray T-shirt and a headset. The van had the same yellow lettering that was on the man's jacket.

KELLY HEART, it said, I realized once I had leisure to read it, BOUNTY HUNTER. Underneath the yellow, in slightly smaller letters, it said: SATURDAYS AT 8PM CENTRAL TIME. CATCHING THE BAD GUYS, ONE AT A TIME.

"Smile," I said grimly to the people who had my back: Zee, Sylvia and her girls, and Sam. "We're on *Candid Camera*." Zee and Sam needed to know there were unfriendly cameras pointed at them.

"Now, just you calm down," said one of the people in black, the woman with bright yellow hair and red lipstick. As she started to talk, she began walking toward us briskly. "You'll want to put down that gun. It's just TV, lady, nothing to get excited about."

I don't take orders. Not from people invading my place. I sent a second shot into the pavement in front of her.

"Tanya, *stop*," shrieked the techie-girl. "Don't make her shoot again. Do you know what those silver bullets cost us?"

"You'll want to stop right there," I told them. Silver was for werewolves. They'd come hunting werewolves. "I was raised in the backwoods of Montana. I can hit a duck on the wing." Maybe. Probably. I'd never shot a duck in my life; I prefer hunting on all fours. "Where I come from, a gun is a weapon, not a TV prop, and if all the bad guys are dead, our side of the story is the only one that gets told. Don't make me decide that would be easier."

Tanya froze, and I pulled the barrel back to center on the man whose face was vaguely familiar once I knew he was a TV star. I was fighting against the growing urge just to pull the trigger and be done with it.

Coyotes, like werewolves, are territorial—and this gun-toting jerk had barged into my place as if he had every right to be here.

"Are the police on their way?" I asked Sylvia, as she hung up the phone. My voice was shaking with adrenaline and anger, but my hands were still very steady.

"He says he'll be here in five. He also said that it would be a good thing to have backup. So there will be some other police as well."

I smiled widely at the bounty hunter, showing my teeth like any good predator. "Tony is a police officer. He's known these kids since they were in diapers. He's *not* going to be happy with you." Tony was also hopelessly in love with Sylvia—though I didn't think she knew that.

There was a movement to my right, and I snuck a quick glance to see Zee and Gabriel coming out the garage door. They must have gone back around. Zee had a crowbar in one hand and held it like another man might hold a sword. Gabriel had—

"Zee," I squeaked. "Tell him to put the torque wrench back and grab something that won't cost me five hundred dollars if he hits someone with it."

"Won't cost five hundred," said Zee, but as I glanced over again, he nodded at the white-faced Gabriel, who looked at what he held as if he'd never seen it before. The boy slipped back into the garage as Zee said, "It wouldn't break it—you'd just have to get it recalibrated."

"We have a whole garage worth of tools—pry bars, tire irons, and even a hammer or two. There's got to be something better than my torque wrench he could have grabbed."

"Listen, lady," Kelly Heart said in a calm, soothing voice. "Let's take a deep breath and discuss this a moment. I didn't mean to scare anyone. That little girl was about to get mauled by a werewolf."

Truth.

It didn't surprise me. Talking to Zee had steadied me, and I'd had a moment or two to think.

There might be a TV reality star somewhere who would point a gun at a cute little girl, but not while he was being filmed. The man behind him had been his cameraman—I could see the camera on the ground where it had been dropped when Heart landed on the second man with all his two-hundred-plus pounds of muscle.

If he'd come here hunting werewolves, he'd have figured out what Sam was right away. There's a bit of wolf magic that encourages humans to see a dog instead of a wolf, but it is only a little bit of magic, and if someone is looking—they'll see a wolf and not a dog.

So. How much to admit. I'd already paused too long to deny what Sam was. "He likes kids," I said instead. "Gentle as a puppy."

Sylvia had been murmuring to her kids, but her voice stopped at my words. There was a short silence, then the littlest one went off like a fire truck, a high-pitched fire truck. At a guess, Sylvia had just snatched her daughter away from the big, bad wolf.

"I have a warrant for him," continued Heart, wincing a little. I couldn't tell if it was the volume that bothered him or the pitch, which was approaching ultrasonic.

I raised my eyebrows and indicated the gun with a jerk of my chin. "Wanted dead or alive?"

Samuel wasn't out. And the only one I was worried about coming after Samuel would never send a bounty hunter. It would be Bran who killed him, when and if the time came. Heart's warrant couldn't be for Samuel.

It didn't take a genius to figure out what werewolf people would expect to find around my place of work: Adam.

How a bounty hunter got a warrant for him, when, to my knowledge, Adam was in good standing as a law-abiding citizen, I didn't know. I was vague on bounty-hunter lore, but I was pretty sure that they mostly hunt down people who are wanted for bail-skipping, and then the bail bondsmen pay them a percentage of the bail money they would have otherwise lost.

The Kennewick Police Department wasn't very far away. Even so, the first vehicle in my parking lot was Adam's. He parked his truck in front of the van, blocking it where it was.

"You're mistaken," I told Kelly Heart, Bounty Hunter, keeping my eyes on him no matter how much I wanted to look at the man who had just closed the door of his new truck. "There aren't any werewolves around here who have a warrant out for their arrest."

"I'm afraid you're wrong," Kelly told me kindly. Against my will, I was impressed by him. He was calm and cool while lying on his back like a turtle—on top of his cameraman, who was scared out of his mind and focused on the mouth of the gun I held.

Another truck door opened and closed—Adam had someone with him. The wind didn't favor me, so I couldn't tell who it was. And I wasn't going to be stupid and look. Not that I really thought the bounty hunter was a threat anymore. At least, not a threat to the children behind me.

I could hear the woman in the T-shirt saying in a frantic voice, "Don't make her shoot again, Kelly. Forty bucks. Forty bucks those cost. Each."

"Don't worry," I called to her. "You can dig them out, and they'll look just about like what they do now. You might even be able to reuse them." Silver doesn't deform as easily as lead, which makes it a lousy ammunition—unless you're shooting at werewolves.

"She doesn't seem too worried about you," I told Kelly with mock sympathy as Adam walked toward us. "I guess silver bullets are harder to find than bounty hunters who look good in black leather."

He smiled. "She thinks so. Look, can I get up? I promise not to try anything, but I outweigh Joe here by a hundred pounds. If I lie on him much longer, he might stop breathing."

"Go ahead and put up the gun, Mercy," said Adam. "Get it out of sight before the police are here. It'll be easier that way. We might even get out of this without anyone getting arrested."

My will broke at the sound of his voice, and my head turned with as much inevitability as a sunflower turning its face to the sun.

Adam was in a three-piece suit with a Mickey Mouse tie his daughter had bought him for Christmas—and he managed to look much, much more dangerous than the man on the ground. I'd known he would come, even after this morning's conversation.

I'd hurt him, and still he'd come when the security cameras he had posted all over the place at my garage told him I was in trouble. I'd never doubted for a minute that he would come; Adam is staunch and true, like the tin soldier in the old children's story. Stauncher and truer than I, who'd pushed him away to save Samuel.

"Sylvia called Tony. The police might already know about the gun."

"Even so," said Adam. "People make mistakes when there are guns about."

Kelly didn't want to take his eyes off me while I was holding a gun on him, but he was caught up in the same spell everyone in Adam's sphere found themselves in. Out of the corner of my eye, I saw the bounty hunter's face turn to Adam, who'd come up from the side so as not to put himself in my line of fire if Kelly had popped up and started running.

"Right," the bounty hunter said. "Just put down the gun, Ms. Thompson. As this gentleman suggests." Maybe he thought Adam would be more reasonable than I was. Kelly Heart wouldn't understand what the bright gold flecks in Adam's eyes meant.

"I came here to bring in a werewolf I have a warrant for," he told Adam, and I could tell he believed it. "I saw the werewolf with the kid and thought there would be trouble."

He was telling the truth—he'd told the truth to me, too. I fumbled a little, putting the safety on the unfamiliar gun. With Adam here, who needed a gun?

Zee came up and held out his hand. "I'll take it and make it disappear," he told me.

Heart rolled off his cameraman, keeping his hands up as he eased himself to the side. He was still mostly paying attention to me, as if I were the threat and not Adam. I ratcheted my estimate of his intelligence downward.

Adam slipped on a pair of sunglasses—but he kept his gaze on the bounty hunter as Heart came to his feet. Adam took a step back when Heart offered a hand to his cameraman, and his foot crunched on something.

Adam knelt, a graceful movement, over in a moment. When he stood up, he was holding the camera.

"I'm afraid this didn't survive the fall."

The cameraman made a moaning sound as if someone had hit him. He snatched the camera and tucked it against his belly as if that could somehow make it better.

Adam looked at the cameraman, then beyond him to the van, where Heart's people were frantically conferring. He glanced at Ben. When he had the other werewolf's attention, he motioned toward the van with his chin. As simply as that, he let Ben know that he wanted him to go keep tabs on Heart's crew. Adam didn't leave things to chance, and he wouldn't ignore possible hostiles on the other side of the parking lot.

"I am sorry for scaring you," Kelly told me, sincerely. This time he was lying. "And for upsetting the children." He wasn't worried about that either. I wondered how many people actually believed that sincere act.

A pair of police cars, followed by Tony's truck, pulled into the parking lot.

"No sirens," said Adam. "Probably Tony didn't tell them about the gun."

Sam stepped around me, making me bump into the door. I dropped one hand and wrapped it in the ruff of his neck—no way was I stupid enough to grab his collar. My touch was a request, not an order . . . but Sam had already stopped beside me. He surveyed the approaching police from the top of the steps, a position that was higher than theirs.

Sam, Heart paid attention to. He glanced longingly at Zee—because the gun was out of sight—and took a step away from the werewolf.

"This is a misunderstanding," he said in a voice designed to carry to the approaching police. "My fault."

I saw the moment the first officer on the scene recognized him because his eyes rounded, and his voice was a little awed as he told the older patrolmen who followed him, "It's all right, Holbrook, Monty. It's Kelly Heart, the bounty hunter from TV."

Monty was probably Tony, whose last name was Montenegro. That would make the older cop Holbrook.

"Green," said the older man quietly—I don't think any of us were supposed to hear him. "It's not all right until you find out what's going on. I don't care if the president himself is in front of you." But then Holbrook took a good look at us, all standing with our hands plainly visible and in the relaxed fashion of people who had not almost killed each other five minutes before. We, all of us, were pretty good at lying with our bodies. "Now, go call it in and tell them situation under control."

Green turned without argument, leaving Tony and Holbrook to approach us alone.

"Mercy?" Unlike the other officers, Tony wasn't in uniform. He was wearing a dark jacket over black jeans, and he wore diamond studs in his pierced ears and looked more like a drug dealer than a cop. "What happened?"

"He came into the office and saw my friend here." I rested my hand on Sam's head. I couldn't call him by name. Tony knew Dr. Samuel Cornick, knew he was my roommate—and wouldn't have any trouble connecting him with a wolf named Sam. And calling him Snowball at this juncture was only going to draw attention to the fact that I was hiding his identity. "And assumed that any werewolf was a danger."

"That's a werewolf?" asked the older cop, who suddenly looked a lot more wary. His hand crept to his holster.

"Yes," I agreed steadily. "And as you can see—despite Heart's precipitous actions"—I didn't tell them what his precipitous actions had been, though Tony's mouth tightened, so I was pretty sure he knew about the gun—"my friend here kept his head. If he hadn't, there would be bodies." I looked at Heart. "Some *people* might learn from his example of self-control and good judgement."

"He's dangerous," said Kelly. "I wouldn't have sh—" He suddenly decided to leave the gun out of it, too, and switched tactics without bothering to finish his sentence. "I have a warrant authorizing the apprehension of the werewolf."

"No, you don't," I told him confidently. No way did he have a warrant for Sam.

"What?" said Tony.

"A werewolf?" said the older cop. "I don't remember hearing anything about a warrant on a werewolf."

He whistled and waved, catching the attention of the young cop who was walking briskly back toward us.

"Green," he said, "you hear anything about a warrant out for one of our local werewolves?"

The young man's eyes widened. He looked at me, looked at Sam, and came to the right conclusion. Sam wagged his tail, and the police officer straightened up, his face going impersonal and professional. I recognized the look—this one had been in the armed forces.

"No, sir," he said. He wasn't afraid, but he was watching Sam closely. "I would have remembered something like that."

"I have proof," the bounty hunter said, nodding toward the van. "I have the warrant in the van."

Tony's eyebrow went up, and he glanced at the other cops. "I can tell you for certain that we haven't had any werewolves arrested and let out on bail. Since when does our department give arrest warrants to bounty hunters? I'm inclined to agree with Mercy—you must be mistaken."

Holbrook kept his attention on Sam, but Green and Tony both showed better sense.

"Officer Holbrook," I said, "you could make things a lot easier on my friend here if you didn't look him in the eye. He won't do anything." I hoped. "But the wolf instincts tell him that direct eye contact is a challenge."

Holbrook looked at me. "Thank you, ma'am," he said. "I appreciate the information."

"The warrant's in the van," said Heart. "I can have my assistant bring it here."

While the police were talking to Heart and me, Adam and Zee had been doing their best to fade into the background. But I caught motion out of the corner of my eye: Zee, catching Adam's attention. When he had it, he tilted his head toward the storage yard across the street.

Like Adam, I followed Zee's gesture with my eyes and spotted it right away. On top of the nearest storage unit was something that blended in with the red metal roof. With enough glamour, a fae can take on the appearance of any living thing, but something inanimate—like a roof—is harder. I couldn't see what he or she was, just that something was there. It took less than an instant, and I pulled my eyes away quickly so as not to alert the fae creature of our notice.

"Ben," Adam said very quietly.

"What did you say?" asked Tony.

Ben was leaning against the van and chatting up Tanya-the-Bounty-Hunter's-Woman, Leather Boy (Heart's too-handsome sidekick), and Tech-Girl. They all must have had really bad instincts, because they were flushed and smiling. When Adam spoke, Ben looked over to his Alpha. The van would hide him from the fae on the rooftop—but it would also hide the fae from him.

"Nothing important," Adam said, while he made a few unobtrusive gestures with his right hand, about hip level. Ben made a gesture in return, and Adam closed his fist, then opened it.

"Who are you, anyway?" asked Heart.

"You were going to show us this warrant?" asked Tony, changing the subject.

By the van, Ben smiled. He ducked his head, said something to the people he was talking with that had them all looking our way, then walked casually around the end of the van. I couldn't see him as he crossed the street because of the van, but I saw the fae notice him and drop off the far side of the warehouse.

Heart said, "Bring it on over, sweetheart." I understood then that they had some sort of mic system that allowed her to hear everything we said. Probably recorded it, too. I supposed that was okay.

Ben hopped the tall chain-link fence without touching it—if any mundane saw him, there would be no question that he wasn't human. But the police, including Tony, were watching the famous TV star.

No one but Adam, Zee, and me—as far as I could tell—
noticed anything. Gabriel was gone. I realized that I'd seen
Gabriel go back through the garage when his sister had
cried out—because Sylvia had pulled her away from the
werewolf.

Paying attention, I could hear him talking in Spanish,
his voice sharp with anger as he and his mother argued
about something—and my name was definitely a part of
the discussion.

I tuned them out as the bounty hunter's tech-girl came
running over with a thick folder that she handed over to
Heart. He leafed through the pages tucked into a pocket of
the folder and produced an official-looking document that
he handed over to Tony.

"He has a warrant," Tony told me, carefully not looking
at Adam. "And you're right. It's not for this werewolf." He
handed the paper to Holbrook.

The older man took one look at it and harrumphed.
"It's a fake," he said, absolute certainty in his voice. "If
you'd have told me the name, I could have told you it was
a fake—without even looking at the elegant signature that
looks less like Judge Fisk's than mine does. No way there's
a warrant out for Hauptman and it's not all over the station."

"That's what I thought," agreed Tony. "Fisk's signature
is barely legible."

"What?" There was enough honest indignation in Kelly's voice that I was pretty sure it was genuine.

Tony, who was watching the bounty hunter pretty closely,
seemed to have the same opinion as I did. He handed the
warrant to the youngest cop. "Green, go call this in and see
if it's real," he said. "Just for the bounty hunter's sake."

Like Tony, Green very carefully didn't look at Adam.
"I haven't heard about this," he said. "And I'd have remem-
bered if we had a warrant for him. We know our local
Alpha. I can sure as heck tell you that he hasn't jumped

bail." Green looked at Tony. "But I'll go call it in." And he strode briskly back to his patrol car.

"My producer told us that the police department didn't want to take on a werewolf and had asked for our help," said Heart, though he didn't sound nearly as certain.

Holbrook snorted indignantly. "If we had a warrant to pick up a werewolf, we'd pick him up. That's our job."

"Your producer told you we didn't want to take on a werewolf," said Tony thoughtfully. "Did your producer give you the warrant?"

"Yes."

"Does he have a name? We'd like contact information for him, too."

"Her," Kelly said. "Daphne Rondo." I wondered if he knew that his heart was in his voice when he said her name. He reached into his back pocket—slowly—and took out his wallet and extracted a card.

"Here." He held it a moment when Tony reached out to take it. "You know this guy, right? That's how you knew this wolf was the wrong one." Then comprehension lit his face, and he let go of the card and looked at Adam. "Adam Hauptman?"

Adam nodded. "I'd say pleasure to meet you, but I don't like lying. What is it I'm supposed to have done?"

The younger cop strolled back from his car, shaking his head.

Kelly looked at the cop, then sighed. "What a cluster. I take it you haven't been killing young women and leaving their half-eaten bodies in the desert?"

Adam was ticked. I could tell it even if he was looking like a reasonably calm businessman. Adam's temper was the reason he wasn't one of Bran's werewolf poster boys. When angered, he often gave in to impulses he wouldn't otherwise have given in to.

"Sorry to disappoint you," Adam told Kelly in silky

tones. "But I prefer rabbits. Humans taste like pork." And then he smiled. Kelly took an involuntary step backward.

Tony gave Adam a sharp look. "Let's not make things worse, if we can help it, gentlemen." He pulled out his cell phone and, looking at the card, dialed the number. It rang until the voice mail picked up. Tony didn't leave a message.

"Okay," Tony said. "I'd like to get a statement from you about this warrant. If we've got someone falsifying warrants, we need to know about it. We can do that here or down at the station."

I left Tony and the police to deal with the fallout, and went back into my office, letting the door shut behind me. I left Sam outside, too. If he hadn't killed anyone yet this morning, he wasn't going to.

I had other matters to deal with.

Gabriel had his youngest sister on his hip, her wet face on his shoulder. The other girls were sitting on the chairs I had for customers, and his mother had her back to me.

She was the only one talking—in Spanish, so I had no idea what she was saying. Gabriel gave me a desperate look, and she turned. Sylvia Sandoval's eyes were glittering with rage as hot as any I'd ever seen on a werewolf.

"You," she said, her accent thick. "I do not like the company you keep, Mercedes Thompson."

I didn't say anything.

"We are going home now. And my family will have nothing further to do with you. Because of you, because of your werewolf, my daughter will have nightmares of a man pointing a gun at her. She could have been shot—any of my children could have been shot. I will have a tow truck come to pick up my car."

"No need," I told her. "Zee has it almost up and running." I assumed. No telling how much he'd done with his magic.

"It is running," Zee said. I hadn't realized he'd come into the office, but he must have come in through the garage. He stood by the inner door, looking grim.

"You will tell me how much I owe you over and above my son's last check."

Gabriel made a protesting sound.

She glanced at him, and he bit back whatever he intended to say, his eyes suspiciously bright.

"My son thinks that because he is almost a man, he can make his own decisions. As long as he lives in my house, that is not true."

I was pretty sure that Gabriel could go off and do all right on his own—but that without his extra income, Sylvia would be hard-pressed to feed their family. Gabriel knew it, too.

"Gabriel," I told him, "I have to let you go. Your mother is right. My office isn't a safe place to work. If your mother were not involved, you still wouldn't have a job here anymore. I'll mail you your last check. When you are looking for work, you can tell them to call me for a recommendation."

"Mercy," he said, his face white and stark.

"I couldn't have lived with myself if something had happened to you or one of your sisters today," I told him.

"Oh, poor Mercy," said Sylvia with false sympathy, her English getting worse. "Poor Mercy, her life it is too dangerous, and she would feel bad if my son were hurt." She pointed her finger at me. "It is not just this. If it were only the gunman, then I would say—no, Gabriel, you cannot work here anymore—but we are friends, still. But you *lied* to me. I say, What is this great big dog? You tell me, Perhaps some mixed breed. You made this decision, to let my daughter play with a werewolf. You did not tell me what he was. You made such a choice about my children's welfare. Do not call at my house. Do not talk to my children on the street, or I will call the police."

"Mamá," said Gabriel. "You're over the top."

"No," I told him wearily. "She's right." I'd known that I made the wrong choice the moment I heard Maia's first cry. It hadn't been Sam—but it might have been. That I'd been sure it was him right up until the moment I saw Kelly Heart with his gun told me that I'd made the wrong choice. I'd endangered Sylvia's children.

"Zee, would you back her car out of the garage, please?"

He bowed his head and turned on his heel. I couldn't tell if he was angry with me, too, or not. Of course, I was pretty sure he had no idea how much of a risk I'd taken. He wasn't a wolf, hadn't lived with the wolves; he wouldn't know what Sam was.

"Mercy," said Gabriel, helplessly.

"Go," I told him. I'd have hugged him, but I thought we'd both cry. I could deal, but Gabriel was seventeen and the man of his family. *"Vaya con Dios."* See, I do know a little Spanish.

"And you also," he said formally.

And his sister started wailing again. "I want my puppy," she cried.

"Go," said his mother.

They left, the girls subdued, following Gabriel, with Sylvia bringing up the rear.

5

~~~~~

WITH SAM AT HIS HEEL, ADAM CAME INTO THE office while Sylvia and her family were still in the garage, waiting for Zee to get the Buick out. From Adam's face I could tell he'd heard every word Sylvia and I had said. He put a hand on my shoulder and kissed my forehead.

"Don't be nice to me," I told him. "I screwed up."

"Not your fault that overeager boy out there came in with guns blazing," Adam said. "Someone sold him a whole pack of lies. Tony and he are trying to get in touch with his producer, but she's not answering her phone. I suppose she wanted a big fight on TV. Man versus werewolf."

"Maybe," I said. "Maybe *he* wasn't my fault. But if it hadn't been Kelly Heart, it could just as easily have been a vampire or a fae. Neither of which would hesitate to kill Gabriel or one of the girls if they thought they were in the way."

The hand on my shoulder slipped down and pulled me into a hug. I leaned into it, knowing I was receiving it under false pretenses—I could tell from the way he was acting that he hadn't realized the full extent of my transgressions yet. Doubtless he'd been too busy to take a good look at Sam—and Sam, miraculously, hadn't done anything to attract anyone's attention. Yet. The day was still young.

I breathed in Adam's scent and took comfort I wasn't entitled to. Sylvia was right. I was feeling far too sorry for myself, and I wasn't entitled to that either.

I pulled away and hopped up to sit on the counter before I enlightened him—I couldn't bear it if he were touching me when he decided he didn't want anything more to do with me. As Sylvia just had.

The sticky black stuff left from where someone in the Dark Ages had taped a piece of paper to the edge of the counter was gone, and I ran my finger over the newly clean spot. She'd left the cookies.

"Mercy?"

I'd betrayed him. For all the good reasons in the world, but I was his mate—and I'd chosen Samuel. I suppose I could have hoped he wouldn't notice, but that seemed wrong in light of this morning. What if Heart hadn't come here first? What if he'd run into Adam and shot him? What if he'd gone to Adam's work or had a photo of him . . . Come to think of it, wasn't that odd? Adam was out to the public, and his face photographed very well.

Someone hadn't wanted Heart to know who Adam was.

"Mercy?"

"Sorry," I told him. "I'm trying to distract myself. You need to look at Samuel." I picked at a mucky spot on my overalls because I couldn't meet his eyes.

If Bran wanted Samuel dead, he'd have to go through me to do it, which he could. But I was through lying to Adam, even if only by omission, merely to keep Bran from finding out.

Sam had trotted past both of us and gone to stand in the

doorway, looking through the garage. I could hear Maia still crying for her puppy.

"Puppy?" said Adam, sounding amused. Sam turned and looked at him—and Adam froze.

I was well on my way to passing stupid for idiotic. It was only when Adam stilled that I had the sudden thought that it might not have been the best idea to show the Columbia Pack Alpha that he had a problem with Sam in the narrow confines of my office.

It was Sam who growled first. Temper flared in Adam's face. Sam was more dominant, but he wasn't Alpha—and Adam was not going to back down in his territory without violence.

I hopped off the counter in between them.

"Settle down, Sam," I snapped, before I remembered what a bad idea that was.

I kept forgetting—not that Samuel was in trouble; I had no trouble remembering that—but that his wolf was not Samuel. Just because he hadn't turned into the ravening beast that the only werewolves I'd seen who lost control to their wolf became, did not mean he was safe. My head knew that—but I kept acting as if he were just Samuel. Because he acted just like Samuel would have. Mostly.

Sam sneezed and turned his back to us—and I started breathing again.

"I'm sorry," I apologized to both of them. "That was a dumb way of doing things."

I didn't want to look at Adam. I didn't want to see if he was angry or hurt or whatever. I'd had just about enough already that day.

And that was a coward's way out.

So I turned and looked up at him, keeping my gaze on his chin—where I could see his reaction without challenging him by meeting his eyes.

"You are so screwed," he said thoughtfully.

"I'm sorry I let you think . . ."

"What?" he asked. "That you needed some time away from the pack, from me? When you really wanted to keep any of us from seeing Samuel?"

He sounded reasonable, but I could see the white line along his jaw where he was gritting his teeth and the tension in his neck.

"Yes," I told him.

Ben boiled into the room—saw our little tableau, and came to an abrupt halt. Adam glanced over his shoulder at him, and Ben flinched and bowed his head.

"I didn't catch it," he said. "Her. The fae thing. But she was armed, and she dropped her weapon when she bolted." He'd been carrying a jacket, and from under it he pulled a rifle that had very little metal on it. If it had been a little prettier, it might have looked like a toy because it was mostly made of plastic.

"Kel-Tec rifle," said Adam, visibly dragging himself into a businesslike manner. "Built to fire pistol cartridges out of pistol magazines."

Ben handed it over, and Adam pulled the magazine. Jerking his hand back with a hiss, he dropped it on my counter. "Nine millimeter," he said. "Silver ammunition." He looked at me. "I'm pretty sure that was a nine millimeter or a thirty-eight you were holding on Heart."

The topic of my transgression was not dropped, just set aside for business. I wished we could just get it over with.

"Nine millimeter," I agreed. "She could have shot someone, and they'd have blamed it on the bounty hunter. How likely is it that someone would have done a ballistics test and noticed one of the bullets didn't come from the same gun?"

"Someone was supposed to die," said Ben. "That's what I think."

"Agreed," said Zee from the garage doorway. Samuel moved—a little stiff-legged, but he moved—so Zee could come into the office.

"Ballistics wouldn't have mattered," said Zee. "Making one bullet match another is cake if the fae is dealing with silver. Even a few with little magic could handle it. Iron is impossible for most fae to work, lead isn't much better, but silver . . . Silver accepts magic easily and keeps it."

My walking stick had silver on it.

Zee continued speaking. "The bullet would take on the appearance of the others. A little more glamour, and the extra bullet disappears. And whoever that was, they weren't minor fae. They had a fair touch of The Hunt—The Wild Hunt."

"I don't know what that means." But our fae assassin had been out to kill werewolves. To kill Adam. I needed to find out as much as I could.

"In this case, mindless violence," Zee told me. "The kind that leaves a man looking at the bodies and wondering why he decided to pull the trigger when he only intended to make a point. If I hadn't been here to counter it . . ." He shrugged and looked at Adam. "Someone wanted you dead with the blame easily placed, so no one would look too closely."

Adam put the rifle down on the counter next to the magazine, grabbed Ben's coat, and tossed it on top of them. "I haven't ticked off the fae recently. Have I?"

Zee shook his head. "If anything, it goes the other way. It must be an individual." He frowned, and said reluctantly, "Someone could have hired her, I suppose."

Ben said, "I've never seen a fae who used modern weaponry." He turned to Adam. "I know she was fae and all—but could she be one of the trophy hunters?"

"Trophy hunters?" Zee asked before I could.

"David has captured two people and killed a third hunting him this year," Adam said. "One was a big-game hunter; one turned out to be a serial killer who'd been prey-ing upon marines from the local base and decided to take on bigger prey. And one was a bounty hunter—though there's no bounty on David's head any more than there is on mine. It looked like he just wanted to try his hand at hunting a werewolf."

"David Christiansen?" I asked. Christiansen was a mercenary whose small troop specialized in rescuing hostages—I'd met him once before he'd become famous. When he retrieved some kids from a terrorist camp in South America, a photographer got a series of really terrific shots that made Christiansen look heroic and sweet. The photos made national news, and the Marrok chose David to be the first werewolf to admit what he was to the public—and thus the most famous werewolf around.

"Yes," Adam said.

" 'The Most Dangerous Game,' " I murmured. See? An education wasn't wasted on me, no matter what my mother says.

"This doesn't feel like that, though," said Adam. "This wasn't personal. Heart wasn't hunting me for thrills, or at least not only for thrills. Someone set him up."

"And not very well either," I added. "He didn't know who you were—and all his producer would have had to do was a simple Internet search for a photo. You'd think someone sending him out after you would make sure he knew who to shoot if you were the target."

Adam tapped his foot. "This feels like a professional job. A lot of planning, a lot of work to kill someone in the most public way possible. And, most telling, when it didn't work according to plan—she withdrew."

"Not 'someone,' " I said. "You. It makes sense. She didn't want Heart killing you; she wanted to do it herself."

"No." It was Ben. "I was wrong to suggest a trophy hunter. This didn't have that feel. It wasn't personal. A woman out for blood—assuming fae females are like the rest of the cu—"

"There's a lady present," growled Adam. "Watch your language."

Ben grinned at me. "Fine. Assuming fae *ladies* are like other *ladies*, this one would have been excited, triumphant over the kill. And enraged when I came along and ruined her fun. She didn't even hesitate when she spotted me. Dropped the gun and ran—no fuss, no bother."

"Well trained," said Adam. "Or just a cool thinker." He looked at me. "And while I admit it looks as though I was the target, it could as easily have been Zee or you. Heart had silver bullets—so the assassin used them, too. It doesn't mean she was hunting werewolves, not when we know Heart was."

Tony opened the front door. "You okay, Mercy?"

"Fine," I lied, but I didn't expect anyone here to believe me anyway.

Tony frowned at me, then turned his attention to Adam. "You have any enemies we should know about? Sounds like Heart's producer wanted some more publicity—but we won't know for certain until we run her down. He had the right paperwork, other than the small fact that it isn't legitimate. There was a series of victim photos, too. We'll look into how she got them when we talk to her."

"Internet," said Ben. "There's a website devoted to pictures of dead bodies."

We all looked at him, and he smirked. "Hey. Don't look at me—it's the job." He saw Tony's blank face and continued. "Information technologies, IT—you know, computers. At work, when we get bored, we issue challenges—like the person who can come up with the worst website gets taken out to lunch. I got the free lunch—the dead-bodies guy was the runner-up. When I chatted up the bounty hunter's people, they showed me the photos of the bodies in the file. The dead-bodies website has a section devoted to animal kills. I recognized one of the photos from that."

"You are a sick, sick man," I told him.

"Thank you," Ben replied, looking modest.

"Someone's after you," Tony told Adam.

"See," I said. "Tony thinks you're the target, too."

Adam shrugged. "I'll be careful."

Werewolves are tough, and Adam tougher than most—but I'd seen a lot of them die.

"Yeah, well, you keep me on speed dial and don't kill anyone if you can help it." Tony looked at me again. "Hey, Mercy. Did you talk to Sylvia? She looked pretty upset when she left. Are they all right?" His heart was in his eyes. He was interested in her and had approached her once. She'd told him she didn't date people she worked with—and that had been that, as far as she was concerned.

"She wasn't happy about Heart pointing a gun at Maia," I told him. "But I think she was madder at me than Heart. He didn't bring in a werewolf for her kids to play with."

His face went police-officer blank. "What?"

"Yeah," I said. "I don't think she'll be coming here to get her car fixed anymore. Gabriel's not coming back either."

"You did *what*?"

"Cut it out," growled Adam. He gestured at Sam. "This wolf would never harm a hair on a child's head, and Mercy knew it."

"Special circumstances today," I reminded Adam harshly—how could he have forgotten that we weren't dealing with Samuel but with his wolf? "She was right to be angry. If I'd remembered Sylvia and the girls were going to be here, I wouldn't have brought him."

"Were they in any danger?" asked Tony.

"No," said Adam, and he meant it.

"Did Mercy know that?"

"Yes," Adam said right over the top of my "no." "She's just feeling guilty because she thinks she should have told Sylvia anyway."

Tony looked at me. "Sylvia's not unreasonable." He paused and gave me a little smile. "Not really. If you explained—"

"They're gone," I told him. "It's for the best. Since I've

started running around with the wolves"—and fae and vampires—"this is not a safe place anymore."

"Is it safe for you?" he asked.

Before I had to answer, the door opened one more time, and Kelly Heart came in. My office isn't too big—and it was already holding me, Zee, Sam, Adam, Ben, and Tony. Kelly was one and a half persons too many. Sam growled at the bounty hunter, but he'd have to go over Zee, Adam, and me to get to him—or hop over the counter.

"Mr. Heart?" I asked.

"My camera people tell me that someone borked the cameras in the van." He looked at Ben. Who smirked. Sam's growls were getting a little louder.

After a moment, Heart shrugged. "Pretty tough to do. It left us with just the data from Joe's camera, which ends with Ms. Thompson disarming me. The cameras aren't coming out of my salary, anyway." He looked at me. "You moved pretty damned fast."

"Not a werewolf," I told him in bored tones as I shoved my way past Ben so I had my back to the counter. Not much better, because Sam could just jump on top of it, then over me, but maybe I'd slow him down.

"I just came to get the gun." He smiled at me. "My crew is extremely concerned that we might lose the silver bullets."

"Mercy," said Tony. "If you are okay, I don't need to know about any gun I might have to include in my report."

"We're fine," I told him. "Adam's here."

"Yeah," said Tony wryly after a quick glance at Adam. "I think you're safe enough, Mercy. I'll get back to work." He opened the door. "You sure you don't want me to talk to Sylvia?"

"I'm sure," I said. "This is easier. Better."

"All right." He left, and there were still too many people in the room.

"So now that the cops are gone, are you going to tell

me what this morning was all about?" Heart asked. "Why someone would get us all the way out here from California to play an elaborate practical joke that could have gotten people killed?"

"No," said Adam.

Heart took two steps forward and stood over Adam. "What did your errand boy go chasing after across the street?"

Before I could mention that threatening a werewolf was a little rash, Adam had the bounty hunter pinned against the door, with a forearm across his throat. Heart was taller, bigger, and more obviously muscled—but he wasn't a werewolf.

"Not your business," said Adam in a low, hungry voice.

"He's not the enemy," I told Adam. "Don't kill him. And, Mr. Heart, if you are going to hunt werewolves, you ought to do your homework. Don't try threatening an Alpha. They don't like it."

Adam increased the pressure against the bounty hunter's throat, but Heart, after an abortive effort to break free, quit struggling.

Adam took a step back, opening and closing his hands several times—maybe to shake off the desire to hit the bounty hunter. When he turned his back on Heart, I think everyone took a relieved breath.

"I'm as upset as you are," Heart told Adam. "Daphne . . . My producer is missing. She's a good person. Someone gave her that file and had her send me after you. She's not in her office, she's not answering her phone, and her housekeeper hasn't seen her for three days. And I don't even know where to look."

Adam sighed and stretched his shoulders to relieve the tension. "I don't know where she is. I don't know who planned this or why—or even if I was the real target. Give me your card. If I find out something that might help, I'll get in touch."

"Is your producer fae?" I asked him. Adam put his hand on my shoulder—a clear signal I should shut up. He didn't want me making Heart curious. I was more worried that he might know something that we needed—something that might tell us if the intended victim was Adam.

"No," Heart said. "Why? Do the fae have something to do with it?"

"Not that we know of," said Adam.

"Then why ask about fae?"

"You sound a little too certain that your producer isn't a fae," observed Ben.

"She's a member of several fae hate groups—which takes guts in Hollywood today—and likes to rant about how the country is succumbing to the wiles of the Wee Folk."

"When did you find out they were sending you here?" I asked.

Heart turned to me, his face thoughtful. "Yesterday morning. Yes, that means that Daphne hadn't been home for two days before that." He smiled at me. "You were supposed to be the Alpha's eye candy."

Adam laughed.

"What?" I asked him. "You don't think I'd be good eye candy?" I looked down at my overalls and grease-stained hands. I'd torn another nail to the quick.

"Honey is eye candy," said Ben apologetically. "You're . . . just you."

"Mine," said Adam, edging between Heart and me. "Mine is what she is."

Heart took out another card and gave it to me. "Call me if you have any more questions. Or if someone knows something that might help me find Daphne. She's good people. I don't see her pulling this as a prank or publicity stunt."

Heart gave Adam a nod and left. Ben followed him out the door—and Sam wiggled through before the door closed.

Zee looked at Adam and me. "I'll just go keep an eye on

Samuel, shall I? That way, if he hunts someone down, I can
share in the spoils."

"And you can give Heart back his gun," I told him.

Zee grinned cheerfully and produced a hunk of metal
that was sort of pretty—steel shot with silver. "I'll be sure
he leaves with it." He shut the door to the garage behind
him, leaving me alone with Adam.

"Mercy," Adam said. And his cell phone rang. He pulled
it out of its case on his belt with an impatient jerk. He
glanced at the number, took a deep breath, and answered it.

"Hauptman," he grunted.

"Adam," said the Marrok's easy voice. "I need you to
locate Mercy and my son."

"I know where they are," Adam said, meeting my eyes.
No such thing as a private phone conversation with me or
any of the wolves around. Adam could have chosen to take
the phone call outside, where he could have talked to Bran
in private.

There was a little pause.

"Ah. Would you be so good as to put one or the other
on the phone?"

"I think," Adam said carefully, "that it might be a little
precipitous to do that."

Another long pause, and Bran's voice was cooler when
he spoke. "I see. Be very careful here, Adam."

"I believe I am," Adam said.

"I can talk to him," I said, knowing Bran would hear
me. Adam was putting himself up as a shield between
Samuel and his father. If something happened, Bran would
hold him responsible.

I love Bran. He, as much as my foster parents, raised
me. But I'm not blind about it. His first directive is to protect the wolves. If that meant killing his son, he would do
it—but he would kill Adam faster.

Adam said, "No. My territory, my responsibility."

"Fine," said the Marrok. "If I or mine can help, you will call me."

"Yes," Adam said. "I'll call you by the end of the week with the results."

"Mercy," Bran said. "I hope this is the best path."

"For Samuel," I said. "For me, for you. I think it is. Maybe not so much for Adam."

"Adam has always had . . . heroic tendencies."

I touched Adam's arm. "He's my hero."

There was another pause. In person, Bran doesn't think out his comments as much. The phone is difficult because wolves communicate so much with their bodies.

"That is the most romantic thing I've ever heard you say," Bran said. "Be careful, Adam, or you'll turn her into a real girl."

Adam looked at me. "I like her just the way she is, Bran." And he meant it, greasy overalls, broken fingernails, and all.

Bran laughed, then stopped. "Take care of my son. And don't wait until it is too late to call me." He hung up.

"Thank you," I told Adam.

He put his cell phone away. "I didn't do it for you," he said. "Wolf in charge or not, Samuel obviously isn't as dangerous as most of us would be. There are some advantages to being very old. But the letter of the law is what Bran has to follow. If he knew exactly what was going on, he'd have to carry out the sentence."

"You don't?"

Adam shrugged. "I guess I'm not much for following orders as written. I prefer the spirit to the letter of the law."

I'd never thought of him that way. I should have remembered . . . the line between black and white is the one he draws.

I looked down. "So, I suppose an apology is too little, too late."

"What are you planning on apologizing for? 'Dear

Adam, I'm so sorry I tried to keep you from knowing that Samuel lost it'? 'I'm sorry I used the problems between us to drive you away so I could deal with it'? Or, and this one is my favorite, 'I'm sorry I couldn't tell you what was going on, but I couldn't trust you to deal with it the way I wanted it dealt with'?" He'd started out sounding amused, but by the last one his voice was sharp enough to cut leather.

I kept quiet. I do know how to do that. Sometimes. When I'm in the wrong.

He sighed. "I don't think an apology will do, Mercy. Because an apology implies that you wouldn't do it again. And, under the circumstances, you wouldn't do anything differently, would you?"

"No."

"And you shouldn't have to apologize for being right," he said, with a sigh. "Much as I'd like to tell you differently."

I jerked my head up and saw that he was perfectly serious.

"If you had called me to tell me that Samuel had lost it, I'd have come over and killed him. Put him down with a bullet because I don't know that I could take him in a fight. I've seen wolves who've lost it before, and so have you."

I swallowed. Nodded.

"What I know, that you do not, is how the wolf longs to hunt, to feel blood in his teeth. The kill . . ." He glanced away and back. "On his own, my wolf would never have let that bounty hunter leave here alive after he held a gun on me. I doubt that he'd have put up with having babies crawl all over him." Sorrow passed over his face. "Even with Jesse, my own daughter . . . I would not trust him. But Samuel's wolf managed to deal. So we'll give him a chance. A week. And after that week, we'll let you go talk to the Marrok and tell him how his son has kept his cool for a solid week. And maybe you can buy more time for him."

"I am sorry," I said in a low voice. "I played on your guilt to keep you away."

He leaned against the counter and folded his arms. "You

didn't lie, though, did you, Mercy? The pack bothers you, and so do I."

"I just need time to get used to it."

He looked at me—and I squirmed just as I'd seen his daughter do under that look.

"Don't lie to me, Mercy. Not to me. No lies between us."

I rubbed my eyes—I was not in tears. I wasn't. It was just the adrenaline letdown after taking on a gunman with a rogue werewolf at my back.

Adam turned his back to me. I thought it was so I wouldn't see the look on his face. Until he grabbed the counter and broke it in half—sending my cash register and a pile of receipts and bookkeeping stuff boiling to the floor.

Oddly, my first reaction to the violence was the dismayed recognition that without Gabriel, it would be *my* job to figure out how all those papers needed to be reorganized to keep the IRS off my back.

Then Adam howled. An unearthly sound to come out of a man's throat—I'd only heard it once before out of a wolf's. My foster father, Bryan, when he held his wife, his mate's body, in his hands.

I took a step toward him—and Sam was standing between us, his head lowered in readiness.

The door between my office and the garage is steel set in steel. After Sam's entrance, it was also bent and broken, dangling from one hinge. I hadn't heard it go; I'd only been able to hear Adam.

Who had made no sound, I realized. His cry had hit me from a different place altogether, where our bond tied me to him and him to me.

Adam didn't turn around. "Don't be afraid of me," he whispered. "Don't leave me."

No lies between us.

I blew out a breath, took a couple steps back, and flopped in one of the battered chairs that lined the wall, trying, with my casual pose, to defuse the situation. "Adam, I don't have the sense to be afraid of Sam in the state he's in now. I don't know why you think I'd be smart enough to be afraid of you." It would be smarter to be more afraid of a werewolf so upset that he took out a counter Zee had built than of a little paperwork and the IRS.

"Ask Samuel to leave us."

"Sam?" I asked. He'd heard Adam.

He growled, and Adam returned the favor. With interest.

"Sam," I said, exasperated. "He's my mate. He's not going to hurt me. Go away."

Sam looked at me, then returned his attention to Adam's back. I could see that back tighten up as if Adam could feel Sam's gaze. Maybe he could.

"Why don't you go see what Zee is up to?" I asked. "You're not helping here."

Sam whined. Took a half step toward Adam.

"Sam, please." I couldn't stand it if they ended up fighting. Someone would die.

The big white werewolf turned reluctantly and walked stiffly, with frequent pauses to see if Adam had moved at all. Finally, he hopped over the wreckage of the door and was gone.

"Adam?" I asked.

But he didn't answer. If he'd been human, I'd have bugged him—just to get it over with. I'd hurt him, and I waited to take my punishment. I'd been taught you make your choices and live with the consequences long before I'd first read Immanuel Kant in college.

But Adam wasn't human. And just then, if I was any judge, he was fighting his wolf. Being Alpha, being dominant, didn't make that fight any easier, maybe the opposite. Being stubborn helped—and Adam was well qualified on that front.

Getting Sam to leave helped more. The only other thing I could do to help was to sit quietly and wait while Adam stared at the wreckage he'd made of my office.

For Adam, screwed-up bonding thing or not, I'd wait forever.

"Really?" he asked in a tone I'd never heard from him before. Softer. Vulnerable. Adam didn't do vulnerable.

"Really what?" I asked.

"Despite the way our bond scares you, despite the way someone in the pack played you, you'd still have me?"

He'd been listening to my thoughts. This time it didn't bother me.

"Adam," I told him, "I'd walk barefoot over hot coals for you."

"You didn't take advantage of this thing with Samuel as a way of putting distance between us," he said.

I sucked in a breath. I could see how he might have interpreted it that way. "You know that section of the Bible, where Jesus tells Peter he'll deny him three times before morning? Peter says, 'Heck no.' But sure enough when he's asked by some people if he's one of Jesus' followers, he says he's not. And after the third time, he hears the cock crow and realizes what he's done. I feel like Peter right now."

Adam started laughing. He turned around, and I saw bright gold eyes looking through me the way wolves' eyes always seem to do. More than that, he'd actually begun to change a little—his jaw was longer, the angle of his cheekbones slightly different. "You're comparing me to Jesus? Like this?" He used his fingers to motion toward his face. "Don't you think you're being a little sacrilegious?"

His voice was bitter.

"No more than I'm Saint Peter," I told him. "But I had Peter's 'what have I done' moment—only his was instantaneous, and mine took a lot longer. It started when I heard Maia scream while I was working in the garage and continued pretty much up until you talked to Bran and bought Samuel a little more time. Funny how making decisions that seem right at the time . . ."

I shook my head. "Peter probably thought that telling the guy he wasn't one of Jesus' followers was the smartest thing to do. Kept him alive, for one. I thought keeping Samuel alive—as he wasn't raving or killing anyone . . . yet—was a good idea. I thought that telling you I needed a little space was good. Give me some time to wrap my head around having other people rattling around in my mind without hurting you because it scared me silly."

"What?" asked Adam incredulously.

I bowed my head, and said, "Because it scared me—scares me—silly."

He shook his head. "Not that part—the keeping it from hurting me part."

"You don't like being a werewolf," I told him. "Oh, you deal with it—but you hate it. You think that it makes you a freak. I didn't want you to know I had problems with some of the werewolf stuff, too." I swallowed. "Okay, more problems than just that whole 'I must control your life because you belong to me' that most of the werewolves I know have."

He stared at me with his yellow eyes and elongated face. His mouth was open slightly because his upper and lower jaw no longer quite matched up. I could see the edges of teeth that were sharper and more uneven than they usually were.

"I *am* a freak, Mercy," he said, and I snorted.

"Yeah, such a freak," I agreed. "That's why I've been drooling over you for years even though I'd sworn off werewolves for life after Samuel. I knew that if I told you being a member of the pack and the bonds and all that were bothering me—it would hurt you. And you are already putting up with . . ." I couldn't wrap my mouth around the ugly word "rape," so I softened it as I often did. "With the aftermath of Tim. I thought if I gave myself a little time, figured out how to keep the pack from turning me into your ex-wife, and bought Samuel a little extra time as well . . ."

Adam leaned against the wall just inside the door—the

wall my counter used to block—and folded his arms across his chest.

"What I'm trying to say," I told him, "is that I'm sorry. It seemed like a good idea at the time. And, no, I did not engineer this to put some distance between us."

"You were trying to keep me from being hurt," he said, still in that odd voice.

"Yes."

He shook his head slowly—and I noticed that sometime while we'd been talking, he'd lost the wolfish aspect and his face had returned to normal. Warm brown eyes caught the light from the windows as one side of his mouth quirked up.

"Do you have any idea how much I love you?" he asked.

"Enough to accept my apologies?" I suggested in a small voice.

"Heck no," he said, and pushed off from the wall, stalking forward.

When he reached me, he put his hands up and touched the sides of my neck with the tips of his fingers—as if I were something fragile.

"No apologies from you," he told me, his voice soft enough to melt my knees and most of my other parts. "First of all, as I already pointed out—you would make the same choices again, right? So an apology doesn't work. Secondly, you, being who you are, could have made no other choice. Since I love you, as you are, where you are—it hardly makes sense for me to kick about it when you act like yourself. Right?"

"People don't always see it that way," I said, stepping into him until our hip bones bumped.

He laughed, a quiet sound that made me happy down to my toes. "Yeah, well, I don't promise I'll always be logical about it." He gave a rueful glance to my broken counter and the cash register on its side. "Especially at first." His smile dropped away. "I thought you were trying to leave me."

"I might be dumb," I told him, putting my nose against his silk tie, "but I'm not that dumb. I've gotcha now, and you aren't getting away."

His arms tightened almost painfully around me.

"So why didn't you tell Bran about Samuel?" I asked him. "I was sure you'd have to tell him. Aren't you bound by blood-sworn oaths?"

"If you'd called me last night and told me what was going on, I'd have called Bran—and shot Samuel myself. But . . . based on what happened this morning, he seems to be holding it together okay. He deserves some time." His arms, which had loosened a little, pulled me against him even harder. "If something like that happens to me— you call Bran and you stay as far from me as you can get. My wolf is not like Samuel's." He gave the counter another look. "If I lose it . . . you just stay away until I'm dead."

6

ONCE MOST EVERYONE ELSE WAS GONE, ADAM tossed the fae's rifle into the backseat of his truck.

"I'll see if I can't find out something from the serial numbers," he said. "The way she just left it probably means that she doesn't think we can trace it to her anyway, but it would be stupid not to check."

"You will be careful," I told him.

"Sweetheart"—he bent down and kissed me—"I am always careful."

"What'll you give me if I watch out for him?" It wasn't what Ben said; it was the way he'd said it. I have no idea how he made those words sound suggestive, but he managed it.

Adam shot him a look. Ben grinned unrepentantly and ducked around the side of the truck and hopped in.

"I was on the way to a job site when I got the call that something was up," Adam told me. "I've got to get back."

"No worries," I said. "I'll lock up. I don't think I'll be doing anything more here today."

He opened his door, and stopped with his head turned away from me. "I'm sorry about your counter."

I took a couple of steps forward until my nose pressed against his back and wrapped my arms around him. "I'm sorry about a lot of things. But I'm glad I have you."

He hugged my arms. "Me, too."

"Get a room," said Ben from inside the truck.

"Stuff it." Adam turned around, kissed me, and hopped in the truck.

Sam and I watched him drive away.

———

I STOPPED AT A SANDWICH SHOP AND BOUGHT ten subs with double meat and cheese. Then I drove the Rabbit to the park on the Kennewick side of the river to eat. There wasn't any snow yet, but it was a cold and dreary day so, other than some distant joggers and a serious-looking biker, we had the place to ourselves. I ate half a sandwich and drank a bottle of water. Sam ate the rest.

"Well, Sam," I asked, when we were both finished, "what do you want to do today?"

He looked at me with interest, which didn't help much.

"We could go run," I told him as I threw our garbage into a can next to where I'd parked the Rabbit.

He shook his head with emphasis.

"Hunting not a good idea?" I asked. "I'd think it would help you to relax."

He lifted his lips to display his fangs, then snapped his teeth five times, each snap faster, more savage, than the one previous to it. When he stopped, he was perfectly calm— except that I could see that he was breathing harder, and there was a deep hunger in his eyes even though he'd just eaten nine and a half feet of loaded submarine sandwiches.

"Okay," I said after a pause to make sure my voice wasn't shaking, "hunting is a bad idea. I get it. Something peaceful."

I opened the passenger door to let him in and saw the towel-wrapped bundle on the backseat.

"Want to help me return a book?" I asked.

THE UPTOWN WAS BUSTLING WITH SATURDAY shoppers, and I had to park a good distance away from the bookstore. I opened the door for Sam. He hopped out, then froze. After a second, he dropped his nose to the ground—but whatever he was looking for he didn't find because he stopped and drew in a deep breath of air.

My nose is better than a normal human's, if not as good as it is in my coyote shape. I took in a deep breath, too, but there were too many people, too many cars, for me to figure out what had set Sam off.

He shook himself, gave me a look I couldn't fathom, and hopped back into the Rabbit. He flattened himself on the seat, stretching across the gap between, and lowered his muzzle to the driver's-side seat.

"You're staying here, I take it?" I asked. It must not be anything dangerous, or he wouldn't let me go on my own—Sam with his wolf ascendant had always been even more protective of me than Samuel himself had.

Maybe one of the other werewolves was nearby. It would make sense for Sam to avoid them. I took another deep breath. I still didn't scent anyone I recognized, but Samuel's nose was better than mine outside of coyote shape.

I moved his tail out of danger and shut his car door. I opened the back door to get the book—and reconsidered. Phin's neighbor might have been fae and faintly creepy, but that didn't mean there was anything wrong. But there could be, and with Sam in the car, the book was just as safe here.

If Phin was at the bookstore, I'd just come back and get it. If his neighbor or someone other than Phin was around instead, I'd regroup.

"I'm going to leave the book in the backseat," I told Sam. "I should be right back."

In the short time since we'd left the park, the temperature had dropped, and the wind had picked up. My light jacket wasn't quite up to the wind and the damp. I gave the gray skies a good look—if it rained tonight and the temperature dropped much from here, we might have a good, hard freezing rain. Montana may have steep, windy roads that are nasty when covered with snow and ice, but those are nothing compared to the Tri-Cities when the freezing rain turns the pavement into a polished ice-skating rink.

I trotted through the parking lot and narrowly avoided getting run over by a Subaru that was backing out without looking. I kept an eye out for other idiots, and so it wasn't until I stepped onto the sidewalk and looked up into the window of the bookstore that I saw a gray-haired woman behind the counter. I felt a frizzle of relief: she wasn't the creepy neighbor.

I reached for the door and saw that the closed sign was still up—with an addition. Someone had taped a piece of white paper with UNTIL FURTHER NOTICE printed in thick black Sharpie.

While I hesitated, the woman inside gave me a cheery smile and walked up to the door, turning the dead bolt so she could open it. Her movements were surprisingly brisk and sprightly for a woman of her grandmotherly roundness and wrinkles.

"Hello, dear," she said. "I'm afraid we're closed today. Did you need something?"

She was fae. I could smell it on her—earth and forest and magic with a touch of something burning, air and salt water. I'd never smelled the like, and I've met two of the Gray Lords, who rule the fae.

Most fae smell to me like one of the elements the old alchemists claimed made up the universe—earth, air, fire, and water. Never more than one. Not until this woman.

Her faded hazel eyes smiled into mine.

"Is Phin around?" I said. "Who are you? I haven't seen you here before." I wasn't a regular customer; maybe she worked with Phin all the time. But I was betting she didn't. If she'd helped often, I'd have smelled her in the store the first time I'd come here. I would have remembered if I'd caught her scent.

Lots of things scare me—like vampires, for instance. Since I've become more intimately acquainted with them, they scare me even more than they used to. I know that they can kill me. But I've killed one and helped to kill two others.

The fae . . .

In the most terrifying horror films, you never see what is killing people. I know that's because the unknown is far scarier than anything some makeup or special-effects person can come up with. The fae are like that, their true faces concealed behind other forms—and designed to blend in with the human race and hide what they truly are.

This sweet-faced person who looked like someone's grandmother might be one of those who ate children who were lost in the woods, or drowned young men who trespassed in her forest. Of course, it was possible that she might be one of the lesser or gentler fae—just as she looked. But I didn't think so.

I'm smarter than Snow White: I wouldn't be eating any apples she gave me.

She ignored my questions—fae don't give out their true names—and said, "Are you a friend of his? You're shivering. I don't suppose it would hurt anything if you came in and sat down a bit to warm up. I'm just helping straighten out the books while Phin is gone."

"Gone?" I wasn't going into that shop alone with her.

Instead, I pounded her with the kind of questions any customer . . . okay, any *obsessive* customer would ask. "Where is he? Do you know how I can get in touch with him? Why isn't the store open?"

She smiled. "I don't know where he is at the moment." Another evasion. She might know that he was in the basement, for instance, but not exactly where he was standing. "He'll probably let me know when he gets a chance to call me. Who should I tell him came asking after him?"

I looked into her guileless eyes and knew that Tad had been right to be worried. All I had was Phin's unresponsive phone, a nasty neighbor, and the store closed—but my instincts were clamoring. Something had happened to Phin, something bad.

I didn't know him well, but I liked him. And, going by the phone call Tad had received, whatever had happened to him was tied to the book he'd loaned to me. Which made it my fault. Maybe if I hadn't kept it to read this past month, he'd still be safe in his store.

I smiled back at her, a polite smile. "Don't worry about it. I'll stop in another time."

She snapped her fingers. "Wait just a minute. My grandson told me that he'd loaned a nice young woman a rather valuable book that she should be returning soon."

I raised my eyebrows. "Right now I'm interested in a first British edition of *Harry Potter and the Philosopher's Stone*." Not really a lie. It would be interesting, and I didn't tell her I was trying to buy one. I don't know if the fae can figure out if someone is lying as well as the werewolves can, but any group that has a prohibition against lying that is as stringent as the fae's probably has a method to detect when it happens.

"He didn't tell me about anything like that," she said suspiciously, as if he would have normally.

But she had lost the chance to convince me that she was Phin's assistant when she allowed my comment that she was a stranger to his store to stand.

"I suspect it'll take him a while," I told her. "I just stopped by to check in with him. I'll come back another time." I stopped the "thanks" that was on the tip of my tongue and substituted "Bye, now" and a casual wave.

I felt her eyes on my back until I was hidden behind rows of cars, and I was glad I'd parked the car a long way from the mall. Sam moved his head off my seat without raising any part of his body enough that he might be seen through the windows. He was hiding.

I looked at him and glanced at the bookstore as I cruised past it on the way out of the parking lot. The woman was back behind the counter going over something that looked like an account book.

Coincidences happen a lot less often in real life than they do in the movies.

"Sam," I said, "are you staying out of sight of a fae? One that smells like all the elements at once?"

He raised his chin and dropped it.

"Is she one of the good guys?" I asked.

He made a gesture that was neither yes nor no.

"Trouble?"

He snorted affirmative.

"Damn it."

I pulled over at a gas station, parked the car, and called Warren, Adam's third in the pack and my friend.

"Hey, Warren," I said when he answered. "Does Kyle have a safe in that monstrosity he lives in?" I could put the book in Adam's safe—and if it weren't fae who were looking for it, I'd feel relatively confident with it hidden and surrounded by werewolves. But Warren's human boyfriend's house would be a much less likely spot to leave it and nearly as safe.

"Several." Warren's voice was dry. "I'm sure he'd be delighted to loan you one. You storin' blackmail material now, Mercy?" There were noises in the background of his phone, people and the kind of echoing you get in a really big building.

"Wouldn't that be something," I said. "How much do you suppose Adam would pay to keep an X-rated video of him off the Internet?"

Warren laughed.

"Yeah," I said sadly, "that's what I think, too. So no riches in my future, and no blackmail either. Can you or Kyle meet Sam and me at Kyle's house sometime soon?"

"I'm on guard duty right now, but I bet Kyle is home. He doesn't always answer the house phone. Do you have his cell number?"

Warren worked for his boyfriend—I know, it's an awkward thing, but Warren hadn't exactly been making rent at the Stop and Rob he'd worked at before. Kyle'd shaken a few trees, bribed a few officials (probably), and maybe blackmailed more, and gotten Warren a private detective's license. Warren guarded clients and did quiet investigations for Kyle's law firm.

"I have it," I told him. "Are you at Wal-Mart?"

"Nope, grocery store. Wal-Mart was an hour ago."

"Poor baby," I said sympathetically.

"Nope," he said, his voice soft. "I'm doin' something useful. This lady deserves to feel safe—though lots of folks seem to think I'm responsible for her black eye."

"You're tough," I said unsympathetically. "You can handle a few nasty looks." Being a gay werewolf for a hundred years gave Warren a skin so thick it might as well be armor. Not much ruffled his feathers except for Kyle.

"I'm kinda hoping her soon-to-be-ex shows up," he said softly; I thought so she wouldn't hear him. "I'd like to get the opportunity to introduce myself to him."

———

KYLE BROOKS'S HOUSE IS IN THE WEST RICHLAND hills, where the rich folks live. Huge and yet somehow delicately designed, it settles in among its neighbors like a sly cat among poodles. The size is right, but it's more graceful and comfortable in the desert light than the rest of them. Divorce lawyering, at least in Kyle's case, pays very well.

I parked the Rabbit on the street, let Sam out, and got the book . . . and the walking stick that was lying beside it.

"Hello," I told it. It didn't do anything magical or warm in my hands, but somehow, it felt smug.

I bumped the Rabbit's door closed with a hip and trotted all the way up to Kyle's front door. The significance of the book had just entered a whole new dimension, once the old woman at the bookstore had mentioned it. So I held it with both hands and tucked the walking stick under my arm.

When I got to the front door, I couldn't ring the bell.

Sam saw my dilemma and caught the doorbell with a gentle nudge of one claw. Kyle must have been right by the door, as he'd promised when we talked, because when he opened the door, he was face-to-fang with Sam.

He didn't even flinch. Instead, he cocked a hip, made a kissy face, then smiled seductively, turning an ordinary pair of jeans and a purple wifebeater into brothel-wear.

"Hey, darling," he told Sam. "I bet you're gorgeous in man shape, hmm?"

"It's Sam," I told Kyle dryly. And even though I knew it would just stir up trouble, I had to warn him again because I really liked him. "You need to be careful about whom you flirt with among the wolves—you might get more than you bargain for."

Kyle could sometimes have a real chip on his shoulder—getting disinherited, then living in a conservative community has had that effect on more than one gay man—and Kyle could take flaming (and bitchy) to an art form when he thought it would make someone who disapproved of him uncomfortable. Luckily, he chose to take my warning in the spirit it was offered.

In an entirely different kind of voice, he said, "Love you, too, Mercy." He dropped the flirtatious act with a speed and completeness that many an Oscar winner would envy.

"Hey, Samuel. Sorry, didn't recognize you with all the fur."
He looked at what I held. "You want to put a towel in my
safe?"

"It's a very special towel," I told him as I ducked around
him and into the house. "Dried Elvis's hair on the day of
the last concert."

"Oooh," he said, stepping back so Sam could follow me.
He shut the door and, almost as an afterthought, turned the
dead bolt. "In that case, you certainly need it someplace
secure. You want the big safe with all the electronics or
something better hidden?"

"Better hidden would be cool." I didn't think that electronics were going to work against the fae.

He led the way through the house, up the stairs, and
past his library—one side filled with beautiful leather-
clad law books, the other with tattered paperbacks that
included Nora Roberts's complete works. I took two steps
and stopped, backed up, and looked in the library again.

If the fae were after the book, and they had some way of
tracking it—certainly they would already have it. Instead, it
had spent the better part of two days in my Rabbit wrapped
in a towel.

Kyle came back and looked at the library, too. "It's a
book, is it? You're thinking of hiding it in plain sight?" He
shook his head. "We can do that, but if someone is looking
for a book, the first place they'll look—after the big safe—
is the library. I have a better idea."

So I followed him to a bedroom. It was painted dark
blue with black splatters, and the twin-sized bunk beds had
comforters with Thomas the Tank Engine chugging around
on his track—not exactly something I expected to ever see
in Kyle's house. I knew that he never had family visit, so it
couldn't be for a nephew. Kyle continued into the bathroom
so I did, too. Sam's claws clicked on the slate floor.

Thomas continued to rule the bathroom, too. A plastic
toothbrush holder in the shape of a train sat next to the

sink, and a set of towels embroidered with Thomas and his friends hung from towel racks shaped like train tracks.

Kyle opened a cupboard next to the sink to reveal two empty shelves and one filled with towels of various colors.

"Give me that," he said, so I handed him the book.

He knelt on the floor and unfolded the towel, repositioned the book, and folded the towel in the same way as all the other towels. He handed it back to me, and I put it on the bottom of one of the stacks.

Kyle looked at my work and straightened the stack. The book towel looked just like the ones around it.

One thing pretending to be another.

For some reason I thought about the incident with the bounty hunter this morning. The bounty hunter—and the fae armed with a plastic gun loaded with silver bullets just like Kelly Heart's gun had been. Because he'd been hunting werewolves.

Maybe . . . maybe that was not what the fae had been hunting. Adam had suggested the silver ammunition might have been used only to match Kelly Heart's, that the shooter might have been after any of us and not just a werewolf. I'd thought he was just trying to draw the spotlight off himself and keep me from worrying about him. But what if he was right? What if the fae had been after me?

I was probably being paranoid. The world didn't revolve around me, after all. Just because this past year I'd had vampires, fae, and werewolves try to kill me at various times didn't mean someone was after me at present. The old woman in the bookstore hadn't known who I was. Surely, if the fae were trying to kill me, she'd have recognized my face. Maybe the fae were willing to kill for the book I'd just hidden in my friend's home. Warren wasn't always here, and Kyle was just human. Maybe I shouldn't leave it here. Maybe I was paranoid and seeing conspiracies where there were none.

"Hey, Kyle?" I said.

He looked at me.

"You don't risk anything for that book," I told him. "If someone comes and threatens you—just give it to them."

He raised a well-groomed eyebrow. "Why don't you give it to them? Whoever 'them' is."

I sorted through a number of answers, but finally said, "That's just it. I don't really know who 'them' is or why they want that book. Or really *if* they want the book." Probably I was overreacting to the whole thing, and Phin would call me in a couple of days and ask for his book back. Probably the bounty-hunter incident was just what everyone thought it was—a publicity-hungry producer. And the armed fae was . . . My imagination failed me. But there could be an explanation that had nothing to do with me or the book.

I couldn't really see someone just killing me outright like that for the book. Wouldn't they at least approach me first? Ask me for it? Tell me that if I didn't give it to them, they'd kill Phin?

Unless they'd already killed Phin.

"You okay, Mercy?" Kyle asked.

"Fine. I'm fine."

WE WERE ON OUR WAY DOWN THE STAIRS BEFORE I finally gave in to curiosity. "Okay. Who's the Thomas the Tank Engine fan—you or Warren?"

Kyle threw back his head and laughed. "Maybe we should have hidden it in the bathroom of the Princess room. Then you could have asked which one of us likes to sleep with a pink canopy over his head." The grin died down. "I have guests, Mercy. Mostly divorces are messy and hurtful for everyone involved. All that hurt can explode on the wrong people. Sometimes people need a place to be safe for a while—and if there's a pool and a hot tub in the backyard, so much the better."

Kyle hid people in his home, children who needed to be safe.

Sam growled.

I reached down and rested my hand on his head, but Kyle didn't seem to recognize that Sam's reaction was a little extreme even from a wolf who loved children. No one was being hurt here and now.

"Yes"—Kyle started down the stairs—"I agree, Samuel. Those are the men I really love sticking it to in court." He paused. "And women, too, sometimes. Abuse and violence goes both ways. Did I ever tell you about the client I had who took a contract out on her husband?"

"You mean a killing-for-hire-type contract?"

He nodded. "It was a first for me, too. Who'd have thought it would happen in our little town? Killer took him out with a single shot. They'd been married for thirty-two years, and he took up with their grandson's girlfriend. Apparently she decided divorce and the lovely settlement I'd gotten her weren't enough. She turned herself in that afternoon. Seemed pretty happy to do so." He paused at the kitchen. "Would you like something to eat?"

"I think I'd better go," I told him. "I'd rather no one realized I stopped by here."

"Weren't you carrying that walking stick of yours? Did you leave it in the bathroom?"

It was gone. I'd been carrying it, and I hadn't noticed when it left. "Don't worry about it," I told him. "It'll show up again when it wants to."

He gave me a delighted smile. "That's right. That's what Warren said. The thing just follows you around like a puppy?"

I shrugged.

"Pretty cool."

At the door, he hugged me and kissed my cheek. Sam gravely raised one paw like a well-trained dog, and Kyle shook the lion-sized foot without flinching.

"You take care of Mercy," he told Sam. "I don't know what she's gotten herself into this time—but danger seems to be her new middle name."

"Hey," I objected.

Kyle looked down his nose at me. "Broken arm, concussion, sprained ankle, stitches, kidnapped . . ." He let his voice trail off. "And that's not the end of the list, is it? You keep Samuel or someone next to you until this blows over. I don't want to be attending your funeral, darling."

"Fine," I said, hoping that he wasn't right. "I'll be careful."

"You just let Warren or me know if we can give you any more help."

I DROVE TO THE BIG MALL IN KENNEWICK BE- cause I felt a strong desire not to park somewhere isolated— and I wanted to call Tad. I had to park in Outer Mongolia because on a Saturday, that was the only place with parking spaces. But I was as far from alone as it was possible to be. Then I called Tad.

"Hey, Mercy," he answered. "Dad told me that you were nearly involved in a shoot-out at the OK Corral in East Kennewick this morning."

"That's right," I told him. "But let me tell you about the whole day and see what you think."

I ran through the whole thing from beginning to end— leaving out only the part where I hid the book.

When I'd finished, there was a small pause while Tad absorbed what I'd said. Then he asked, "Just what is in that book anyway?"

"It's a book written about the fae by someone who was fae," I told him. "I don't think there's anything magical about it—or if there is, I can't tell, and I usually can. There's a lot of information in it and a lot of fairy tales retold from the other side." I had to laugh. "Gave me a whole new perspective on 'Rumplestiltskin' and a real aversion to ever reading 'Hansel and Gretel' again."

"Nothing shocking?"

"Not that I read. Not a whole lot that isn't already out in the realm of folklore—though this is more organized. Particularly in regard to the variety of the fae and the fae artifacts. I suppose there could be something shocking in the part I haven't gotten through yet—or there's something concealed by magic or a secret code . . . Invisible ink, maybe?" My imagination failed me.

"Let me tell Dad all of this," Tad said. "I can't think that there would be that much interest in that old book. Sure, it's valuable—and there would be a desire, I think, to keep it out of the hands of the humans. But it wouldn't be disastrous if there's nothing in it but fairy tales not that much different from books already available . . . Wait a minute." He paused. "Maybe that old woman in the shop was Phin's grandmother."

"His grandmother? She was older, but not that old. Phin is . . ." It had been difficult to pin his age, I remembered. But he had been an adult—at least in his thirties, possibly as old as a well-preserved fifty. "Anyway, this woman was maybe early sixties, no older than that."

Tad cleared his throat. "If she's fae, Mercy, it doesn't matter how old she looks."

"Phin doesn't have much fae in his background," I said. I was certain of that. "This woman was big-time old-school Gray Lord kind of fae."

Tad laughed. "The woman he calls his grandmother is probably more like his great, great, great . . . Add a lot more 'great's to the end of it. He told me that one time, when he was a kid, she drove off a bunch of fae who were unhappy that he was so human . . . or maybe that he, a human, had a touch of fae blood at all. After that, she'd drop in now and then until she started to keep up with him just by cell phone."

"So she's a good guy? You think I should talk to her? Tell her about the book and ask her where Phin is?"

"I don't know if this piece has any good guys or villains, Mercy," he said. "And I certainly don't know if the fae you saw was Phin's grandmother or a Gray Lord. And if it was . . . there's no surety that she's safe to deal with. Fae are not human, Mercy. Some of them could eat their own children without anger or regret. Power motivates them more than love—if they can love. Some of them are so alone . . . You have no idea. I'll call Dad, then get back to you."

He hung up.

"Well," I asked Sam, "excitement enough for one day? Do you want to go home?"

He looked up at me, and I saw that he was tired, too. More tired than a day mostly running around in a car could account for. *Sad*, I thought suddenly.

"Don't worry," I told him, bending down until my forehead was on the back of his neck. "Don't worry, we'll find some answers for you, too."

He sighed and wiggled until his muzzle was on my lap. I drove home that way.

I MADE MEAT LOAF—SAMUEL'S RECIPE, WHICH included plenty of jalapeños and several other peppers. Day-old and out of the refrigerator, it could burn the skin off the roof of your mouth if you weren't careful.

My phone rang, and I looked at the number. I set the timer on the oven, and it was still ringing.

"Bran," I answered.

"You're playing with fire," he said. He sounded tired.

"How did you know I'm making Samuel's meat loaf?"

"Mercedes."

"You're supposed to give us some time," I told him. My stomach roiled. I needed more time to prove Sam's ability to keep the peace.

"I love my son," Bran said, "but I love you, too."

I heard everything that he didn't say. He'd chosen his son over me before—that was how he saw it. That was how I might have seen it at the time, too.

"He's not going to hurt me," I said, looking into Sam's white eyes. He stiffened, and I remembered to drop my gaze—though he hadn't been making me do that after last night. Usually, once the wolf knows you've acknowledged he's the boss, those kinds of things only crop up when the more dominant wolf is upset.

"You don't know that."

"I do, actually," I replied. "I had a gunman break into the garage and point a gun at him, and he didn't attack because I asked him not to—and because someone, a child, might have gotten hurt in the cross fire."

There was a very long pause.

"I need you to be very clear on what is wrong," he said.

But I interrupted him. "No, you don't. If I tell you that Samuel's wolf is in charge, you will have to kill him."

He didn't say anything.

"Maybe if he weren't your son, you could afford to be more lenient. Or if you hadn't used your position as Marrok to force wolves who would rather have stayed hidden out into the open. But that lost you a lot of moral support that you haven't recovered yet. If you loosen those rules even a little . . . well, you probably won't lose your position—but there might be a lot of dead bodies on the ground. Maybe more than can be explained away to the humans." I'd been doing a lot of thinking about this.

I let that hang in the air for a little while. We needed that week to justify Sam's reprieve to the other wolves.

"Stay by the phone," he said, and hung up.

Sam looked at me and sighed, then flattened out on the floor on his side like a big fur rug.

When the phone rang next, it was Charles, Samuel's brother and Bran's enforcer. "Mercy?"

"Right here," I answered.

"Tell me about Samuel."

"Is it safe?"

"I won't know until you tell me, will I?"

Was he trying to be funny? With Charles, I could never tell. Of all the Marrok's wolves, his younger son was the most intimidating—at least to me.

"I meant for Samuel," I said.

"I'm under orders," he said, with a cool smile in his voice, "to keep the contents of our conversation to myself."

"All right." I cleared my throat and took Charles through my discovery that Samuel had tried to commit suicide all the way to Kelly Heart trying to apprehend Adam.

"He played with the children?" Charles asked.

"Yes. I told you. Maia got on his back and rode him like a pony. It's a good thing for him she wasn't wearing spurs."

Still flat on the floor, Sam thumped it with his tail twice—otherwise, he might have been asleep.

"That's good, isn't it?" I asked. "It means he has some time."

"Maybe," Charles answered. "Mercy, for werewolves— all of us have different relations with our wolves." Charles didn't usually talk a lot, and when he did, his speech was deliberate, as if he thought through everything twice before saying anything out loud. Bran sounded that way on the phone, but Charles did it all the time, even in person.

"Think of werewolves as conjoined twins. Some of us are quite separate, barely sharing anything at all with our wolves. Just two entities under the same skin—we all start out that way. When our human side is able to take control, wolf and man work out a . . . 'Truce' is the wrong word. 'Balance' is better. And just as our human soul loses parts of what it was to be human, our wolf loses part of what it means to be wolf."

"So Samuel's wolf isn't dangerous?"

"No," he said quickly, and Sam picked up his head, rolled

up to his belly, and took a more sphinxlike stance. "Never think that. He's not whole anymore—he isn't equipped to be in charge. Like a conjoined twin, he shares his heart and head with Samuel. And if he succeeds in wresting complete control from Samuel, or if Samuel lets him do it, that heart will quit beating."

I dropped to my knees and put a hand on Sam's shoulder because the pain in Charles's voice found its echo in mine.

"I doubt he'll survive for very long that way—do you hear me, wolf?"

Sam's upper lip curled, showing teeth.

"He does," I said.

"He'll grow tired and more hungry than usual. He'll slowly lose the chains that Samuel forged to control him, and all that will be left is a ravenous beast. A new wolf, a whole wolf in charge, kills easily and often, but usually there is a reason for it, even if that reason is that he doesn't like the way his victim smelled. What will be left of Samuel will kill and destroy until he drops dead."

"How do you know?" Charles was only a couple of centuries old. He hadn't ever lived in a place outside of the Marrok's control, and the Marrok killed the wolves who lost control. But he sounded absolutely certain.

"Let's say that, like you, I once had a friend I wished to help, and I kept him out of sight of my father in a place he could do no harm. It would have been kinder to kill him from the first."

My fingers sank into Sam's fur.

"How long do we have?"

"My friend was old, but not as old as Samuel. He lost his humanity over a few days, became sick and lethargic toward the end of that. I thought he was just fading—but he went into a frenzy." He stopped speaking for a moment. "Then just dropped dead. Less than a week. I have no idea how long Samuel will last."

"If he'd lost it when the wolf took over?" I asked. "Like

the new wolves do? He'd have been better off?" I'd been so happy that he'd been different.

"Then he'd have lived until our father caught up with him—but you would have died along with the people in the hospital where you found him. This is better, Mercedes. But do not trust him too much."

"Do you have any suggestions how I can help him?"

"The first is to convince the wolf to allow Samuel back in the driver's seat, if only for a short period of time."

"He wants to survive," I told them both. "That's why he took over from Samuel in the first place. If that means letting Samuel back in, he'll do it." I sounded much more convinced of that than I felt, but Sam sighed and gave me a tired, faint whine.

"And then you have to convince Samuel that he wants to survive."

"And if I can't? If the wolf lets Samuel out, and he still wants to kill himself?"

"Then the wolf will have to fight for control again—or my brother dies." Charles let out a breath of air. "All things die, Mercedes. Some just take longer than others."

7

I TOOK SAM WITH ME TO THE BOOKSTORE THAT
night, which was inconvenient.

I suppose we both could have stayed home, but I wanted
in to look at Phin's bookstore. The woman had been search-
ing for something; maybe I could figure out what it had
been. Maybe I'd find Phin there, happy and healthy. Maybe I
wouldn't sit home all night, worrying about things I couldn't
change.

I couldn't leave Sam by himself, not after my little talk
with Charles. But he wasn't the best partner to bring with
me to break into the store.

People would overlook a woman wandering around
the Uptown mall in Richland even after most of the stores
were closed. It wasn't that late, a little after nine at night.
The crime rate is relatively low in Richland—and most of
what crime there is tends to be committed by gang members or teenagers. Sam . . .

I imagined the hypothetical conversation as I drove down the interstate.

Officer: "Tell me, did you see anything unusual last night?"

Random witness: "There was this big white dog. Huge. And really white, stood out in the darkness like a beacon."

Yep. Sam made matters more difficult. So I would just act like I knew what I was doing and hope no one ever called the police to investigate.

"I don't know what I hope to discover in the bookstore," I said. "There is hardly going to be a note telling me where Phin is, right? Still, it's a start. If we don't find anything, maybe we'll go break into his apartment. It's better than sitting around at home, right?"

And the pack was meeting at Adam's house that night. I knew why he'd called the meeting. He wanted to find out who'd been playing games with me. He'd called me to tell me what he was doing—and asked me to stay away because he hadn't had a chance to show me how to defend myself from pack members crawling around in my head.

I should have gone over anyway, confronted my enemies. But it was different when all your enemies could do was kill you.

"I don't want to stay home knowing how much of a coward I am," I told Sam. "I should have gone to Adam's when I saw them all arrive."

He grunted.

"But the thought of them being able to make me do something I would never . . ."

I was pretty sure that it hadn't just been lack of opportunity that kept Adam from teaching me how to protect myself. He'd said that if he'd known what was happening at the time when whoever it was started influencing me, he could have discovered their identity. I think he planned on trying to force a confession tonight—and if he couldn't, he would wait until they tried it again. If that was his motivation, I approved in spirit, but at the same time, I really didn't want to wait around until someone tried to make me do their bidding again.

I parked in the corner of the Uptown parking lot where an all-night restaurant was located. There weren't a lot of cars there but enough that the Rabbit didn't stand out.

I opened Sam's door, and he sniffed the air carefully.

"Are you scenting for the fae woman who was here today?" I asked.

He didn't give me any kind of answer, just shook himself and looked at me expectantly—as if he really were the dog we were pretending he was. Was he slower? Did his tail droop more than usual? Or was I letting Charles's words make me paranoid?

I glanced at him and was pretty sure it was both. Just because you're paranoid doesn't mean you aren't right. He wasn't quite as responsive either, as if it took him a moment to translate words into meanings.

I didn't notice anyone who seemed to be watching us as we crossed the parking lot—but we were out where people could see us. All I could do was act as if I weren't breaking into the shop. It took me two full minutes to crack the lock on the door of the bookstore, which was about one and a half minutes longer than I was comfortable standing there with my back to the parking lot and the busy street beyond. I was hopeful that someone from the street couldn't tell that I was playing with my lockpicks instead of fumbling with a stiff lock. There was a bar that was still open about three stores over, but no one had come or gone while I struggled. Sheer good luck, something I couldn't always count on. I was going to have to get some practice in if I kept having to break into buildings.

The door handle turned, and I started to move on to the dead bolt, when I realized that the door had popped open when I'd unlocked the handle. Someone hadn't engaged the dead bolt.

I held the door for Sam, then slipped inside myself. He couldn't shut the door—and if there was something unfriendly in the store, he was better able to deal with it.

I turned the dead bolt and looked around. My eyesight is good in the dark, so we didn't need to attract even more attention by turning on the light. It was darker in the store than it was outside and the windows were already tinted, so it would be hard for anyone looking to see anything but the reflection of the outside lights.

At first I observed a neat and tidy store that smelled of incense and old books. Paper holds the memory of any strong scent, so in a used bookstore, it wasn't uncommon to get little trickles of food, tobacco, and perfume. I took a deep breath to see if I could find anything that stood out.

Blood and fear and rage are a little out of the ordinary.

I stopped where I was and sucked in several deep breaths. Each time the smell grew stronger and stronger.

Fae glamour—a type of illusion—is strongly effective on sight, sound, taste, and touch. I'm told it is sufficient for a human sense of smell, but mine is better than that. By the third breath I smelled the sharp smell of broken wood, and the ammonia-like scent that fae magic sometimes leaves behind.

I closed my eyes, bowed my head, and let my nose be right. My ears cleared with a pop, and when I looked up, the tidy bookcases filled with tidy books had disappeared, leaving destruction in their place.

"Sam." I kept my voice down, though I don't think anyone outside would have heard me if I'd shouted. It was a reflex thing—we were sneaking around, so I needed to be quiet. "Do you smell it? The blood? There's a glamour here. Can you break it, too? Do you see the mess the fae left behind when they searched the place?"

He cocked an ear at me, then looked around. With a movement swifter than thought, he turned and sank his teeth into my arm.

Maybe if I'd thought there was a chance of him attacking me, I could have gotten out of the way or defended myself somehow. Instead, I stared at him dumbly as his fangs slid through skin and into flesh. He released me almost immediately, leaving behind two clean marks that could have been a vampire bite except that they were too far apart and too big. Vampires have smaller fangs.

Blood trickled out of one mark, then the other, dribbling down my forearm. Sam licked it clean, mostly, ignoring my surprised squeak and the way I backed away from him.

He looked around the shop again. I clamped my arm to my mouth—I didn't want to be bleeding anywhere in enemy territory. Witches can use blood and hair and other body parts to do nasty things. I didn't think the fae worked quite the same way, but I didn't want to chance it.

I checked under the counter for tissues and found something better—a first-aid kit. It wasn't as good as the one I had, but it was good enough to have gauze and an Ace bandage.

Wrapped and no longer in danger of dripping bits of myself all over, I walked back to Sam. He was still where I'd left him, staring as hard as he could at something I could no longer see.

It hadn't been a hard bite, and I wouldn't let myself be afraid of Sam. My foster father's SIG was in its holster across my shoulder, full of regular ammunition that generally worked just fine on fae—and did nothing to werewolves but make them mad. I tuned out Charles's warning voice and put the hand of my uninjured arm on Sam's neck. I refused to believe he was regressing into a vicious killer. A bite did not a killer make.

"Damn it all, Sam, why'd you bite me?" If I yelled at him, I couldn't be afraid of him. So I yelled at him.

Sam glanced at me, then knocked one of the fallen books aside with one paw. It was a cloth-bound copy of Felix Salten's *Bambi's Children*. In the glamour version of the shop, there had been no books on the floor. He'd bitten me on purpose—hadn't I asked him if he could break the glamour, too? Evidently, the bite was his answer. My blood must have allowed him to see what I did, some sort of sympathetic magic or something.

"Cool," I said. "That's cool." Pushing out of my head the knowledge that neither Samuel nor Sam, my friend, would have bitten me so casually, I turned my attention to the bookstore.

I have a pretty good memory for scents, and I picked up Phin's without any trouble. If I'd been looking for purely human assailants, I'd have been in trouble. This was a bookstore and had had a lot of people running through it. There weren't many fae aside from Phin, who barely qualified to my nose. However, several of the fae had been here recently, without many people in to cover up their trail.

"I've got Phin, the old woman from this afternoon, and three other fae," I told Sam.

Sam raised himself on the edge of one of the dominoed bookcases and put his nose against the back, moving and sniffing until he'd found what he wanted. He stepped back in obvious invitation.

Without touching it, I bent until my nose was nearly touching the wood. I smelled it, too, right where someone had put their magic-laden hand on the wood and pushed the bookcase over.

"That's one of them," I told Sam. "Some kind of woodland fae, I think—air and growing things."

I followed Sam's lead and sniffed and crawled and sniffed some more until we had a handle of sorts on what had happened here. I could have done it easier if I took coyote form. But if someone came upon us, I'd have a better chance of explaining myself and keeping things calm if I was human. Calm was good, because I didn't want Sam eating anyone he shouldn't.

I told myself all these good reasons to keep my human

shape on because they *were* good reasons. But I knew the real reason was because that bite had made me concerned that Sam would forget that I was his friend if I were running around as a coyote instead of a human who could remind him of it.

"So," I told him, my hands on my hips as I surveyed a patch of blood belonging to Phin. "They came in the door, and the last one locked it behind him. Let's call him Fishy Boy, because he's a water fae of some sort. He seems to be the one running the show because all the damage to the store was done by the other two."

Sam's icy gaze speared me, and I looked down and away—like the salute of a fencer. Acknowledging his state as the big, bad wolf without submitting to it. It must have been enough, because he didn't act any more aggressive.

Again with the dominance stuff, it wasn't something Sam usually indulged in unless he was really upset or meeting a wolf for the first time. When you are the top dog for long enough, I guess you don't feel like you have to rub people's noses in it.

If he hadn't bitten me, I'd have just dropped my eyes, but that didn't feel safe anymore. Not after he bit me. I needed to remind him that I was an Alpha's mate, predator and not prey.

A week, Charles had said, based on one example who had been a lot younger than Samuel was. I was starting to worry that he'd been optimistic—which is something I've never felt compelled to accuse Charles of being. How much time did Sam have?

"So Fishy Boy grabs Phin, and says, 'We know youse got it, see.'" I used my best Jimmy Cagney voice as I recited the scene I had pieced together. "And then he nods to his minions—Jolly Green Giants One and Two, because they both smell like green beans to me. Giant One, she pushes over a bookcase that topples a few more." I couldn't always tell the sex of the person whose scent trail I was following, but Giant One was definitely female, though not necessarily big. "Two, he's a little stronger. He gets some loft on his and tosses it about halfway across the room, taking down a couple of more bookcases along the way in a much more destructive fashion."

The original bookcase Two had tossed was in pieces, having broken apart when it hit. I could see the action running like a film through my head; the steps had been laid out before my nose and eyes—with a little imagination thrown in. I wasn't sure even a werewolf could have picked up a bookcase stuffed full of books.

"But Phin doesn't tell right away," I told Sam.

I thought about Tad, my morning visitor-with-gun, and the dried blood on the floor. "So Fishy Boy continues working on Phin while the Giant Twins go looking for it in the store. They're pretty convinced it is here because they take apart everything. I'm thinking that the ripped-up books might just be frustration—because it wasn't done in a methodical way. I suppose, even so, it could be that they are looking for something that is not a book." I looked around. "Maybe it could be hidden in a book or behind a book. They stopped because Phin started talking."

Sam sneezed a quick agreement—or maybe it was just dust. I was worried it was just dust.

"Did he know they were coming and call Tad to warn me?" I asked. "Or did they make him call Tad, and he managed to leave a vague warning instead? Either way, isn't it interesting that he didn't say what it was I'd borrowed?"

I tapped my fingers on a bookcase that was still upright. "So maybe they don't know it was a book, and he was afraid they could hear him—or they could read Tad's message."

Sam sneezed again. I glanced at him and saw the intelligent gleam that told me he was listening—and made me realize that he hadn't been just a few minutes ago.

"Maybe they really are after something entirely different. It could even be that Phin got clever and sent them after me to throw them off the trail. He does know that I have more protection than most people."

I let go of the bookcase so I could start pacing. "And this is where I'm going to be adding one and one and getting fifty—but bear with me." I walked twice around the shop and came to a halt where I'd started in the first place.

"Assume that at some point yesterday, Phin breaks down and tells them exactly who I am: things like who I'm dating and how many people would be angry if they just came after me. This next part is the weakest part of my story, Sam, but my instincts are screaming at me that the incident with Kelly Heart this morning and what happened to Phin are connected—it's that fae waiting up on the roof that makes me certain of it. I just don't know exactly why they wanted me dead."

Sam growled.

"Think about it," I told him, as if I were sure that he was growling at the threat to me. "This isn't the work of the Gray Lords. If it were, I'd be dead. We know there are at least three of the fae. Four if the woman on the roof of the storage building wasn't Giant One . . . Five if the old woman I saw here earlier today, who may or may not be Phin's grandmother, is one of them. But still, I don't think it's a huge group. It wouldn't be a happy thing for them if the werewolves went out hunting them. So they set up an incident, and Kelly Heart's producer is encouraged—by charm or by harm, as Zee would say—to send Kelly to my garage to find Adam."

I stopped and looked out past the parking lot to the headlights of the cars driving by.

"If they were after Adam, there are better ways to find him than coming to my garage. He's not hard to find. He goes to work six days a week, and his home address is a matter of public record. I had put it down to Heart's producer looking for the best drama . . ."

I took a deep breath and gauged Sam for his reaction.

Sam's stance—intent on my words—told me that he was making the leap with me. Or at least his wolf was. Just how smart was the wolf half of the werewolf?

"But things didn't go quite as they planned. I disarmed Heart right off the bat. They could hardly shoot me while I held the gun I was supposed to be shot with, right? But when Adam showed up, then the police, they decided to try to create a little chaos: a feeding frenzy fueled by magic. But Zee took care of that—and spotted their shooter. They had to run from Ben and leave the field."

I rubbed my damp palms on my thighs. "It sounds far-fetched, I know. But there is the book and the phone call to Tad that ties me to the fae who came into Phin's bookshop and destroyed it. They beat Phin until he bled, then took off with him. Violence and fae—just like this morning. And the only common factor is me. Coincidences happen, I know. Maybe I'm just egocentric, thinking it's all about me."

I waited in the bookstore until I realized I was waiting for Samuel to say something. But Samuel wasn't here: it was just Sam and me.

"Okay, that's enough make-believe for me." I dusted off my jeans. I'd have been hoping that I was wrong, but the way my life had been going the past year—this almost sounded tame. No vampires or ghosts, right? No Gray Lords who terrified even other fae. If I was wrong, I was afraid that it was only because the reality was even worse. "Let's keep looking. I'd feel really dumb if Phin turns out to be hidden in the basement."

Sam found a door behind about three bookcases. Happily, it opened away from us, so we just had to scramble over the top to drop to a landing. Straight ahead was a brick wall; to the right of the door we'd entered through was a set of narrow and steep stairs that led down into a pit of inky blackness: the bookstore had a basement.

I didn't think that anyone would notice if I turned on the

lights here because I was pretty sure that there weren't any windows in the basement. I'd have noticed.

It took me a minute to find the light switch. Sam, apparently unfazed by the darkness, had already continued down on his own when my hand found the right place.

With light to guide my way, I could see that the basement was mostly a storage facility with cardboard boxes set in piles. It reminded me of the hospital's X-ray storage room in that there was obvious order to the stacks. The ceiling height was deeper than usual for basements this near the river, but I could detect no trace of dampness.

Just to the right of the stairway, a section had been used as an office. A Persian rug delineated the space and stretched out beneath an old-fashioned oak desk complete with clamp-on desk lamp. There was a large framed oil painting of an English-type garden placed just in front of the desk, where someone sitting might use it as a mock window.

At one time the desk had held a computer monitor. I could tell because the monitor was lying in pieces on the cement floor next to the rug. There were more broken things on the ground—what looked to be the remains of a scentless jar candle, a mug that might have held the pens and pencils that had scattered when they hit the cement, and an office chair minus a wheel and the backrest.

"Be careful," I told Sam. "You'll end up with glass in your paws."

The stack of boxes nearest the desk was the only one that had been disturbed. Five or six boxes had been knocked around, spilling their contents on the floor.

"No blood here," I told him, and tried not to be relieved. I did not want to discover Phin's body. Not while I was alone with Sam, the wolf. "They were just looking—and not very seriously at that. Maybe they were interrupted, or this is how far they got when Phin finally broke down and started to talk."

"Fee fie foe feral," said a man's voice, hitting my ears like the blast of a barge's horn. "I smell the blood of a little girl." He rhymed "girl" with "feral," something only possible because of his cockney-accented English. "Be she hot, be she cold, I'll wager this, me lads—she won't get more old."

All I could see was two feet on the stairs. I'd had no warning that the man was in the building at all—and from Sam's sudden movement, he hadn't heard or smelled anything either. I had no idea that fae could hide themselves like that. No telling whether he'd been there all the time, or if he'd followed us in.

The fae was wearing big, black boots, the kind that should go clomp-clomp-clomp. And he was in no hurry to come down and kill us—which told me that he was one of the kind that enjoyed the hunt.

He wasn't a giant, despite my facetious naming of the two forest fae, because the giants were beast-minded, more instinct than intelligent. The beast-minded fae who had survived the rise of metal-wielding humans had died at the hands of the Gray Lords. Instinctive behaviors weren't good enough to make sure you'd hide your nature from the humans, and for centuries the fae had tried to pretend that they had never existed outside of folklore and fairy tales. But from the size of those feet, he was big enough.

Sam caught my attention by bumping his head against my hip—then ducked under the desk. He planned on taking the fae by surprise. Good to know Sam was still with me.

"That's possibly the worst doggerel verse I've heard since I was thirteen and wrote a poem for an English assignment," I told the waiting fae as I walked around so I could look up the stairs.

The one who stood at the top of the stairs was maybe six feet or a little under, though his feet were five inches longer than I've ever seen on any normal human. He had curly red hair and a pleasantly cheerful face—if you didn't look too hard at his eyes. He was wearing slacks and a red shirt with a blue tie that matched the red canvas apron that covered his clothes. Embroidered across the top of the apron was the name of a grocery store.

In his right hand he held a butcher knife.

He smelled of the iron and sweetness that was blood, with an undertone that made him the second of the Jolly Green Giants who'd trashed the place. The damned strong one who'd hefted a filled bookcase.

"Ah," he said, "a hintruder. How droll." He loosened his neck by pulling his head to one side, then the other. His accent was so heavy it was hard to decipher. *Intruder,* I thought, *not hintruder.*

"Droll?" I tried it, then shook my head. "Fateful, rather. At least for you." When in doubt, sound confident—it confuses the guys who are about to wipe the floor with you. It helped that I had a secret weapon. "What have you done with Phin?"

"Phin?" He came down three steps and paused with a smile. I think he was waiting for me to run—or, like a bored cat, drawing out the pleasure of the kill. A lot of fae are predators by nature, and among the things they like to eat are people.

"Phin is the owner of this bookstore." My voice was steady. I don't think I was getting braver, but after all the things that had happened lately, being frightened had lost its novelty.

"Maybe oye et 'im." He smiled. His teeth were sharper than a human's—and there were more of them.

"Maybe you're a fae and can't lie," I told him. "So you should stick to the facts instead of trying my patience with 'maybes.' Like where is Phin?"

He raised his left hand and gestured at me. Faint green sparkles stretched out between us and hung in the air for a moment until one touched me. It fell and took the others with it. They glittered on the floor, then winked out.

"What are you?" he asked, tilting his head like a puzzled wolf. "You ain't witch. Oi can feels witches in moy 'ead."

"Stop right there," I said, pulling the SIG from its holster.
"Are you threatening me with that?" He laughed.

So I shot him. Three times over the heart. It knocked him back but not down. I remembered, from my reading of Phin's book, that not all the fae have their organs in exactly the same places that we do. Maybe I should have aimed for his head. I raised the gun to make certain of my target and watched him sink through the wooden stairs like a ghost. He left the butcher knife and his apron behind.

Stone hands rose from the floor and grabbed my ankles, pulling my feet out from under me. I fell too fast to react.

———

I WOKE UP LYING IN THE DARK AND HURTING ALL over, but especially on the back of my head. My ankles were also sore when I tried to move them. I blinked, but I still couldn't see anything—which is very unusual for me.

I smelled blood and felt something ridged under my shoulder. Old sensory memory, left over from late-night studying in college, told me it was a pen. I waited for more recent memory to kick in—the last thing I remembered was the fae grabbing my ankles. When nothing more made itself known, I decided that there were no memories to come back. I must have been knocked out when my head hit the cement.

Odd as it might seem, I was still alive even though I'd been lying helpless before the fae.

I almost sat up, but there was a sound I couldn't place, a wet sound. Not a drip, but a slop, slop, slop. Rip. Slop, slop, slop.

Something was eating. Once I worked that out, I could smell death and all the undignified things it brought to a body. I waited a long time, listening to the sounds of something with sharp teeth feeding, before I forced myself to move.

It didn't really matter who had died. If it was Sam, I stood no chance against something that could kill a werewolf after I shot it three times in the chest—whether its heart was there or not, it still should have hurt it.

If it wasn't Sam . . . either he would kill me, too, or we'd both walk out of the basement. But I had to wait until I'd considered every possibility before I rolled stiffly to my feet.

The sound didn't change as I shuffled around, crunching glass under my feet until the edge of my shoe caught the edge of the rug. I used the rug to find the desk and fumbled around until I could turn on the desk light.

It wasn't very bright, but it showed me that the lighting fixtures on the ceiling had been torn loose and were dangling by wires. The neat stacks of boxes were mostly gone, leaving tumbled books, ripped-up cardboard, and shreds of paper in their place. There was also blood. A lot of it.

Some of the fae bleed odd colors, but this was all a dark red that pooled black in the dim light a yard or so from the edge of the rug where the kill had been made. It hadn't been too long because the edge of the pool of fluid was still wet. But the victor had dragged the body over a pile of book boxes and found a secluded place hidden behind several leaning stacks in the far corner of the basement where the weak light I held wouldn't penetrate.

"Sam?" I asked. "Sam?"

The sound of feeding paused. Then a shadow darker than the things around it flowed over the stacks and crouched on top of the remaining piles of books, flattened to keep from bumping into the ceiling. For a moment, I thought it was the fae, because the wolf was so drenched in blood that he was almost black. Then white eyes caught my desk light, and Sam growled.

"SO," I ASKED SAM AS WE HEADED BACK TOWARD Kennewick, "what do you think we can do to resurrect the love of life in your human half? Because I don't think that this is working. You almost lost it there, my friend."

Sam whined softly and put his head on my lap. I'd cleaned both of us in Phin's bathroom as best I could. His white fur was more pink than white still, and he was soaking wet. Thank goodness the Rabbit had a powerful heater.

"Well, if you don't know," I muttered, "how am I supposed to figure it out?"

He pressed his head harder on my thigh.

He'd almost killed me tonight. I'd seen the intent in his eyes as he'd raised his hindquarters—and knocked over the boxes he was perched on, already precariously tipped during his battle with the fae.

It was the kind of mistake that Samuel would never have made, and it had thrown off his attack. He'd landed short of me, on top of the broken office chair. He'd put a foot through the space between the arm and the seat, and during the struggle to free himself had remembered that we were friends.

From the lowered tail and head, I think he'd scared himself almost as much as he'd scared me.

We'd spent a long time in that bookstore, so the traffic had subsided somewhat, though it was still pretty busy.

I took my right hand off the steering wheel and ran my fingers through the fur behind Sam's ears. His whole body relaxed as I rubbed. "We'll manage it," I told him. "Don't you worry. I'm a lot more stubborn than Samuel is. Let's go home and dry us both off. Then I think . . . it's time to call Zee—"

MERCY!

Adam's voice in my head screamed at such volume that I couldn't move. A blasting yet soundless noise that grew and grew until . . . there was nothing at all. The cry left me with a headache that made the one I'd woken up with in Phin's basement seem like a pinprick.

"Sam," I said urgently, both hands on the wheel again—for all the good it was going to do me. I'd only just barely kept from hitting the brakes as hard as I could, which doubtless would have caused a big pileup on the busy high-way behind me. On the other hand, I could hardly keep traveling the way I was. "Sam. Sam, I can't see."

A mouth closed on my right wrist and tugged down and then back. As soon as he was guiding me straight, I put on my brake, gently, and rolled to a stop.

The Rabbit shook as cars blasted past us, but no one honked, so we must have made it to the shoulder. After some indefinable amount of time, the pain faded finally and left me shaken and sweating and feeling as if I'd been run over by a semi.

"We have to get home," I said, restarting the car. My hands were shaking as I put the Rabbit in gear and made a beeline toward Finley.

I'd left Adam to deal with his pack. If something had happened to him, I'd never forgive myself for my cowardice.

8

WE WERE ON CHEMICAL DRIVE, THE HIGHWAY that led out of the city to the countryside, when the ambulance passed us going the other direction, lights flashing but sirens off. I almost turned to follow.

No. Better to find out exactly what's happened first. Sam isn't a doctor today, and I can't help anyone better than the hospital where they're taking the victim. And maybe it wasn't anyone I knew in the ambulance at all.

As soon as I turned down my road, I put my foot down on the gas pedal and forgot about speed limits. Ahead of us, something was billowing black smoke. There were red flashing lights—fire engines at my house, which was well on its way to becoming so much kindling.

Adam would have thought I was in there. I hadn't told him I was leaving—because he'd have sent someone with me, someone he trusted, and I wanted him to have all of those people with him.

Adam's cry suddenly made sense, but I was terrified of what he'd done when the connection had blown. It might have felt like I had died or fallen unconscious. I should have called him instead of waiting until I could drive here.

Adam's pack surrounded the trailer, staying out of the way of the fire department. The fire must have started while the meeting was still taking place or shortly thereafter—I firmly squelched the notion that they might have set it on fire in effigy. My eye slipped over familiar faces—there was Darryl, Auriele, Paul—and some not so familiar— Henry and George. I couldn't find Adam anywhere in the bunch. My stomach clenched in fear at his absence.

I parked by the side of the road as close as I could get with the fire trucks everywhere, but it was still well back from the fire.

I sprinted up to the closest of Adam's pack and grabbed her by the arm—Auriele.

"Where is Adam?" I asked.

Her irises widened in shock. "Mercy? Adam thought you were in there when it blew."

Blew? I looked around and realized that it did look as though the trailer had simply exploded. Bits of siding, glass, and trailer were scattered a dozen yards from the burning hulk that used to be my house. The trailer had gas heat; maybe there had been a leak. How long would it have had to leak before blowing up? If it had been leaking when I left, I would have smelled gas.

Tomorrow, I'll feel bad about losing my home and the things that are important, like my photos . . . poor Medea. I left her locked in because I always lock her in at night so she'll be safe. I don't want to think about what happened to her. Tonight, I have more urgent fears.

"Auriele," I said slowly and clearly, "where is Adam?"

"Mercy!"

Arms snagged me hard and pulled me close. "Oh God,

oh God, Mercy. He thought you were effing dead. Went through the side of the bloody trailer to find you." Ben's voice was hoarse from the smoke and almost unrecognizable. If it hadn't been for the British accent, I wouldn't have been certain it was him.

"Ben?" I peeled myself out of his embrace with some difficulty—and care, because the hands that clutched me convulsively were burned and blistered—but I had to be able to breathe. "Ben. Tell me where Adam is."

"Hospital," said Darryl, trotting over to us from where he'd been talking to some of the firemen. Darryl was Auriele's mate and Adam's second. "Mary Jo was able to ride in with him on the strength of her job." Mary Jo was a werewolf whose day job was as a fireman and a trained EMT. "I'll take you."

I was already running back to the Rabbit. Sam somehow slithered past me when I was getting in, and when the passenger door opened, he hopped into the backseat so Ben could sit down.

"Warren's on his way," Ben said. His teeth were chattering with shock, and his eyes were bright wolf eyes. "He was working, couldn't get off in time for the meeting. But I called him and told him that Adam was at the hospital."

"Good," I said, pulling out in a storm of gravel. "Why didn't they take you to the hospital, too?"

Away from the fire, the scent of burnt flesh and his pain was impossible to miss. The little car's engine roared as I opened it up on the highway. Ben closed his eyes and braced himself against the seat.

"I was still in the building," he said. He coughed, rolled down his window, and hung out the side, choking and hacking for a while. I handed him a half-empty water bottle, and he rinsed his mouth out and spit.

He rolled up the window and took a drink. "Adam went for your bedroom, and I went for Samuel's." His voice was even rougher than it had been.

"How bad are you?"

"I'll be all right. Smoke inhalation sucks."

WE THREE BARGED INTO THE EMERGENCY ROOM.
Even for a place that was used to odd things, we must have
looked a sight. I glanced at Sam. He'd rolled on the ground
when I wasn't looking, covering up the remnants of bloodstains with dirt. All of us looked bedraggled, but at least I
didn't think Sam and I looked as if we'd been killing fae.
Of course, we didn't look like we'd been fighting a fire, like
Ben did, either. I'd come up with some story if someone
asked.

I'd forgotten that there was something more shocking about us than dirt, burns, and old, mostly washed-out
bloodstains.

"Hey, you can't bring a dog in here!" The triage nurse
took three quick strides to us and met my eyes . . . and she
stumbled to a halt. "Ms. Thompson? Is that a werewolf?"

"Where is Adam Hauptman?"

But a roar from the emergency room told me all I needed
to know.

"Whose bright idea was it to bring him here?" I muttered, running for the double doors between the waiting
room and the emergency room, Ben and Sam flanking me.

"Not me," Ben said, sounding a little more cheerful. I
think he'd been worried about what we'd find, too. "I am
absolved of guilt. I was in the trailer getting toasty-warm
when they sent him here."

A gray werewolf whose fur darkened around his muzzle
stood in the aisle between the patient rooms and the central counter, his change so recent that I could still see the
muscles of his back realigning themselves.

He was missing large patches of fur where his skin
was blackened and had bubbled up like wax. All four of
his feet were hideously burnt, the singed skin a horrible

imitation of the black fur that usually covered them. The curtain from the room was caught over his tail.

I stopped just inside the doors, assessing the situation.

Jody, the nurse I'd talked to the night of Samuel's accident, was standing very still—and someone had coached her on how to behave around werewolves, because her eyes were fixed on the floor. But even from where I stood, I could smell her fear, an appetite-rousing scent for any werewolf. Mary Jo crouched in front of Adam, one hand resting on the floor, her head bowed in submission—and her tough athletic body, so fragile-appearing next to the wolf, was directly between the bystanders and her Alpha.

I glanced down at Sam, but apparently he'd fed enough on the dead fae that his attention was all on Adam, though he stayed next to me. Ben waited on my other side, holding himself very still, as if he was trying really hard not to attract Adam's attention.

In other circumstances I wouldn't have been as worried. Werewolves tend to lose their human halves when badly injured, but they can be recalled to themselves by a mate or by a more dominant wolf. Samuel was more dominant than Adam, and I was Adam's mate. Either of us should have been able to bring him back.

Unfortunately, Samuel wasn't himself this evening and Adam had fried our mate bond in his panic when he thought I was trapped in the trailer. I didn't know what that meant in terms of how he would respond to me. He lowered his head and took a step forward, and my time to dither ran out.

"Adam," I said.

His whole body froze.

"Adam?" I stepped away from Ben and Sam. "Adam, it's all right. These are the good guys. They're trying to help—you've been hurt."

I'm fast, and I have good reflexes, and I didn't even see him move. He pinned me back against the doorframe, rising on his poor burnt hind legs until his face and mine were at the same height. The scent of smoke and burning things wrapped around us as his hot breath touched my cheeks. He inhaled, and his whole body began shaking.

He'd really thought I was dead.

"I'm okay," I murmured while I closed my eyes and tilted my chin to expose my throat. "I wasn't in the trailer when it blew."

His nose brushed from my jaw to my collarbone, and he let out a low, wheezing cough that seemed to go on forever. When it was finally over, he laid his head on my shoulder and began to change.

It would be safer for everyone if he were human, which was probably why he'd done it. But he'd just been badly hurt—and only just completed a change from human to wolf. To attempt to reverse the shift within minutes was miserably difficult. That he chose to do it anyway made it obvious to me that he was in very bad shape.

He'd never have started changing while he was touching me if he'd been fully aware. The change is agonizing enough in itself; skin-on-skin contact makes it even worse. Add to that his awkward position and the pain Adam was already in because of his burns, and I didn't know what would happen. I slid slowly down the wall, bringing him with me as his skin stretched and the bones moved. Watching a wolf change is not a beautiful thing.

I put my palms flat on the floor, so as not to give in to the temptation to touch him. As much as my head knew more skin contact was the last thing he needed, my body was curiously convinced that I could alleviate the agony of the change.

I looked up at Ben and jerked my chin toward the nurse . . . and the doctor who'd pulled the curtain back to join the fuss out front. Ben gave me a "why me?" look. In return, I glanced at Adam—obviously incapacitated—and then Sam, who was a wolf.

Ben looked up at the sky, invoking God's pity, I supposed. He trudged over, hands cradled in front of his body, to solve the problems he could. I caught Mary Jo's eye and interrupted a look directed at me . . . such a look. As soon as she realized I was looking at her, her face cleared. I couldn't interpret the emotion I'd seen, just that it was very strong.

"Anybody hurt?" asked Ben. When he extends himself beyond his usual nasty personality, people tend to find Ben reassuring. I think it's the nifty British accent and composed appearance—and even with the burns and the charred clothing, he looked somehow more civilized than anyone else.

"No," said the doctor, whose name tag read REX FOURNIER, MD. He looked to be in his late forties. "I surprised him when I opened the curtains." And then in a spirit of fairness seldom seen in terrified people, he said, "He was pretty careful not to hurt anyone, just knocked me aside. If I hadn't stumbled over the stool, I'd have kept my feet."

"He was unconscious when I left," Mary Jo told Ben, half-apologetically. "I came out to see if I could find someone to help him—we'd been here for a while. I didn't realize I'd been away long enough for him to change."

"Not so long," I said. "I saw the ambulance pass us. You can't have been here more than a half hour, and it takes about half of that for him to complete the change. Whose bright idea was it to bring Adam to the hospital in his condition anyway?"

It had been Mary Jo's. I could see it in her face.

"All he needed was the dead flesh peeled off," she said.

A really, really painful procedure—and no painkillers work on werewolves for long. It was such a bad idea that we all stared at her, all of us who knew, anyway—Ben, Sam, and I. Adam was preoccupied with his change.

"I didn't realize how bad it was," she defended herself. "I thought it was just his hands. I didn't see his feet until we were already in the ambulance on the way over here. If it had just been his hands, it would have been okay."

Maybe. Probably.

"I thought you and Samuel were dead," she said. "And that left it my problem as the pack medic. And as medic and as my Alpha's loyal follower, I deemed the hospital the safer option."

She'd just lied.

Not about Adam being safer at the hospital than home. With the recent upheavals, she was probably right that a badly wounded Adam wasn't safe with the pack in his condition. They'd tear him apart and apologize and maybe even feel bad afterward. But that first statement . . .

Maybe she thought we were too overwrought to notice— and Ben was sometimes not as aware of subtle cues as some of the other wolves. But maybe Mary Jo didn't realize that I could tell when she was lying as well as any of the wolves could have.

"You knew we weren't in the house," I said slowly. And then the light dawned about what that meant. "Did Adam send you out to keep watch over me while he met with the others? Did you see us leave?"

She had. It was in her face—and she didn't bother denying it. She might be able to lie to the humans in this room, but not to the rest of us.

"Why didn't you tell him?" asked Ben. "Why didn't you stop him before he went into the fire?"

"Answer him," I said.

She met my eyes for a long count of three before finally dropping them. "I was supposed to follow you if you left. Make sure you didn't get hurt. But you see, I think everyone would be better off if one of the vampires had killed you."

"So you chose to defy Adam's orders because you disagreed with him," said Ben. "He picked you to watch Mercy because he trusted you to take care of business while he dealt with the pack—and you betrayed that trust."

I was grateful that Ben kept talking.

Mary Jo was one of the people in Adam's pack I'd thought was my friend. Not because a debt the fae owed me had kept her from dying a little while ago . . . I suspected that had been a mixed blessing, like most fairy gifts. But we'd spent a lot of hours in each other's company because Adam liked to use her as a guard when he felt I needed one.

Mary Jo wanted me dead. That was what that look had been about.

It was such a shock that I might have missed her answer to Ben's question if she hadn't sounded so defensive.

"It wasn't like that. She was safe enough; she left with Samuel. There's nothing I could do that would protect her better than Samuel could."

"So why didn't you stop the arsonists?"

Arsonists? There had been arsonists?

"I wasn't ordered to protect her place. She wasn't in there."

Ben smiled in such satisfaction that I realized he hadn't known there were arsonists either. "Who were they, Mary Jo?"

"Fae," she said. "No one I knew. Just more trouble she's bringing to my pack's door. If they wanted to burn down Mercy's house, what did I care?" She looked at me, and said viciously, "I wish they'd burned it up with you in it."

"Ben!"

How he managed to stop his hand before it hit her face, I don't know. But he did. She'd have wiped the floor with him afterward. She might be nominally below him in the pack hierarchy, but that was only because unmated women were at the bottom of the pack.

She wanted to fight him. I could see it in her face.

I couldn't move with Adam mostly on my lap. "That's enough." I kept my voice soft.

Ben was panting, his hands shaking in rage . . . or pain. His hands were really damaged.

"He could have died," Ben said to me, his voice rough

with the wolf. "He could have died because this—" He stopped himself.

And the violence was gone from Mary Jo's posture as quickly as if someone had hit a switch. Her eyes brightened with tears. "Don't you think I know that? He came running from the house, calling her name. I tried to tell him it was too late, but he just pulled the wall apart and jumped through the hole he'd made. He didn't even hear me."

"He'd have heard you if you told him she wasn't in there," said Ben, unaffected by the tears. "I was right behind him. You didn't even try. You could have just told him she was alive."

"Enough," I said. Adam's change was nearly finished. "Adam can settle this himself later."

I looked over at Sam. "Two changes is bad when there's tissue damage, right? It heals wrong." The human ear I could see was scarred, and the top half of Adam's head from his eyebrows up seemed to be as well. He must have had a wet towel or something over his head to cover his face, but it had fallen down at some point and hadn't protected his scalp.

Sam sighed.

The doctor had been listening to Mary Jo's story with fascination—I bet he watched soap operas, too. "I'm sorry," he told me, sounding it. "Unless you have some means of effectively restraining him, I cannot treat him here. I won't risk my staff."

"Can we have a room, then?" I asked.

Time wasn't our friend. We could take him back to his house and take care of him . . . but once Mary Jo had reminded me of the danger he'd be in wounded, in the middle of his pack, I really didn't want to take him back there and hurt him.

Sam caught my eye and looked down the line of curtained rooms to the one I'd retrieved him from.

I looked back at the doctor. "A real room would be best. Could we use the X-ray storage room?"

The doctor frowned, but Jody came to my rescue. "This is Doc Cornick's Mercy," she said. "She's dating Adam Hauptman, the pack Alpha."

"Who is lying in my lap," I told them. "I'm sorry. If it were anyone except for Adam who was hurt, we could make sure your personnel were safe—but Adam's the only one who could keep a lid on it reliably. You are right not to risk your people. But I've got a couple of wolves here—Mary Jo's an EMT—and we can manage on our own. If it weren't urgent that we get started, I'd just take him home. But if we don't do something soon, the scars will be permanent."

His feet were the worst. Wholly human and . . . I could see bone under blackened skin. He was unconscious, sweaty, and four shades paler than usual.

"What can we get you?" Fournier asked.

"A stretcher," said Mary Jo. She looked at Sam, waiting for him to take over. Then she realized that in this place he couldn't possibly show them he was a werewolf. I don't think she had noticed the full extent of Samuel's problem yet. She just turned to the doctor and started speaking medical gibberish.

A gurney appeared, and Ben lifted Adam out of my lap and onto it. A host of hospital personnel showed up and emptied the X-ray storage room of boxes—with very little respect for the existing organization. Someone was going to be upset about that. Dr. Fournier was paged to the third floor and left with the same brisk efficiency with which he seemed to manage everything—including werewolves in his ER.

With everything out, there was room, if only just, for all of us, the gurney, and the tray of tools Jody brought in.

"Fournier isn't as good as Doc Cornick when things go bad." Jody gave me a sharp look as Mary Jo and Ben maneuvered Adam to the center of the little room, and I

wondered if she was thinking about how many werewolves
I seemed to know and connecting it to the fact that I was
Samuel's roommate. If so, she didn't seem to be hysterical
at the thought of all the werewolves who were here at the
moment, so maybe she'd keep quiet about her suspicions.

"Fournier didn't get hurt," I said. "He didn't make anything worse. That's good enough for me."

"Do you need help?" she asked bravely.

I smiled at her. "No. I think that Mary Jo can handle it."
I'd have rather had Jody and the doctor, but Adam wouldn't
thank me for putting humans at risk. Like Jody, I'd really
rather have had Samuel . . . who had disappeared from my
side.

"It's not a sterile environment, but it sounds like that's
not important."

"No," I told Jody distractedly. Where had Sam gotten
to? "Werewolves deal with germs better than people do.
Looks like they're ready to go."

I closed the door, took a deep breath, and turned to
Mary Jo. "Do you know what to do? I have to find Sam."

"I'm here." Samuel was naked as the day he was born,
and sweating freely from the speed of his change. His skin
was filthy with dust and fae blood—a condition he was
remedying with a bucket of water and a towel that must
have been among the things Mary Jo had required. His
eyes were gray, a shade or two lighter than normal, but the
other wolves would doubtless put it to changing. "I'll take
care of it."

"Samuel," I said.

But he looked away and took up something that looked
like a scrub brush, with stiff bristles. "I need you to hold
him down. Ben, lie across his hips. Mary Jo, I'll tell you
where I need you. Hands will be the worst, so we'll start
with them."

"What about me?" I asked.

"You talk to him. Keep telling him we're helping him

with this torture. If he hears you and believes you, he won't fight us as hard. I'll give him some morphine. It won't help much or for long, so we'll need to move fast."

So while Samuel scrubbed the dead skin and almost-healed scabs off Adam with a stiff-bristled brush, I talked and talked. The burns had killed tissue that had to be removed. Once it was gone, the raw wounds would heal cleanly and without scars.

Adam kept going into coughing fits. When they'd happen, everyone backed off and let him cough until he spit up blood with great hunks of black in it. Ben had a few of those fits, too, but he rode them out while still keeping his weight on Adam.

Every so often, Samuel would stop and dose Adam with more morphine. The worst of it was that Adam never made a noise or struggled against the people holding him down. He just kept his eyes on mine while he sweat and his body shook with small tremors that grew and subsided with whatever Samuel did.

"I thought you were dead," he said, his voice a bare rasp while Samuel moved from his hands to his feet. It didn't seem to hurt as much—at a guess there weren't a lot of nerves left. He'd jumped into a burning building barefoot to save me.

"Stupid," I said, blinking hard. "As if I'd die without taking you with me."

He smiled faintly. "Was it Mary Jo who betrayed us at the bowling alley?" he asked, proving he hadn't been entirely unaware of what had been going on while he was changing.

Both of us ignored the pained sound Mary Jo made.

"I'll ask her later."

He nodded. "Better—" He quit talking, and his pupils contracted despite the morphine he'd been given.

He arched up and twisted so he could press his face into my belly, making a noise somewhere between a scream and a growl. I held him there while Samuel snarled at Ben and Mary Jo to hold him still.

Another shot of morphine, and Samuel moved us all around. Ben across Adam's legs—"And don't think I haven't noticed your hands, Ben. You're next up." Mary Jo on one arm, just above the elbow. Me on the other.

"Can you hold him?" asked Samuel.

"Not if he doesn't want me to," I told him.

"It'll be all right," Adam said. "I won't hurt her."

Samuel smiled tightly. "No, I didn't think you would."

When Samuel started on Adam's face with the brush, I had to close my eyes.

"Shh," Adam comforted me. "It'll be over soon."

WARREN ARRIVED NOT LONG AFTER THAT. TOO late to help with Adam, but he and Mary Jo held on to Ben while Samuel scrubbed his hands free of black skin and blisters. He hadn't changed twice and started healing wrong, but it was still bad enough.

Adam had closed his eyes and was resting while I stood with my hands wrapped around his upper arm, one of the places where he hadn't lost any skin. The connection between us hadn't reset yet, and I had to rely on my senses to tell me what he felt. It surprised me, given how unhappy I'd been with that bond, that I missed the connection when it was gone. My ears told me that he wasn't fully asleep, just catnapping.

Ben wasn't as quiet as Adam had been, but he was obviously doing his best to keep his cries down. Finally, he sank his teeth into Warren's biceps and dug in.

"Attaboy," Warren drawled without flinching. "Go ahead and chew some if it helps. Too far from the heart to do me much harm. Dang, but I hate fires. Guns, knives, fangs, and claws are tough—but fires are the worst."

Adam's hands looked like raw hamburger, but at least

they didn't look like burnt hamburger—and one of them reached over and closed over my fingers. I tried to let go of him, but he opened his eyes and held on to me.

"Okay, that's it," Samuel said, and he stepped back from Ben. "Sit him down on the stool and leave him alone a bit."

"I brought an ice chest filled with beef roasts," Warren said. "It's out in the truck, so we can feed them."

Samuel jerked his head up. "Your Alpha was in trouble, and you stopped and went grocery shopping?"

Warren smiled with cool eyes while blood dripped to the floor from the arm Ben had gnawed on. "Nope."

Samuel stared at him—and Warren gazed at the wall beyond him without backing down a bit. He might like Samuel, but Samuel wasn't his Alpha. He wouldn't cede the lone wolf the right to question his actions.

I sighed. "Warren. Why do you have an ice chest filled with roast on hand?"

The cowboy turned to me and gave me a wide smile. "Kyle's idea of a joke. Don't ask." A light blush bloomed on his cheekbones. "The freezer and the fridge are already full at Kyle's house. We put them in the ice chest out in the garage to take back to my apartment, where I have an empty freezer, but I hadn't gotten around to it yet." He looked toward Samuel. "Bit snappy, aren't you?"

"He's waiting for Mercy to start in on him," said Adam. His voice was faint, but, hey, we all had good hearing. "And Mercy is wondering if she should do it with all of us listening in or not."

"What's Mercy got on you?" asked Warren. When it was obvious Samuel wasn't going to answer, Warren looked at me.

I was watching Samuel.

"I just can't do it any longer," he said, finally. "It's better to go now, before I hurt someone."

I was too tired to put up with his garbage. "The hell you can't. 'Do not go gentle into that good night,' Samuel. 'Rage, rage against the dying of the light.'" He'd helped me memorize that poem when I was in high school. I knew he'd remember.

"'Life's but a walking shadow,' Mercy, 'a poor player, that struts and frets his hour upon the stage, and then is heard no more.'" He countered my Dylan Thomas with Shakespeare, spoken with as much weary bleakness as any stage actor ever managed. "'It is a tale. Told by an idiot, full of sound and fury, signifying . . . *nothing.*'" He said the last word with a bite of bitterness.

I was so angry I could have hit him. Instead, I clapped my hands in mock appreciation.

"Very moving," I said. "And stupid. Macbeth killed his overlord and followed his ambition, bringing misery and death to everyone involved. Your life is worth more, I think, than his was. More to me—and to every patient who crosses your path. Tonight, it was Adam and Ben."

"Count me in on that," said Warren. He might not have been in on the cause of the conversation, but any wolf would have caught the gist of what we were talking about. "If you hadn't been here when that demon got ahold of me not so long ago, I'd be dead."

Samuel's reaction was not what I expected. He ducked his head and snarled at Warren, "I am not responsible for you."

"Yes, you are," said Adam, opening his eyes.

"That chap your hide?" suggested Warren gently. He shrugged. "People die. I know that; you know that. Even wolves like us die. Fewer people die when you are around. Those are the facts. Being upset about them don't make them false."

Samuel stalked away from us all. There wasn't much room to get away, though, and he stopped with his head down. "I was hoping this could be easier, Mercy. But I forgot—you don't do easy." He turned around and met my eyes. When he spoke again, it was in that gentle, patronizing tone I thought I'd cured him of a long time ago. "You can't save me, Mercy. Not when I don't want to be saved."

"Samuel," said Adam in a demanding tone, much stronger than his condition allowed. He raised himself up on his elbows and stared at the other wolf.

Samuel met Adam's eyes . . . and I saw shock in his face for just an instant before he began to shift to wolf. It was a dirty trick, something Alphas—strong Alphas—could do, forcing the change on another wolf. I suspected that if Adam hadn't caught Samuel by surprise, it would never have worked. Adam held Samuel's gaze while we waited with bated breath. Fifteen minutes is a long time to hold still. And at the end of it, Samuel was gone, leaving the white-eyed wolf in his place. The wolf smiled at Adam.

"Might not be able to save you, old son," Adam said, lying back again and closing his eyes. "But I can buy us a little time to kick you in the butt hard enough you stop thinking about 'tomorrow and tomorrow' and start thinking about how much your butt hurts."

"Sometimes," said Warren, "it's real easy to see you were in the military, boss."

"Butt kicking being part and parcel of the service, both on the giving and receiving end," agreed Adam, without opening his eyes.

Mary Jo had been staring at Sam. "His wolf is in control," she said, horrified.

"Has been for a couple of days," agreed Adam. "No bodies yet."

He didn't know about the fae at the bookstore . . . but I wasn't sure the fae counted. It had been a defensive killing rather than an uncontrolled killing spree, though Sam had nearly taken me as dessert afterward.

Sam met my eyes thoughtfully, and I realized that he seemed . . . different, more expressive, than he had in Phin's bookstore—just as I was used to seeing Samuel's wolf. I'd thought he was getting more aggressive earlier, but I could see that he'd also been becoming . . . less

Samuel, even less Sam. Our little disaster might have bought us a little more time.

"Ah take it that the Marrok does not know about Samuel?" Warren broke the silence, sounding very cowboy, very laid-back—which was usually a sign that he wasn't.

"Sort of," I said. "I told him he didn't want to know yet, and he believed me. But only on the condition that I'd talk to Charles. According to Charles, the good news is that if Samuel's wolf was more independent of him, he'd have started causing mayhem right away. Bad news is that if we don't get Samuel out of his funk soon, his wolf is going to fade, too." As he had been doing. "And we'll be left with a dead Samuel anyway, but only after a bonus of lots of other dead bodies."

"A regular Vikin' funeral," commented Warren.

Mary Jo gave him a sharp look, which he returned.

"Ah can read, as long as they's lotsa good pictures," he said, speaking even slower than usual and using a lot more Texas-cowboy grammar.

"That's my line," I told Warren. "I resent your stealing it."

Ben laughed. But then asked, "How is fading different from just having the wolf in control?"

Wolves are blunt creatures, mostly impatient with the soft-pedaling that the rest of the world considers politeness.

"I gather Sam will turn all fang and no brain, and will eventually just fall over dead," I told them. "Probably less damage than what normally happens when the wolf is in charge. Especially since the wolf doesn't stop until someone stops him. But not good."

"He'll be easier to kill if it comes to it," said Warren, recognizing the advantages. Samuel was old, powerful, and clever—if his wolf was half as smart, it would take Bran or Charles to take him. This way, any of us with a silver-loaded gun could do it.

Sam didn't seem bothered by the conversation. He half

closed his eyes and snapped his teeth at Warren with mock fierceness. His ears were up, showing that he was only playing.

They hurt my heart with their fierce full-on acceptance of reality.

"Pack up, kids," said Adam, with his eyes still closed. "It's time to take this party home."

Home.

I glanced worriedly at Warren. Adam would be up and functional in a day or two—thanks to nifty werewolf superpowers of healing. But the pack was still a mess.

"Right, boss." Warren nodded at me and continued to talk to Adam. "I reckon I'll stick by you for a bit, though, if you don't mind. Darryl will be there, too."

WE PACKED ADAM INTO THE BACK OF WARREN'S truck on top of a thick camping pad and underneath a sleeping bag. Werewolves are pretty immune to the cold— especially the kind of cold the Tri-Cities could manage most winters. But we weren't taking any chances with him. He accepted our fussing with a sort of royal amusement that managed to be appreciative, too, though he didn't say a word.

"Camping?" I murmured to Warren under my breath after we'd gotten Adam settled. "You actually got Kyle to go out camping?" Kyle was very happy with the comforts of civilization. I couldn't see him spending a weekend in the woods voluntarily.

"Nah," he muttered. "Not overnight anyhow. But I'm hopeful for next spring."

"But you had sleeping bags and camp pads in your truck." I couldn't help the smile that grew on my face. "Does this have anything to do with the ice chest full of meat?"

He ducked his head, but he was grinning. "You don't ask me what you don't want to know, Mercy."

Mary Jo rode in the back of the truck with Adam while

I drove my car with Ben beside me and Sam in the back. Ben had offered to drive the Rabbit so I could ride with Adam, but his hands were raw and painful. Mary Jo wasn't going to do anything to hurt Adam; whatever resentment or hatred she felt for me didn't interfere with her desire to keep him safe.

As soon as I started driving, Ben said, "You need to find out who the second man on watch was."

"What?"

"The other wolf Adam had watching with Mary Jo. She doesn't want to tell, and she's a higher rank than I am, so I can't ask her. If Warren asked . . . She's one of the crowd that thinks he shouldn't be pack."

"What?" I'd thought the homophobic elements in the pack were all men.

Ben nodded. "She's quieter about it than most, but she's also more stubborn. If Warren gave her an order she didn't want to comply with—like one that would make her narc on someone she cares about—she's likely to defy him. He'd have to hurt her, and that would hurt him more because he likes her—and doesn't have any idea that she's one of the stupid people."

I'd always thought Ben was one of the stupid people, too. I guess that must have shown in my face because he laughed.

"I was bitter when I first came here. Eastern Washington is a big comedown from London." He didn't say anything for a while, but about the time I turned onto the highway he continued in a soft voice. "Warren's okay. He cares about the pack, and that's not as common in the upper echelon as you'd think. Took me a while to appreciate—and that's on me."

I patted his arm. "Took us a while to warm up to you, too," I said. "Must be your charming personality."

He laughed again, and this time it was with genuine humor. "Yes. No doubt. You're a right bitch sometimes, you know?"

The response was elementary-school automatic. "Takes one to know one," I said. "You think there was someone else who watched Adam jump into a burning building to save me and didn't do anything to stop him?"

"I think that Adam sends us out in pairs. One man on point, the second as backup. Always. Mary Jo wasn't out there alone when you and Samuel left. She wasn't the only one who watched whoever set fire to your house."

He paused. "I think I know who it is, but I'm prejudiced, so I'll keep my mouth shut. Just remember: Mary Jo . . . she's good folk when it comes down to it. She's been a firefighter since they allowed women to be on the teams. She may not like you that much, but she's got no bone to pick with Samuel. I don't think she'd have stood by and watched arson taking place without someone stepping in and influencing her. There aren't many of the pack who could override her good sense like that."

"You think someone else made the decision to disobey orders."

Ben nodded slowly. "I do. Yes."

"Someone Adam trusted enough that he didn't insist on their attending the meeting he held at his house."

"Yes."

"Damn it."

9

~~~~~~

AT THREE IN THE MORNING, I FOUND MYSELF
drinking hot chocolate at the kitchen table in Adam's
house with Jesse, Darryl, Auriele, and Mary Jo. Given my
druthers, I'd have had a couple of people between Mary
Jo and me—because I don't believe in throwing water on
boiling oil—but by the time I'd finished pouring cocoa, the
seat between Jesse and her was the only one open.

The one good thing was that most of the wolves had
returned to their homes, and Adam was still safe. Sam and
Warren were in Adam's room, doing guard duty, while the
rest of us tried to decide how to proceed until Adam was
up and about. All the other wolves who'd shown up had
been sent away.

I planned on joining Adam as soon as we were done
here, but I knew he was all right without me. He'd eaten
about ten pounds of meat and lapsed into a sleep so deep it
resembled a coma. Warren was a big enough wolf to take

on any two of the rest of the pack as long as the group
didn't contain Darryl, who outranked him. Mostly.

Sam was a little unpredictable, but in his current state
I was pretty sure he would be on our team. When a wolf
is hurt, he is vulnerable. In the best scenario, an injured
wolf will be protected by his pack mates—but when the
pack is uneasy, as Adam's was just then, it is best to keep
trustworthy guards around.

Between the two of them, Warren and Sam, they'd see
to it that no harm came to Adam.

Ben trudged in, towing one of the dining-room chairs.
He slid it between Jesse and Auriele, painfully pulled his
gory fingers off the chair back, and dropped to the seat.
Jesse slid a cup of hot cocoa in front of him, then reached
across with the can of nondairy whipped cream and
squirted a bunch of sweet artificial white goo on top. Jesse's curly hair had grown out a little, and she'd dyed it pink.

"Thanks, darling," Ben told her in a suggestive voice, and
she scooted her chair away from him. He tipped his head
so she couldn't see his face and smiled until he realized I
was watching him. I narrowed my eyes, and he cleared his
throat. "E-mail's out to the list, detailing what happened
and that Adam'll be up and about in a day or two."

That there was a mailing list had been news to me. I
wasn't on it, probably so they could all complain about
me without hurting my feelings. Given the state of Ben's
hands, Auriele had offered to send out the report, but he'd
said that computer work was his duty, and as he still had
ten fingers, he figured he could complete it.

He leaned forward and sipped his cocoa without touching the hot cup.

"It's instant," I apologized. "My stash of spicy real stuff
went up with the house." I wished I hadn't said it as soon as
the words were out of my mouth. I had been doing just fine
at forgetting that out in the darkness beyond the kitchen
windows, my house was a pile of black scraps.

"It's chocolate," Ben said. "At this point, that is sufficient."

Silence fell, and I remembered that I was supposed to be running this. It reminded me in an odd way of the time I'd had to take over my sister's Girl Scout troop when my mother had been sick. Fourteen preteen girls, a tableful of werewolves—there were certain monstrous similarities.

I ran my hands over my face. "So what else needs to be dealt with before we can go to bed?"

Darryl folded his big hands on the table. "The fire marshal hasn't made it out yet—but the firemen seemed pretty convinced it was the wiring. The fire started near the fuse box in the hall. Apparently, the old manufactured homes sometimes go up like that, especially the first few weeks the heating system kicks in in the winter." He glanced at me. "Do we accept that, or have you been riling people up again?"

He might owe his ebony skin and his size to his African father, but he could do Chinese inscrutable better than anyone I'd ever met who was wholly Chinese instead of just half. It was hard to tell whether he meant the last sentence as a joke or a justifiable criticism.

"It was the fae," I said with a sigh, bumping the nearest table leg halfheartedly with my ankle.

"What—all of them?" asked Ben humorously. I slid down in my chair so I could reach past Jesse and kicked his foot, which was more satisfying.

"No, not all of them," I said, after he yipped with mock pain.

"You just bring us one damned thing after another don't you, Mercy," said Mary Jo, looking out the window.

"Bitch," said Ben. It seemed to be his word of the day—which was better than the usual assortment. He hadn't actually sworn much around me that day, if I didn't include the time while Samuel was fixing his hands. And if the only words that counted were the ones that got movies an "R" rating. I wondered if it was coincidental, if he was trying to improve himself—or if I hadn't spent enough time with him.

Mary Jo's lip curled. "Suck-up."

"You have some nerve throwing stones," he told her, "when you just sat there and watched them set fire to Mercy's house."

"What?" said Darryl in a very, very soft voice.

But Mary Jo wasn't listening to Darryl. Instead, she half rose to her feet and leaned on the table, threatening Ben. "So what? You think I should have taken on a bunch of unknown fae for *her*?"

Auriele stood up and gave the table a hard shove, pinning Mary Jo against the wall behind her with a bang that must have hurt. If someone didn't know her very well, I suppose it might be possible to underestimate Auriele. She was delicately built, as some Hispanic women are, and looked as though she'd never gotten her beautifully manicured hands dirty.

Most of the pack would rather have Darryl mad at them than Auriele.

Darryl's mate's voice was frozen as she asked, "You just watched a bunch of fae burn down the house of a pack member?"

I'd picked my cocoa up off the table when it moved and managed to save Jesse's, too. With my hip, I altered the trajectory of the table just enough to make certain that it didn't hit Jesse. Darryl caught Ben's cup—he'd finished his own. So it was only Mary Jo's and Auriele's cocoa that spilled across the table and down on the floor.

Into the tense silence of that moment, the interruption of my ringing phone seemed decidedly welcome. I thumped the two mugs I held down onto the table and pulled the phone out of my pocket.

I didn't recognize either the number or the area code. Usually, I recognize the number of people who call me in the middle of the night.

"Hello?"

"Mercedes Thompson, you have something that belongs to me. I have something that belongs to you. Shall we play?"

I hit the speaker button and set the phone in the middle of the table. Of course, everyone except for Jesse could have overheard the call anyway—but with all of us listening full volume, maybe someone would hear something different. My cell was relatively new, and I'd paid extra to get one with good sound quality.

Darryl pulled out *his* phone—one of those miniature computers with every gadget known to man—hit the screen a couple of times, and set it next to mine. "Recording," he mouthed.

"Everything I have went up in flames last night," I told my unknown caller, and after I said it, the truth of that hit me again. Poor Medea. I set my jaw with determination that this person—who sounded female to me, though a female with a deep smoker's voice—would never hear the pain she'd caused me. Assuming that this was one of the fae who set the fire.

"It wasn't there," she said—and I was growing more confident it was a "she." Her next words made me certain that she was one of the fae, too. "It would have revealed itself in fire or in death. We watched your home burn, watched the fire eat your life, and what you took from Phineas Brewster wasn't in the coals or in the ashes."

Fae often say things that sound odd to human ears. I've found myself spouting Zee's sayings and having people stop to look at me.

"In fire or in death," I said, repeating the phrase that had sounded like a quote of some kind.

"It reveals itself when the one who holds it dies or if it burns," she clarified impatiently.

"Your bounty hunter seemed like the kind of man who gets things done," I said. "Why didn't you have him kill

me instead of relying on backup?" Growing up with werewolves has taught me several ways of controlling the situation without being too aggressive. Asking a question a little
off topic is one way of doing it—and if the question is hidden as another question, my chances of getting information
are even better.

"Kelly?" she said, her voice incredulous. But she knew
who I was talking about. She must be the fae who'd created the incident that had almost gotten Maia hurt. "Kelly
would never hurt a woman. But the police wouldn't have
believed it."

There was a tone to the woman's voice that told me she
knew Kelly Heart personally—and felt a veiled contempt
for something in him that she thought was a weakness.

"I take it I am speaking to the one who calls herself
Daphne Rondo?" I'd remembered the missing producer's
name because she shared the first with Scooby Doo's token
cute girl and it had caught my attention. I phrased the question carefully because the fae cannot lie—and it probably
wasn't her real name. Mostly the fae don't give their true
names to anyone.

"Sometimes," she said, but she didn't like it that I'd figured her out. She could have refused to answer, of course,
but that would have been as good as an answer anyway. A
fae who wasn't Kelly Heart's missing producer would take
great pleasure in informing me I was mistaken.

"Mr. Heart is worried about you," I told her. And then
could have bitten my tongue. This woman did not deserve
to know about his concern—she'd sent him here to die.
If Adam had believed that Kelly had killed me, he would
have personally seen to Heart's death. Anyone who knew I
was dating the local Alpha would understand that much—
it was why she had contrived to set the bounty hunter up.
"He'd feel differently if he knew what you planned for
him."

"If he knew what I was after, he would support me with

his whole heart," she said with a sudden passion that told me she had her doubts, and they bothered her. "He is my soldier, and he follows my orders."

I'd heard that kind of talk before and felt my lips curl in anger—on behalf of a stranger who'd mainly just ticked me off . . . but mostly for a friend of mine, Stefan, another soldier who'd been used too hard and had finally broken.

"You are overburdened with self-importance," I told her. "But that is a common condition with the fae." I was tired, and it was hard to keep to the fine line that kept her from taking the upper hand without enraging her. Who did she have? Stefan? I hadn't seen the vampire for weeks. Zee? I hadn't called him as I'd planned to before my house burned down.

"You are overburdened with stupidity," she replied with icy contempt. I'd pricked her about Kelly . . . not that she'd hurt him, but that he might not do her bidding if he knew what she wanted. "But that is a common problem with *humans*. Especially humans who involve themselves in matters that are none of their business." There was a pause as if she was weighing some matter. Then she said, "You would be wise not to irk me when I hold something you value."

There were two distinct sounds right as she finished. The first was something striking flesh, the second a muffled cry. We all stilled, listening for a hint of identity.

"Male," mouthed Darryl.

I nodded. I'd caught that as well. The cry was followed by a third sound: someone who was gagged trying to talk. He was furious. There was something about the sound . . . not Stefan, not Zee.

Mary Jo caught my shoulder. Her face was pale and pinched. "Gabriel," she mouthed.

That was it. Mary Jo had spent some time doing guard-Mercy-at-work duty this summer, working with me and Gabriel. She knew him, too.

I hadn't been listening for Gabriel—because I thought he was safe. I closed my eyes in momentary despair. Stefan was a vampire; Zee was a fae other fae gave a good deal of respectful space to. Gabriel was a seventeen-year-old with no supernatural powers. He didn't stand a chance against one of the fae.

Jesse made a little sound, then jerked her hands to her mouth, but the fae on the other end caught the noise.

"Angry, child?" she asked. She thought she'd heard me. "Do you know who we caught? I'll give you a hint. He was stealing a car from you. We almost disposed of him—but he belongs to you, doesn't he? We decided to bring him along and see if you would play the game."

"Gabriel is welcome to drive anything I own," I told her in clear tones—and hoped that even Gabriel's human ears could hear me. "The Gray Lords are not going to be happy that you brought a human into fae matters."

She laughed. Her laughter caught me completely by surprise. Any woman with a voice as deep as hers usually has a complementary laugh. But hers was delicate and light—completely inhuman, like silver bells ringing—and the sound of it told me what kind of fae she was, which only made my stomach clench harder. Gabriel was in more than one kind of danger.

There was a pad of paper next to the phone on the wall. I pointed at it, and Auriele got up soundlessly and brought it back to me.

"So you figured out who we have," the fae woman said. "Did his mommy call you? He's awfully sweet-looking, don't you think?" There was a wistfulness in her voice. "If this were a different age, I would keep him for my own." I waited for the diatribe about how it was different in the old days—I've heard a lot of variations on that over the years. But there was only silence.

I wrote, *Fairy queen. Travels with five to twenty fairy followers. Used to capture humans to use as servants/*

lovers. Takes them to her own realm, sort of like Underhill but different. Enchantment: humans perceive time passing oddly. "Rip Van Winkle" (100 years) or "Thomas the Rhymer" (seven days became seven years). I underlined Thomas the Rhymer's name because it was history and Rip was a story by Irving that might or might not have been based on various legends—including Thomas's. *Her laughter is like tinkling of silver bells. Also some sort of mesmerizing spells. Robs victims of free will—might have the same effect on her fae followers, too. Rule bound more than most fae, but powerful within those rules.*

That book had taught me a lot more about the fae than I'd known before. I hoped something would help us find Gabriel before the fairy queen decided to keep him.

"You are patient," she said. "That doesn't match what I've heard of you."

"Not so patient," I told her. "I don't think I'll play your game by myself. I think the Gray Lords might as well take care of my problems for me." They wouldn't, of course, and I wasn't so stupid as to invite them in. But I wanted to hear what her reaction would be to it.

She laughed again. "You do that. You just do that, Mercedes Thompson. And if they figure out what you have—and have any inkling that you might know what it is—they will kill you, werewolves or no. They'd kill you to get it, too—and trust me, it is easier to kill you, human, than it is to bother looking for it wherever you have it stashed."

I didn't doubt that she was telling the truth about the Gray Lords. Fae always tell the truth. They usually respond to taunts, too—which is why I added a smug tone to my voice as I said, "Most especially because you don't know what it is either."

"The Silver Borne," she said.

She wasn't looking for the book. I had no idea what "the silver borne" was, but the book was made of leather and embossed with gold; there wasn't anything silver about it.

I had nothing to bargain with for Gabriel. So we'd have to find them and take him back in such a way that she never bothered us again. A lot of fairy tales ended "and the evil fairy never bothered them from that day until this."

"You don't know what it looks like," I said confidently. "You think I have it because Phin is dead, and it didn't reveal itself to his killers as it would have if he were in possession of it." I told her as if I knew it to be fact.

"Do you have it?" she asked. "Maybe he did give it to someone else. Though if you don't have it, I shall take this beautiful young man as consolation and continue looking for it."

I bit my lip. Phin was dead.

"I have something of Phin's," I said with obvious caution. In the morning, I'd feel bad about the man who'd stuck his neck out to help me in defiance of the Gray Lords, who loved books and old things—and who'd had a grandmother who'd called him and worried about him. As things were, I needed to keep my wits. I was tired, and Adam's pain and fatigue were starting to trickle through me as our bond chose this inconvenient time to begin to mend itself.

"You will not tell the wolves," she said. "That is the first step. I will know if you break your word. Then I will take the boy and redouble my efforts to see you dead."

I glanced at the wolves around the table. "You didn't seem so anxious to kill me that you would risk my mate's ire yesterday morning."

She hissed. "When I have that which is silver borne, I shall have no need to fear. Not wolves, not Gray Lords. The only thing that saves you at this moment is that it might take some time after you die for it to reveal itself. If you make this too difficult for me, I will risk it."

"What did you want me to do?" I asked her.

"Tell me you won't tell any of the werewolves about me, about what you have, and that Gabriel is in any kind of distress or danger."

"Okay," I said reluctantly. "I won't tell any of the wolves about you, about the thing I have that was Phin's, or about Gabriel's current danger."

"You will not tell any of the fae. Not the Gray Lords, not the old fae who was at your place of work this morning."

I looked at Darryl, and he nodded grimly. He'd tell Zee for me.

"I will not tell any fae I know about you, about the thing I have that was Phin's, or about Gabriel's current danger."

"I can't force you to adhere to that agreement," she told me. "That magic is no longer mine. But I will know the instant you break your word—and our deal will be off. This young and beautiful man will be mine, and you will die."

Jesse's cold hand gripped mine. She and Gabriel had been sort of dating for a while. "Sort of" because he was concentrating on school since he needed scholarships for college.

"All right," I told the fae.

"Second. You will bring this thing to the bookstore and give it to my knight of the water."

Fishy Boy, I thought. Though "knight of the water" didn't ring any bells. Maybe it was a title rather than a type of fae.

"Nope. I'm not bringing it to the bookstore to your knight." One of her people could kill us all and leave her not foresworn. We needed to deal only with her.

"You will—"

"Not trust you unless it is a full exchange. *You* bring Gabriel, and I get him safe and unharmed in exchange for this thing I will bring you."

"I cannot bring you Gabriel unharmed," she said, sounding amused.

Mary Jo gave a very soft rumbling growl, and I poked her to stop it. Maybe the fae wasn't paying attention. She'd heard the earlier sound Jesse had made, but as Bran liked to tell me, you can have the best senses in the world, but if you forget to use them, they can do you no good.

"No more harmed than now," I said. "Himself, in his own mind, his body no more bruised than it is at this instant."

"That I can manage," she said, still sounding amused.

"I would consider death as further damage."

She laughed. The sound was beginning to get on my nerves. "So distrustful, Mercedes. Don't you read your fairy tales? It is the humans who betray their bargains. Get a good night's sleep . . . Whoops, too late. Rest, then. I'll call you at this number sometime tomorrow when I have had a chance to organize a safe meeting place."

I wracked my brain because she was too happy, like she knew something we didn't.

"Gabriel is the only human you have," I said, suddenly worried that she had more hostages.

She laughed again. "You don't really think I'll answer that, do you?"

And she hung up.

"Does anyone know what area code 333 belongs to?" I asked.

"There isn't one," said Ben. "No 333, no 666. Phone company doesn't officially believe in numerology, but they have a lot of customers who do."

"You want me to call Zee right now?" rumbled Darryl. "Or does he get grumpy when you wake him up?"

I looked at him. "I can't answer your first question. And Zee is almost always grumpy. Don't let it bother you."

"I'll call him," said Auriele.

"Wait before . . ." I hesitated to say anything about her calling Zee, not knowing just how far I could go without triggering the fae's spell. But Auriele understood and sat back down.

"Did anyone hear anything that might pinpoint where she was calling from?" asked Jesse—who watched several forensic police procedural TV shows regularly.

"No trains," Mary Jo said dryly. She pushed the table so she wasn't pinned anymore. "No water noises. No highway or car sounds. No airplanes. No distinctive church chimes. No dolphins playing in the background."

"Which eliminates a lot of places," said Auriele. "I'm pretty sure it was indoors. I heard a hum that might have been a fluorescent light fixture."

"I heard echoes, like she was in a room with hard sides," said Darryl. "Not a huge room, though. It didn't sound hollow."

"When—" I couldn't say "she hit him," because I'd promised not to talk about the fairy queen or Gabriel's danger to the werewolves. "When Mary Jo heard something, there was a slight scuffing sound," I said. "Like a chair sliding on cement." I closed my eyes and thought about the feel of the background sounds.

"The lack of outdoor noises might mean that she was in a basement instead of just indoors," said Darryl. "If she's not from around here, she'd need to acquire someplace secure—not a hotel. Rentals are hard to find in the area right now—one of my coworkers was complaining about it. If Phin is dead, maybe the fae is using his house."

"He lived in an apartment, one of the newer ones in West Pasco—and he has nosy neighbors." I got up and got a dishcloth and wet it down so I could clean up the cocoa.

"The bookstore, then," said Auriele. She took the cloth and tossed it to Mary Jo. "Your mess, you clean it up."

Mary Jo's shoulders were tight, but she started to clean up without protest.

"Sam and I were in the bookstore's basement tonight," I said. "But the lighting there is incandescent—no buzzing. Beyond that, the sound was wrong. There were a lot of books down there, so it wasn't as echoey. The room in the phone call sounded emptier."

"You were at the bookstore? Did you catch a scent?" Ben had been dozing, I thought. Even after he spoke, his eyes were closed. The stress of his wounds and the full belly from Warren's mysterious ice chest of roasts would work like a narcotic.

"Do you need to go downstairs and sleep?" I asked.

"No, I'm fine. Did you find out anything?"

"We picked up Phin's scent—and four other fae who had been in there. One of them, some kind of forest fae, came back, and Sam killed it. There was another forest fae, a female we didn't meet. She was the same kind as the one Sam killed—I'm pretty sure of it. And then there was one who smelled of swamps and wet things who hopefully is her knight of the water. The fewer allies she has, the happier I am. I met the fourth, who left traces in the bookstore earlier today . . . I guess that's yesterday now. She looked like a happy-grandmother type. I couldn't tell what she was."

"Was it her?" asked Ben, and nodded at the phone.

"I can't answer that," I told him.

"But you can answer me," said Jesse. "Was the old woman the one who took Gabriel?"

"I don't know," I said. I closed my eyes and thought about what had happened and when. "No. She was looking through Phin's records, trying to find out who Phin gave something to. The bad guys had already tried to kill me once—if you didn't pick up on it, the incident at my garage yesterday morning was aimed at me. They knew where they were looking." Maybe if I could have talked to her, we'd know more about what it was that the fairy queen wanted.

"She's not smart, this fairy queen," said Ben. "If she were, she'd have known that you weren't human."

"I don't exactly advertise," I told him. "And, other than my connection to Adam and the Marrok, I'm not important. There's no reason that she should know. Especially since she's been producing shows in California."

"She makes assumptions," Darryl said. "Most people look at you, Mercy, and wonder if you are fae or wolf and just hiding it, because you're mated to a wolf and working with a fae." He stopped and raised a speculative eyebrow.

"Or she thinks you are one or the other and might react and tell her which one if she kept taunting you with being human."

"That sounds about right," I said.

"Why not just give them whatever she wants and get Gabriel back," Mary Jo said. "It's not yours, and it sounds like the rightful owner is dead anyway."

Ben snorted. "You aren't usually this dumb. You want to hand a woman like this fairy queen an object of power that she believes can protect her from us?"

Darryl tilted his head and looked at Mary Jo. She flushed and dropped her gaze. "Don't think I don't remember that you disobeyed Adam," he said. "You have no standing here, and you will not leave this house until your punishment." He waited, then answered her question. "Ben's right. Besides, you really think she's going to let anyone live who knows what she has? I don't know a damn thing about what she wants. If the Gray Lords are willing to kill Mercy just because she knows about it—Mercy who has their favor and is beloved by our Alpha—don't you think they'd kill one of those under their power, who has no such protections? If I can figure that out from one phone conversation, this Daphne, she knows it, too. She has no intention of letting anyone go. She'd make the exchange, then kill both Mercy and the boy."

"Or keep the boy and kill Mercy," added Jesse, who had her dad's clear eye for strategy. "Gabriel would rather be dead." She was still a teenager with a streak of drama, though. I wasn't so sure Gabriel would rather be dead than serve the fairy queen—from all accounts it was fairly pleasant from the victim's side because they had no will-power to object.

I'd rather be dead. Maybe she was right.

"Mercy," grumbled Darryl, "she was right about one thing: you need some sleep. Go to bed." His voice soft-ened. "You, too, Jesse. We can all help your boy better on a full night's sleep."

He was right. I was so tired I could hardly keep my eyes open.

I yawned and hooked my arm through Jesse's. "Okay."

———————

AFTER DROPPING JESSE OFF AT HER ROOM, I opened the door to Adam's as quietly as I could. Someone had stripped the comforter and thrown it on the floor. Adam was sprawled naked on top of the sheet—and he looked horrible. A mass of dark red scabs covered most of his extremities as well as here and there on the rest of his body.

Warren had taken off his boots and was lying on the near side of the bed on his side, facing the doorway. Sam was curled up between them at the foot of the bed.

I'd worried a little about leaving him with a wounded Alpha, but apparently he was still behaving atypically for an uncontrolled werewolf. While I closed the door, he rolled flat on his side and half looked at me. He wiggled a bit and let out a satisfied *oof* as he pushed Warren's feet over a few inches. I noticed that he didn't touch Adam.

Warren was awake—even if he looked like he was deeply asleep. I crawled over him and the corners of his mouth tipped up. I settled in between him and Adam, curling my legs up so I didn't kick Sam.

I tried not to touch Adam, but he rolled over and threw an arm over my hip. It felt warm and safe and good—and probably hurt him. His eyes opened a slit, then closed.

I lay there a while in simple appreciation that he'd survived the fire. The door opened just as I was drifting off to sleep.

"Is there room for one more?" asked Ben. I lifted up my head to see him standing in the doorway in a pair of baggy sweats. His hair was ruffled on one side as if he'd been lying down before he came up. "If not, I can go—"

"Come on in," rumbled Warren. "I'll go take the upstairs guest room."

Warren rolled off the bed, and Ben crawled on. He put one foot on mine, then let out a sigh and collapsed like a puppy who'd been playing for too long. Pack is for comfort when you hurt, I thought, putting my head back down. And for the first time in a long time, maybe the first time ever, I appreciated being a part of one.

I WOKE UP BECAUSE THE TOP OF MY HEAD WAS too warm. The sensation was vaguely familiar so I started to go back to sleep when sharp, pokey things started digging into my scalp. And then I remembered why there shouldn't be a cat sleeping on my head.

I sat up and stared into the cool gaze of the slightly singed calico Manx who expressed her irritation with my abrupt change of position with an irritated meow. She smelled of smoke, and there was a raw spot on the top of her back, but otherwise she seemed to be fine.

Adam didn't move, but Ben rolled over and opened his eyes.

"Hey, cat," I said, tearing up, as she adjusted to my new position and maneuvered herself so she was within easy petting distance of both Ben and me. "I thought you were toast."

She pushed her head under my hand and rolled so my hand slid through her coat. Ben started to reach out but stopped as soon as he moved his fingers. They looked better than they had before—though they still looked like something that might appear in a horror movie.

"I didn't realize you didn't know," Ben said, his voice still rough. "I should have told you. Adam went to your room. I went to Sam's and found her under the bed."

I wiped my eyes and nose on my shoulder (both hands

being occupied with cat and covered with cat hair anyway).
Then I leaned forward and kissed Ben's nose.

"Thanks," I said. "I'd have missed her a lot."

"Yeah." He stretched out on his back, hands carefully
laid across his belly. "We'd have missed her, too. Only
cat I've ever seen who tolerates werewolves." He sounded
oddly vulnerable. I don't think he was used to being the
hero.

"Don't feel too flattered," said Adam dryly. "Medea
likes vampires, too."

"Adam?" I said.

But he was asleep again. And I could feel him in my
head, just as he should be.

10

I WOKE UP, AND MY FIRST THOUGHT WAS SUR-
prise that I was so sore. Then I remembered the huge fae
who'd knocked me silly. In the wake of my home burning
down and Adam getting hurt, the encounter with the fae in
the bookstore had become incidental. There was a goose-
egg-sized knot on the back of my head, nothing wanted to
move very much, and my ankles—both of them—ached.

Sam was snoring, something he actually didn't do very
often. He was stretched out across my feet, which couldn't
have been very comfortable for him, though he seemed
happy enough. He must have felt my attention because
he rolled onto his back and stretched—an instant of half
wakefulness that ended with him going back to snoring.

Adam was still sleeping like the dead, as he had for
most of the night—except when he woke up coughing
blood tinged gray with smoke particles. Sometime during
the night, he'd rolled away from me, and now he slept on

his side. I ran a hand over his shoulder blade, and he moved into my touch without waking up.

"Hey," I told him. "I love you."

He didn't answer, but I didn't need one—I knew how he felt. Only after I rolled painfully off the edge of the bed did it occur to me that Ben was missing. A glance out the window told me it was still morning, not early, but not late enough to make me feel like a slugabed either.

I limped stiffly to the bathroom. One hot shower later I could move again. And even if my clothes were on their second day—and smelled of blood and smoke and all—I felt ready to face the morning. After a little dithering, I put my shoulder holster back on.

I didn't feel any urgent need to go armed—but I didn't have anywhere to put the SIG out of harm's way either. Adam probably had a gun safe around somewhere, but I didn't know where it was. So I wore the shoulder harness under my T-shirt, which was loose enough to conceal it. I'd have a hard time drawing the gun, but that shouldn't matter: it was loaded with lead bullets, and the house was full of werewolves. If I had to draw the gun, I was probably dead anyway.

On that cheery thought, I left the bedroom and shut the door quietly behind me. The lovely smell of sausage and butter pulled me into the kitchen.

Darryl was cooking.

Auriele grinned at my expression. "Sundays," she said with satisfaction, "he cooks, and I wash dishes. Mostly we end up here at Pack Central, and when Darryl cooks, everyone stops by. It's a pretty big job."

The way werewolves eat, it certainly was. A big job that was one of those little things that pulled a pack together: Sunday breakfasts at Adam's house.

"If you're doing dishes while he cooks, does he do the dishes when you cook?" I asked.

"Nope," Darryl said, serving each of us a plate of sausage, eggs, hash browns, and French toast with a snap that looked awfully professional, and returned to the stove. "Not that enlightened."

She smiled at his back. "He vacuums, though." And Darryl made an irritated noise.

"Have you seen Ben?" I asked, then said, involuntarily, "This is really good." The French toast was spiked with real vanilla, cinnamon, and a host of other things, including authentic bittersweet maple syrup.

"Mmmm." Auriele nodded, taking a bite of her hash browns. "He cooked his way through grad school."

"Made good money at it, too," Darryl agreed. "Ben's been down, eaten breakfast, and gone. He'll be back soon. I called Zee last night."

I set down my fork. "What did he say?"

"Nothing, if you are going to let my good food go cold."

I took a hasty bite, and he went back to cooking—and talking. "I played last night's ransom call back to him, and he picked me clean of everything you told us. Then he said he'd see what he could do. He called an hour or so ago and told me to tell you he'd be over here as soon as he could. It might be a couple of hours, though, so stall the villainess if she wants you to move before he gets here."

"How did he sound?"

"Grumpy. Coffee or orange juice?"

"Water is fine."

His eyebrows went up.

"Uh-oh," Auriele said, but she was smiling.

Darryl was not. "Are you implying that my coffee is not the best in four counties? Or my fresh-squeezed orange juice is less than perfect?"

Jesse breezed in and squealed. "Oh my goodness, *Darryl* is cooking. I'd almost forgotten it was Sunday. Orange juice, please." She glanced at me and laughed. "Mercy doesn't do orange juice or coffee," she said, grabbing a glass out of the cupboard and filling it out of the pitcher Darryl had set out. "So sad. More orange juice for me."

She was being cute and upbeat, but there were dark circles under her eyes. She took the plate Darryl handed her and sat down next to Auriele.

"So," she said. Her pink hair helped her cheerful act—hard to look sad with pink hair—even if her eyes were a little pink, too. "How are we going to save Gabriel?"

"Have you ever noticed that everyone who knows Mercy eventually needs saving?" asked Mary Jo as she walked into the kitchen.

I was going to have to do something about Mary Jo. I took another bite of French toast and put the fork down on the plate. Sooner was probably better than later.

I stood up. "Excuse me," I said to Darryl. To Jesse I said, "I'm borrowing your bedroom—any complaints?"

She stared at me a moment. "No?" she said, her voice rising as if her answer were a question. Which maybe it was.

"Your stereo is pretty effective at keeping voices from being overheard by all the werewolves in this house. And from the noise coming from downstairs, there are a lot of werewolves here."

"It's Darryl's cooking," said Auriele, sounding a little apologetic.

"I can see why," I said. "I'd appreciate it if you would guard my plate until I come back." I looked at Mary Jo. "You. Come with me."

And without looking behind me, I led the way up the stairs to Jesse's room. I walked into Jesse's room and turned on her stereo until it was almost painfully loud. The CD wasn't something I'd have chosen to listen to, but it was loud, and that was all I was interested in.

"Shut the door," I told Mary Jo. I was almost surprised she'd just followed me up as I'd asked.

Face blank, she did as I'd requested.

"Okay. Now, if you come over here by the window, it's almost impossible for anyone to overhear us."

All the precautions weren't really necessary. With this many people in Adam's house, no one, no matter how good their hearing was, could really listen from one room to the next—there were simply too many conversations going on. But the stereo made our privacy virtually certain.

"What do you want?" she asked, not moving from the center of the room.

I leaned against the wall next to the window and crossed my arms over my stomach. It felt wrong to be in this position. I've been a solitary person my whole life. Even when I lived in Aspen Creek with the Marrok's pack, even then I'd really been alone, a coyote among wolves. But Adam needed his pack behind him—and because of me, they weren't. If I was going to be the problem, I owed it to him to be part of the solution. So I was going to see if all those times I had watched the Marrok twist people in little knots would allow me to use his techniques to achieve the same results.

I smiled at her. "I want you to tell me what your problem with me is. Right here, right now, where there is no one else to interfere."

"*You* are the problem, Mercedes," she snapped. "A scavenger coyote among wolves. You don't belong here."

"Oh, come on. You can do better than that," I goaded her. "You sound like you're Jesse's age—and Jesse doesn't sound like that."

Her eyes veiled as she considered what I said.

"All right," she said after a minute. "Point to you. First problem—you let Adam rot for two years after he claimed you as his mate. And during that two years our pack fell apart because Adam could barely keep himself calm—and was nearly useless at helping anyone else keep their wolf in check."

"Agreed," I said. "But I have to point out in my defense that Adam never asked *me* if I wanted to be his mate during that time—or before he declared it in front of the pack. He never asked me either before or after. I wasn't a pack member—and his declaration was to keep the rest of the wolves away—so I didn't even find out about this until well after it happened. Even then, no one told me the consequences until just a few months ago, and as soon as I figured out what was happening to the pack and to Adam because of that claim, I made a decision."

"How kind of you," she snapped, her eyes brightening with temper. "To become Adam's mate for the pack's sake."

"Point to me," I told her calmly. "The choice I made had nothing to do with the problems in the pack—all Adam needed was an answer, and 'no' would have worked just as well to set the pack back in order. I agreed because . . . because he's Adam." *Mine,* whispered a voice in my head, but I was pretty sure that it was my own voice.

"Second problem," she said between gritted teeth. "It was your invitation to the stray that led to Adam being almost killed and Jesse kidnapped."

"Nope." I shook my head. "You can't lay that one on me. That was werewolf business from beginning to end. I got involved because I was in the wrong place at the wrong time. No more, no less. Point to me."

"I disagree," she said. She was standing in the classic "at ease" position, I noticed, like a soldier. I wondered if it was something Adam taught them while he had them in training because, to my knowledge, Mary Jo had never been in the military.

"Fine," I said, shrugging. "It's a free country. You can feel as you wish."

"You can't deny who nearly got our third killed when the demon came to town, you and your connection to the vampires," she said.

Her voice was cool, her heartbeat steady. Warren wasn't important to her; Ben had been right. She hadn't even called him by name because she felt the rank was more valuable than the man.

"Once it was known that there was a demon in town, it was inevitable that the wolves would have to go after it," I told her. "And you could care less about Warren, so don't pretend you were concerned about him."

That had her head up and her eyes on me. She actually looked a little worried. She had been trying to pretend that she wasn't one of the wolves that Warren bothered.

"Warren is worth ten of you," I told her. "He's here when he's needed, and he doesn't do his best to undermine Adam whenever his orders are inconvenient." I waved off her impending argument because I was saving the discussions of her more recent activities until later, when I'd broken her down enough to answer my questions. "Back to business. What else?"

"It's your fault I died," she said. "Poor Alec—when he tore my jugular, he didn't know what hit him. None of us did. The vampires targeted us because of you."

The vampires had set a trap at Uncle Mike's, the local tavern where the fae and assorted other supernatural people went to relax. They'd laid a spell that drove anything with ties to wolves to bloodshed. Mary Jo's bad luck that she and two other werewolves—Paul and Alec—had gone there on the wrong night. By the time Adam and I got there, Mary Jo was dead. But apparently if you die when there is a Gray Lord present, at least when one particular Gray Lord is present, dead isn't as permanent as it might otherwise have been.

"Point to you," I said, deliberately relaxing against the wall so she could see it didn't bother me in the slightest. I can't lie with my mouth, but sometimes body language does it for me. "I'd tell you that accepting the blame for the bad guys is a stupid thing to do—the proper people to blame for your almost death are the vampires. But if I hadn't been dating Adam, they wouldn't have targeted the wolves, so I suppose you could be justified in blaming me."

I waited for her to look up again, so I could read her

face. When she looked at me, her control was back in full. There were two things that could explain her sudden dislike of me. The first one was the incident at Uncle Mike's, but she wasn't angry enough about it. Which left me with the second—I'd hit her with that when it would do me more good.

"But," I told her, "if I accept the blame, I'd like to point out that I'm also the reason you are still standing here. The Gray Lord healed you because she thought she owed *me* a favor."

She sneered. "I hope to God that someone does you that kind of favor someday. It hurt . . . It still hurts. Some days I can't feel different body parts."

I'd known about that, and it worried me though the fae had given her word that Mary Jo would be back to normal. I expect that she'd left out the word "eventually" because Mary Jo's suffering didn't really matter to the fae.

"Next time, I'll tell her not to bother bringing you back," I promised. I tapped my foot and wondered how far I really wanted to push this. Some of it depended upon what role I wanted to take in the pack. Just then I was channeling my inner Bran, using the techniques I'd grown up watching the Marrok use, techniques that came so easily to me it made me a little uncomfortable—I don't see myself as a manipulative person. For the moment, though, I set that aside and considered the case at hand.

"Figure out the results you want and do what you can to get them" was one of Bran's favorite sayings. Well, then, exactly what results did I want?

Part of that really depended upon how much of her recent activities were directed at me and how much at Adam. I found that I could excuse her actions against me, but I was less inclined to be forgiving about Adam.

I remembered that look she'd given me when I was sitting on the floor of the hospital with Adam changing in my lap—Adam, who'd damn near burned to death trying to rescue me because she hadn't told him I was safe. The look that said she'd have been happier with him dead than with him on my lap.

Had that been a momentary thing, or had her anger that Adam was mine become a force driving her past the point of no return?

"Mary Jo," I said pleasantly, "you and I know all of that is garbage. It is all true, or mostly, but it isn't why you are so angry with me."

Her chin jerked up.

"Adam is mine," I told her. "And you can't handle it. Does it bother you that I'm a coyote? That we have sort of an extreme case of an interracial—in our case maybe even cross-species—mating? Darryl is African and Chinese, and Auriele is Hispanic, and they don't seem to bother you." It wasn't that I was a coyote shifter that bothered her. I knew it. I just wondered if she knew it. It did bother some of the pack; maybe Auriele and Darryl bothered some of them, too. If so, those pack members were smart enough to keep it to themselves.

Mary Jo tightened her lips but didn't say anything.

"How long have you wanted him?" I asked her. "You had all these years since Jesse's mother left."

Bran's methods sucked. I watched her eyes darken with pain and wanted to kick myself. But she'd been at least partially responsible for Adam's wounds. And I agreed with Warren about fire after watching Samuel scrub dead flesh from live. Mary Jo had been stupid. I was betting she hadn't hurt Adam on purpose, but I had to know.

I observed the anger that followed pain rise in her face and just watched her.

"You are *nothing*," she spit. "I'm nothing, too. That's how I know. Adam deserves the best. A wolf strong and beautiful, a woman who is—"

"More?" I suggested. "Smart, well-bred?"

"Not a half-breed coyote," she snapped. Her wolf was

in her eyes, and her voice was raw. "Not a stupid mechanic or a freaking fireman. There isn't even a proper word for what I am. Fireman. He needs someone soft, someone feminine."

"He deserves so much," I said slowly. I had her, even though it made me sick. Coyotes aren't cats; we don't play with our prey. "I think he deserves a pack who has his back."

"I have his back," she said. I couldn't see her hands. Through all this she'd held to parade rest, and her hands were hidden behind her back. From the flex of her biceps I would bet that they were clenched in fists, and her voice wasn't as hard and certain as she meant it to be. But her words told me what I'd been watching for, told me that she hadn't wanted him dead. That made the rest of this both harder and easier. Harder because she was going to be hurting even more before this was over—easier because she would survive it.

"You have his back, do you?" I kept my voice soft, my body relaxed. "Funny, I could have sworn that you just set him up to be killed."

"I got him out," she said. "I ran in after him with Darryl and pulled him out."

"Not soon enough, Mary Jo," I said. "He could have easily died in there." I had to take a breath so I could maintain my relaxed posture. *He could have died.* But I had to keep up the momentum, make her listen to me, make her listen to herself.

"Who was it that was out there with you?" I asked coolly. "Ben says whoever it was, he has to be more dominant than you. It wasn't Warren or Darryl." Ben would have noticed if Darryl hadn't been at the meeting. He'd have said something to me because if it was Darryl who was running the show, it would have been too dangerous to hold his tongue. The same was true of Auriele.

"How does the pack run from there?" I watched her sweat. Ben was right that it was someone higher up. She was expecting me to name him soon, so not too far down the pack hierarchy. "Auriele. It wasn't her either, was it? She likes Adam. *She'd* never send him into a burning building to rescue someone who wasn't there."

She stiffened at the dig.

"Then there is Paul." That got her—wasn't that interesting? But I knew better. "It wasn't him, though. Adam doesn't trust Paul at his back. He'd have kept him right here through the whole pack meeting." Paul had been my pick for the jerk who'd influenced me at the bowling alley before I'd understood how angry Mary Jo was. He'd probably been Adam's pick, too. Paul was still angry about losing a fight to Warren, and he'd put the blame on Adam for that. Like Ben, Paul was a bitter and difficult person who didn't like many people. Mary Jo was one he did like, her and her boyfriend, Henry.

I watched her face closely. She was worried I'd guess. Not Paul, then who? Further down the ranks things could get murky to an outsider as I had been and really still was. I ran the wolves I knew well through my head, then stopped. Henry? He was a nice guy. Smart and quick. A banker, I thought, but I wasn't sure, something with finances. He would never— Hmm. "Never" was an awfully strong word.

I wondered how Henry felt about Mary Jo's crush on Adam.

"Henry," I said experimentally and watched her face whiten. Maybe she didn't know how much she was telling me without opening her mouth at all. "Henry was out with you last night. Henry told you to leave the fae alone when they set my house on fire."

Jesse's door opened, and Adam came in and shut it gently behind him. He was obviously stiff, and, from the set of his jaw and the tightness of the skin around his eyes, he was in pain as well. If I could see it, he was hurting a lot more than he showed. And the Alpha didn't show weakness if he could help it.

He was dressed only in a pair of *gi* bottoms that ended midcalf, leaving the weepy wounds on his feet clearly visible. Oh, there were other bits in rough shape, but next to his feet, nothing looked all that bad.

"I heard your voice," he told me, pulling my eyes away from his feet and up to his face. "So I pressed my ear to the door, and even with the noise my daughter calls music blaring, I overheard what you said, Mercy." He looked at Mary Jo, who had turned around to face him and lost her formal parade-rest stance. She just stood there, looking vulnerable.

Had it been Samuel standing there, I'd have worried that he would be too soft on her. But Adam didn't really see women as the weaker sex, and he knew how to organize and how to recognize organization when he saw it.

His unreadable face was focused on Mary Jo. "So Henry was there when the fae set Mercy's house on fire. And here I thought you were out there alone. Because I knew Henry was in the house when I had plainly told him to back you up last night. Doubtless if I asked him, he'd tell me that he thought I only meant for him to be there while the meeting was going on . . . or he'd come up with some other explanation."

"Henry was the one to tell you my house was on fire, wasn't he?" I said. Like Adam, I was watching Mary Jo. I couldn't see her face, but her shoulders tightened. A friend of mine from college, a drama major, told me that the shoulders are the most expressive part of the body. I had to agree with him. She was almost to the point of seeing the big picture, because she expected Adam to say yes.

"I see you've followed this to its logical conclusion, Mercy," he told me, but his eyes were on Mary Jo. "I wonder if she's seen it yet—or if she's part of it."

"Henry ran in and got you out to the trailer before anyone else came out of the house?" Mary Jo's voice was stark, but she wasn't arguing.

"That's right," Adam agreed. "More or less. He wandered into the kitchen. Before I could ask him why he wasn't out watching Mercy, he looked out the window, and said, 'What's that? Is that a fire? My God, the house is on fire.'"

"He knew," Mary Jo said uncertainly. "He saw them start it. He wouldn't let me confront them because he was afraid I'd get hurt. He said Mercy and Sam were gone, what was the harm if the upstart coyote's house went up in flames? She deserved a little hurt because of all the pain she'd caused."

Mary Jo looked at Adam. "He meant to me. He was really angry about how the vampires had attacked us . . . how I was hurt because they were trying to get to Mercy. He wanted to get back at Mercy."

"He could care less about me," I told her. "His girlfriend didn't like *me* better than she liked him. Henry was interested in Adam. He saw an opportunity to get back at Adam, and he jumped at it." I looked at Adam. "The next time you leap into a burning building after me, you'd better make damned sure I'm in there. And wear your shoes, damn it." I looked at his feet again. "You're leaking nasty burn ooze on the carpet."

He smiled. "I love you, too, sweetheart. And thanks to the time you bled all over it, I now know a place that can clean almost anything off the carpet."

"He wanted Adam hurt," I told Mary Jo. "Because if he's hurt, then he's vulnerable. An Alpha can be challenged at any time. Since Adam is hurt, usually he could put it off without anyone complaining, especially since the Marrok doesn't allow fights for an Alpha position without his consent. But the pack is—" I looked at Adam. "Sorry, I know it's my fault. But the pack is broken. Adam can't put this off—not when the pack is in this much turmoil. If he does, he's liable to have worse than a formal fight on his hands—he'll have a rebellion."

See, I grew up in a werewolf pack. I know the dangers.

Not even fear of the Marrok can completely control the nature of the pack. That's why an Alpha will do anything in his power to hide his weakness in front of the pack.

"Henry challenged you?" Mary Jo's voice was shocked. "The Marrok will kill him, if you don't manage it first."

"Almost right," said Adam. "Paul is actually the one who challenged me. Climbed in the window of the bedroom about four minutes ago and challenged me in front of Ben, Alec, and Henry. Henry having volunteered to drive Ben to pick up some clothes for Mercy because Ben's hands are still too sore for him to drive easily and suggested Alec tag along."

He paused, and said heavily, "Henry is helpful like that."

Mary Jo nodded. "And Alec is known as a neutral party. Not one of your biggest fans, but not one of the hotheads either."

Adam continued in a gentler voice. "They must have had some signal so that he and Paul appeared in my bedroom at virtually the same moment when neither Warren nor Darryl was there to interfere. Ben and Henry witnessed the challenge. Henry was appalled that Paul would challenge me when I was hurt."

"They set you up," said Mary Jo numbly. "They used me to set you up."

"That's what I was trying to tell you," I said, then added a question casually. "Was it just you and Henry at the bowling alley, or did Paul help, too?"

She nodded, not even noticing all the assumptions I'd made because she was too distracted by the realization that things might not have been as she'd thought they were. "Paul, Henry, and I. Paul suggested it to me. 'Can't have a coyote second in rank in a respectable pack.'" Mary Jo looked at Adam. "He said she wasn't good enough for you—and I agreed. Henry was pretty reluctant. I had to talk him into it. He set me up, didn't he? Both of them set me up."

I felt sorry for her. But I'd felt more sorry for her before I'd found out that the wolf who'd challenged Adam was Paul. Henry was a good fighter—I'd seen him play fight a time or two—but he wasn't a tithe on Paul. Paul . . . Normally I wouldn't worry about Paul taking Adam either, but normally Adam's feet weren't oozing goo on the carpet, and his hands weren't swollen and raw.

That was why I wasn't sorry enough for Mary Jo that I'd let her escape blame by pointing her finger at the other two.

"The bowling alley was you," I said. "Oh, Paul wouldn't cry if Adam and I broke up—but he wants to get rid of Adam more than he wants to get rid of me. Henry . . . Maybe that was the straw that broke the camel's back for Henry—you'd know better than I. Was that the first time he realized how much you wanted Adam?"

Adam jerked his head toward me. I guess he hadn't noticed how Mary Jo felt.

"Paul," began Mary Jo. Then she stopped. Closed her eyes and shook her head. "Not Paul." She gave Adam a wry smile. "Paul is tough, and he's not stupid—but he's not a planner. He'd never have figured out how to force you to accept a challenge before you were ready. She's right. It's Henry. What can I do?"

"Not a darn thing," he said. "Just be smarter next time."

"When's the fight?" I asked, trying to be cool, trying to be a good coyote who lets her mate go out and fight a duel to the death when it hurts him to walk. I had to do it, because sobbing and fussing wouldn't change anything except make his job harder. If he refused the challenge, Paul would be Alpha—and if I knew Paul, his first act would be to kill Adam. Henry was hoping so, anyway.

And the reason it was Paul who challenged and not Henry was because as soon as the Marrok heard about this—Paul was a dead man. And that would leave Darryl in charge of the pack with Warren as his second. The pack would not tolerate having a gay man in the second position because if something happened to Darryl, Warren would run the pack. So Warren would be killed or be moved by Bran—leaving Henry as the second in the pack.

Of course, Adam would have to lose to Paul for that to happen. I felt sick.

Adam looked at Jesse's clock, which read 9:15. "Fifteen minutes from now in the dojo," he said. "Would you go down and let Darryl and Warren know they'll be wanted for witnesses? I think I'll go lie down for another ten minutes." He was in the hallway when he said, "If I survive, Mary Jo, we'll have to come up with a suitable reparation for the bowling alley. You ruined a very promising evening, and I won't forget about it."

"YOUR FOOD IS COLD," GROWLED DARRYL, AS I entered the kitchen. "I hope your business was important."

Jesse was still there, drying, while Auriele washed. There was no saving this, not if Paul specified the fight be here—no chance of talking Jesse into waiting this one out somewhere safe; she was too much her father's daughter.

"Paul's challenged Adam," I told them. "Fifteen minutes from now in the dojo in the garage."

Darryl whirled around with a growl, and Auriele stepped between him and Jesse, though I don't think Jesse realized it because she was staring at me.

"How did he get to Adam?" said Auriele. "Who was supposed to be watching him?"

"Me," I said after a stunned moment. "I guess that would be me."

"No," said Auriele. "That would have been Samuel. Ben said he left Adam with Samuel and you."

"Samuel's not pack," growled Darryl, eyes light gold in the darkness of his face.

Sam wasn't Samuel, I thought. In the normal course of things Samuel would have kept that challenge from happening. I wondered if Paul or Henry had realized that. Probably not.

"My fault," I said.

"No." I'd left Mary Jo in Jesse's room, but she must have followed me down. "Not your fault," Mary Jo said. "Maybe Warren or Darryl could have stopped Paul, but Henry was very careful to make sure they weren't there." She gave me an inscrutable look that would have done credit to Darryl, inscrutable but not overtly hostile. "They wouldn't have thought Samuel would interfere. They think of him as a lone wolf, not as Adam's friend."

The look, I realized, was to let me know that she wouldn't tell them about Samuel unless I did.

"Henry?" Darryl was shocked into dropping his anger. "Henry?"

Mary Jo lifted her chin. "He planned it." She looked at me, then away. "He wants Adam dead and is using Paul . . . used me, too, in order to accomplish it."

"Is that what they told you?" Henry himself came into the kitchen. He was a compact man, a little taller than me, with a quick smile and hazel eyes that could look either gray or gold rather than the more usual brown and green. He wore his hair in a conservative cut and almost certainly shaved with a regular razor rather than an electric because an electric never produces quite the same well-groomed look. "Mary Jo—"

"Inconvenient," I murmured. "Not being able to lie to another werewolf."

If Mary Jo hadn't stepped in front of me, he'd have hit me. She took the hit for me, and it knocked her into the center island. The granite top broke loose under the impact and slid—Jesse caught the granite slab before it overbalanced and fell on the floor, shoving it back on its base. If he'd hit me that hard, I wouldn't have gotten up the way Mary Jo did—and she was holding her ribs.

Auriele stepped in front of Henry when he would have

gone to her. Her lips peeled back. *"¡Hijo de perra!"* she said, her voice alive with anger.

Henry flushed, so the insult hit home. Calling someone a son of a dog is a good insult among werewolves.

"Hijo de Chihuahua," said Mary Jo.

Auriele shook her head. "Darryl kept saying that it couldn't be Paul behind the unrest we've been having for the last couple of years. No one would listen to Paul. We knew he was right, but no one else fit. I would have suspected Peter before I suspected you."

Peter was the lone submissive wolf in the pack. It was inconceivable that a submissive wolf would play power games. If Auriele was right, this had started long before the disastrous bowling-alley incident.

"How long have you known that Mary Jo would have dropped you like a hot potato for Adam?" I asked.

He snarled something rude.

"You have no common sense whatsoever," said Auriele. I assume she was talking to me, so I answered her.

"He's not going to do anything with you between us," I told her. "He's smart enough to be afraid of you."

"Since I was killed for certain," said Mary Jo, answering the question I'd asked Henry. "Isn't that right? The first time I regained consciousness. You kissed my forehead, and I called you by Adam's name. But it sounds like you had a pretty good idea about it even earlier."

"Get out of here," said Darryl, his voice low with anger. "Get out of this house, Henry. When you come back to see this fight, you come in from the outside door. And you'd better hope Adam wins this fight, or I'll wipe the ground with you so hard they won't need a box to bury you in. All they'll need is a mop."

Henry flushed, went white, then flushed again. He left the room without a word. The outside door opened and slammed shut.

Ben strolled in, looking grim, Sam right behind him.

"Where's Henry going in such a hurry? Darryl, good—I was looking for you. I just got through talking to Warren downstairs. Have you heard . . . ?" His voice trailed off when he saw Jesse standing there. He took a good look at all of us. "I see you have."

Darryl stiffened. "Samuel?" His voice was soft.

"He's been like this a couple of days," offered Ben. "So far, so good. It's a long story, and you can hear it later: we're due in the garage in five."

11

THE ONLY REASON THE GARAGE WASN'T PACKED
with werewolves was that there hadn't been enough time
for the word to go around.

Instead of thirty or so, we only had eighteen, not including Sam, who wasn't pack. But I had to keep looking around
and counting because there seemed to be fewer people than
my count showed. Most dominance fights, like boxing or
wrestling matches, are full of jostling, cheering, jeering,
and betting. This one was eerily silent, and only one person
was moving.

Paul jogged in place on one side of the padded floor,
stopping every ten or fifteen seconds to stretch or do a little
shadowboxing. He was a tall man with blond hair and a
short red beard. His skin was the kind that is usual for red-
heads, pale and freckled. The excitement of the impending
fight left him flushed. Like Adam, he wore only a pair of
gi pants.

There is no tradition that dictates dominance fights have

to be done in human form. It is common, though, because it makes the challenge more about skill and strength. When you are armed with fangs and claws, a lucky hit can take out a more skilled opponent.

On the far side of the mats from Paul, Adam stood in horse stance, head bowed, eyes closed, and shoulders relaxed. All signs of pain were gone from his face, but he hadn't been able to eliminate the pain-caused stiffness in the time that he'd walked from the house to the mat. Even if he had, only an idiot would look at the broken scabs on his feet and hands and not understand that he was in trouble.

As Alpha, even as badly hurt as he had been, he really should have been healing faster than this. Granted that werewolves, even the same werewolf, will heal wounds at different rates depending upon a number of things. He might have been hurt worse than he'd shown us, or the trouble he'd been having with his pack could be interfering with his ability to heal. I tried not to look worried.

Jesse and I had the equivalent of ringside seats at the edge of the mat on the side where Adam stood—traditional for the family of the Alpha, but not smart when neither of us could reasonably defend ourselves if the fight rolled off the mats. Sam stood beside Jesse, and Warren stood between us, presumably to keep the combatants from hurting us.

Adam wasn't wearing a watch, but at exactly nine thirty by the clock on the wall, he raised his head, opened his eyes, and nodded at Darryl.

Wolves aren't much given to long speech-making. Darryl strode from the sidelines to the center of the mat. "Paul has chosen today to challenge our Alpha," he announced baldly. His lips twisted as he said, "He eschewed the formality of running the challenge by the Marrok."

No one murmured or looked surprised. They all knew what Paul had done.

There was the bare chance that the Marrok would look at the mess the pack was in and allow that Paul had no choice

but to challenge. The chance that the Marrok wouldn't kill
Paul would have been slightly greater if Adam hadn't been
hurt already. But Paul probably thought that he was in the
right and that he could convince the Marrok of the same
thing.

I suppose anything is possible. I don't think Paul understood just how unlikely that was. He'd never, to my knowledge, actually met the Marrok. Henry, who had, probably
told Paul that it would be all right. People like Henry are
good at getting others to believe them.

Darryl looked around the audience. "My job is to see
that you stay off the mats. I am willing to ensure that this
is a fair fight with your life. Are we clear?"

"Excuse me," said Mary Jo's voice.

She was just this side of five feet tall so I didn't see her
until she stepped onto the mat in front of Darryl.

"I call challenge on Paul," she said.

And then there was noise, a great howl of noise as the
whole garage full of werewolves objected—women don't
fight in challenge fights.

Darryl raised his hand and quiet spread reluctantly.

"I'm within three of his rank," she said. Her eyes were
properly on Darryl's feet, though her face was turned to
him. "It is within my right to challenge him for the right to
fight the Alpha."

I stared at her. This was not something I'd have expected
of the Mary Jo who had allowed the fae to set fire to my
house while she was supposed to be standing guard.

"You're not within three ranks," growled Darryl.

She held up her hand. "Paul," she said. Then she held
up one finger "Henry." Another finger. "George and me."

She was right. That was where I'd have put her, too.

"You are an unmated woman," Darryl said. "That puts
your rank at the bottom. Alec is after George."

"Alec," she called, not taking her attention away from
Darryl. "Who is more dominant, you or me?"

Alec stepped around the other wolves and looked from her to Paul. I could see the answer he wanted to make, and Darryl started to relax. Adam, I noticed, was watching Mary Jo with surprised respect.

Alec opened his mouth, then hesitated. "You all could tell if I lied," he said. He raised up both his hands in a gesture of surrender. "I hope you know what you're doing, Mary Jo." He looked Darryl in the eye, and said, "Mary Jo outranks me."

And chaos reigned. Paul stuck his head in Darryl's face and raved. He was one of the very few people in the pack tall enough to stand eye to eye with Darryl. If there hadn't been so much noise, I'd have been able to hear what he said—but I could guess. Paul liked Mary Jo. He didn't want to kill her.

Mary Jo stood there; like Adam, she was an island of quiet in the uproar. She was small, but every ounce of weight she had was muscle. She was tough as boot leather, quick, and agile. I wasn't as certain as Paul was that she'd lose—I wouldn't want to fight against her. If she won, she could yield to Adam. If she decided to fight—and I didn't think she would—she'd be coming into the challenge tired and possibly hurt.

Then I remembered the way Henry had thrown her into the island in the kitchen. She had either broken or cracked her ribs when she hit. Though I couldn't see it in the way she was moving, there had not been enough time for her to heal. No one healed that fast unless they were an Alpha with a full moon outside.

"Enough," roared Warren suddenly, his voice ringing out over the hubbub like a shot fired in a crowd.

Darryl turned to Mary Jo, and said, "No."

"Not your call to make," she informed him. "Adam?"

"I have a problem," he said. "Justice demands that I must step away from this determination because I am more than a little vested in the decision. In the name of justice, then, let it fall to the next three in rank—Mercy, Darryl, and Auriele."

He looked at me.

I know what I wanted to say. Auriele was likely to agree with Mary Jo—and we'd already heard what Darryl's viewpoint was. Even if Mary Jo lost, it would help Adam. I looked at the wolves and saw a lot of resentful faces—they had done the math as well, and they were very unhappy with me being a part of the decision.

Then I saw some wiggle room.

"It seems to me that there is another problem," I said. "If we agree that Mary Jo can fight because she ranks within three people of Paul. I submit that Paul does not stand within three people of Adam." Like Mary Jo, I held up my hand. "Adam, then me." I held up a finger. "Darryl—and Auriele, then Warren."

"Then Honey," said Warren with a little smile. "Then Paul."

Paul snarled. "He has already accepted my challenge. That presupposes I have the right."

I looked at Adam.

"Nice try," he told me. "But I agree with Paul."

"And the official code of conduct," said Ben grumpily, "which I had to damn well *memorize* before I was allowed in the pack, says challenge within quote *three men* unquote. The important word being 'men.'"

"So Mary Jo can't fight," said Paul with a relieved grin. "She's not a man."

"So Mary Jo's claim is still valid," I pointed out. "She's within three men of your rank. Does the code of conduct say that the challenger has to be a man?" Kyle told me that one of the secrets of being a lawyer was never to ask a witness a question you didn't know the answer to. I knew what it said, but it would sound better coming from someone else.

"No," said Ben.

I'd done all I could do. Adam's silent urging pushing me, I looked at Mary Jo, and said, "Like Adam, I have too much of a stake in this."

"Mercy," whispered Jesse fiercely. "What are you doing?" I patted the hand she'd locked on my wrist.

"Darryl, Auriele, and Warren will decide this, then," said Adam.

Because my mate bond with Adam was sort of functioning again, I knew he believed that if I'd been part of the decision, it would have just become another point of contention. Another stupid thing that allowing a coyote into a pack of wolves had accomplished—instead of what it should be, a recognition of Mary Jo's right to challenge regardless of her sex. I figured he was right.

"There are only three females in this pack," said Darryl. I don't think he forgot about me so much as he really meant three women werewolves instead of females in general. "That is typical for all packs. Most werewolves die before they have spent a decade as a wolf, but for women who are wolves, that life span is almost doubled because they do not fight men for dominance. And still they are so few. You are too precious to us to allow you to risk so much."

It took me a while to realize he wasn't talking to the whole pack, but to his mate.

Auriele crossed her arms. "That makes sense in a species where women are important to survival. But we aren't. We cannot have children—and so are no more valuable to the pack than anyone else."

It had the ring of an old argument.

"I vote no," said Darryl, snapping his teeth as he spoke.

"I vote yes," responded Auriele coolly.

"Damn it," said Warren. "Y'all are going to throw me in the middle of a marital spat on top of everything else?"

"Up to you," Auriele said grimly.

"Hell," said Warren, "if this ain't a whole can of worms, I don't know what is. Mary Jo?"

"Yes?"

"You sure about this, darlin'?"

It felt as if the whole pack drew a breath.

"This is my fault," she told him. "That Adam got hurt, that the pack has been in an upheaval. I didn't cause it all, but I didn't stop it either. I think it's time I make suitable reparations, don't you? Try to fix the damage?"

Warren stared at her, and I saw the wolf come and go in his eye. "All right. All right. You go fight him, Mary Jo— and you damn well better win. You hear me?"

She nodded. "I'll do my best."

"You do better than that," he said grimly.

"Mary Jo." Paul's voice was plaintive. "I don't want to hurt you, woman."

She kicked off her shoes and started pulling off her socks. "Do you yield?" she asked him, while she stood on one foot.

He stared at her, his body tight with growing anger. "I stuck my neck out for you," he said.

She nodded. "Yes. And I was wrong to ask you to." She tossed her second sock aside and looked at him. "But Henry used both of us to ruin our pack. Are you going to let him get away with it?"

It was very quiet in the garage. I'm not sure anyone was even breathing. Henry's name had been a shock. Heads turned toward Henry, who was leaning against the wall between the garage doors, as far as he could get from Adam's side of the mat.

Paul looked at him, too. For a moment, I thought it was going to work.

"Are you going to let some girl lead you around by your tail like I did?" Henry said, sounding miserable. "She wants Adam, and she's willing to throw both of us away to get him." It was a masterful performance, and Paul bought it—hook, line, and sinker.

"The hell with you, then," Paul said to her. "The hell

with you, Mary Jo. I accept your challenge." He looked
at Adam. "You'll have to wait. I guess I'll eat my dessert
first."

And he strode to the far end of the mat, next to Henry.
Mary Jo walked up to where Adam was standing.

"Reparations accepted," he said. "You remember he
fights with his heart and not his head."

"And he moves slower to the left than the right," she
agreed.

Adam left her. As he walked across the white mat, he
left little traces of blood wherever his foot hit. Blood was
better than yellow pus, right?

"Good job," he murmured when he came up to me.
"Thank you. I couldn't tell if you could hear me or not."

Warren yielded Adam his place between Jesse and me,
moving around Jesse so he could still help her if he was
needed. Sam moved around to my side and lay down on the
cement with a sigh.

"See if you congratulate me when she's lying dead,"
I said, very quietly. I'd have told him about her ribs, but
I was afraid that the wrong person would hear, and Paul
would find out. Henry knew, of course . . . but somehow I
didn't think he would tell Paul that he'd broken Mary Jo's
ribs. Paul wouldn't understand—and Henry was smart
enough to know that.

Mary Jo adopted Adam's horse stance and faced Paul,
whose back was to her.

"Challenge given and accepted," Darryl said. "Fight to
the death with the winner having the option to accept a
yield."

"Agreed," said Mary Jo.

"Yes," said Paul.

Mary Jo was faster, and she was a better-trained fighter.
But when she hit, she didn't hit as hard. If Paul had been
nearer to her size instead of four inches over six feet, she'd
have had a good chance. But he had over a foot of height,

which translated into reach. I'd remembered from his fight with Warren that he was surprisingly fast for such big man.

Eventually, he landed a fist on her shoulder that put her down like she'd been hammered.

"Yield," he said.

She stuck her feet between his and knocked them apart. Then she rolled like a monkey between his spread legs, elbowing him in the kidneys as she rose behind him. A second kick behind the knee almost had him on the ground, but he recovered.

"Yield like hell," she gritted, when she was a few body lengths from him.

"Quit being easy on her," said Darryl heavily. "This is a fight to the death, Paul. She will kill you if she can. If you accepted her challenge, you have to give her the respect of fighting her honestly."

"Right," said Adam.

Paul snarled soundlessly and stepped back to the edge of the ring, raising both arms to a high-block position, his feet perpendicular to each other, hands loosely fisted, deliberately inviting a strike to the torso.

Trouble with baiting a trap like that was that if Mary Jo handled it right, she might be able to turn it into a very big mistake. I grabbed hold of Adam's arm and tried not to dig in my fingernails. He was tense beside me, muttering, "Watch out, watch out. He's faster than he looks."

Mary Jo went slowly left, then right, and Paul turned easily to face her. She shifted her weight to the right—but with a blur of speed, she broke left and moved to the attack, dropping into a long, low lunge that looked almost like something a fencer might use, her fist blurring as hip and shoulder rotated into line, driving it forward like a lance. It was a perfect strike, delivered with superhuman speed.

Paul rotated smoothly as her fist flashed through empty air, just grazing his stomach. He brought both fists down like hammers on her unprotected back, driving her flat to the ground with a sound like distant thunder. Next to me Adam grunted, as if he felt the impact of Paul's fists himself.

Mary Jo was obviously dazed. She lay on her stomach, blinking myopically. Her mouth and throat worked like a fish's out of water. Then she drew in a long, shuddering breath and her eyes focused. If her ribs had been hurt before, she must be in agony after the blow she'd just taken.

Any sane person would know the fight was over and beg to yield, but she was slowly struggling to get her elbows under her and lift her body from the mat. Paul's mouth twisted in a mirthless smile as he watched her efforts.

"Stay down," he told her. "Stay down. Yield, damn it. I don't want to hurt you anymore."

She'd gotten to her elbows and was pulling her knees up when he did a flashy skip-step and brought the edge of his foot down on the back of her thigh, driving her flat to the mats again. A short scream tore from her throat, but she jerked her knees underneath her and popped to her feet.

Her guard was too low, her right elbow pressed tightly against her injured ribs. Below her elbow, a small stain of bright red blood was slowly spreading. Every wolf in the room could smell it, and so could I. I was afraid that one of those damaged ribs had punctured a lung. Her left leg wasn't working quite right, and she took a simple stance with most of her weight on the ball of her right foot. She stood at the very edge of the ring, which eliminated her ability to retreat but also meant Paul couldn't circle behind her.

Paul advanced slowly, carefully, a predator stalking wounded prey. But I saw him frowning at Mary Jo's ribs. He was trying to figure out how she'd hurt them.

He moved left and right, forcing her to use the injured leg, his head tilted. He must have heard the same thing I could—the faint burble of a collapsing lung. Her mouth was open as she tried to get more oxygen.

Paul struck with a powerful front kick with no trace of finesse, but power to spare. Mary Jo snapped both arms down and slowed the blow, which had been aimed at her injured leg, but it still flung her stumbling backward off the mats.

She kept her balance, barely, but the leg was obviously almost useless. A ragged sea of hands pushed her, not ungently, back into the ring where Paul was waiting for her.

"It's okay," Adam said. "It's okay. Yield, Mary Jo."

Mary Jo looked beaten, but as she entered the ring, her injured leg suddenly shot up, toes pointed like a prima ballerina's. Her kick was as simple as Paul's had been. Straight up, angling between his thighs.

He tried to block, but it was already too late. There was a muffled impact, and Paul's breath exploded outward. He backed up rapidly, bent forward with fists crossed over his groin, every muscle in his torso tensed in sudden pain. Mary Jo followed, though I could tell that it hurt, and took advantage of his dropped guard to hit him with a hammer fist to the back of the head.

A perfect nerve strike, I thought. *Good for you, Mary Jo.*

If he hadn't been a werewolf, he'd have been seeing lights and hearing bells for weeks. His eyes were wolf-pale, and his arms moved strangely as bones began to shift beneath the skin. Paul shook his head, trying to shake off the effects of the strike. If she'd been in better shape, she could have finished him.

But Mary Jo was too slow. He straightened and pulled his hands back to guard position with obvious effort. Then he came at her slowly, implacably, simply walking to close the distance. Her right fist shot toward his throat, but he blocked it with his right hand, then pushed her elbow with his left, turning her body, then smashed a knee into her injured ribs, hard. She went to the mats, facedown and coughing blood. Paul followed her to the mats, landing astride her shoulders. He grabbed one of her legs and began to bend it back, bowing her back into a tight arch. There were faint popping sounds, and Mary Jo scrabbled at the mat frantically, her control shattered and the wolf fighting for survival.

"God *damn* it," he said. "Yield. Don't make me kill you."

For some reason at that moment I looked at Henry. The bastard was watching without any emotion on his face at all.

"Yield," Adam roared. "Mary Jo. Yield."

Mary Jo hit the mat with her right hand, twice.

"She yields," Paul said, looking at Darryl.

"Paul wins," said Darryl. "Do you accept her yield?"

"Yes, yes."

"It is over," declared Darryl.

Paul jumped off of her and rolled her over. "Medic," he said, sounding frantic. "Medic."

A few heads turned to Sam. He stayed where he was, but he all but vibrated with the need to help. He closed his eyes and finally turned his back to the scene. It was Warren who pulled up Mary Jo's T-shirt, and Adam who grabbed the first-aid kit.

I grabbed Jesse, and we both stayed back. Within a few seconds I couldn't see what was happening for all the people who crowded closer.

"Got to pull the rib out of her lung," said Adam tightly. Then, "Just toss the broken bits. They'll regrow." Medicine among werewolves is, in many ways, much simpler—if more brutal—than for humans. "Hold her down, Paul. The more she struggles, the more this is going to hurt." Then in a much softer voice, Adam crooned, "Just bear with us a bit, baby. We'll get you so you can breathe better in just a second."

"I didn't hit her in the ribs," Paul said.

"Henry knocked her across the kitchen," said Auriele. "Here. Don't get that Vaseline all over. Just a little around the wound to seal the Teflon pad, but you've got to tape three sides of the pad, and *that* will work better if you aren't taping to Vaseline-covered skin."

There was a wave of relieved silence as whatever they'd managed to do seemed to work and Mary Jo could breathe again. People backed away, giving her space since she was out of immediate danger.

The dojo came equipped with a stretcher—a very basic piece of equipment, just a metal frame with canvas stretched around it and a pair of grips on each end. Alec and Auriele picked Mary Jo up on it and carried her into the house. A human would be down for a long time with a punctured lung. With a few pounds of raw meat, Mary Jo's lung would probably be fine in a few hours, if not sooner. The ribs would take longer, but she would be back to normal in a few days, a week at most. No worries about infections or secondary infections while missing pieces of rib or lung regrew.

Henry hadn't moved from his place. I noticed that he was getting looks from the rest of the pack. And when they started to move back off the mats in preparation for the final battle, there was a space around Henry—and there hadn't been before.

As a couple of wolves swabbed up the mess, Paul retreated to his corner of the mat and Adam to his.

I kept my eye on Paul. That nerve strike of Mary Jo's . . .

At first I thought he'd just shrugged it off; his walk to his end of the mats had been pretty steady. But before Mary Jo's blood was completely cleaned off the mat, Paul shook his head slowly and raised a hand to rub at his ear, avoiding the spot where he'd been struck. He blinked rapidly and seemed to be having trouble focusing.

Then Paul blew out a long, even breath and found his center. His body stilled, and his breathing became deep and regular. He stood like a statue, bare chest coated with a light sheen of sweat. There was no fat on the man, and he looked like a cross between a Calvin Klein ad and an army recruitment poster.

After the wet spots on the mats were perfunctorily dried, Darryl stepped back into the center.

"Paul, do you still want to continue with your challenge?"

He looked at Henry. "You hit Mary Jo?"

Was he still a little off balance? I couldn't tell.

"It was an accident," Henry said. "Mercy said . . ." He looked at me. "You know, something as fragile as you are should learn to keep your mouth shut, then other people wouldn't have to take the fall for you."

"People with as much to lose as you have," I said, "should control their tempers better." As an insult it lacked . . . substance. But it was more important to get a quick reply out than it was to be clever. I looked at Paul. "Mary Jo stepped between me and Henry."

"And you still let her fight?" Paul asked me incredulously. "You didn't think that might be dangerous?"

"A fight to the death is dangerous," I told him. "She knew about her ribs. I knew you didn't want to kill her."

He stared at me. Glanced at Henry. To Darryl, he said, "Yes. Let's get this over with."

Darryl gave him a half bow, stepped off the mat, and said, "Gentlemen, you may begin."

It started slowly.

With most of the expanse of the dojo between them, Paul made some fancy salute that I didn't recognize; a graceful flutter of the hands and forearms combined with a half step forward, then back. He made a breathy, hissing noise that sounded alien and predatory.

Adam placed his fists together at his chest, then lowered them slowly and silently, flowing smoothly into an open-handed guard: a more common salute, simple and direct. It looked very similar to the salute my sensei had taught me. The scabs on his hands broke as he moved his fingers.

Paul advanced, a quick series of zigzag steps that let him glide across the mat while making it virtually impossible to predict where his next step would take him. His left arm was high, almost vertical, while his right maintained a low guard, his hand positioned unconsciously near his groin.

Adam watched him, pivoting slightly to face him squarely as he crossed the mat. Had he seen what I had? That Paul was blinking as if he were trying to clear his vision.

Adam smiled just a little. For me? I decided that I'd do better to try to keep out of his head if I could figure out how—and let him concentrate on Paul.

Paul's foot flashed out in a low, scything kick to the knee, and Adam's weight shifted as he raised his foot in response. As Adam completed the block, Paul's foot stopped short, then zipped up toward Adam's right cheek in a modified roundhouse. Paul was strong enough to put some serious muscle behind the kick despite the short distance. Adam barely blocked in time, and the force of the kick made him stumble a half step. Paul danced back out of range.

Adam moved forward slowly, deliberately, a couple of bold steps, eyes on his quarry. Paul retreated, automatically giving ground to the Alpha. He caught himself and glared at Adam, who met his eyes and held them. With weres, a battle could be waged on multiple fronts.

To get away from Adam's gaze, Paul threw another roundhouse with his left foot, but he was too far away to connect effectively. Stupid waste of energy, I thought, but at least the move let him break eye contact without actually losing the contest. He was using his legs more than his arms, and I wondered if he had hurt his hands in the fight with Mary Jo. If so, it wasn't enough to matter.

Paul used the momentum from the wasted kick to spin sharply and drive his right heel in a savage back kick aimed at Adam's stomach. He might be a jerk, but Paul knew how to move, and he was blazingly fast.

Adam again managed to block the kick, but the block

only muted the force. Adam let the kick fold him over and throw him back across the mat, springing back with it. Paul came in right behind, arms rising to the high-block position he'd used on Mary Jo. Adam regained his balance just as Paul closed with him, and spun on his left foot and drove his right leg in a side kick. There was the crisp pop of fabric snapping as his leg flashed out to full extension, but it missed Paul by a handspan or more.

The kick hadn't missed; it was the start of something beautiful and dangerous. Adam's left leg hit Paul's shoulder with such force that Paul's blow went wide, flailing at empty space, as he spun in midair before crashing to the mats.

Paul hit like a pine tree falling, and the sound of his arm breaking was loud enough for everyone to hear. Adam landed on his stomach, one leg trapped under Paul's body, which was perpendicular to Adam's. Unlike Paul, Adam's landing was deliberate and controlled. Before Paul could react, Adam twisted his body and drove the shin of his free leg into Paul's chest.

In karate movies, they break celery to mimic the sound of breaking bones. Trust me, my hearing is acute, and I know these things: Paul's ribs didn't sound anything like celery. A human might have died from that blow; he certainly would have needed CPR. Werewolves are tougher than that.

Paul's hand slammed the mat.

"He yields," said Adam.

"Adam wins," announced Darryl. "Do you accept Paul's yield, Alpha?"

"I do," replied Adam.

"This fight is over," said Darryl.

Adam leaned down to Paul. "That edge you lost in your fight with Mary Jo is what allowed me to take the time to find something that would hurt you—instead of kill you. You can thank her for your life."

Paul moved his head, exposing his throat to Adam. "I will, Alpha."

Adam smiled. "I'd give you a hand up—but we'd better have Warren look at your ribs first. One punctured lung is enough."

I'd been keeping an eye on Henry throughout the fight. I glanced at him just as he stepped onto the mat.

"Alpha," he called. "I chal—"

He never got the whole word out—because I drew my foster father's SIG and shot him in the throat before he could.

For a split second everyone stared at him, as if they couldn't figure out where all that blood had come from.

"Stop the bleeding," I said. Though I made no move to do it myself. The rat could die for all I cared. "That was a lead bullet. He'll be fine." Though he wouldn't be talking— or challenging Adam—for a while. "When he's stable, put him in the holding cell, where he can't do any more harm."

Adam looked at me. "Trust you to bring a gun to a fist-fight," he said with every evidence of admiration. Then he looked at his pack. Our pack. "What she said," he told them.

12

~~~~~~

WHEN THE PACK ESCORTED ADAM IN A TRIUM-
phant procession into the house, I hung back with Jesse and
Sam—both of whom looked pretty wrung out.

Paul had left the dojo the same way Mary Jo had, on the
stretcher—and he should be resting beside her in one of
the downstairs bedrooms that were considered pack prop-
erty rather than Adam's. Any member of the pack could
and did claim one for sleeping or reading or whatever they
needed. With Adam in the house, neither Paul nor Mary
Jo would have a problem with control while they healed—
their wolves knew their Alpha was in residence to keep
them safe.

There were some awful things about being a werewolf.
Lots of them. But there were some okay parts, too—and
some that were nice. One of those was knowing that as
long as the Alpha was around, you had a safe place to be.

Henry hadn't died from the blood loss, so far as I knew,
and had probably already healed. A bullet is a small thing,

and the hole it cuts is clean if it doesn't hit anything hard on the way through—like bone. He'd be up before either Mary Jo or Paul. Of course, what happened to him after that was in question. I suppose it would be Adam's decision.

Warren hung back until everyone else except for me, Sam, and Jesse were gone. And then he shut the door.

"Adam will miss you in about five minutes," he told me. "And in six minutes you're going to need to get him upstairs and in bed without letting the whole pack know that in ten minutes that man is going to be unconscious on the floor."

"I know," I told him.

The big cowboy smiled tiredly, though, like me, all he'd done was watch the challenge. "That was a nice bit of fighting. I suspect he could have taken Paul without Mary Jo stepping in."

I nodded. "But now Paul is back in the pack again, happier than before. And I don't think that could have happened without Mary Jo."

"I hate this part," said Jesse shakily.

"The part where everyone is safe, and you want to find a quiet corner and bawl like a newborn?" Warren glanced at me. "I reckon it's better than when people aren't safe—but it's not my favorite either." He wrapped his arm around Adam's daughter's shoulder, and she snuggled into him.

"There you go," he said. "You go ahead and cry, baby. Ain't no one going to say you don't have the right. Get it over with and cry some for me—'cause if Kyle catches me crying, he's gonna think I turned into one of those sissy boys."

Jesse laughed but left her head where it was.

Warren looked at me. "You go on. You got someone else's shoulder to cry on. You tell him I got Jesse's back. And, Samuel, you stay with me, too. We don't need any more drama, and I doubt that Adam is up to showing his weakness to someone who could be his rival until the adrenaline eases a bit."

Sam stretched, yawned, and lay down.

"Thanks, Warren," I said.

He smiled and tipped the front of his imaginary cowboy hat. "Shucks, ma'am, I'm only doin' my job. Darryl's gonna feed the masses again, and I'm riding herd on the stragglers."

Jesse pulled back and wiped her eyes, a smile on her face. "Have I ever told you that you're my favorite cowboy?"

"Of course I am," he said smugly.

"You're the only cowboy she knows," I informed him.

He glanced at his watch. "You got about two minutes left."

"Mercy?" Jesse asked, catching my arm before I could go. "What about Gabriel?"

"We'll find him," Warren said, before I could respond. He smiled at me. "I have good hearing, and the house was plenty quiet enough last night to hear a phone call in the kitchen." He bent down so he could look Jesse in the eye. "Running around when we don't know anything won't help him. Zee's looking into it, and waiting for him is our best option at the moment."

"If Zee couldn't help us, he'd have told us by now," I said, looking only at Jesse. I wasn't talking to Warren; I was talking to Jesse. No oath breaking here. "We'll get Gabriel out of this."

"Maybe we'll sic Sylvia on them," said Warren.

"You heard?" Of course he had. News travels fast in the pack.

"Heard what?" Jesse was coming back online, I thought. Warren's hug had been exactly what she needed.

"Sylvia threatened to set the police on me if I darkened their doorstep again. Gabriel isn't working for me anymore." I frowned. I hadn't thought about it, but it might affect Jesse, too. "I don't know if you're considered one of the prohibited people—but since she got mad because I didn't warn her that Sam was a werewolf before Maia adopted him as her new pony, I expect that werewolves of any kind are going to be a hot button for a little while. Once we get him home, you need to talk it over with Gabriel."

She nodded. "If we get him home, I'll be happy to fight with Sylvia about my right to hang out with Gabriel."

"Good for you," said Warren.

She stepped back from him and almost fell over Sam. "Hey," she said to him. "How come you let Warren and Dad take care of Mary Jo?"

"He's not himself," I said. "It wouldn't have been a good idea."

Sam gave me a look full of guilt and turned his head away.

I thought about that guilty look all the way to the house and into the living room, where the pack was scattered all over the furniture and the floor. There were more wolves— latecomers receiving the blow-by-blow account of the fight. And I hadn't seen Adam's pack this relaxed since . . . ever. I hadn't hung out with the werewolves much until this last year—and it hadn't been a peaceful one for the pack.

Honey caught me on my way to get Adam, who was sitting on one end of the leather couch. I hadn't noticed her in the garage—and I would have because Honey doesn't go unnoticed, partly because she is very dominant and partly because she is very beautiful—so she must have been one of the latecomers.

"Mary Jo was recognized as more dominant than Alec?" she asked. She didn't sound happy, which was odd. Because her mate, Peter, was a submissive wolf, Honey was considered the lowest member of the pack except for Mary Jo, though by personality and fighting power she was actually closer to the top. Maybe the idea that they might rank her where she belonged offended her idea of what a lady should be. Maybe she worried it would cause trouble in the pack, or between her and her mate. Maybe she was afraid that she was going to get targeted in the dominance fights. Whatever it was, her trouble ranked way down in my priorities at the moment—Adam was listing to the right. In a few moments, someone else was bound to notice.

"Yes," I said, sliding by her and stepping over someone who was lying on their side on the floor. "Don't ask me what it means long-term; I don't think anyone knows. Adam?"

He looked up, and I wondered if Warren should have knocked a minute off his countdown to the crash; he looked that bad.

"You should come with me. We need to call the Marrok." Invoking the Marrok's name should make it unlikely that anyone would follow us. I ensured that by adding, "He's not going to be happy about being left out of this. The sooner he hears, the better."

There was a twinkle in Adam's eyes, though he kept the rest of his face stoic. "Better be in my bedroom, if I'm going to get chewed on. Give me a hand up, would you? Paul gave me a few good ones."

He held up one of his poor, sore hands, and I took it without wincing for the pain that closing his hand over mine must have given him. It was a show to reassure the pack he was as strong as ever. The twinkle left his eyes though his mouth turned up in a smile as he stood up easily, without pulling on my hand at all.

When we got to the moron who was sitting in the only path to the stairway, Adam caught my waist and lifted me over before stepping over the man himself.

"Scott?" Adam said as we headed upstairs.

"Yeah?"

"Unless someone shoots you, skins you, and throws the results on the floor, I don't want to see you lying in the walkway again."

"Yessir!"

When we reached the top of the stairway, his hand was heavy on my shoulder, and he leaned harder on me all the way to the bedroom.

Someone—and I was betting it was Darryl—had left three huge roast beef sandwiches, a cup of hot coffee, and a glass of ice water on the table by the side of the bed. Medea was sleeping on the pillow in the middle of the bed. She looked up at us and, when I didn't make any move to oust her, closed her eyes and went back to sleep.

"Crumbs on the sheets," muttered Adam, watching the sandwiches intently as I pushed him down on the bed.

"Bet there are clean sheets in this mausoleum some-where," I told him. "We can find them tonight and remake the bed. Presto, no more crumbs." I took half a sandwich and held it up to his face. "Eat."

He smiled and bit my finger with a playfulness I'd have thought beyond him, as beat as he was.

"Eat," I said sternly. "Food, then sleep. Rescue—" I bit my lip. Adam was a wolf. I couldn't talk to him about Gabriel, no matter how wrong that felt. "Food, then sleep. Everything else can wait."

But it was too late. He'd never let that word go by with-out a challenge. He accepted the sandwich from me, took a bite, and swallowed it. "Rescue?"

"I can't talk about it. Talk to Jesse or Darryl."

Mercy?

His voice wrapped around my head like a bracing win-ter wind, fresh and sweet to my taste. Here was a way I could communicate without speech—if I could just figure out how. I stared at him intently.

Finally, he smiled. "You can't talk about it. You prom-ised . . . someone. I got that much. I keep a notebook in my briefcase in the closet. Why don't you get that and spend some time writing a letter to me about whatever it is you can't say."

I kissed his nose. "You've been hanging out with the fae again, haven't you? Wolves are usually a little better about keeping the spirit as well as the letter of the law."

"Good thing you aren't a werewolf, then." His voice was gravelly with fatigue and smoke damage.

"You really think so?" I asked. When I was growing up, I'd wanted to be a werewolf so I could really belong to the Marrok's pack. I'd always wondered whether, if I had been a werewolf instead of a coyote, my foster father would have reconsidered his decision to follow his mate in death. But when Adam said he was glad I wasn't a werewolf, it sounded like he meant it.

"I wouldn't change a hair on your head," he told me. "Now, go get the notebook and write it all down before I die of curiosity."

"I will if you eat."

He obligingly took another bite, so I rummaged through his closet until I found the briefcase. He scooted over, making Medea protest until he scooped her into his lap so I could sit on the edge of the bed. While I sat beside him and wrote down everything I could think of, he finished all but half a sandwich ("Yours," he said. "Eat.") and fell asleep while I was still writing.

I finished. "Adam?"

He didn't move, but I noticed that his hands were looking better. His pack was behind him again—for the moment at least. Or maybe it was just the way his magic chose to work this time. People who try too hard to explain how magic works end up in funny farms.

I added "Sweet Dreams" at the bottom of the last page and left the notebook beside him. I slipped out of the bedroom and closed the door. I hadn't taken two steps before my phone rang. It was Zee.

"Get somewhere you won't be overheard," he said.

I stepped through the open door of Jesse's room—which was empty—shut the door, and turned on the music again.

Adam was sleeping like the dead; it might last five minutes or several hours. No one else would hear anything.

"Okay."

"I know you can't talk to me about the woman who took our Gabriel," Zee said. "So you'll just have to hear me out."

"I'm listening."

"I have Phin's grandmother here, and we need to talk. But no werewolves."

"Why is that?" It wasn't about the kidnapping, so I figured it was a safe thing to say without ticking off the fairy queen.

"Because she's scared to death of them, was nearly killed by them. She can't even look at one without a panic attack. And you don't want to be around this lady when she has a panic attack."

I wondered if I'd have been as sympathetic if I didn't have my own panic attacks. "Fine. Where?"

"Good question. Your house is no more," he said. "She doesn't live here, so she doesn't have a place. My house is no good. She won't go where there are so many fae."

"What about the garage?"

"In fifteen," he agreed. "Do you have anything that belongs to Gabriel?"

I opened my mouth and closed it again. How specific would the spell be? Better to play it safe. "I can't answer that question."

"Get something."

A woman's voice said, "Something that is *his*. Something he is connected to, that matters to him or that has belonged to him for a long time."

"You heard her?" Zee asked.

I didn't say anything.

"Good."

He hung up.

I didn't have anything like that. Gabriel was incredibly organized; he didn't just leave stuff lying around.

I looked around the room. Jesse would have something. It was either that or go face down Sylvia.

Thinking of Sylvia made me realize that I should have called her as soon as I found out about Gabriel. I would rather be stripped naked and walked through the mall with a pink feather boa. I would rather be boiled in oil. Rancid oil.

I could call her on the way to the garage. First I needed to find Jesse, in the hope that she had something of Gabriel's I could use.

Conveniently, Jesse walked into her room just when I was about to leave and hunt her down. "I'm looking for Samuel," she said. "He went walkabout. Ben says he ought to be fed because he didn't eat anything this morning, and for some reason Ben's pretty frantic about it. I didn't expect to find Samuel here—but I didn't expect to find you here either."

"I was just coming to find you."

She looked at me, then at her stereo. "You like *Bullet for My Valentine*?" she asked. "Just like you were sharing my Eyes Set to Kill CD with Mary Jo earlier?"

"Sarcasm isn't lost on me," I told her. "You could tone it down, and I'd still get the point. I was having a private conversation."

She gave me a tight smile. "Let me guess. Stuff I shouldn't know because I'm a girl. I'm only human. I can't be risked."

"You know how to use a gun?" I hadn't meant to ask that. I'd meant to just ask her for something of Gabriel's. But I knew what it was like to sit around while people were in trouble, and you couldn't do anything about it.

At my question, she stilled—just like her father did when something important was going on. "I have a sweet forty-cal 1911 Dad got me for my last birthday," she said. "Tell me you found Gabriel?"

And the intensity of her voice made my decision for me.

They were young—he was trying not to be serious because he was aiming for college; she was trying not to be serious because she knew he felt that way. Nothing might ever come out of it, but she cared a lot for him. That gave her a great big stake in this mess—and if she could shoot, she could protect herself.

Jesse was her father's daughter. Smart, quick-witted, and tough. And yet I already had one of my fragile humans in danger, and I was considering another.

But I couldn't talk to the fae or the werewolves about Gabriel, and writing, as my attempt to write down everything for Adam had demonstrated, was too time-consuming. I needed Jesse.

I pulled Jesse all the way into the room and shut the door. "Zee called and wants me to meet him at the garage in fifteen minutes. He has a fae who is terrified of werewolves who can help us. We need to find something that belongs to Gabriel that he's pretty attached to. I don't think she intends to hunt for him by scent, so it can be something hard like a ring instead of just things that carry smell, like a sock or shirt."

"I get to come?"

"You get to come to this meeting," I told her. "I need you. But you need to understand that I will not be exchanging Gabriel for you. I'm not going to get you hurt." I gave her the best smile I could manage because the fae scare the pants off me. "I need you. But I need you to listen to me when I send you home, too."

She watched me with her father's eyes, and I saw the moment when she decided. "Okay. Shall we tell them we're going out to get you stuff that you need because your house burned down yesterday?"

"Secret girl stuff," I said. "Remember they can tell if you lie. So when this is all done, I'm going to go get a gallon of chocolate mint chip ice cream."

"Secret girl stuff," she said. "And if they try to send

Warren with us because for some reason they think he ought to be interested in girlie things—which really makes no sense, since Kyle likes men, after all, the more manly the better—what do we do?"

"Preemptive strike," I told her. "Let's find Warren first and send him up to keep an eye on your father, who is sleeping."

And then Sam crawled out from under the bed.

———

IT WORKED. WE MADE IT ALL THE WAY OUT TO MY car with only Sam beside us. All the wolves in the house were fine with Jesse and me going out together—because we had Sam.

"You have to stay here, Sam," I said. And then stopped. Looked at him. Really looked at him.

Sam the wolf wouldn't have turned his back while everyone was trying to fix Mary Jo—and he wouldn't have looked like he felt guilty about it. Because Sam the wolf wasn't a doctor—he was a wolf. This morning, Darryl had recognized pretty quickly that Samuel was in trouble. But in the garage, not one of the wolves even looked funny at Sam. *Because it had been Samuel.*

"Welcome back," I said, trying to act like it was no big thing. I didn't know why he'd decided to take charge again—or if it was a good thing—but I figured the less drama about it, the happier Samuel would be. But . . .

"You can't come with us," I told him. "You heard Zee. We're going to see a lady who—" I stopped. "How do the fae manage this lying-without-lying stuff? It really sucks. Look, Samuel, we're going to see the lady who is scared to death of wolves. You have to stay here. You can't come as a wolf, and you don't have any clothes."

He just stood there looking at me.

"Stubborn," I said.

"We're going to be late," said Jesse. "And Darryl is looking out the window and frowning at us."

I grabbed my purse out of my car and held the back door of Adam's truck open for Samuel. "There should be jeans and sweats and stuff in a pack in the backseat if you want to dress," I told Samuel. "And when we get to the garage, you need to stay outside and leave her to us. Hopefully, we'll find out . . . what we need to find out . . . and I expect that we'll be really glad we have you with us then."

ON THE WAY TO THE GARAGE, I CALLED SYLVIA. She might insist on bringing the police into it—but I hoped I could talk her out of that. Her phone rang until the answering machine picked up.

"Sylvia, this is Mercy—I have news about Gabriel. You need to call me as soon—"

"I told you," she said, coming on the line. "My family doesn't want to talk to you. And if Gabriel chooses you over his family—"

"He's been kidnapped," I told her, before she could say something that would break her heart later. She wasn't as tough as she liked to pretend—I knew, because I pretended to be tougher than I was a lot, too.

Into the silence that followed, I said, "Apparently he walked to the garage last night and tried to take one of the cars—which he has my permanent permission to do. You'd know better than I why he'd do that and where he was going. I have a friend who is in trouble, and that trouble crashed down on Gabriel."

"Your kind of trouble, right?" she asked. "Let me guess. Werewolf trouble."

"Not werewolf trouble," I said, abruptly irritated with her assumption that all werewolves were horrible. Me, she could be mad at, but she would have to hold her tongue around me about the wolves.

"Tell Maia that her werewolf buddy is going to put his neck in the noose trying to save her big brother, who got himself kidnapped by the bad guys." Because I knew that Samuel—my Samuel who was at that very moment dressing in the backseat—would never stand by and watch a human get hurt. He was the only werewolf I knew who cared that much about mundane humans, just because they were mundane humans. Most werewolves, even the ones who liked being werewolves, actively resented, if not hated, normal people for being what they could no longer be.

Sylvia was silent. I supposed the information that Gabriel was in trouble was finally catching up to her.

"Gabriel is alive," I told her. "And we've managed to make sure his kidnappers know that his continued health is important to their goals. Police wouldn't help, Sylvia. They just don't have the tools to deal with these people. All that bringing the police into it will do is make things worse and get someone killed." Like Phin. "My werewolf friend is a little better equipped. I promise I'll let you know when I find out something more—or if you or the police can help." And I hung up.

"Wow," said Jesse. "I've never heard anyone hand Sylvia her head like that. Even Gabriel is a little afraid of her, I think." She settled back into her seat. "Good for you. Maybe it'll make her think. I mean, werewolves *are* scary, they *are* dangerous—but . . ."

"They're our scary-dangerous werewolves, and they only eat people they don't like."

She flashed a quick smile at me. "I guess that's what I meant. Maybe, when you put it that way, I can understand how she got so upset. But it seems to me that what she was saying when she made Gabriel quit working with you was that she didn't trust Gabriel's judgement. As if he were stupid and would work someplace that was dangerous."

"Someplace he might get kidnapped by a band of nasty fae?" I asked dryly, but then I went on. "As if he were her son whose diapers she'd changed. You have to forgive parents for acting like parents even though their children aren't four years old anymore. As a not-unrelated example, when your dad finds out I took you to meet a strange fae, he's going to have my hide."

She did grin then. "All you have to do is let him yell at you, then sleep with him. Men will forgive you anything for sex."

"Jessica Tamarind Hauptman, who taught you that?" I said in mock horror. Funny how she made me feel better at snapping at a mother whose son had just been kidnapped by a fairy queen . . . It sounded like "The Snow Queen" when I put it that way. I hoped that we didn't find Gabriel like poor Gerda found her Kai in the story—with a shard of ice in his heart.

ZEE'S TRUCK WAS ALREADY AT THE GARAGE when I got there. The Bug I'd loaned Sylvia was parked where she'd left it, but it was trashed. Someone had pulled the driver's-side door off its hinges, the front window was smashed, and there was blood on the seat of the car.

Samuel wasn't through changing.

"Stay here," I told him, and got out of Adam's truck.

"He's not a dog," Jesse said on the way to the shop.

"I know." I sighed. "And he's not going to listen to me anyway. Let's get this done as fast as possible."

Zee had moved the chairs around in the office, pulling them out of their usual line so that three of them were facing one another—all that was missing was a kitchen table. When he saw Jesse with me, he looked a little surprised but pulled out another chair.

"I'm the facilitator," Jesse explained. "She can talk to me instead of you."

I wasn't surprised to see that Zee's companion was the older woman from the bookstore—though I wouldn't have been surprised to see a complete stranger either. She was subtly different from the grandmotherly woman I'd met earlier. The kind of difference that made Little Red Riding Hood say, "What big teeth you have, Grandmother."

"Mercy," Zee said, "you may call this woman Alicia Brewster. Alicia, this is Mercedes Thompson and"—he paused—"Jesse."

He gave me a look. "I hope you know what you're doing," he said.

"Having her here will speed things up," I said. "When we're finished, she's going home."

"All right," he said, and sat down next to Alicia.

"You came to my grandson's store looking for him," the fae woman said to me without acknowledging the introductions. "And to return what you'd borrowed."

I looked at Jesse. "When I saw Alicia at Phin's store, I was trying to bring Phin's book back to him. He'd called Tad—Zee's son—to have him ask me to take care of it. It was odd, that phone call, and the fae who'd moved in next door to Phin was odder. By the time I got to the bookstore, I was ready to believe that there was a problem. When I saw Alicia at the counter, and she couldn't tell me anything about where Phin was or when he was coming back, I decided that I wasn't going to give her the book to return to him. I also decided that someone needed to see if they could figure out where Phin was."

"So you came back at night and looked for him at the store?"

"I thought," I said to Jesse, "that we were coming here to find out where Gabriel is and how to rescue him."

"And I choose to ask questions of you first so that I may decide how much I want to tell you," Alicia said.

That implied heavily that if I chose not to answer her questions, she'd tell us nothing. If she knew anything. I looked at Zee, who shrugged and lifted his hands an inch off his lap—he had no influence with her.

My other option was to wait for the fairy queen's call.

"All right," I told Jesse. "You already know that Sam

and I went to check out the bookstore at night to find out if something had happened to Phin. We found that his store had been trashed by a water fae and two forest fae of some sort."

"There was a glamour in the store," said Alicia. "A strong glamour that I couldn't penetrate, though I knew it was there. I was so afraid that my grandson's body was lying next to me, and I could not sense it."

"There's a cost for magic," said Zee, folding his age-spotted hands over his little potbelly. "Glamour has less than most now, but there is still a cost for sight and sound, a cost for physical dimensions. There are few fae with good noses, so less effort is spent there and more on the other senses. Magic works . . ." He glanced my way.

" 'Oddly' is what I usually say," I told him.

"Oddly on Mercedes. Some works fine, some not so well. But she has a keen nose, and that allows her to penetrate glamours. I've seen her break through a glamour set by a Gray Lord. This one we are after is no Gray Lord."

"Phin bled on that floor, Jesse," I said. "I don't have much hope that he survived his encounter. But we didn't find his body. We went down to the basement—which was also trashed—and while we were down there, one of the fae who had destroyed the store turned up on the stairs."

"That's the one who was dead in the basement," Alicia said in an odd tone. "The one someone started to eat."

"Sam's not been himself lately," I told Jesse. "The fae knocked me cold, and when I woke up, Sam had killed him and . . ."

"Sam," the fae said softly—and her hands clenched on her lap. "You have friends who are werewolves, Zee tells me. This Sam is a werewolf?"

"Sam is a werewolf and my friend," I told her. Maybe my tone was a little sharp, but I was getting tired of people attacking Samuel. "Who saved my life by killing the not-so-jolly green giant. I'm okay with it if he helped himself

to a little snack." If it squicked my thou-shalt-not-be-a-
cannibal button, that was a button my mother gave me, not the
werewolves. He hadn't violated any werewolf taboos—eating
your prey is better than leaving the bodies lying around.

Alicia didn't seem to be too upset about my snapping at
her, though.

"Samuel Cornick," she said, her eyes catching mine.
"Samuel Marrokson, Samuel Branson, Samuel Whitewolf,
Samuel Swiftfoot, Samuel Deathbringer, Samuel Avenger."
I couldn't remember what color her eyes had been in the
bookstore, but I knew it hadn't been green. Not hazel, not a
human color at all, but a brilliant grass green that darkened
to blue and brightened.

"That would be me," said Samuel, standing in the doorway. He was wearing a gray sweatshirt and had managed
to find a pair of jeans that were only a little baggy. "Hello,
Ari. It's been a few centuries." His voice was soft. "I didn't
know you had a talent for true naming."

She looked at him, and I saw the pupils of her eyes widen
past her changeable irises until her eyes were as black as a
starless night. And then her glamour went all funky.

I've seen fae drop their glamour before. Sometimes it's
cool, with colors sliding and mixing; sometimes it's like
when I shapeshift—just blink and the man in front of you
suddenly has antennae and six-inch-long hair growing
from his hands.

But this was different. It reminded me of an electri-
cal appliance shorting out, complete with quiet fizzling
noises. A patch of skin appeared on her arm that had been
covered by the sweater she wore, and on the patch of skin
was a little scar. Then there was a sound and the sweater
reappeared and there was a six-inch-by-four-inch section of skin revealed on her thigh, but most of that space
was taken up by a horrendous scar that looked deep and
stiff—a wound that healed badly enough that it probably
interfered with her ability to use her leg. After an instant it

disappeared, and three scarred areas appeared on her face, hand, and neck. Her skin tone around the scars was darker than the one she wore to hide from the world. The color was nothing outlandish, a few shades darker than mine or lighter than Darryl's, but to my eyes the texture was softer than human skin. It appeared as if the old wounds were presenting themselves to us—or rather to Samuel, because she never took her attention off him.

Jesse reached out and grabbed my knee, but her face didn't change as the fae woman slowly stood up. She began to breathe hard as she took several steps back, sliding her chair behind her until it bumped into the shelving in back of her, and she couldn't retreat anymore. Her mouth opened and she began panting, and I realized what I was seeing was a full-blown panic attack done fae-style.

Zee had said her panic attacks were dangerous.

"Ariana," Samuel said, in a voice like Medea's gentlest purr. He didn't move from the door, giving her space. "Ari. Your father is dead and so are his beasts. I promise you are safe."

"Don't move," Zee told Jesse and me in a low voice, his eyes on the fae woman. "This could go very badly. I told you not to bring any of the wolves."

"I brought myself, old man," said Samuel. "And I told Ariana that if she ever needed me, I would come. It was a promise and a threat, though I didn't mean it that way at the time."

Alicia Brewster—whom Samuel had apparently known as Ariana—hummed three notes and started to talk.

"A long time past in a land far from this one," said Alicia in a storyteller's voice, "there was a fae daughter who could work magic in silver and so she was named. In a time where fae were dying from cold iron, their magics fading as the One God's ignorant followers built their churches in our places of power, the metals loved her touch, her magic flourished, and her father grew envious."

"He was a nasty piece of work," said Samuel, his eyes on the woman's wrinkled face that sometimes wore scars on her cheek or at the corner of her eye. "Mercy would call him a real rat-bastard. He was a forest lord whose greatest magic was to command beasts. When the last of the giants—who were beasts controlled by his magic—died, it left him a forest lord with no great power, and he resented it as Ariana's power grew. When the fae lost their ability to imprint their magic on things—like your walking staff, Mercy—she could still manage it. People found out."

"A great lord of the fae came," continued Ariana. She didn't seem to be listening to Samuel, but she waited for him to quit speaking before she started. "He required that she build an abomination—an artifact that would consume the fae magic of his enemies and give it back to him. She refused, but her father accepted and sealed the bargain in blood."

She stopped talking, and after a moment Samuel picked up the story. "He beat her, and she still refused. His was a magic sort of like the fairy queen's, in that he could influence others. It might have been more useful, but he could only influence beasts."

"So he turned her into a beast." Ariana's voice echoed even though my office was full enough that a gunshot shouldn't echo, and it was eerie enough that Jesse scooted nearer to me.

Ariana wasn't looking at Samuel anymore, but I couldn't tell where she was looking instead. I don't think it was a happy place.

"In those days, the fae's magic was still strong enough that it was harder to kill them unless you had iron or steel," said Samuel.

He didn't seem worried about Ariana, but Zee was. Zee had gradually moved off his chair until he was crouched between Jesse and the scarred fae woman.

"He used his powers to torture her," Samuel said. "He

had a pair of hounds who were fae hounds. Their howls would drop a stag in its path, and their gaze could scare a man to death. He set them at her every morning for an hour, knowing that as long as he went not one moment more than an hour, she could not die—because that was part of these fear hounds' magic."

"She broke," Ariana said hoarsely. "She broke and followed his will as faithfully as his hounds. She knew nothing but his commands, and she built as he desired, forged it of silver and magic and her blood."

"You didn't break," said Samuel confidently. "You fought him every day."

Ariana's voice changed, and she snapped, "She couldn't fight him."

"You fought him," Samuel said again. "You fought, and he called his hounds until his magic failed him because he used it one time too often. I had this story from someone who was there, Ariana. You fought him and stopped, leaving the artifact incomplete."

"It is *my* story," she growled, and she turned those black eyes on Samuel. "She failed. She built it."

"Truth belongs to no one," Samuel told her. "Ariana's father visited a witch because his magic was insufficient to work his will." There was something in his voice that made me think that he knew and hated that witch. "He paid the price she demanded for a spell that combined witchcraft with his magic."

"His right hand," said Ariana.

Samuel waited for her, but she just stared at him.

"I think he wanted to call his hounds," Samuel said. "But they had strayed too far for him to influence. He got something quite different."

"Werewolves," said Ariana, then she turned her back to us, hunching her shoulders. I saw that there were scars on her back, too.

"We attacked because we had to," Samuel said gently.

"But my father was stronger than we were, and resisted. He killed her father. We stopped, but she was so badly hurt. A human would have died or been reborn as one of us. She only suffered."

"You doctored her," I said. "You helped her heal. You saved her."

Ariana crumpled—and Samuel leaped over all of us and caught her before she hit the floor. Her body was limp, her eyes closed, and the scars were hidden safely behind her glamour again.

"Did I?" Samuel asked, looking down at her with his heart in his eyes. "The scar on the top of her shoulder was one I gave her."

Hot damn, I thought, watching him. *Hot damn, Charles. I found something for Samuel to live for.*

Samuel had been upstairs with Adam when the fairy queen called to tell us what she was looking for. Silver Borne. The mention of the artifact alone was enough to make it impossible for him to yield to his wolf. But it had been when Zee had called me and Ariana spoke that he'd come back to us.

"You saved her," I told him. "And you loved her."

"She didn't know, did she?" said Jesse, sounding as caught up in the story as Ariana had been. "You doctored her up, and she fell for you—and you couldn't tell her what you were. That's really romantic, Doc."

"And tragic," said Zee sourly.

"How do you know it's tragic?" sputtered Jesse.

The old fae scowled and gestured toward Samuel. "I'm not seeing a happy-ever-after ending here, are you?"

Samuel pulled the fae woman against him. It looked odd, a young man holding a woman who could have been his grandmother indeed. But fae don't age, they fade. Her grandmotherly appearance was a glamour. The scars were real—but I saw his face and knew that he only cared about the pain they represented.

"Endings are relative," I said, and Samuel jerked his head up. "I mean, as long as no one is dead, they get the chance to rewrite their endings, don't you think? Take it from me, Samuel, a little time can heal some awfully big wounds."

"Did she look healed to you?" he said, and his eyes were the color of winter ice.

"We're all alive," said Zee dryly. "And she didn't disappear on us—which she still has the magic to do. I'd say you have a chance."

13

SAMUEL STARTED TO SAY SOMETHING TO ZEE when the woman he held opened her eyes, which were green again. She gave us all a bewildered look, as if she could not imagine how she'd gotten where she was.

I knew exactly how she felt.

As soon as he saw that she was awake, Samuel set her down with careful haste. "I'm sorry, Ari. You were falling . . . I wouldn't have touched—"

I had never in my life seen anything like it. Samuel, the son of a Welsh bard, who shared his father's gift for words, stammering like an infatuated teenager.

She grabbed Samuel's sweatshirt and looked up at him in utter astonishment. "Samuel?"

He stepped away from her, but stopped short of pulling the shirt from her grasp. "I can't give you space unless you let me go," he told her.

"Samuel?" she said, and, though it hadn't caught my notice before, I realized that her voice had changed sometime in the middle of her panic attack and sounded way too young for the late-middle-age face she wore. It was also lightly accented, some combination of British and Welsh or a related language. "I thought . . . I looked but I never could find you. You just disappeared and left me nothing. Not a shirt or a name."

He pulled away again, and this time she let him go. Free, he retreated to the damaged door that separated my office from the garage. "I'm a werewolf."

Ariana nodded and took two steps forward. "I did notice that when you killed the hounds who had come for me." There was a hint of humor in her voice. Good, I thought. Any woman I'd allow to have Samuel would have to have a sense of humor. "The fangs gave it away—or maybe the tail. You saved me again—and then you left, and all I knew was your first name."

"I scared you," he said starkly.

She gave him a half smile but clenched her hands. "Well, yes. But it seems I scared you worse because you ran away for . . . a very, very long time, Samuel."

He looked away from her gaze—the most dominant werewolf in the Tri-Cities, and he couldn't meet her gaze. Didn't he see that even if he scared her, she still wanted him?

She tried to take another step toward him and stopped. I could smell her terror, sharp and sour. She backed away from him with a little sigh.

"It is very good to see you again, Samuel," she said. "Because of you I am whole and here all these centuries after my father would have destroyed me. Instead, his body long ago fed his beasts and the trees of his forests."

Samuel bowed his head, and, to the floor, he said, "I'm glad you are well—and apologize for causing your panic attack today. I should have stayed out . . ."

"Yes. Panic attacks. They can be pretty . . ." She looked at Zee, who was back in his chair looking as relaxed as if he'd spent the last ten minutes watching a very boring soap opera. "Did I hurt anyone, Siebold?"

"No," he said, folding his arms. "Just true-named our wolf, and told Mercedes and Jesse the story of the Silver Borne."

She looked at me, then at Jesse, maybe to see how frightened we were. Whatever she saw reassured her because she gave a shy smile.

"Oh, that's good. Good." Her shoulders relaxed, and she turned her attention back to Samuel. "I don't have them often anymore. Not at all with mortal canines. It's just the fae dogs, the magic ones—black dogs and hounds—that set me off. Only when I am overcome with—" She bit her lip.

"Fear?" Samuel suggested, and she didn't answer. She also had left off werewolves, I noticed.

"I am glad to see that your magic has returned," he said. "You thought it was gone."

She took a deep breath. "Yes. And for a while I was glad of it." She looked at me. "And that has bearing on the present situation. You are Samuel's friend, Mercedes?"

"And mate of the local Alpha werewolf—Jesse's father," I told her. I could hardly tell her that Samuel was single— that was a little too obvious. I saw that it mattered to her that Samuel didn't belong to me.

"You were going to—" I was so caught up in matchmaking that I almost flubbed it then and there. I shut my mouth and grabbed Jesse's hand.

"—help us find Gabriel." Jesse completed my sentence for me.

Ariana didn't move like a human at all when she came back to where we sat, with her chair in hand; she moved like a . . . wolf, bold and graceful and strong. Without a glance at Samuel, she sat down.

"Ask her about the thing the fairy queen wants," I told Jesse.

"Zee said she wants the Silver Borne," Ariana said. "That is the object of power I built for my father—although it never quite worked as the one who commissioned it would have liked. For many years I thought I had destroyed all my magic by making it." She closed her eyes and smiled. "I lived as a human, except for my long life span. I married, had children . . ." She glanced at Samuel, who was looking over our heads and out the window. His face was composed, but I could see the pulse beating fast in his throat.

Ariana continued her story quickly. "It took me nearly a century to make the connection between my lack of magic and the Silver Borne."

She gave me a wry smile. "I know. I had no magic anymore, and the last thing I made was something that was supposed to eat magic. You'd think I'd have made the connection. But all I knew was that it wasn't finished . . . and I couldn't remember how far I'd gotten when my father called the wolves. After a while it was not as important to me—it was only a broken thing that did nothing. Someone stole it, and I thought, good riddance. I left it to them, and after a few months my magic returned. It was then that I first understood I'd succeeded, in part. It does consume fae magic—but mostly just the magic of the person who currently possesses it."

"Why would a fairy queen want it, then?" I asked, then added a belated, "Jesse?"

"It eats fae magic, Mercy," said Zee. "How easy to change a formidable opponent to someone more vulnerable than a human—at least a human knows he has no power. Dueling is still allowed among the fae."

"Or maybe she doesn't really understand what it does," suggested Ariana. "She could believe it does as it was built to do: take power from one fae and give it to another. I've heard the stories—and I do not bother to correct them. Now I have answered a question, I have one for you. Mercy, did Phin give that book to you?"

I took in a breath to answer, and Jesse clamped her hand over my mouth and jumped in. "It would work better if you ask me," she said. "Then it would be less likely that Mercy breaks her word." She dropped her hand. "Did Phin give you the book?"

"But what does the book have to do with it?"

"Glamour," said Samuel suddenly. "By all that's holy, Ari, how did you manage to do that? You disguised that thing as a book, and you gave it to your grandson?"

"He is mostly human," she answered him without looking his way. "And I told him to keep it locked away so it wouldn't eat the magic he has."

"What if he'd sold it?" I asked. "Jesse?"

"It is my blood that it was born in," Ariana said. "It finds its way back to me eventually. Jesse, please ask her. Did Phin give you the book?"

"No. I might have bought it if I could have afforded—" I stopped talking because she slumped down and put both hands over her face.

"I'm sorry, I'm sorry," Ariana said, hiccuping and wiping her face with her hands. Samuel surged toward her, then stopped where he was. She'd flinched, just a little.

"It's just been such a . . . I was so sure Phin was dead—that they'd killed him trying to get it, and it would be my fault." She wiped her eyes again. "I'm not usually like this, but Phin is . . . I adore Phin. He is so much like my son who I lost a long time ago . . . And I thought he was dead."

"Now you know he lives?" Samuel asked.

"In fire or in death," Jesse said, understanding it before any of the rest of us did. "That's what the fairy queen said. That if she killed Mercy, or if they burned it, it would reveal itself. But if it still belongs to Phin . . ."

"If they had killed him, the Silver Borne would have revealed itself to them," Ariana agreed. "They wouldn't still be looking for it."

"Why did you make it that way?" asked Jesse.

Ariana smiled at her. "I didn't. But things of power . . . evolve around the limits they are given. That's why, even though I thought it did nothing, I kept it with me. Because even unfinished, it was a thing of power."

"How did you figure out that it . . . Oh." There was comprehension in Jesse's voice.

"Right. It's a very old thing, and many of its owners have died in various ways. The fire thing came later." Her face grew contemplative. "And quite spectacularly."

"Aren't you its owner?" Jesse asked.

"Not if I want to keep my magic—I'm only its maker. That's why it's called the Silver Borne."

"*Ariana* means silver in Welsh." Samuel sat down on the floor and leaned against the end of the nearest metal shelving unit. He'd had a rough couple of days, too—but I hoped that Ariana's obvious fear of him wouldn't send him sliding back into despair.

"Jesse," I said. "Ask her how we find Gabriel."

"What did you bring me that belongs to this young man?"

Jesse handed her a white plastic bag. "It's a sweater he loaned me when I was cold."

"Phin told me that his magic was that he could sometimes feel things from objects," I said. "Things like how old an object is. Psychometry."

"Something he inherited from me." Ariana pulled the sweater out and put it against her face. "Oh dear. This won't work."

"Why not?" Samuel asked. "It is his. I can smell his scent on it from here."

"I don't work off scents," she told him, her eyes on the sweater. "I work off ties, the threads that bind us to those things that are ours." She looked at Jesse. "This sweater means far more to you, as a gift of love, than it did to him when he wore it. So I can use it to find you, but not him." She hesitated. "Does he feel the same way about you?"

Jesse blushed and shook her head. "I don't know."

"Give me your hand," said the fae woman.

Jesse reached out and Ariana held it—and smiled like a wolf scenting her prey. "Oh yes, you are a lodestone." She turned to look at Zee. "With her I can find him. He is that way." She pointed toward the back of the garage.

WE LOADED INTO ADAM'S TRUCK BECAUSE ZEE'S truck wouldn't hold us all—and Zee drove. Ariana sat in the front and Samuel sat behind Zee, as far as he could get from her in the big truck.

The sound of the big engine brought a smile to Zee's face; he appreciates modern technology more than I do.

"Adam has good taste," was all he said.

Looking for Gabriel was frustrating because it took us a while to figure out that we had to cross the river, and the roads didn't always lead where Ariana was pointing. Adam had a map in his jockey box, and Samuel used it to figure out how to work our way around to the most likely destinations.

We ended up in an empty, flat meadow up a winding dirt road (not marked on Adam's map) that might have been an hour's drive from the Tri-Cities if we'd known where we were going in the first place. There was a fence around the field we'd all had to climb over. Maybe ten years ago it might have held in livestock, but the barbwire drooped and T posts were tipped over. Near where we'd parked the car were the remnants of someone's old cabin.

Ariana, looking out of place in her cardigan and stretch-knit pants, stopped in the middle of the field between a thatch of bunchgrass and a couple of sagebrush.

"Here," she said, sounding worried.

"Here?" Jesse said incredulously.

I took advantage of our halt to start picking cheatgrass out of my socks. If I'd realized we'd be running around out there, I'd have worn boots—and a thicker jacket.

"The fairy queen has set up her Elphame," Zee observed soberly.

"That's bad?" I asked.

"Very bad," he said. "It means she is stronger than I thought—and probably she has more fae at her command than we suspected if she still has the ability to build a home."

"How could she have done that here?" asked Ariana. "She must be able to tap into Underhill to create her own land. The gates to the Secret Place have been lost to us for centuries—and Underhill never was in this land."

I looked at Zee. I couldn't help it, because I'd been to Underhill—and then sworn to silence.

"Underhill was wherever it chose to be," Zee said. "The reservation is no more than ten miles away as the crow flies. Most of the fae who live there aren't the powerful among the fae—but there are a lot of us, more than appear on the government's rolls. There is power in that kind of concentration." He was careful not to say that the reservation had reopened a path or two to Underhill.

Ariana held her hand out, palm down, and closed her eyes briefly. "You're right, Zee. There is power here that tastes of the Old Place. I had wondered why she bothered to keep Phin alive when killing him would have been the most logical path for her to take. She outsmarted herself when she took him to Elphame."

"Fairy queens follow rules," agreed Zee. "Mortals who are taken to the Elphame cannot be killed or permanently harmed—it's part of the magic of building a place apart."

Ariana gave him a little smile. "My Phin must be too human for her to kill. I wonder if she knew that when she took him to her lair? If he is human, she cannot, of her own volition, release him for a year and a day."

"Does that mean she can't kill Gabriel?" Jesse rubbed her arms to keep warm. "And that we can't get him for a year and a day either?"

"She can't kill Gabriel either." It was Samuel who answered. "That doesn't mean she won't hurt or enthrall them. Fairy prisoners can be rescued by stealth, by battle, or by bargaining."

"Bargaining? Like in the song 'The Devil Went Down to Georgia' but with a fairy?" I asked. It seemed to me that I'd heard a similar tale with fairies in it.

"Right," Samuel agreed. "It can be a contest—usually musical, because fairy queens tend to be musically talented. But there are stories of footraces or swimming contests. My father has a wonderful old song about a young man who challenged a fairy to an eating contest and won."

"How do we get in?" asked Jesse.

"The only way I know of getting into Elphame is by following the queen in," Ariana said.

"I might be able to open a way," said Zee. "I think I can manage to keep her from knowing what I've done. But I'll have to stay here and hold the door open—and I won't be able to keep it open forever. An hour at most and you have to be out. If the door closes . . . As it does in Underhill, time passes differently in Elphame. If the door closes, even if you manage to escape, there is no telling how much time will have passed when you get out."

"Okay," said Jesse.

"Oh, no," I said. "Not you, Jess. No."

"I'll be the safest person there," she told me. "I'm strictly a mortal human—they can't kill me."

"They can make you want to be dead," said Samuel.

"You need me to find Gabriel." Jesse set her chin. "I'm coming."

I looked at Ariana, who nodded. "The Elphame is entirely under the control of its maker. If we want to find your young man quickly and get him out, we'll need her to do it."

"Then let me call Adam and get the wolves." I should have stopped at Sylvia's to pick up something that Ariana could have found Gabriel with that wasn't living. I didn't

want to cause Adam's pack any more trouble than I already
had—but I wanted even more to get Gabriel and Phin out
of the fairy's hold and still keep Jesse safe.

Ariana sucked in a quick breath. "I am sorry," she said.
"Samuel is . . . I could not do it with strange werewolves.
If it were just fear, I would do it. But the panic attacks can
be dangerous to anyone around me." She looked at Zee.
"Could they find them without me, do you think?"

"No," said Zee. "If I have to stay out here, then they
will need you to keep them from being lost. Moreover, I
think that the wolves might be a mistake. Samuel is old
enough and powerful in his own right—I think he could
resist the will of one such as a fairy queen. But all of the
wolves . . . The chances are too great that she would turn
our own against us. If she turns you or Jesse, Ariana and
Sam can still get you out. If you go in with the pack, even
one wolf who turns would mean death."

"It's all right, Mercy," said Jesse. "I'm not helpless, and
I . . . Would you be able to wait out here if it were Dad in
there?"

"No."

"Are you ready?" asked Zee.

"All right," I said, painfully aware that Adam would not
be happy with me, but Jesse was right. She was probably
the safest among us. "Let's get them out of here."

"Good," said Zee—and he dropped his glamour without fanfare or drama.

One moment he was the tallish skinny old man with a
little rounded belly and age spots on his neck and hands,
and the next he was a tall, sleek warrior with skin dark as
wet bark. Sunlight tinted his hair gold. It hung in a thick
braid that flowed over one shoulder and hung lower than
his belt. The last time I'd seen him, his pointed ears had
been pierced many times, and he had worn bone earrings
in the piercings. There were no decorations at all.

His was a body that didn't belong in the jeans and plaid

flannel shirt he still wore. The clothing fit him as well in his current shape as they had in the one I was used to. I supposed that made sense because it was the Zee I knew who was the illusion and this man, and his clothes, that were real.

Zee's true face was uncanny—beautiful, proud, and cruel. I remembered the stories I'd found about the Dark Smith of Drontheim. Zee had never been the kind of fairy who cleaned houses or rescued lost children. He'd been one to avoid if you could and to treat very, very courteously if you couldn't. He'd mellowed a little with age and didn't disembowel anyone who displeased him anymore. Not that I'd seen anyway.

"Wow," said Jesse. "You are beautiful. Scary. But beautiful."

He looked at her a moment, then said, "I have heard Gabriel say the same of you, Jesse Adamstochter. It was meant as a compliment, I believe." He turned to Ariana. "You'll have to leave the glamour behind. The only glamour that works in Elphame is the queen's, and if you wait until the Elphame rips it from you, it will alert those inside that they have an intruder."

She clenched her fists and glanced at Samuel and away.

"I've seen your scars," he said. "I am a doctor and a werewolf. I saw those wounds when they were new and raw—scars do not bother me. They are the laurels of the survivor."

Like Zee, she didn't bother with theatrics. Without glamour, her skin was a warmer color than Zee's and several shades lighter. It was beautiful against silver-lavender hair that was no more than a finger-length long anywhere and floated out from her scalp more like plumage than hair—a lot like Jesse's current hairstyle. Ariana's clothes altered when her glamour dropped as well, into a simple knee-length dress of an off-white color with a handkerchief hem.

She wasn't conventionally beautiful—her face was too inhuman for that, with eyes that were too big and a nose too small for humanity. Her scars weren't as bad as they'd appeared when I'd seen them before. They looked older and less angry . . . but there were a lot of them.

"We are ready," Samuel said, looking at Ariana with a hunger that had nothing to do with his stomach.

Zee reached behind his head and drew his dagger, dark-bladed and elegant in its deadly simplicity, from beneath the collar of his shirt. Either it was magic or a sheath, I couldn't tell, and with Zee it could be either one. He used it to make a single clean cut on his forearm. For a moment, nothing happened, and then blood, dark and red, welled up. He knelt and let the blood drip into the dirt.

"Mother," he said. "Hear me, your child."

He put the hand of his uninjured arm into the soil and mixed his blood into the powdery earth. In German he whispered, *"Erde, geliebte Mutter, dein Kind ruft. Schmecke mein Blut. Erkenne deine Schöpfung, gewähre Einlass."*

Magic made my feet tingle and my nose itch—but nothing else happened. Zee stood up and counted off four paces before he sliced his other forearm.

Kneeling, he bowed his head, and this time there was power in his voice. *"Erde mein, lass mich ein."*

Blood slid over his skin and down onto the backs of his hands, which were flat on the ground. *"Gibst mir Mut!"* he shouted—and rolled his hands over, wiping the blood on the ground.

"Trinkst mein Blut. Erkenne mich." He leaned forward and put his weight on his arms. First his hands, then his arms sank into the ground until they were buried past the wounds he'd given himself. He leaned down until his mouth was nearly in the dirt, and said quietly, *"Öffne Dich."*

The ground under my feet vibrated, and a crack appeared between the place Zee sat and the place where he'd mixed his blood with the soil.

"Erde mein," he said. The ground quivered with the vibrations of his voice, which sounded darker, as if he were dragging it out of a deep cavern. *"Lass mich ein. Gibst mir Glut."* He put his forehead on the ground. *"Trinke mein Blut. Es quillt für Dich hervor. Öffne mir ein Tor!"*

There was a flash, and a large square of dirt just disappeared, leaving in its place a stone staircase that went straight down for eight steps, then began to turn upon its inner edge. I couldn't see any farther because a thick fog rose from the depths of the hole and obscured the stairway about ten feet down.

Zee jerked his hands out of the ground. There was dirt on his arms, but no wounds and no blood. He raised one hand and held it out to Ariana, giving her a stone that glowed.

"I can hold it for about an hour," Zee told us. "Ariana can use the stone to find the way back to me. If you see the light begin to flicker, it means I am at the end of my strength, and you need to get back here. So long as this door is open, the time in the Elphame will sync with the time outside. If this door closes, you might get out, but I don't know when you'll find yourselves if you do."

———————

SAMUEL LED THE WAY DOWN, FOLLOWED BY ARI-ana. I sent Jesse ahead of me and took up the rear. The light above us grew quickly dimmer until we were traveling in virtual darkness. Jesse stumbled, and I caught her before she could fall.

"Here," said Ariana. "Put your hand on my shoulder, Jesse."

"I'll put mine on yours," I told Jesse. "Samuel, can you see anything?"

"I can now," he said. "It's getting lighter ahead."

"Lighter" was a relative term, but the ten stairs we went down I could see. The stairs ended in a dirt tunnel that was lit by gems embedded in the ground that were as big around as oranges. The ceiling of the tunnel was about six inches lower than Samuel was tall, and the roof and sides were thick with tree roots.

"There aren't any trees above us," I said. "And even if there were, we've come down a long way past where I'd have thought there would be roots."

"She has a forest lord in her court," said Ariana, reaching to the side where strings of roots made a rough curtain for the dirt wall beyond. The roots moved toward her, caressing her fingers briefly before falling back where they had been.

"What kind of fae are you, Ariana?" asked Jesse. "Are you a forest lord, too? Or a gremlin like Zee, because you can work silver?"

"There are no others like Zee," she told us. "He is unique. Almost all fae can work with silver to one extent or another—silver loves fae magic. But you are right: there are iron-kissed fae in my background, and steel holds no terrors for me."

We were talking quietly, but I wasn't too worried about being discovered. There was a feeling of . . . emptiness here that told me that there was no life other than the roots that tangled in my hair and tripped my feet.

"We—" I stopped, remembering that I wasn't supposed to discuss anything about the fairy queen. Had I already broken my word? Did it matter when we were storming the castle?

"Jesse," I said, deciding to play it safe, "we haven't planned anything at all about the rescue."

"There's no planning when you're running through Elphame," said Samuel, who was walking bent over, with one hand up to ward off the roots. "It's not that kind of place. Ariana will lead us to her grandson and Gabriel, and we'll try to get out by coping with anything that happens along the way."

"That sounds . . . simple," I said.

"It could *be* simple," Ariana told me. "She cannot be expecting visitors—there just aren't very many fae who could open a back entrance into a fairy queen's lair. Thralls will not react to us—they know nothing and are not much more than automata who follow the queen's orders. We may be able to find Phin and Gabriel and leave with them before anyone realizes there is something wrong."

"Should we have brought—" Ariana's fingers touched my lips.

"Best we not talk about what that one so desires in her lair," she told me. "I expect she might hear that. And no. It is powerful, and even if it will not do as she wants, it will still do great harm in the wrong hands."

"All right," I said.

Samuel raised his head. "Best we not talk anymore at all. I'm starting to pick up the scent of people now."

I could smell them, too, once he'd pointed it out. We were coming upon more-traveled ways. The loose dirt of the floor became packed earth, and the roots thinned and were replaced with rough-cut square blocks as the dirt floor became cobbles, and the ceiling rose so Samuel could stand up straight again.

There were already other tunnels joining ours.

I caught the scent before Samuel, but I think it was only because the woman came upon us from behind, and I was walking last. It didn't matter, though, because I only had time to whirl around, and she was upon us.

She wore a torn jacket and filthy jeans and carried a large wooden cutting board in both her hands. She walked right into me and bounced off. When she tried to walk around me, I blocked her a second time.

"Take this to the kitchen," she said, without looking up at me. She shifted her weight from one foot to the other, all of her attention on the board she held. Her hair hung in ragged clumps, and there was dirt on her knuckles. Around her neck was a thin silver collar. "The kitchen, child. The kitchen. Take this to the kitchen."

I moved out of her way, and she all but sprinted past us.

"She's not taking care of her thralls," said Ariana disapprovingly.

"Thrall?" asked Jesse.

"Slave," I answered. "You know when someone is *enthralled* with a movie or a boyfriend—that's from the same root word."

"Follow her," said Ariana. "The kitchen should be at the heart of Elphame."

We jogged after her, passing by a young man in a police uniform, a woman in a jogging suit, and an older woman carrying a steaming teapot, all wearing silver collars, and all moving with unnatural intentness. The floor switched from cobbles to stone tiles, and the ceiling rose again until it was fifteen feet or more above our heads.

The gems that had lit the passage we had been in were lining the walls and dangling from the ceiling from something that could equally well have been fine silver wire or spiderwebs. Whatever it was, it didn't look strong enough to hold them. Samuel's head would hit the lower gemstones once in a while, sending them swinging.

We came into the kitchen, which could have been imported from a 1950s TV set—a very large cooking set, since there were two six-burner stoves in a room that was bigger than my now-deceased trailer. I looked around, but none of the people in the kitchen was Donna Reed or June Cleaver . . . or Gabriel Sandoval either. The glistening white appliances were rounded in a manner my eyes found odd, and the three refrigerators had silver latching handles and *Frigidaire* stenciled in silver across the top. People with silver collars were preparing food and drink—and didn't seem to notice our presence at all. The woman we'd followed here put the cutting board on the counter next to one of the sinks and began to fill the sink with water by working the hand pump that it had instead of a faucet.

"Excuse me," said Ariana, walking up to a man who was stirring something in a pot that looked like oatmeal.

"Stir the pot seventy times seven," he said.

"Where are they keeping the prisoners?" Samuel asked, putting the push into his voice that the really dominant wolves could. His voice echoed oddly in the room.

Slowly, all the action in the kitchen came to a stop. One by one, the six people wearing silver circlets around their throats turned to look at Samuel. The man Ariana had spoken to stopped moving last. He pulled his spoon out of the pot and pointed to one of the seven rounded doorways. The others, one by one, pointed the same way.

"Forty-seven steps," the oatmeal stirrer said.

"Take the right tunnel," said a man who'd been chopping turnips.

"Eighteen steps and turn," said a girl kneading bread. "The key is on the hook. The door is yellow."

"Do not let them out," said a boy who looked about thirteen and had been filling glasses with water from a pitcher.

"Resume your tasks," said Samuel, and one at a time they did so.

"I think that's the creepiest thing I've ever seen," said Jesse. "Are we just going to leave these people here?"

"We're going to get Gabriel out and Phin," said Ariana. "And then we'll take this to the Gray Lords, who have forbidden the keeping of thralls. Only the fairy queen can release her thralls, and the Gray Lords are the only ones who have a chance of making her do that. In the Elphame, she rules utterly."

"What if she's enthralled Gabriel?"

"She won't have," said Ariana positively. "She promised Mercy, and breaking her promise would have dire consequences. And my Phin is protected against such a thing."

The path we took from the kitchen was less grand than the one we'd taken into it. The floor was made of those small white octagonal tiles with a line of black tiles running about a foot from either wall. Forty-seven paces from the kitchen, the tunnel widened into a small room. The black tiles formed a complicated Celtic knot in the center of the room. There were passageways that opened across from ours, and one to either side.

We took the one to the right. Here the floor was rough wooden planks that showed the marks of being hand hewn. It creaked a little under Samuel, who was the heaviest of us.

"Eighteen," he said, and there was a yellow door with an old-fashioned key hanging off a hook—the first door we'd seen in the Elphame.

Samuel took the key from the lock and opened the door.

"Doc?" said Gabriel. "What are you doing here?"

"Gabriel." Jesse pushed past Samuel.

Key in hand, Samuel followed her in. Ariana and I brought up the rear.

Gabriel was hugging Jesse. "What are all of you doing here? Did she get you, too?"

The room was white. White stone walls, white ceiling with clear crystals hanging down to light the room. The floors were made of a single slab of polished white marble. There were two beds with white bedding.

The only color in the room came from Gabriel and the man who was lying on one of the beds. He looked dreadful, and I'd never have recognized him if Ariana hadn't whispered his name.

Phin sat up slowly, as if his ribs hurt, and Ariana rushed to kneel beside his bed on one knee.

He frowned at her. "Who?"

"Grandma Alicia," she said.

He looked startled, then he smiled. "Has anyone ever told you that you don't look like anyone's grandmother? Is it a rescue, then? Like in the old stories?"

"No," said Samuel, who had turned to face the doorway. "It's a trap."

"Welcome to my home," said a familiar dark voice. "I'm so happy you came to call."

The woman who stood in the doorway of the cell was lovely. Her hair was dark smoke, pulled back in a complicated braid composed of many small plaits. It flowed down her back and dragged the ground like an Arabian show horse's tail and set off the porcelain of her skin and the rose of her lips.

She was looking at me. "I am so glad to have you in my home, Mercedes Thompson. I was just trying to call you on my cell when—imagine my surprise—I discovered that you were here. But you did not bring it." Having a fairy queen talking about cell phones almost was enough to make me laugh. Almost.

I raised my chin. By stealth, by strength, by bargain. "I am not such a poor bargainer, fairy queen. If I had brought it, we could not play."

She smiled, and her silver-gray eyes warmed. "By all means," she said. "Let us play."

14

"BUT THIS IS NOT THE PROPER PLACE FOR BARgaining," she said. "Follow me."

Ariana picked up Phin in her arms. Samuel looked at Gabriel.

"I'm okay, Doc," he said. He glanced at Ariana, then looked at me. "Werewolf?" he mouthed.

"No," said Samuel. "That's me. Ariana is fae."

Gabriel jerked his head to Samuel. "You're . . ." And then his face cleared. "That explains a few things . . . Snowball?"

Samuel smiled. "Are you sure you don't need help?"

"Phin's the one who was really hurt," he said. "He's gotten a lot better over the past week, but he didn't start off good."

I gave Gabriel a sharp look, but I supposed it wasn't really important to tell him that he'd only been gone a day, out in the real world—if we didn't get out before Zee had to stop holding the door open, then it really wouldn't matter.

The fairy queen's voice floated through the doorway. "Are you coming?"

Ariana nodded to Samuel, who took point again out the door, following the fairy queen. Ariana went next, and I waved my hand for Gabriel and Jesse to precede me. I took a deep breath, the kind that cleared your mind and lungs before some extreme endeavor—and smelled earth and growing things in this cold marble room.

Only the fairy queen's glamour would work in her Elphame, Zee had said. I paid attention to my nose as we walked down the hall in the wake of the fairy queen.

Question, I thought, as I tried to sniff out the scents that were real from the ones produced by the queen's illusions. *If it looks like a hallway, feels like a hallway, and acts like a hallway—is it important to figure out that it isn't a hallway?*

But curiosity is very nearly my besetting sin. Gradually, as we walked, the scent of dirt, of the sap of wounded wood, and of something that might have been sorrow grew. I glanced up at the dangling lights and saw tree roots instead of silver wires, and shining rocks instead of gemstones, rocks much like the one Zee had given Ariana. I blinked, and the gems were back, but I didn't believe in them anymore, and they wavered.

I stumbled and looked down, momentarily seeing a root sticking up from a soft dirt floor, then my vision changed and the tiny white tiles, laid flat and even with nothing to trip over, were back.

"Mercy?" Jesse asked. "Are you all right?"

The queen looked back at me, and her face—though still beautiful—was different from the woman she'd been just a few minutes ago. It was elongated from chin to forehead, and her eyelashes were longer than humanly possible without glue and fake eyelashes. Narrow, clear wings, like a damselfly's, poked up from her shoulders. They were too small to lift her body off the ground without magic.

"Fine," I said.

The long silver gown the queen had been wearing was

real enough, but there were dark brown stains that might
have been old blood on the hem and near her wrists. The
necklace she wore, which had looked like a silver-and-
diamond waterfall, was of tarnished black metal, and the
set stones were uncut.

My first sight of the great hall she led us to was jaw-
dropping, if only for ostentatiousness. The floors were white
marble shot with gray and silver, and pillars of green jade
rose gracefully to support an arching ceiling that would not
have looked out of place at the Notre Dame Cathedral. Silver trees with jade leaves grew out of the marble floor and
shivered, disturbed by a wind I could not feel. When the
leaves knocked together, they chimed musically. Graceful
benches carved out of pale and dark woods, like a wooden
chess set, were placed artfully around the room, occupied
by lovely women and beautiful men, who all looked at us
when we entered the room.

At the far side of the hall there was a raised dais with a
silver throne, delicately made and decorated with gems of
green and red, each as big as my hand. Curled up next to
the chair was a cat that looked like a small cheetah until it
lifted its head, displaying huge ears. Serval, I thought, or
something that looked a lot like the medium-sized African hunting cat. But I didn't smell a cat: the whole room
smelled of rotting wood and dying things.

And then the room I was walking through wasn't a
room at all.

I didn't think there were any naturally occurring caves
in this area. There are a few man-made caves because
some of the wineries have carved their own caverns into
the basalt to age their wines. Most of our geology is igne-
ous, which allows for lava tubes, but no limestone caves
like the ones in Carlsbad. I suppose magic, if it is strong
enough, doesn't care much about geology—because we
were in a huge cave whose walls, ceiling, and floor were
not stone but earth and roots.

The Elphame was magic made, but I wondered if it was the fairy queen's magic that had created it. Ariana had looked at the tree roots in the cave Zee's entrance had brought us to, and she said that there must be a forest lord about. Looking around, I thought she was right.

The floor was woven from tree roots—I had to look sharp not to trip and draw attention to myself again. The fairy queen's throne was the only thing in the whole room that had not altered when I saw through the glamour. The pillars were thick roots hanging from the ceiling or bursting from the floor like living stalactites and stalagmites. The benches were formed of living wood, not so pretty as the queen's illusions, but more beautiful.

Most of the fae in the room were not pretty—though there were a few as long as your tastes weren't hung up on humanity as a standard for beauty. None of them looked like lords and ladies—Ariana and the fairy queen herself were the most human-appearing among them, and neither would have been able to walk into a store without everyone knowing that she was other.

I didn't waste much time looking at the court fae, though. It was the creature that lay behind the fairy queen's throne that caught my attention. It lay huge and still, like a great redwood cut down by the woodsman's axe. It had bark and evergreen needles—but it also had four eyes as big as dinner plates that glowed like ruby glass lanterns. It was bound with iron chains that glittered with magic. I didn't know what a forest lord looked like, but a giant tree with eyes seemed like a strong possibility.

Next to the throne was a middle-aged woman who had the strong features and coloring of the Mediterranean people—Greek or Italian or possibly even Turkish. She wore the collar I'd begun to associate with the fairy queen's thralls, but she was also chained to the throne. My nose told me that somewhere among the fae, the humans, and the dying forest lord, there was a witch. I could see a witch being tough enough that the fairy queen would want more than just a silver ring around her throat to ensure she was controlled.

Among those who call themselves witches, there are various types. Least troublesome are the humans who have adopted Wicca as their religion. Some of them have a spark of power, enough to enrich their faith, but not so much as to attract the attention of bigger and nastier things.

Then there are the white witches—people born to the witch families who have chosen to do no harm. Like the mundane-born witches, white witches are usually not very powerful—because witch magic gets its power from death, pain, and sacrifice, and white witches have chosen to eschew that.

Most witches of any power are black witches. They smell of it, some more than others. There are black witches who skirt the doing of actual evil. Elizaveta Arkadyevna, our pack's witch, is one of those. She is very powerful as witches—even as black witches—go. But, as I understand it, skirting evil is difficult, time-consuming, and requires a lot more from a practitioner than true black magic does. It is so much easier to use the suffering of others to make magic, and the results are more predictable.

This witch—and as we closed toward the throne, the smell got stronger and stronger, making my supposition more and more likely—this witch stank of the blackest magic. In her neighborhood, pets and small children would go missing, and even the occasional homeless man. I was betting that the iron chains binding the forest lord were hers.

The room the others saw, for all its height, was not a terribly big one. The cave I could see was bigger, but almost half of it was taken up by the forest lord behind the throne. It didn't take long for us to reach the dais.

The fairy queen sat on the edge of the seat of the silver throne and reached down to pet her witch—who didn't seem to appreciate it much. The queen's wings fluttered as she sat, then folded so she could lean against the back of the throne.

Her eyelids fluttered with a faint *wrip-wrip* sound. Once I was facing her, I could tell that her eyes were just . . . wrong. She would stare and stare, then blink rapidly. It was hard to watch.

"Jesse," she said. "Tell me your name?"

"Jessica Tamarind Hauptman," Jesse said, her voice not quite right.

"Jessica," said the queen. "Isn't that a pretty name? Come sit at my feet, Jessica." She looked at me and smiled as Jesse did as she was bid.

The queen leaned forward to pet her head—Jesse seemed to appreciate it more than the witch had. "She is half-mine already," the queen told me. "Your young man, Gabriel, and I have already done this as well. Haven't we?"

"Yes, my queen," he murmured tightly.

"I haven't collared him because of our bargain, Mercedes Thompson, but while a human is in my presence, unless I suppress my magic, they belong to me. It was not smart of you to bring me another thrall." She patted Jesse one last time, then sat back. "But that is not all you brought into my Elphame. Tell me, Mercedes, how is it that you managed to bring not only a fae, but a wolf with you when you were not to speak of this to them?"

I gave her the short version. "I taped our phone conversation."

"I see." She looked like she'd swallowed a lemon, but didn't complain. "So, Mercedes Thompson, you would cry bargain." She smiled coolly. "You want to exchange the Silver Borne for your life?"

Ariana gave me a sharp look, but I knew how to listen—and I knew about fairy bargains that left you ruing the day you made them, even before I'd read Phin's book. If I wasn't really careful, I could bargain the book for my life—and end up wishing myself dead. For instance, I could get out of here and be forced to leave Jesse and Gabriel behind.

"I don't know," I said, squirming under the weight of the fairy queen's gaze. I bit the inside of my lip until it bled—and it hurt because human-shaped teeth aren't sharp enough to cut through skin easily.

"Samuel," I said, "a kiss for courage and clear-seeing, my love?"

Samuel turned to me, startled—a kiss was probably the last thing that he'd been thinking of. I stood on my tiptoes and damn near had to climb him to get to his mouth. I clamped my open lips to his and tried to get as much blood into his mouth as I could. After the barest instant he seemed to understand what I was doing. He participated fully, licked my lip, and set me down gently.

I hoped the blood would work as it had in the bookstore, and that he saw what I did. It was hard to say from Samuel's reaction, but I thought it had. Maybe it wouldn't matter, but outside of the gun in my shoulder holster and the one in the small of Jesse's back, Samuel was our best weapon against the fae. Maybe he was better than the guns because he'd be a lot harder to stop. It couldn't hurt to have him know what he was fighting.

"Very affecting," the queen said, sounding bored. "Are you courageous and clear-sighted enough to give me the Silver Borne yet?"

"That is not a bargain," I said, trying to keep her from seeing the blood on my mouth. "It is an exchange. I would consider such an exchange only if my comrades are allowed to leave. It is having them leave here safely and soon that I'm interested in bargaining for."

"A true bargain?" she said. "Do you play an instrument?"

The piano and I have a hate-hate relationship. I didn't consider that playing, and I know my piano teacher hadn't either. "No."

"A different bargain, then. You hold something of my choosing while it changes. For each time it changes, I release one person."

She snapped her finger, and the witch muttered to herself, and the fae nearest us—a short and fine-boned creature with skin like a peach and pinkish green hair—burst into flame. It wasn't glamour because the room didn't change. They were real flames even though they didn't seem to hurt the fae.

"She can't hold flame, without dying," said Ariana. She hadn't looked at Samuel or me since I had kissed him. I don't know if she suspected something was up—or if she thought we were lovers. "And that breaks the heart of the bargain. It must be something that is possible—however unlikely—for the challenger to accomplish."

"Fine," said the queen. "If you are so particular, Silver, you may be the challenger." She laughed, and the roots in the ceiling writhed as the sound of bells echoed in the room. "Of course I knew who you were, dear Silver—how could you think otherwise? Are there so many of us who chose to live so disfigured by the fangs of hounds and wolves? No. Only Silver. So you may take this bargain, and the alternative is that I will kill this almost-mortal woman who is not so human as your Phin or the boy. Half-blood is not human enough to be saved by the guesting laws of the Elphame."

Ariana didn't seem to hear the queen's taunts. Instead, she said clearly and slowly, "I take hold of this fae, who will change—the first shape of fire counts as one. After that, for every time he changes, one of my comrades will go free. He will change five more times, three minutes each form, and if I succeed, all shall leave. If I don't, one leaves for each shape I hold."

As she was talking, Ariana set Phin down next to Gabriel. Even under the queen's thrall, Gabriel put a hand on Phin's shoulder to steady him.

"Four times," said the queen. "Five shapes. I will not let go of Mercedes Thompson, who holds the Silver Borne."

"It's all right," I told Ariana. "I'm a survivor. Ask anyone. I can deal with the queen about the book when all of you are safe."

"Six forms," said Ariana. "One for each. It is in the rules. 'The bargain requested, *all* prisoners invested in the outcome tested.'"

The poetry didn't flow well, but I suppose that it didn't need to be very good poetry to record the rules of a fairy queen.

The queen's eyes fluttered in irritation. I had a hard time not looking away—or blinking too fast myself.

"Agreed," she snarled. "But Mercedes is the last to be freed and your grandson first."

Samuel said, "Phin, Jesse, Gabriel, Ariana, me, and Mercedes, then."

"Phin, Ariana, then the rest followed at the end by Mercedes," counteroffered the queen.

I saw what she was doing. By putting Ariana and Phin at the beginning, she thought she was reducing Ariana's motivation even as the bargain became harder and harder to keep.

Samuel shook his head. "Phin, Jesse, Gabriel, Ariana, me, and Mercedes."

"I am getting bored," said the queen. "Agreed. The bargain is struck."

Ariana gave Samuel a narrow-eyed look—I think it was because he put her before him. But I agreed with him. Get the helpless ones out first, then those who could best protect themselves. That meant Ariana before Samuel.

"The bargain is accepted," agreed Ariana, and she stepped forward, embracing the flaming fae. As soon as she touched him, her hair burst into flame as did her clothing, and what was not burnable dropped to the ground, including the stone Zee had given her to hold. Its steady light was almost unnoticeable against the flames as the rest of Ariana smoldered a moment before lighting up as well.

"She holds earth, air, fire, and water," Samuel told me. If I hadn't known him as well as I did, I might have thought he was disinterested. "It is what made her able to do great magic after most of Underhill was out of reach. Magic fire will do her no harm."

The queen was speaking to the witch. After she was finished talking, the witch stood up, a steel knife in her hand. She gathered up her chains and moved to the far-thest extent, which left her just able to reach the forest lord. She plunged the knife into the treelike creature, and it bel-lowed, shook, and bled amber fluid onto the knife. The floor moved under my feet and the ceiling roots contracted and wiggled.

Samuel put a hand under my elbow to steady me—so I knew the blood had worked. He could see through the glamour to the reality of what we dealt with.

The witch licked the knife and dipped a finger into the cut she'd made in the trapped fae. She used that fin-ger to draw symbols that hung in the air where she'd put them, and glowed a sickly yellow. She pulled up her shirt to expose the skin of her belly, then she reached into the air and grabbed the symbols and slapped them onto her bare skin. When she was finished, she walked back to the throne, sat down, and finished cleaning the blade with her tongue. She caught me watching her and smiled.

Maybe she didn't know about the glamour, or maybe she thought I was afraid of cats. One thing was for sure: she knew that I was scared of her. I wished I knew what she had done.

Whatever it was, it was unlikely to be helpful to us. And we needed help. Three minutes times six is eighteen— and Zee had already been holding the entrance open for a while. Adding eighteen minutes was going to push him well beyond the hour he'd promised. The fairy queen wouldn't need Zee's opening to allow them to leave—but if it was still open, then they would walk out on the same day they'd entered.

The time was up at last, and the fae Ariana held turned to ice. Three minutes is a long time to hold on to a giant ice cube. I couldn't understand why Ariana continued to hug him close instead of holding him more loosely so not as much of her was against him. Especially as all of her clothes had burned away and she was naked, with nothing between her and the ice.

"Flesh to flesh, remember," said the fairy queen in such a grumpy tone that I knew she'd hoped Ariana would back off.

I heard some murmurs from the fae around us, remarking upon Ariana's scars. How ugly they were, how shameful. I thought they might be commenting on purpose, as some subterfuge of the fairy queen, but if so, their taunts seemed to have no effect I could see on Ariana.

Three minutes was up, and Jesse was safe—and the fae Ariana was holding turned into smoke. She seemed to have been prepared for it, though, because as the ends of him started to dissolve, she reached out and snagged the cloak of the fae who was nearest her. She wrapped the cloak around herself and the fae, then touched the cloak with her cold hand, and a layer of ice covered it, trapping the smoke in the frozen cloth.

Surreptitiously, I glanced around at the fae who were in the room with us. There had been a few in the hall when we'd gotten here, but the others had entered more purposefully afterward, as if she'd summoned them all. I counted twenty-eight, not including the forest lord, who, I suspected, couldn't be numbered among her followers.

I looked at their faces, and they seemed to be less . . . blank than the thralls, but I didn't think that they were free agents either. Maybe it was the way all twenty-eight stared hungrily at the queen, as if they were waiting for any task, any order—anything at all that they could do for their true love whom they worshipped. I've been around the fae. I've seldom seen any three of them see eye to eye on anything, let alone twenty-eight.

"Look at the scars her father gave her," said one.

"How could she live through that—it looks as though she's been mauled by beasts."

"Don't you know the story?" said a third. They all looked at Ariana, instead of the fairy queen, as the third one continued. "Her father called his beasts to torture her every morning for three years."

Ariana's mouth tightened as she remembered, too. And then that three minutes was up as well—she'd won freedom for Gabriel.

The fae under the cloak began to grow, and Ariana let the cloth fall to the ground. At first I couldn't figure out the challenge. The creature had changed into another fae, a large male with almost human features. His skin was the color and texture of a silver birch, some places smooth and white and others rough and dark gray or black. His hair looked like shredded bark and hung around his face. He wasn't ugly or horrible—but then Ariana started to shake.

Beside me, Samuel stiffened, a low growl beginning in his throat.

"Hello, daughter mine," the fae-man with bark skin said. After that, he switched to Welsh; the accent was so obscure I couldn't tell what he said. He raised his right arm—and I saw that it had no hand on the end of it—and petted her hair with it.

Ariana's father had been a forest lord, but evidently not the same kind of forest lord as the one the fairy queen held, because he looked quite a bit different.

The fairy queen had been using her people to weaken Ariana for this moment, to remind her of what had been done to her by this man. But she had underestimated Ariana if she thought Ariana was going to lose this easily. Her arms tightened on the man and pulled him next to her.

Samuel's Welsh I could understand: he wasn't talking over the phone, he was speaking slowly, and what he said was pretty simple. "He can't call his hounds, Ari, my love. Don't worry. They are dead and gone. I made sure of it. He's not real, not real. She doesn't have that kind of power. My da, he killed yours. I killed the hounds, and they are not coming back."

Patiently, he kept up the refrain, giving her something to listen to other than the fae, who evidently wore the face and form of her abusive father.

I was watching the face of the witch, and I wasn't as certain as Samuel that her father wasn't real. Witches can do some very scary things. The first three things the fae turned into—fire, ice, and smoke—those all smelled of fae magic to me. This one—other than the scent he bore, which was his own—this one reeked of black magic, witch's magic, and witches could call back the dead.

For three minutes, Ariana held the man who had been willing to torture her until she was mindless. At the end of the three minutes, she could have let go and walked out of the Elphame, leaving Samuel and me to stand prisoner. She was tougher than that. So when her father turned into a snarling werewolf that bore more than a passing resemblance to Samuel, she went to her knees so she could pull him close and stared—at Samuel. Her eyes grew black, and her face went blank, but she held on, mouthing one word over and over—Samuel's name.

Samuel went to his knees, too, his eyes white and wild.

"Not here," I told him, and it was my turn to talk. "You cannot change here, Samuel. You have to get her, Phin, and the kids out of here. You have to—she's not going to be in any shape to do anything. Hold on."

She wasn't going to be able to free me: first her father, then a werewolf, and I could take a pretty good guess at what the final shape would be because the fairy queen had no intention of letting me go.

She who had been Daphne thought I was the proper owner of the Silver Borne. She thought that when she released Gabriel, our bargain about my safety would be over. Evidently, I wasn't human enough to benefit from the guesting laws that prevented a fairy queen from killing the humans who came into her realm. She could kill me and get the book.

She'd have been right had it not been for one thing. I didn't own the Silver Borne; Phin did. When she killed me, all she'd get was a boatful of trouble—and I'd do my best to convince her of that once the others were free. All I'd have to do would be hold out until Adam came to get me.

Of course, if Ariana managed to hold on to the last shape the fae took, it would make my life a lot easier.

For three minutes, Ariana held on to the werewolf—and then it changed. The hound looked a little like a giant beagle: white with brown spots, rounded ears that hung on either side of its face, but there was no sign of the friendly expression that most beagles live and die with.

Ariana looked at the hound she held, her arms wrapped around its throat and her legs tucked almost under its body. For a moment, nothing happened, and, despite myself, I felt a great leap of hope. I didn't want to be left alone with the fairy queen, who wanted to kill me.

Then Ariana rolled away from the hound, who must have looked like one of the hounds her father had tortured her with, and curled into a fetal position, her mouth open and screaming, but the sounds locked in by terror. Samuel picked her up and crooned to her. Not saying anything, just giving her his voice. He hadn't forgotten who the enemy was, though. His eyes were on the fairy queen.

"Five," said the fairy queen, sounding moderately grumpy. "I thought I might get to keep you, werewolf, too, but she was stronger than I thought."

Samuel snarled at her.

I noticed that Zee's rock, lying on the ground under

the belly of the hound, who was focused on Ariana, was flickering.

"Samuel," I told him urgently. "Zee will be waiting. Get the kids and *Phin*, too—" Especially Phin. Any fae willing to use a black witch and allow her to torture another being was not someone I wanted to give more power to. We needed to get Phin out of here and safe so the Silver Borne was out of her reach. "Take them and get out of here."

"Can't you help me up?" Phin asked Gabriel. He knew what we needed.

There was a momentary pause, but when the queen didn't interfere with Phin's request, Gabriel helped him to his feet.

"You," said the queen, pointing to the fae nearest to her. "You take them to Outside and let them leave. You'll have to carry the human man." She looked at Jesse, then glanced at Gabriel. "Go, children, and when you are outside my Elphame, be thou as thou wert."

The fae she'd pointed to bowed deeply and picked Phin up with the same ease that Ariana had displayed. Not all fae are so strong. Silently, Jesse and Gabriel followed him when he started out the door.

Samuel stopped and kissed my cheek, still holding Ariana, who was shivering in terror. "Stay alive," he told me.

"Planning on it," I said. I gave Ariana, who was very deep into a panic attack, a wary look. I remembered her concern when she'd returned to herself last time, and so I added, "You stay alive, too. Now get out while the getting is good."

"*Semper Fi*," he said, glancing down at Zee's rock. Then he hurried after the others.

So far as I knew, Samuel had never been a marine. But he'd known I'd catch the reference. The marines never leave a man behind. He'd be back, and so would Adam. All I had to do was survive.

We all waited until the fae who had escorted them out

returned. He bowed to the queen, and said, "They are Outside, safe and alive, my queen."

I took a deep breath, and a few seconds later Zee's stone was just another gray rock among the roots in the floor of the cave. They'd made it with almost two minutes to spare by my rough count—though probably Zee had held the opening until he saw them.

"My bargain is done," the queen told me.

"Fine," I said.

"You will exchange the book for your life."

"Nope." I shook my head. "I've considered it—and decided that it is not going to happen."

There were no humans to protect anymore. Just me. Worry over what the witch might do if I freed her made me hesitate before I pulled my gun—and it was one hesitation too many. I reached under my T-shirt, and two of the queen's people grabbed my arms. The gun fell on the ground, and the fairy queen kicked it aside—well out of the witch's reach.

"You misunderstand," she told me. "I will take your life, and you will give me the book with your death."

"I thought I had to own the book before that worked," I said in a puzzled voice.

The fairy queen stared at me. "Did you give the book to someone before you came down here?"

"Not the way you mean it," I answered.

"How would you mean it?" she said softly.

"Why would I answer that?" I asked. The fairy queen gave a sharp nod, and the witch reached out and touched me.

I CAME BACK TO MYSELF LYING ON THE BED where Phin had been. At least it smelled like Phin, but the room was made of roots and dirt rather than marble. I was confused for a moment, but then I woke more fully and

realized that I'd never seen it without the glamour—just
smelled it.

My whole body hurt, though I had no additional bruises.
I'd held out as long as I could, to give Samuel and Adam
time to make everyone safe. I didn't know if it was long
enough. I'd expected to be dead when it was over. But I
could work with unexpected results—even if it involved
using a chamber pot. That had to be what the white porcelain vessel under the other bed was. The fairy queen had
a kitchen with fridges and everything, and didn't have a
bathroom? I considered it a minute and decided that maybe
she just didn't have a bathroom for prisoners.

After a very long time that was probably no more than
an hour after I woke up, the door opened, and the queen
walked in with two female attendants and two male.

The first man was the fae who had seen Samuel and the
rest out. He was tall, taller than Samuel, with seafoam eyes.
For the first time, I realized he was the water fae who'd
broken into the bookstore. The second man was short by
human standards but not oddly so. His skin was green and
rippled like the waves of an ocean at sea. Like the fairy
queen, he had wings on his back, though his were grayish
and leathery and less insectlike.

One of the women was carrying a chair. She was nearly
human in appearance except that her eyes were orange and
her skin pale, pale blue. The second woman was covered,
head to toe, with sleek brown hair about two inches long,
and her arms were a third again as long as they should have
been. She was carrying a narrow silver ring just big enough
to fit around my neck.

At the sight of the silver ring, I tried to run. The tall man
caught me and sat me in the chair while the woman who'd
carried it in tied me into it: wrists, elbows, and ankles.

Then they put the silver collar around my neck.

Once she has them in thrall, only she can release them.

"It took me too long to find your secrets, Mercedes,"

she said. "Phin was the owner, but Ariana has him safely guarded in the reservation, where none of mine can get him. You gave it to your friend, but he has given it over to the werewolves, and we cannot go there either."

How long had I been out, and what had I told her? I didn't remember all of it, and that worried me.

The fairy queen was wearing a different dress than she had been. This one was blue and gold. Did that mean it was a different day? Or just that she'd gotten things on her dress and had to change?

"They have left me only vengeance for now." Her eyes gave that weird flutter. "Eventually, they will not guard the Silver Borne as diligently, and I will have it. Until then, I'll take what I can get. I hope you enjoy your victory.

"Mercedes Athena Thompson," she said, putting a hand on my forehead. *Look at me.*

The "Look at me" part was inside my head. It reminded me of the way Mary Jo's voice had entered my head in the bowling alley. Maybe without that experience, the queen's voice wouldn't have seemed so clearly foreign.

You want to serve me. Nothing else matters.

Adam mattered.

If I didn't make it out of here alive, he'd think it was his fault. That if he'd been in better shape, I'd have brought him with me, and he'd have saved the day. He'd take responsibility for the world if someone (like me) wasn't around to shake him up. So I had to survive—because Adam mattered to me.

The fairy queen had continued to talk in my head, but I wasn't paying attention to what she said.

"Whom do you serve?" she asked aloud, pulling her hand away from my head. Not as though she were interested in the answer.

" 'Choose this day whom you will serve,' " I murmured. " 'But as for me and my house, we will serve the Lord.' " It seemed appropriate to quote Joshua at her.

"What?" she asked, startled.

"What were you expecting me to answer?" I asked, feeling a little let down. Some of the very old fae react poorly to scripture, but this one didn't seem to mind—not the scriptures anyway.

"Bring her to the hall," she said, her eyelashes beating her cheekbones with the force of her temper.

The men picked me up, chair and all, and hauled me back to the hall. I had only vague memories of what had happened to me there at the hands of the witch—my mother once told me that childbirth was like that. All that pain, then nothing. But if my mind had blocked out the worst of it, my body seemed to make up for it. As we got closer and closer, my stomach clenched, and I broke out in a sweat. By the time we made it into the hall, I wouldn't have been surprised if the men carrying me could smell my fear.

They brought me right up to the throne before setting me down.

"What did you do?" the queen hissed at the witch, who shrank back from her. "What did you do that she resists me?"

"Nothing, my queen," the witch said. "Nothing that would allow her to resist you. She is only half-human. Perhaps that is the problem."

The queen released her and stormed back to me. She took a silver knife out of her belt and cut my arm right over the bite Samuel had given me. The bite marks were still fresh-looking, so I hadn't lost a lot of time.

She rubbed her fingers in my blood and put them in her mouth. Then she cut herself and dribbled three drops into the open wound on my arm.

She was going to use old magic to bind us together. This was the stuff the wolves got out to make someone pack.

I had a sudden panicky thought. If she got me, could she get to the pack through me? Zee had been worried about her enthralling the wolves.

"My blood to yours," she said, and it was too late to do

anything about what she was doing. "My silver, my magic, our blood makes you mine." Because it was done.

A fog rolled over my head.

I struggled and struggled, but there was nothing to struggle against; it was only fog that seemed to cover everything and muffle my thoughts.

15

AFTER STRUGGLING AND STRUGGLING, I FOUND myself alone, standing on a great barren field of snow. The cold was so great that it froze my nose when I breathed in, but, although I was naked, I wasn't uncomfortable.

"Mercedes," Bran's voice was breathless. "Here you are! Finally."

I turned all around and couldn't see him.

"Mercedes," he told me, "I can talk to you because you are part of Adam's pack and his pack is mine, too. But you need to listen because I can't hear you. All I can do is show you what I think you need."

"All right," I told him. It felt lonely knowing he couldn't hear me. Lonely because it wasn't Adam who'd found me there in the snow. I shivered though I still wasn't feeling the cold.

"The biggest weapon in the arsenal of a fairy queen is enthrallment. As a member of a pack, you should be all but immune to that. But yours is a special case, and I am told that no one thought to teach you how the pack magic should work for you. Apparently my son and Adam, who should know better, assumed that it would all be instinctive because that's how it works for a wolf. When Adam found that it was not the case, he chose to wait so he could find out who had been messing with you—instead of making you safe."

"There were complications," I told him sharply. I didn't like to hear him being critical of Adam. I'd known what he was doing and approved of the way his mind worked.

A pause followed, and I had the distinct impression of surprise.

"I'm sorry for offending you," he said slowly. "That I know you are offended is . . . interesting." I got the impression of a shrug, and he continued with his message. "You should know that thrall magic is not so different from the pack bonds, Mercedes. The pack bonds are not built to subdue individuality to the Alpha or enforce behavior of any kind. A pack needs all its differences, and we find strength in that: a lot more strength than *one stupid fairy queen who is stealing magic and using a witch. You understand me?*" His fury shook my whole being, he was so angry.

He wasn't angry with me, though, so it wasn't my concern.

"I understand," I told him, even though he couldn't hear me. Or mostly couldn't hear me.

"I'm going to show you something," he said. And suddenly in the white snow there was a silver garland. "This is one of your pack bonds," he told me. I couldn't see him, but I could feel him walking beside me as we followed the garland. We stopped by the end, and there was a rock tied . . . enveloped in a soft cage of silver. The rock glowed a warm yellow that was very welcome in this cold place.

"Christmas garlands and a rock?" he said, a smile in his voice. "Why not an ornament?"

"Wolves aren't fragile," I told him. "And they're . . . stubborn and hard to move."

"I guess that imagery works as well as anything," he

allowed. "Do you know who this is? Can you feel how worried she is for you?"

"Mary Jo," I said. And once he'd pointed it out to me, I could feel it, too. Could feel that she was looking for me, running on four feet to use her nose to its best advantage. She wasn't hot on the trail—and I had the impression of miles traveled and miles to go stretching out both ways in weary infinity.

"It is not usually so clear," Bran said, pulling me out of Mary Jo. "Partially it is because I am with you—and I am the Marrok. Another part is that the fairy has locked you into your own head—I can tell that by the quality of my contact with you. That she has done this is *an unforgivable offense*"—once more I felt him try to contain his anger—"but that will give you strength here you would not otherwise have had." He paused. "The connection between you and me is stronger than it should be, too. I'm not getting words back, but there is something . . . No use getting distracted with the why of that now. We have other tasks."

He took me to another silver garland and had me tell him whom it belonged to. After the third, I could find the strands myself without his guidance. The fourth was Paul's. He was running with Mary Jo—and just as anxious to find me. He still didn't like Warren, though. I could see that his garland and Mary Jo's were intertwined and connected to all the other garlands, too. One by one we walked by the rocks that were the wolves in the pack.

Bran held me at Darryl's, when I would have hurried on because I wanted to find Adam.

"No," he said. "I want you to look here for a bit. Can you find Darryl's connection to Auriele? It's different from the pack bonds."

I looked and looked. I found Auriele's rock nearby, but I couldn't see anything. Finally, in desperation, I picked up Darryl's rock and saw that it moved Auriele's, too—as if they were tied together . . . and then I couldn't understand how I'd missed the blazing gold rope between them, it was so obvious. Maybe I'd been looking too hard for a silver garland and instead their bond was very different—softer, stronger, and deeper. Unlike the pack bond, it wasn't tied onto the rocks; it originated in one and ended in the other.

Bran took me by the elbow. "Okay, quit playing with them. You're making Darryl unhappy. I have another one to show you."

He led me to the center of all the strands of silver.

All but buried in the pack magic was a very, very black rock. It radiated anger and fear and sorrow so strongly it was hard to go near it.

"Don't be frightened," Bran said, and there was a rough affection in his voice. "Adam has been frightening quite enough people lately. Look and tell me what you see."

This was Adam? I ran up to the rock and put both hands on it. "He's hurt," I said, then corrected myself. "He's hurting."

"Where is your mate bond?"

It lay in the snow, a fragile and worn thing. There were a lot of places where it had been roughly knotted, just to keep it together.

"Hastily made in need, which isn't necessarily a bad thing," the Marrok said, "but that was compounded by rough handling by a bunch of idiots. Most of whom should have known better."

I could see that around the knotted places, the rope was worn, as if a dog . . . or a wolf had chewed on it until someone had tied it to keep it from breaking.

"Henry isn't in the pack anymore," said Bran. "Just in case you hadn't noticed. I've brought him to my pack for a little one-on-one. In a few months, I might let him go out on his own again. Most of that mess is his doing."

But I wasn't worried about the chewed sections anymore.

"It's broken," I said, kneeling in the deep snow. In front of me the rope came to an abrupt ending, as if sliced by a

sharp knife. I'd thought that the reason I hadn't been able to
feel Adam was still the overload from when he'd thought I
was dead. Though it had been recovering from that, hadn't
it? When had I lost the connection?

It hurt to know that it was broken.

"Now, that," Bran growled, *"was cut by black magic."*

His voice was so strong in my right ear that I turned—
and got a glimpse of something huge and awful that didn't
look anything at all like Bran in any form I'd ever seen.

"I couldn't see how it would be possible until Samuel
told me there was a witch involved. Between the witch and
the queen, they found a weakness and broke it," he told me.
And then, in a curiously amused tone, he said, "And I don't
scare you a bit, do I?"

"Why would I be afraid of you?" I asked—but my focus
was on the broken rope. Would I hurt Adam if I touched it?

"Go ahead," said Bran. "He would give anything for
you to touch it again."

"Mine," I said. "Mine."

But I still didn't touch it.

With that superior humor he occasionally used, which
made me want to hit him every time, Bran said, "I'm sure
he can find someone else who wants it."

I grabbed it with both hands—and not because I was
worried there would be someone else, no matter what Bran
thought. But because we belonged together, Adam bound
to me, me to him. I loved it when he let me make him
laugh—he was a serious man by nature and weighed down
by the responsibility he held. I knew he would never leave
me, never let me down—because the man had never abandoned anything in his long life. If I hadn't taken the gold
rope of our bond, I knew Adam would have sat on me and
hog-tied me with it. I liked that. A lot.

"Mercy!" This voice wasn't Bran's. This voice was demanding and half-crazed. A short pause, then much more

controlled, Adam said, "About damned time. Found you. Mercy, we're coming to get you. Just sit tight."

I wrapped his voice around me and held on tighter to the rope between us until it settled into my bones, and I didn't have to hold on anymore. "Adam," I said, happily. And then added, because he'd know I was teasing, "Took you long enough. You were waiting for me to get myself out?"

I looked around my field of snow, by then littered with cheery garland and glowing rocks. I closed my eyes and wrapped the feel of pack around me like a warm cloak. I felt the fairy queen's magic touch the golden rope I shared with Adam—and this time it was the queen's magic that shattered.

MY GAZE WAS LOCKED WITH THAT OF THE trapped forest lord. He blinked, and I jerked my eyes down—and saw that my arm was still dripping blood. From the amount I'd lost, I hadn't been out of it for more than a few seconds.

"There," said the fairy queen. "Now you are mine."

I blinked at her and tried to mold my features into the stupid expression I'd seen on the other thralls as she cut the ropes that held me to the chair.

"Go to the kitchens and get something to wipe the blood off the floor," she told me.

I stood up and started walking. She quit paying attention to me, because I wasn't interesting anymore. I started walking a little faster because I saw my gun on the floor by one of the benches, where someone must have kicked it. I suppose that made sense. There weren't many fae who could have picked it up without hurting themselves. None of the thralls would dream of using it—but I could see that the fae might hesitate to have a thrall dispose of it.

I picked it up and turned around. Slowly, so as not to

attract the attention of the fae in the room—who were all looking at the fairy queen and not at her new thrall. The queen was leaning over the arm of her throne, talking to her witch. I shot the queen three times in the heart. The witch was watching me and smiled as I pulled the trigger.

"Huh," said a voice right next to me. I turned my head and had to look down at a human-seeming child who appeared to be no more than eight or nine years old.

She smiled at me. "And they were afraid something would happen to you if we waited until everyone could come to the party. Just like a coyote to spoil the fun for everyone."

The last time I'd seen this fae, she'd been playing with a yo-yo in the front yard of a murder scene she was guarding. I didn't know her name, just that she was plenty powerful, people were scared of her, and she was a lot older than she looked.

For an instant I almost saw something completely different standing beside me, then she smiled at me, and said, "Not my glamour you don't, Mercedes."

The other fae in the room didn't move, frozen in the moment of the fairy queen's death.

Yo-yo Girl walked forward to the dead queen, and I followed her. The witch had grabbed the body and was taking handfuls of the queen's blood and painting it over the silver thrall necklace around her neck.

"I don't think so," said Yo-yo Girl. She bent and touched the remains, and said something that might have been a word. The queen's body turned to dust.

Yo-yo Girl started to back away—and then saw the forest lord in his chains beyond the throne. Somehow I don't think that she'd seen him before reducing the queen to so many ashes.

The silver ring popped off the witch's neck—only to be replaced by small fingers. I heard only the echo of a whisper, then the witch was dust, too. Yo-yo Girl took a handful of the resultant gray mass, lifted it to her mouth, and licked it like an ice-cream cone.

"Yum," she said to me. Her hands, her clothes, and her mouth were covered with ashes. "I love witches."

"I'll take chocolate, if it is all the same to you," I told her.

"*Mercy!*" roared Adam from somewhere beyond the hall.

"Uh-oh," said Yo-yo Girl. "Someone missed out on all the killing."

"Here!" I called. "We're okay."

And then it was true. Because Adam was there and he had his arms around me and that made everything all right.

———————

I KICKED THE SNOW AND STUBBED MY TOE ON the kitchen sink. It was the night of the big rescue, and everyone was partying over at Adam's house. I'd been hugged and fussed over until I decided that it was a good time to go check out the remains of my home.

The snow hid a lot, and the pack had cleaned it up. They'd had the whole month that I'd been missing to do it. I suppose I was lucky it hadn't been a year or a century.

They hadn't been able to find the Elphame after Zee had been forced to let his door close. Apparently, as Zee explained it to me, the Elphame moved in relation to the reservation, and Ariana hadn't been able to find me.

It was only when the bond between Adam and me reconnected that they were able to locate the Elphame. While Zee worked to make another entrance, they'd sent Yo-yo Girl ahead to make sure I was safe. She apparently didn't need anything as crude as an entrance to find her way to the Elphame. She probably had a name besides Yo-yo Girl, but the fae are funny about names, and no one wanted to give her a real one.

The fae who had belonged to the fairy queen were being

housed in the reservation temporarily. Some of them had
no memory of how they'd come to follow the fairy queen.
Some of them were angry that I'd killed her, but not so
angry they'd made any move against me. Zee said that the
Gray Lords were torn between anger at the way the fairy
queen had used a forest lord and a black witch, and triumph
at the proof that Underhill was returning some power to all
of the fae.

There wasn't much left of my trailer except for a small
pile of things that might be reused. I hadn't lost the pole barn
with my Vanagon inside. I hadn't lost Medea or Samuel.

The first time I'd seen the place, there had been a coyote
hiding under the porch, and I'd taken it as an omen. When
I'd finally bought it, I'd felt like I had a home for the first
time in my life. A home no one could take away from me.

"Saying good-bye?"

I hadn't heard the Marrok, but Bran was like that.

"Yeah." I smiled at him so he'd know I didn't mind his
presence.

"I meant to thank you for Samuel," Bran said.

I shook my head. "It wasn't me. It was Ariana—have
you seen them together? Aren't they cute?" Ariana wasn't
at Adam's house, though Samuel was. She wasn't quite up
to bearing a pack of werewolves celebrating madly. Samuel
had talked about her for twenty minutes, though.

Ariana hadn't managed to touch Samuel when he was a
wolf—yet—Samuel had told me. But she didn't have any trouble with Samuel the man, and she didn't have panic attacks
around any of the werewolves—as long as they were calm
and approached her one at a time in human form. She'd just
needed a reason to work on her phobias, he'd explained with
great pride. Bran had smiled when Samuel said that, the
smile that said the Marrok had been up to something. So he
might have had something to do with her finding her way
among the wolves. Or maybe he just wanted me to think

that. I've found that I do better when I don't worry too hard about what Bran can and can't do.

"Ariana is a gift," said Bran. "But if it hadn't been for what you did, Samuel wouldn't have been around to receive it."

"That's what friends are for," I told him. "Lift you when you're down—and kick you in the rump when you need it. Adam helped. Speaking of friends, thank you for the Pack Magic 101 that kept me from being Zombie Mercy."

He smiled, an expression that made him look about sixteen. If you didn't know him, it would be hard to believe that this young man with the diffident expression was the Marrok.

"Did you get all of that?" he asked. "I wasn't sure how much made it through."

I looked at his innocent expression. "How much did you get back?"

He gave me wide eyes, then grinned. "I think that we both were getting a bit of a boost from an interested party."

"Who?"

"Zee had no trouble freeing the forest lord from his chains. He's a charming fellow, by the way, very gracious as well as powerful. She kidnapped him from his own place in Northern California about a year, year and a half ago. His wife and family were very glad to hear that he'll be coming home soon. Daphne, the fairy queen, apparently visited the reservation and decided this would be a good place to roost. She enthralled a nasty witch and used her to grab the forest lord— because she didn't have enough power to enthrall *him*."

"You think he helped us?"

"Someone did. I'd just about given up." He looked around at the remnants of my home. "I have a more probable answer, but I'm having a little trouble wrapping my head around it. Have you decided what you are going to do with this yet?"

"It was insured," I told him. "I might as well replace it." Gabriel might need to live somewhere.

He and Zee had kept the shop going for the month I'd been missing. His mother wasn't happy with his doing that, so he was living at Adam's house. In the basement—as far from Jesse's bedroom as Adam could manage.

"Look," said Bran. "Your oak tree didn't burn down."

"Yeah," I said, pleased. "Scorched a bit, but I think it'll be okay." I took a step toward it, and my foot caught something and moved it. I thought at first it was a broom handle, but when I bent down to retrieve it, it turned out to be my old friend the walking stick.

"Ah," said Bran. "I wondered where that had gotten off to."

I gave it a thoughtful look. "You've seen it?"

"It was sitting on the couch in Adam's basement," he said. "When I picked it up—suddenly all my efforts bore fruit at last, and I found you among the pack bonds as if you had never been missing."

I gave him a wry smile. "It does seem to show up at interesting moments."

"So," he said, "have you given any thought to raising sheep?"

"Not at the present time," I replied dryly. "No."

We walked a little more in companionable silence.

"I have some photos," Bran said abruptly. "Of Bryan and Evelyn." My werewolf foster family. "Some of your old school pictures, too, if you want them."

"I'd like that," I said.

He looked back toward Adam's house, and I saw that someone else was headed over.

"Looks like you've been missed. I'll leave you alone." He kissed my forehead and jogged off.

He met Adam at the barbed-wire fence, and Adam said something I couldn't quite hear that made Bran laugh.

"Hey," I said, as Adam approached me. His response was a blast of warmth that had me blushing.

"Do you have keys to your van?" he asked, his voice a

dark caress that gave me goose bumps. He smelled of need and impatience.

"They're in the van."

"Good," he said, taking my arm and walking briskly toward the pole barn that had survived the fire without a scorch mark. "If I had to go get my truck, someone might notice us leaving. I have keys to Warren's apartment. He said the guest room has clean sheets."

He stopped at the van. "I need to drive."

Normally, I'd have argued with him just on general principle, but sometimes, especially with Adam so intense that he was ready to explode, it was just better to give Alpha males their way. Without a word, I headed toward the passenger side of the van.

He didn't speed and he didn't talk. We made it to Richland without hitting a red light, but there our luck ran out.

"Adam," I said gently, "if you break my steering wheel, we'll have to walk the rest of the way to Warren's house."

He loosened his hands but didn't look at me. I put a hand on his thigh, and it vibrated under my palm.

"*If* you want to make it to Warren's," he said, his voice almost guttural, "you'll have to keep your hands to yourself."

There is something incredibly arousing about being *wanted*. I pulled my hand back and sucked in a deep breath. "Adam," I said.

The light turned green at last. I had the whimsical thought that my time in Elphame had completely skewed my internal clock, because I could have sworn we were there for hours instead of seconds.

Warren lived in an A house, one of a group of "Alphabet Houses" built during World War II to accommodate the exploding population of nuclear-industry workers in Richland. The one he lived in was still a duplex. Both sides were dark—and the other duplex had a FOR RENT sign on the window.

Adam parked the van and slid out without looking at

me. He closed the door with exquisite gentleness that said a lot about his state of mind. I got out and didn't even bother to worry about whether my prized Vanagon Syncro was locked—which I suppose said equally as much about *my* state of mind.

Adam unlocked the door of Warren's apartment and held it open for me. As soon as we were both inside, he closed the door and locked it.

When he turned to face me, his eyes were bright gold and his cheeks were flushed. "If you don't want this," he told me, as he had since the . . . incident with Tim, "you can say no."

"Race you to the bedroom," I said, and started for the stairs.

He caught my arm in a very careful grip before I took more than two steps. "Running . . . would not be a good idea right now." He was ashamed of his lack of control; maybe someone else would have missed it in his voice. Maybe I would have, too, if it weren't for the bond between us.

I put my hand over his and patted it. "Okay," I said. "Why don't you take me to bed?"

I hadn't been ready for him to grab me and pick me up that fast or I wouldn't have squeaked.

He froze.

"Sorry," I said. "I'm fine."

He took me at my word and carried me to the stairs. I halfway expected him to run, but instead his pace was deliberate, his step almost heavy. The stairs were narrow and steep, and he was careful not to bang my head or feet.

He set me down just inside the guest bedroom and closed the door. He stood there, his back to me, breathing heavily.

"A month," he said. "And neither Zee nor any of the fae we knew could tell us if we'd ever get you back. Samuel's woman couldn't find you—everything you had burned up in the fire. Neither the van nor the Rabbit worked as a close enough tie. She tried to approach me to see if she could use me, but she couldn't even walk into the same room as me—not half-crazed as I was. Touching me was out of the question. I thought I had lost you."

I remembered feeling Mary Jo and Paul hunting me. "You looked for me."

"We did," he agreed. Abruptly he turned and hauled me against him. He was shaking, and he hid his face in my hair. It was useless, if he was trying to prevent me from understanding what he was feeling. I had a Technicolor view through our bond.

I hugged him as hard as I could so he'd know I was real, that I didn't mind him holding me hard. "I'm here," I said.

"I couldn't find you either," he told me, his voice a bare whisper. "Our bond was broken, and I couldn't tell if you'd done it on purpose, if the queen had managed it—or if you were dead. We could feel you in the pack bonds, but that's been known to happen when people die. Bran came and he couldn't find you either. Then yesterday, Darryl was feeding us lunch and dropped the pan on the floor."

I'd heard about that already, from various people, but I didn't interrupt.

"Darryl thought someone was messing with Auriele, and stormed halfway up the stairs—only to be met by Auriele, who was worried about him for the same reason. That's when Bran came up from the basement and said . . ." He stopped speaking.

"He said, 'I've done the hard part, Alpha. Now tell us where your mate is,'" I said. "And he was holding the walking stick in his hand."

"And there you were," Adam told me. "Inside of me, just where you belonged."

He drew back, moving his hands to my cheeks. The heat of his skin felt precious to me, his hot amber eyes feeding the fires in my heart—and my body.

His nostrils flared, like a stallion scenting a mare. His hands dropped to my coat, and he ripped it down the back and threw it on the floor before backing away from me.

"Damn it," he said gruffly, his head against the door.
"Damn it . . . I can't do this."

I pulled my shirt over my head and stripped off my
jeans and underwear. Warren didn't keep his house at seventy degrees—since he was mostly sleeping at Kyle's these
days. But I didn't feel the cold, not while I could feel the
force of Adam's need roaring like a welding torch.

"What can't you do?" I asked gently, pulling back the
bedding and lying down on the sheets.

"I can't be gentle. I know . . . I know you need care, and
I can't do that right now." He pulled open the door. "I've
got to go. I'll send—"

"If you leave me naked and waiting on the bed without
making love to me, I'll—"

I didn't get to finish the threat. I think it was the word
"naked," though maybe it was "bed," but before I finished
my sentence, he was on me.

He was right; he wasn't gentle. Up until that point in our
relationship, our lovemaking had been passion tempered
with humor and sweetness. I'd been hurt and he'd been so
careful of me.

In the darkness of Warren's guest bedroom, sweetness
and humor had no place in him. And though there was care
in his touch, he was anything but careful. Not that he hurt
me—quite the contrary. But he was fire and need that went
so far beyond simple desire that it consumed me—and like
the phoenix, I found myself reborn in the crucible.

I met his urgency with my own, digging my fingers
into the silk-covered stone of his arms as his sinful mouth
tasted my skin wherever it fell. He was hot and hard, his
need forcing me to rise to meet his fire with my own. Sweat
dripped onto my skin, and the scent of it was an aphrodi-
siac because it was all Adam. If he needed me, I needed
him every bit as much.

He rose over me, closing his golden eyes as he pushed
through me, into me, became a part of me with one heavy

thrust. Only when he was all the way in did he look at me again, and in that look was triumph and a claiming so basic that it should have scared me.

"Mine," he said, rocking his hips against my own in a move that was more about possession than passion.

I raised my chin and held his eyes in a challenge only I could make without consequences. I tightened my belly and dug my heels into the mattress to give my own thrust power. "Mine," I said.

Adam's wolf smiled at me and nipped my shoulder. "I can live with that," he said. And then he demonstrated what that possession would mean when it involved an Alpha werewolf who knew how to be patient and thorough when hunting coyotes.

———

I DREAMED I WALKED IN THE SNOW, BUT I WASN'T afraid. There was a thick golden rope wrapped securely around me. It was free of fray or knot and led me into the forest, lighting my way with its bright warmth. I followed it with a light heart and the humming anticipation of finding something wonderful. At last I came to the end of the rope and a blue-gray wolf with golden eyes.

"Hello, Adam," I told him.

———

"SHH," SAID ADAM SLEEPILY. HE PULLED ME tighter against him and rolled over the top of me as if that would make me be quiet. "Sleep."

My body was tired. I was warm and safe. A return to sleep should have come easily, especially since I'd awakened from such a good dream. But it had reminded me of what it had felt like to be lost.

"I couldn't find you either," I told Adam, burrowing against him. He was thinner than he'd been the last time I'd been in bed with him. The fire had left no scars, and he

kept his hair short anyway, but the ribs I could feel told me
I had cost him.

"I quit trying," I admitted. "I was so afraid she was going
to use me to enthrall the whole pack. I didn't understand
that she couldn't do that, that she didn't have the power."
I closed my eyes and let myself remember how terrified I
had been. I opened them again, almost immediately, need-
ing to see him to feel safe. "In that place, it felt like she had
all the power to do anything."

He was so still that I thought he might have gone back to
sleep, until he spoke. "She hurt you." It wasn't a question.

"She did." I wouldn't lie to him. "But it was just pain, not
real damage. I knew you would come for me if I could just
hold out." I let him hear the sureness of that in my voice.

He rolled over until I was on top of him. His hands moved
to my shoulders, and he gave me a little shake. "Don't ever
make me go through that again. I couldn't bear it."

"I won't," I promised him rashly. "Never again."

He laughed then and hugged me tight. "Didn't Bran
teach you not to make promises you can't keep?" He
sighed. "I suppose if you won't shut up so I can sleep, I
might as well find something to do with the time."

When he was through, we both slept.

ADAM WENT WITH ME TO RETURN THE BOOK TO
Phin the next morning, an hour before the store opened.
The book was still wrapped in Kyle's towel and had apparently traveled from Kyle's linen closet to Adam's with no
fuss. Darryl and Auriele had brought it to us, along with
a new coat for me and clothes for Adam, since his hadn't
survived. Darryl didn't crack a smile, though it would have
been obvious to him what we'd been doing, even if he'd
been a human and didn't have the nose of a wolf. Instead,
both he and Auriele had observed us with a satisfaction I
found a little disconcerting. I was glad when they'd left us.

Phin was at his desk in the bookstore, looking very much as he had the first time I'd seen him, except that he'd lost a little weight: a man of indeterminate age with fading golden hair and good-humored eyes. There were a few new bookcases, but otherwise the bookstore looked much as it had the first time I'd seen it.

"Hey, Mercy. Adam," Phin said with a friendly smile.

"Hey. I have something for you." I unrolled the towel carefully and set the book on the counter.

When I touched it, the leather was butter soft under my fingertips.

"Ariana has a fine sense of irony," observed Adam, reading the title for the first time—*Magic Made* was embossed on the cover and spine in gold. "Hard to believe that is glamour."

"It isn't, quite," said Ariana, coming around the end of a bookshelf.

She'd changed her appearance. She didn't look like a middle-aged woman anymore; instead, she'd altered her real appearance just enough that she looked human. Her skin was tanned and human-smooth, her eyes gray, and her hair as blond as Phin's must have been when he was a young man.

She looked at Adam for a moment, and he stayed still with the coaxing quietness of a man trying not to startle a wild creature.

"You've changed," she told him, relaxing a little. "She contents your wolf."

"I'm sorry I frightened you." Adam's voice was carefully gentle, and I remembered that he'd said she hadn't been able to stay in the same room with him.

She shook her head. "Not your fault—neither the old fear or the new. But still, you are not so terrifying now." With a resolute breath and raised chin, she strode across the store to us.

She looked at the book and shook her head. "You cause me more trouble." To Adam and me, she said, almost shyly, "Would you like to see what it really looks like?"

"Please," I said.

She put both of her hands on the book, and I felt a wave of magic. She picked up the book, and when she moved it, a small silver statue of a bird was left behind. A lark, I thought, though I was no expert. It was no bigger than the palm of my hand and amazingly realistic. I looked at the book sitting next to it.

"The best disguises are real," she said. "I just used the book to hide the artifact."

Adam put his hand on my shoulder, bent down, and said, "Such a small thing to cause so much trouble." And he kissed the top of my ear.